GRANTA BOOKS

VOX

Nicholson Baker was born in 1957. He has written three books, *The Mezzanine*, *Room Temperature* and *U and I*. He lives in upstate New York with his wife and child.

NICHOLSON BAKER

VOX

GRANTA BOOKS

LONDON

in association with

PENGUIN BOOKS

GRANTA BOOKS
2/3 Hanover Yard, Noel Road, Islington, London N1 8BE

Published in association with the Penguin Group
Penguin Books Ltd, 27 Wrights Lane, London W8 5TZ, England
Viking Penguin, a division of Penguin Books USA Inc.,
375 Hudson Street, New York 10014, USA
Penguin Books Australia Ltd, Ringwood, Victoria, Australia
Penguin Books Canada Ltd, 2801 John Street, Markham,
Ontario, Canada L3R 1B4
Penguin Books (NZ) Ltd, 182-190 Wairau Road,
Auckland 10, New Zealand

Penguin Books Ltd, Registered Offices: Harmondsworth,
Middlesex, England

First published in the USA by Random House Inc. 1992
First published in Great Britain by Granta Books 1992

3 5 7 9 10 8 6 4

Made and printed in Great Britain by Clays Ltd, St Ives plc

A CIP catalogue for this book is available from the British Library

"What are you wearing?" he asked.

She said, "I'm wearing a white shirt with little stars, green and black stars, on it, and black pants, and socks the color of the green stars, and a pair of black sneakers I got for nine dollars."

"What are you doing?"

"I'm lying on my bed, which is made. That's an unusual thing. I made my bed this morning. A few months ago my mother gave me a chenille bedspread, exactly the kind we used to have, and I felt bad that it was still folded up unused and this morning I finally made the bed with it."

"I don't know what chenille is," he said. "It's some kind of silky material?"

"No, it's cotton. Cotton chenille. It's got those little tufts, in conventional patterns. Like in bed-and-breakfasts."

"Oh oh oh, the patterns of *tufts*. I'm relieved."

"Why?" she asked.

"Silk is somehow . . . you think of ads for escort services where the type is set in fake-o eighteenth-century script—*For the Discriminating Gentleman*—that kind of thing. Or Deliques Intimates, you know that catalog?"

"I get one about every week."

7

"Right, a deluge. Lace filigree, Aubrey Beardsley, no thank you. All I can think of is, ma'am, those silk tap pants you've got on are going to stain."

"You're right about that," she said. "Someone gave me this exotic chemisey thing, not from Deliques but the same idea, silk with lace. I get quite . . . I get very *moist* when I'm aroused, it's almost embarrassing actually. So this chemisey thing got soaked. He said, the person who bought it for me said, 'So what, throw it away, use it once.' But I don't know, I thought I might want to wear it again. It's really nice to wear silk, you know. So I took it to the dry cleaners. I didn't mention it specifically, I bunched it in with a lot of work clothes. It came back with a little tag on it, with a little dancing man with a tragic expression, wearing a hat, who says, you know, 'Sorry! We did everything we could, we took extraordinary measures, but the stains on this garment could not come out!' I took a look at it, and it was very odd, there were these five *dot* stains on it, little ovals, not down where I'd been wet, but higher up, on the front."

"Weird."

"And the guy who gave it to me had *not* come on me. He came elsewhere—that much I was sure of. So my theory is that someone at the dry cleaners . . ."

"No! Do you still give them your business?"

"Well, they're convenient."

"Where do you live?"

"In an eastern city."

"Oh. I live in a western city."

"How nice."

"It is nice," he said. "From my window I can see a streetlight with lots of spike holes in it, from utility workers—I mean a wooden telephone pole with a streetlight on it—"

"Of course."

"And a few houses. The streetlight is photo-activated, and watching it come on is really one of the most beautiful things."

"What time is it there?"

"Um—six-twelve," he said.

"Is it dark there yet?"

"No. Is it there?"

"Not completely," she said. "It doesn't feel really dark to me until the little lights on my stereo receiver are the brightest things in the room. That's not strictly true, but it sounds good, don't you think? What hand are you holding the phone with?"

"My left," he said.

"What are you doing with your right hand?"

"My right hand is, at the moment, my fingers are resting in the soil of a potted plant somebody gave me, that isn't doing too well. I'm sort of moving my fingers in the soil."

"What kind of a plant?"

"I can't remember," he said. "The soil has several round polished stones stuck in it. Oh wait, here's the tag.

9

No, that's just the price tag. An anonymous mystery plant."

"You haven't told me what *you're* wearing," she said.

"I am wearing . . . I'm wearing, well, a bathrobe, and flip-flops with blue soles and red holder-onners. I'm new to flip-flops—I mean since moving out here. They're good in the morning for waking up. On weekends I put them on and I walk down to the corner and buy the paper, and the feeling of that thong right in the crotch of your toe—man, it pulls you together, it starts your day. It's like putting your feet in a bridle."

"Are you 'into' feet?" she asked.

"No no no no no no no no. On women? No. They're neutral. They're about like elbows. In my *own* case, I do . . ."

"What?"

"Well, I do very often, when I'm about to come, I seem to like to rise up on the balls of my feet. It's something about the tension of all the leg muscles and the, you know, the ass muscles, it puts all the nerves in communication, it's as if I'm coming with my legs. On the other hand, when I do it I sometimes feel like some kind of high school teacher, bouncing on his heels, or like some kind of demagogue, rising up on tiptoe and roaring out something about destiny."

"And then, at the very top of your *relevé*, you come into a tissue," she said.

"Yep."

"The things we do for love. I knew this person, a doctor, who once told me that he liked to hyperventilate when he was masturbating, like a puppy. He got very scientific about it. He said that hyperventilating decreases the ionized calcium in the blood, alters neural conductivity, does this, does that. I tried it once. He said when you're almost there, after panting and panting, he-a-he-a-he-a, you're supposed to do this thing called a Valsalva, which is where you take a breath and you clamp your throat shut and push *hard*, and if you do it right, you're supposed to have a mind-blowing orgasm—tingling extremities, tingling roots of your hair, tingling teeth, I don't know, the whole business. I didn't have much success with the technique, but he was this huge man, huge coarse beard, huge arms, he loved large meatball subs, with that orange grease—and he was so big and so innocent and actually quite shy that the idea of him gasping—"

"His eyes squinted shut."

"Right, hunched over his male organ, though I have to say I was never quite able to picture his male organ, but the idea of him intentionally, deliberately gasping and swallowing was enough to help me toward a moment or two of pleasure myself."

"Ooo. On that very bed?"

"On this very bed."

"But without the chenille bedspread."

"Without the chenille bedspread, which I notice is

leaving little white pieces of fluff on my pants, mm, mm, mm, get off, you. You see, a pretentiously sexy silk bedspread from Deliques would have been more practical after all."

"Well, right, no, I can see that the things in Deliques might be sexy," he said. "Garters and all that. They don't do much for me—in fact, the whole Victorian flavor of a certain kind of smirky kinkiness puts me off—but still, I have to admit that when the catalogs started coming, week after week, early fall, midfall, late fall, this persistent gush of half-dressed women flowing toward me in the mail, on such expensive paper, with the bee-stung lips and all that, it did start to interest me."

"Ah, now you're admitting it," she said. "The male models are quite good-looking, too."

"Well, but still for me it wasn't the lace hemi-demi-camisoles or any of that. I'll tell you what it was, in fact. It was this one picture of a woman wearing a loose green shirt, lying on her back, with her legs in the air, crossed at the ankles, wearing a pair of tights. Not black tights. I was, I was absolutely entranced by this picture. I remember coming home from work and sitting at the kitchen table, studying this picture for about . . . ten minutes, reading the little description of the tights, looking at the picture again, reading, looking. She had very long legs. Now, did I have anybody I could buy these tights for? No, not really. Not at that moment. They were made of a certain kind of stitch, not chenille, not chenille. Pointelle! She was wearing these beigey-green pointelle tights. See, to me the word 'tights' is much more exciting than just 'stockings.' Anyway I went into the living room and put the phone on the floor, and then I lay down on the floor next to the phone and I just studied this shot, went through the rest of the catalog, but back to this one picture again, until my arms started to get tired from holding the pages in the air, and I put the catalog face-down on my chest, and I went into a state of pure bliss, rolling my head back and forth on the rug. If you roll your head back and forth on the floor it usually increases any feeling of awe or wonder that you've got going. But no tingling of the extremities, unfortunately."

"No."

"And I don't eat lots of meatball subs. I mean I *do* enjoy a meatball sub occasionally, with mushrooms—I just want to differentiate myself from, you know . . ."

"Oh don't worry about that," she said. "Your accent is very different from his, your voice is quite . . . compelling."

"I'm glad to hear that. I was nervous when I called. My temperature dropped about fifteen degrees as I was deciding to dial the number."

"Really. Where did you see the ad?"

"Ah, a men's magazine."

"Which one?" she asked.

"This is oddly embarrassing. *Juggs*. *Juggs* magazine. Where did you see the ad?"

There was a pause. *"Forum."*

"What does your ad say?" he asked.

"Let me see," she said. "There's a line drawing of a man and a woman, each holding a telephone, and the headline is ANYTIME AT ALL. I liked the drawing."

"I've seen that one," he said. "That's very different from my ad. My ad has a color shot of a woman with a phone cord wrapped around her leg and one arm kind of covering her breasts, and the headline over the phone number is, MAKE IT HAPPEN. But there *is* something intangibly classier about this ad than the other ads, something about the layout and the type that the phone number is in, despite the usual woman-plus-phone image, and I thought that maybe it might attract a different sort of caller. Although, boy, that flurry of assholic horniness from the men on the line when you first spoke was not exactly cucumber sandwich conversation. That *one* guy that kept interrupting—'You like to *sock* on a big *caulk*?' 'How big and brown are your nips?' But then, I suppose we aren't calling for cucumber sandwich conversation."

"I wouldn't object—cucumber away. But I guess not. Anyhow, here we are, 'one on one,' as they say, in the famous fiber-optical 'back room.' "

"True enough."

"So go on," she said. "You were telling me how you were on the floor rolling your head back and forth?"

"Oh, right. Well, I was on the floor with the catalog

facedown on my chest, entranced by those tights, and a conception, this conception of thrilling wrongness, took shape in my brain stem. I had a vision of myself jerking off while I ordered that pair of tights, specifically the vision was of, of, of . . ."

"Of?"

"Of being in the bathtub, but on the phone with the order-taker from Deliques, who's got, you know, this nice innocent voice, a mistaken but lovable overfrizzed perm, a hint of twang, bland face, freshly laundered jeans, cute socks, but probably wearing a pair of Deliques finest 'fusion panties' with a chevron of lace or something over her mound, which she's bought at the employee discount, while I'm in my bathtub, which is ridiculous since I never take baths, but I'm in my bathtub moving so carefully so she won't hear any aquatic splips or splaps and know that I've taken the portable phone into the bathroom and that I'm semi-submerged, and she says, 'Let me check to be sure we have that in stock for you, sir,' and during the pause, I arch myself up out of the water and sort of point the phone at my Werner Heisenberg so she can see it somehow or get its vibes, and at the moment she says, 'Yes, we do have the pointelle tights in faun,' I come, in perfect silence, making a Smurf grimace."

"That's awful."

"I know, but I don't know, I was there on the living-room floor. I don't often lie down there."

"Were you actually . . . playing with yourself as you envisioned this?"

"Certainly not! I had one hand on the telephone, just *toying* with the number keys, teasing them, and the other hand was lying on the facedown catalog on my chest. Anyway, then I thought I would be embarrassed to order a pair of tights for myself—maybe the order-taker would assume that I was a transsexual, when in fact I am not a transsexual at all, I'm a telephone clitician."

"An obscene phone caller."

"Exactly. And I started to think of who I could order them for, and I thought of this woman at work, a very nice woman, some might say plain, but very nice, who once startled me and this other guy by telling a story out of the blue about some friends of hers who'd just had a large wedding at a museum during which some thieves backed a van up and loaded all the wedding gifts in and drove away."

"The wedding gifts were on display?" she asked.

"Yes."

"Ah, well, that was their mistake."

"Well, they were punished for it. Anyway, one of the gifts, this woman from work told us, was one of those sex slings that I guess you bolt to a stud in the ceiling, so that the woman is . . ."

"Yeah, I know," she said.

"And this woman from work had joked about the difficulty of trying to fence the stolen sex sling, and the

memory of her talking about this oddball device came back to me and I wanted to order the tights for her, so she'd come home from work one day, and she'd go, 'Hey, what's this, a slim little package for me from Deliques?' She'd open it up and slip out this plastic packet with tights in it, and there's the order slip in her hand, and somehow I've convinced the order-taker that I don't want my name on the slip."

"Sure, sure."

"So she knows she's got a secret admirer. And there on the packing slip is the line of printout that says, all in abbreviations, 1 PR PTL TIGHTS, FN, SM, $12.95, and I just thought of her looking at the packing slip and thinking, Well, gee, I suppose I *should* at least see if they fit."

"Ah, but wait," she said. "No, what catches her eye, what catches her eye is . . ."

"Tell me," he said.

"Is that on the packing slip, over the numeral one, for one pair of tights, is this *check mark*, in blunt pencil."

"That's right, there is."

"And she looks closely at that check mark, and she imagines a male hand making it, a surprisingly refined hand, because there has been a strike at the Deliques warehouse, and what's happened is that Deliques management has had to hire the male models from the catalog on an emergency basis to fill in for the normal pickers and packers, who are of course mostly middle-aged Laotian women. And they were right in the middle of a catalog shoot, all these male models, when the walk-out took place, so they're wearing exactly what they were wearing on the shoot, which are the usual aubergine paisley boxer shorts, and Henri Rousseau bathrobes, and Erté pajamas, and that sort of thing, but there was no time for them to change, they had to be herded barefoot into this giant warehouse because the company was bombed with orders. April was their biggest month. So—one male model takes this woman's order slip, and studies it, looks at her name on it—what's her name?"

"Jill."

"Looks at her name, Jill Smith, and then takes the order slip and crumples it against the piece of horseradish in his foulard silk boxer shorts, and he hands it to the next male model, a gorgeous peasant with strange slitty nipples, who smooths it out, studies it, duh, Jill Smith, squeezes his asscheeks together, and passes it to the next guy, who smooths it out, studies it, bites one corner, and hands it to the next guy, and so on down this row of male models, each one broader-shouldered and sinewier-stomached than the last, until finally the order slip gets to the last guy, who's fallen asleep sitting on one tang of the forklift, a much slighter gentleman, with a beautiful throat with a softly pulsing jugular you just wanted to *eat* it looked so good, and of course wearing a green moiré silk codpiece, pushed forward and upward by the one tang of the forklift. This male model rouses himself, smacks his lips sleepily, studies the slip of paper, gets in the forklift, and drives off, weaves off, toward the distant vault where they keep the pointelle tights."

"Yes?"

"And he reaches the mountain of crates marked FAUN, and he slides the forklift into the highest pallet and lifts it off and, *vvvvvvv*, brings it down, and he pries it open . . ."

"Probably with his dick."

"No, no, with his powerful refined *hands*," she said. "The packing tape goes *pap! pap! pap!* as he tears the mighty box asunder. But now that you mention it, as he's reaching in, deep into the box filled with . . . with one metric ton of cotton pointelle, his cock *is* pressing against the cardboard, pressing, pressing, and it starts to fight against the tethers of that codpiece. So he climbs back in the forklift, puts the pair of tights in his lap, and drives back. Well, while he was gone, Todd, Rod, Sod, and Wadd, the other male models, all heterosexual, of course, who've been standing in a row waiting for him, have been thinking about Jill Smith wearing those tights and by now their bobolinks have all gotten thoroughly hard, and even the sleepy forklift driver, perhaps because of the faun tights in his lap, is embarrassed to get out because there's this frank erection that has now gotten so big and bone-hard that it's angling right out of his codpiece. He takes his place in the row of male models, his cock swaying slightly, and he holds the tights to his face and exhales through them, then nods, takes a pencil with a surprisingly sharp point, and makes a check mark over the numeral one on the packing slip. He hands it to the next guy—by this time all the male models have abandoned their shame in each other's presence and they are all standing there in a row with their various organs pronging at various angles out of their various robes and boxers and sex-briefs. So the forklift guy hands it to the next guy, who almost ritualistically takes the tights and winds them around and around his cock, pulls once hard, and then unwinds them and makes a check mark exactly superimposed over the first check mark on the numeral one on the packing slip. And he hands the tights to the next guy, who also winds the tights around his cock, many winds, it's *very* long, and he pulls, and he makes a superimposing check mark, too, and so on down the row, wind unwind check, wind unwind check, and the final guy folds the tights up with neat agile movements that belie his enormous forearms and slides them into the sheer plastic envelope and puts the last check mark over the numeral one, so that it now looks as if only one blunt pencil check-marked over it, when really there were *nine* check marks. And so together, humming 'The Volga Boatman' in unison, they seal the package up with Jill Smith's address on it and send it off to her."

"Well, maybe that *is* what happened," he said. "No, in reality, there wasn't any strike at Deliques when I called. Their computer was down, though."

"Oh, so you really *did* call?" she said. "That's very wicked of you. In the bath?"

"No, in the end that seemed like too much trouble. I called from the living-room floor. First I worked myself up to a creditable state of engorgement, then I dialed the 800 number."

"All right . . ."

"A woman answered and said something like 'Hello and welcome to Deliques Intimates, this is Clititia speaking, how may we help you today?' She had a young high voice, exactly the sort of voice I'd imagined. Well, my fourteen-and-a-half-inch sperm-dowel instantly shrank to less than three inches. Which is the opposite of what was supposed to happen. I told her what I wanted to order, and she said the computer was down, but she would take the order 'by hand,' right? Why wasn't I enough of a leerer to come back with something insinuating? Just something basic, like 'Heh heh, honey, I hope you *do* take it all by hand.' But instead I just said, 'Boy oh boy, that must be a lot of trouble for you.' I gave her my address, my card number, and she said, 'I've got that, sir, now, is there anything else you would like to order this evening?' I said, 'Well, I'm torn, there *is* one other thing I'd like to get this person, just a pair of very simple panties, but I'm torn.' I said, 'Now you see the so-called Deliques *minimes* on page thirty-eight? You see those? Do you have the catalog there right in front of you?' She said she did. I said, 'Okay. I'm not sure I can tell the difference between these *minimes* and the so-called *nadja pants* on page, ah, forty-six. To the naked eye they seem identical.' She said, 'Just one moment,' and I heard her flipping through the catalog, and I made a last valiant attempt to stroke myself off, because the idea of her looking carefully at those pictures of women in those tiny weightless panties, with the darkness of pubic hair visible right *there* through the material, at the very same time I was looking at those same cuppable curves of pubic hair on my end, should have been enough to make me shoot instantly, but I don't know, she sounded so well-meaning, and I knew that there was a very good chance that she would not like to know that I was there trying to . . . I mean, she didn't want to work at a job where men called her and ordered a few items of merchandise just so they could . . . right? That wasn't what she'd had in mind at all in taking the job, or possibly wasn't, at least, so even when she said, finally, 'Well, the nadja pants ride a little lower on the hip,' which is a statement that any normal jacker-offer should be able to come to easily, because what does it imply? It implies her own hip, it implies that the nadja panties have ridden *her own hip*. But even then I could not achieve and maintain. So I said, 'Oh well, no, thanks, I'll see how the tights go over and then order the *minimes* later.' And a week afterward, I was the owner of a pair of tights. I still have them, unopened. Give me your address and I'll be glad to forward them to you."

"Why don't you give them to Jill?" she asked.

"Oh, a million reasons. But that's not quite the end. I hung up from making the order and instantly I got hard

again, naturally, and I thought for a second, and I hit the
redial button, and a different woman answered, with a
much lower and smarter voice, with some name like
Vulva, and I said, 'Vulva, I have what may sound like an
unorthodox question, and you don't have to answer it if
you don't want to. But what I'm curious about is, well,
of the men who order from your catalog, do you think
some of them are in a subtle or maybe not-so-subtle way
obscene phone callers?' She laughed and she said, 'That's
a good question.' And then there was a long pause, a very
long pause. I said, 'Hello?' And right there I knew I'd
blown it—I knew the tone of my hello, that slight reed-
iness in my voice that betrayed sexual tension, blew away
the potential rapport I might have had with Vulva. See,
I'd sounded quite confident when I actually asked her the
question."

"What did she say?"

"She just said, in a more official voice, but still a
friendly voice, 'I don't think I'm going to answer your
question.' And I said, 'Fine, I understand, okay, sure.'
And she said 'Bye.' Not 'Good-bye,' you notice—still the
slight vestige of amused intimacy there. If she'd said
'Good-bye' I would have felt absolutely crushed."

"What did you do then?"

"I sat up and ordered a pizza and read the paper. So
you see, I'm not an obscene phone caller, really. I can't
smother an orgasm."

"Ho ho. I·can," she said.

23

"Can you? Well, I mean I can physically do it."

"*I know what you mean.*"

There was a pause.

"I hear ice cubes," he said.

"Diet Coke."

"Ah. Tell me more things. Tell me about the room you're in. Tell me the chain of events that led up to your calling this number."

"Okay," she said. "I'm not in the bedroom anymore. I'm sitting on the couch in my living room slash dining room. My feet are on the coffee table, which would have been impossible yesterday, because the coffee table was piled so high with mail and work stuff, but now it is possible, and the whole room, the whole apartment, is really and truly in order. I took a sick day today, without being sick, which is something I haven't done up to now at this job. I called the receptionist and told her I had a fever. The moment of lying to her was awful, but gosh what freedom when I hung up the phone! And I didn't leave the apartment all day. I just organized my imme-diate surroundings, I picked up things, I vacuumed, and I laid out all the silver that I've inherited—three different very incomplete patterns—laid it out on the dining-room table and looked at it and I gave some serious thought to polishing it, but I didn't go so far as to polish it, but it looked beautiful all laid out, a big arch of forks, a little arch of knives, five big serving spoons, some tiny salt spoons, and a little grouping of novelty items, like oyster forks. No teaspoons at all. One of the dinner forks from my great aunt's set fell into the dishwasher once when I was visiting her and it got badly notched by that twirly splasher in the bottom, and someone at work was telling me he knew a jeweler who fixed hurt silverware, so I'm planning to have that fixed, it's all ready to go. And I even got together all my broken sets of beads—I sorted them all out—the sight of all those beads jumbled together on my bedside table was making me unhappy every morning, and now they're ready to be restrung, the pink ones in one envelope, and the green ones in one envelope, and the parti-colored Venetian ones in one envelope—and I have them on my dining-room table too, ready to go."

"The same jeweler who fixes silverware restrings beads?" he asked.

"Yes!"

"How did your beads get broken?"

"They seem to break in the morning when I'm rushing to get dressed. They catch on something. The jade ones, my favorite set, which my father gave me, caught on the open door of the microwave when I was standing up too quickly after picking a piece of paper up off the floor. That was the latest tragedy. And of course my sister's babe yanked one set off my neck. But they can all be repaired and they will all be repaired."

"Good going."

"Anyway, this apartment is transformed, I mean it,

not just superficially but with new hidden pockets of order in it, and I waited until the midafternoon to have a shower, and I did *not* masturbate, because the illicitness of calling in sick without justification made me want to be pure and virtuous all day long, and I had an early dinner of Carr's Table Water crackers with cream cheese and sliced pieces of sweet red kosher peppers on them, just delicious, and I did *not* turn on the TV but instead I turned on the stereo, which I haven't used much lately. It's a very fancy stereo."

"Yes?"

"I think I spent something like fourteen hundred dollars on it," she said. "I bought it from someone who was buying an even fancier system. It was true insanity. I had a crush on this person. He liked the Thompson Twins and the S.O.S. Band and, gee, what were the other groups he liked so much? The Gap Band was one. Midnight Star. And Cameo. This was a while ago. He was not a particularly intelligent man, in fact in a way he was a very dimwitted narrow-minded man, but he was *so* infectiously convinced that what he liked everyone would like if they were exposed to it. And good-looking. For about four months, while I was in his thrall, I really *listened* to that stuff. I gave my life up to it. My own taste in music stopped evolving in grade school with the Beatles, the early early Beatles—in fact I used to dislike any song that didn't end—you know, end with a chord, but simply faded out."

"But then you met this guy," he said.

"Exactly!" she said. "All of the songs he liked faded out, or most of them did. And so I became a connoisseur of fade-outs. I bought cassettes. I used to turn them up very loud—with the headphones on—and listen very closely, trying to catch that precise moment when the person in the recording studio had begun to turn my volume dial down, or whatever it was he did. Sometimes I'd turn the volume dial up at just the speed I thought he—I mean the ghostly hand of the record producer— was turning it down, so that the sound stayed on an even plane. I'd get in this sort of trance, like you on the rug, where I thought if I kept turning it up—and this is a very powerful amplifier, mind you—the song would not stop, it would just continue indefinitely. And so what I had thought of before as just a kind of artistic sloppiness, this attempt to imply that oh yeah, we're a bunch of endlessly creative folks who jam all night, and the bad old record producer finally has to turn down the volume on us just so we don't fill the whole album with one monster song, became for me instead this kind of, this kind of summa- tion of hopefulness. I first felt it in a song called 'Ain't Nobody,' which was a song that this man I had the crush on was particularly keen on. '*Ain't nobody, loves me better.*' You know that one?"

"You sing well!" he said.

"I do not. But that's the song, and as you get toward the end of it, a change takes place in the way you hear it, which is that the knowledge that the song is going to end starts to be more important than the specific ups and downs of the melody, and even though the singer is singing just as loud as ever, in fact she's really pouring it on now, she's fighting to be heard, it's as if you are hearing the inevitable waning of popularity of that hit, its slippage down the charts, and the twilight of the career of the singer, despite all of the beautiful subtle things she's able to do with a plain old dumb old bunch of notes, and even as she goes for one last high note, full of daring and hope and passionateness and everything worthwhile, she's lost, she's sinking down."

"Oh! Don't *cry!*" he said. "I'm not equipped . . . I mean my comforting skills don't have that kind of range."

There was another sound of ice cubes. She said, "It's just that I really liked him. Vain bum. We went dancing one night, and I made the mistake of suggesting to him as we were on the dance floor that maybe he should take his pen out of his shirt pocket and put it in his back pocket. And that was it, he never called me again."

"That little scum-twirler! Tell me his address, I'll fade *him* out, I'll rip his arms off."

"No. I got over it. Anyway, that wasn't what I meant to talk about. I just mean I was here in my wonderfully orderly apartment after dinner and I saw this big joke of a stereo system and I switched it on, and the sky got darker and all the little red and green lights on the receiver were like ocean buoys or something, and I started to feel what you'd expect, sad, happy, resigned, horny, some combination of all of them, and I felt suddenly that I'd been virtuous for long enough and probably should definitely masturbate, and I thought wait, let's not just have a perfunctory masturbation session, Abby, let's do something just a little bit special tonight, to round out a special day, right? So I brought out a copy of *Forum* that I rather bravely bought one day a while ago. But I'd read all the stories and all the letters and it just wasn't working. So I started looking at the ads, really almost for the first time. And there was this headline: ANYTIME AT ALL."

"MAKE IT HAPPEN."

"That's right. And I *like* the sound of the pauses in long-distance conversations—the cassette hiss sound. And yet I didn't really want to talk to anyone I knew. So that's more or less why I called. Now I've answered your questions, now you tell me something."

"Do you want to hear something true, or something imaginary?"

"First true, then imaginary," she said.

"Once," he said, "I was listening to the stereo with the headphones on, I was about sixteen, and the stereo receiver was on the floor of a little room off the living room, I don't know why it was on the floor, I guess because my father was repainting the living room—that must have been it—and the headphone cord was quite short, but I was very interested in learning how to dance. It was winter, it was maybe eight o'clock at night, very dark, I hadn't turned on the light in the room. And I was trying to learn all these moves, but tethered to the stereo, so I was almost completely doubled over, like I was tracking some animal, but I was really ecstatic—dancing, sweating, out of breath, flailing my arms, doing little jumps . . . once I got a little too excited and did a *big* sideways bob of my head and the headphones came off and pulled my glasses off with them—but no problem, I just stylized the motions of picking up my glasses and putting them on and repeated them a few times, incorporated them in. And then suddenly I hear, 'Jim, *what* are you doing?' in this horrified voice. My younger sister had heard all this breathing and panting coming from me in the darkness and thought of course that I was . . ."

"Right."

"I said, 'I'm dancing.' And she went away. I danced for a while longer, but with somewhat less conviction. That was my year of heavy stereo use. Unlike you I didn't have a big crush on anyone at the time. I think it was more that I had a crush on the tuner itself, frankly. I used to imagine that the megahertz markings were the skyline of a city at night. The FM markings were all the buildings, and the AM markings were their reflection in water . . ."

"Ah," she said, "but you're supposed to be telling me something true, not something imagined."

"Yes, but the true thing is shading into the imagined thing, all right? And the little moving indicator on our stereo was lit with a yellow light, and I knew where all the

stations were on the dial, and I'd spin the knob and the
yellow indicator would glide up and down the radio cityscape like a cab up and down some big central boulevard,
and each station was an intersection, in a neighborhood
with a different ethnic mix, and if the red sign came on
saying STEREO I might idle there for a while, or the
cabbie might run the light, passing the whole thing by as
it exploded and disappeared behind me. And sometimes
I'd thumb the dial very slowly, sort of like I was palming
a steering wheel, and move up, move up, in the silence
of the muted stretches, and then suddenly I'd pierce the
rind of a station and there would be this crackling
hopped-up luridly colored version of a song that sounded
for a second much better than I knew the song really was,
like that moment in solar eclipses when the whole co-
rona is visible, and then you slide down into the fertile
valley of the station itself, and it spreads out beneath you,
in stereo, with a whole range of middle and misty dis-
tances."

"That's true!" she said.

"It *is* true? That's bad, because it means that I still
have to come up with an imaginary thing, right?"

"I'm afraid so."

"But my imagination doesn't work that way," he said.
"It doesn't just hop to at the snap of a finger. What do
you want the imaginary thing I tell you to be about?"

"I think that it should be about . . . my beads and my
silverware, since they're all laid out for us."

"Well," he said. There was a pause. "Once there was

31

a guy who, um, needed his fork repaired. No, I can't. I'm sorry. You tell me something more."

"It's *your* turn."

"I need more confidences from you first. I need to be charged up with a stream of confidences flowing from you to me."

"Come on now," she said. "Give it a try."

"Yeah, but I don't think I can just be handed an assignment like that. I'm pedestrian. I think I have to stay with the truth."

"All right, tell me what the most recent thing or event was that aroused you."

"The idea of making this call," he said.

"Before that."

"Let me think back," he said. "The Walt Disney character of Tinker Bell. I was just leaving the video store, and I came to this big cardboard display of *Peter Pan*, the Walt Disney cartoon *Peter Pan*, which has just been rereleased, with a TV beside it playing the movie."

"When was this?"

"This was today, about an hour and a half ago, I guess. I rented three X-rated tapes."

"And you're going to play them later this evening?"

"Maybe. Maybe not, I don't know. I was going to play them when I got home."

"The second you got home."

"That's right."

"What about dinner?"

"I ate at a pizza place."

"What kind?"

"Small mushroom anchovy."

"All right. So you got home with the tapes . . ."

"Yeah, and I put them on top of the TV and got out of my work clothes and put on a bathrobe . . ."

"Just a bathrobe?"

"Well, I have my T-shirt and underwear on underneath, of course."

"White underwear?"

"Gray, white, somewhere in that range. Anyway, I came out and saw the pile of X-rated tapes on top of my TV, and they're in these orange boxes. The store uses brown boxes for their normal tapes, like adventure, comedy, slasher, etcetera, and then they use a whole different color, an orange box, for the adult tapes. It's to avoid confusion, because now there are so many X-rated Christmas tapes and X-rated versions of *Cinderella* and all that. And I'd never seen two of these particular tapes before, but of course I knew what was in them anyway, and I heartily approved of it, I'm enthusiastically pro-pornography, obviously, but suddenly I foresaw my own crude arousal—I saw myself fast-forwarding through the numbing parts, trying to find some image that was good, or at least good enough to come to, and the sound of the VCR as it fast-forwards, that industrial robot sound, and I suddenly thought no, no, even though one of the tapes has got Lisa Melendez in it, who I think is just . . ."

delightful, I thought no, I don't want to see these right now. Fortunately, I'd also bought a *Juggs* magazine, because this anti-orange-tape reaction has hit me before. There are just times when you want a fixed image."

"There's always the pause button," she suggested.

"Well, but then you get those white sawtooth lines across the screen."

"Four heads are better than two, as they say. Of course, the resolution is better on the magazine page, I imagine."

"It certainly is," he said. "But it's much more than that! Don't laugh, really. No movie still is ever as good as a photograph. A photograph catches a woman at a point where her frans are at their perfect point of expressiveness—the soul of her frans is revealed, or rather the souls *are* revealed, because each has a separate personality. Nipples in still pictures are as varied and as communicative as women's eyes, or almost."

"Frans?"

"Yeah, sometimes I don't like the word 'breasts' and all those slangish synonyms. I mean, just look at the drop in arousingness between *Playboy* magazine and the exact same women when they're *moving* from pose to pose on the *Playboy* channel. It's true that I don't actually get the *Playboy* channel, so I see everything on it through those houndstooth and herringbone cycles of the scrambling circuit, and I keep flipping back and forth between it and the two channels on either side of it because sometimes for an instant the picture is startled into visibility just after you switch the channel, and you'll catch this bright yellow torso and one full fran with a fire-engine-red nipple, and then it teeters, it falters, and collapses—and I've noticed that the scrambling works least well and you can see things best when nothing is moving in the TV image, i.e., when it's a TV image *of* a magazine image, sort of as if the scrambling circuitry is overcome in the same way I am sometimes overcome by the power of fixed pictures. I once stayed up until two-thirty in the morning doing this, flipping."

"Anyway."

"Right. Anyway, I looked through my brand-new *Juggs* magazine with high hopes, but I don't know—again, the sexiest woman was in a poolside setting, and I find poolside settings unerotic—that is to say, in general I find them unerotic, since God knows I've certainly come to an enormous number of poolside layouts in magazines, but there's something about the publicness of its being outside, in the sun—it's not as bad as a beach setting, which is a complete turnoff—I mean, again, if I were exiled to a desert island with nothing but some pages of a men's magazine showing a nude woman on a desert island, with the arty kidney shapes of sand on the asscheeks and all that, I would probably break down and masturbate to it . . . what do you think of that word?"

" 'Masturbate'? I don't hate it. I don't love it."

"Let's get a new word for it," he said.

"To myself, I sometimes call it 'dithering myself off.' "

"Okay, a possibility. What about just 'fiddle'? Fiddlin' yourself off? The dropped *g* is kind of racy. No, no. *Strum.*"

"Strum."

"That's it. I looked through the *Juggs*, and even though it was a poolside scene, I tried to *strum*, and there *was* one shot where the woman was looking straight at me, on her elbows on a yellow pool raft, and her frans were at their point of perfect beauty, not erect nipples but soft rounded tolerant nipples, which you have to have in a poolside photo set because as soon as you see those erect nipples in a poolside layout you think *cold water*, you don't think arousal. I want you to know, by the way, that I am not one of these sad individuals who hang out at the frozen fried-chicken section of the supermarket where it's extra cold just to see women's nipples get hard. I don't get the least thrill from wet T-shirt contests either, because I have to have an answering arousal there in the woman, and cold water is anti-sexual, except if in the case of the wet T-shirt contest I can convince myself that this woman is using the shock of the cold water, the giggliness and the splutteriness of it, to make something possible that otherwise wouldn't be possible and yet is arousing to her: I mean if she *wants* to show off her breasts, if she's proud of them and yet knows she's not the kind of person who's going to go off and become a stripper or whatever, and the douse of cold water is distracting enough to keep her sense of its all being in innocent fun in the end, *then* I can get turned on by shots of a wet T-shirt contest. You know?"

"I can see how that works. So you're looking at the woman in *Juggs*."

"Yes, and she was looking right at me, so appealingly, with such a lucid joyful amused look and her elbows were really digging into the pillow of the yellow raft, so it looked as if it might burst, and I could almost imagine strumming myself off to this, but then, no, there were too many things wrong—the photographer had put her hair in pigtails, tied with some kind of thick purply pink polyester yarn, and it just seemed so awful somehow, the age-old thing of men wanting to pretend that twenty-eight-year-old women are little girls by forcing this icon of girlishness, pigtails, on them, when really, when was the last time you saw a real little girl wearing pigtails? Not to *mention* the incidental fact that little girls are a turnoff. Here's this beautiful, alert, lovely woman, of at least twenty-seven, and all I could see was the dickhead photographer handing her some polyester yarn and saying, 'Uhright, now tie this purple stuff in your hair.' And I felt at that moment that I wanted to talk to a real woman, no more images of any kind, no fast forward, no pause, no magazine pictures. And there was the ad."

"But you've called these numbers before, haven't you?" she asked.

"A few times, but with no real success. And I don't

think I've ever called this very number before—2VOX."

"What do you mean by 'success'?"

"No women with any kind of spark. Or, actually, honestly, few women at all, period, except the ones who are paid by the phone service to make mechanical sexual small talk and moan occasionally. It's mostly just men saying 'Hey, any ladies out there?' But then once in a while a real woman will call. And at least with this, as opposed to pictures, at least there's the remote possibility of something clicking. Perhaps it's presumptuous of me to say that we, you and I, click, but there is that possibility."

"Yes."

"In a way it's like the radio. Do you know that I've never actually gone to a store and bought a record? That's probably why I never learned to appreciate the fade-out, as you describe it, since on the radio, one song melts into the next. But it seems to me that you really need the feeling of radio luck in listening to pop music, since after all it's about somebody meeting, out of all the zillions of people in the world, this one other nice person, or at least several adequate people. And so, if you buy the record, or the tape, then you *control* when you can hear it, when what you want is for it to be like luck, and like fate, and to zoom up and down the dial, looking for the song you want, hoping some station will play it—and the joy when it finally rotates around is so intense. You're not hearing it, you're overhearing it."

"On the other hand," she said, "if you own the tape, you show you've got some self-knowledge: you know what you like, you know how to make yourself happy, you're not just wandering in this welter of chance occurrences, passively hoping the disk jockey will come through. Maybe when you're a little kid you find yourself out on a balcony in the sun and you think, My oh my, this feels unexpectedly nice. But later on you think, I know that I will feel a particular kind of pleasure if I walk out onto this balcony and sit in that chair, and I wish to experience that pleasure now."

"Well, right, and so the reason I called this line was that the pleasures I'd sought out weren't doing it for me and there was this hope of luck, that I, that there would be a conversation . . ."

"You never said what it was about the Disney Tinker Bell exactly, at the video store."

"Well, in the scene I saw, and this is the first time I've seen any of this particular Disney by the way, and you have to remember that I'm in an altered state there in the movie store, with my three orange movies and my men's magazine in my briefcase, but in the scene, Tinker Bell zips around in a sprightly way, with lots of zings of the xylophone and little sparkly stars trailing her flight, and you think, right, typical fairy image, ho hum. And she's *tiny*, she's a tiny suburbanite, she's about five inches tall. This insubstantial, magical, cutely Walt Disneyish woman. But then this thing happens. She pauses in mid-air, and she looks down at herself, and she's got quite small breasts—"

"I thought you didn't like that word."

"You're right, but sometimes it seems right. Actually most of the time it's the right word. Anyway, she's got quite small breasts but quite *large* little hips, and *large* little thighs, and she's wearing this tiny little outfit that's torn or jaggedly cut and barely covers her, and she looks down at herself, a lovely little pouty face, and she puts her hands on her hips as if to measure them, and she shakes her head sadly—too wide, too wide. *Oh* that got me hot! This tiny sprite with *big hips*. And then a second later she gets caught in a dresser drawer among a lot of sewing things and she tries to fly out the keyhole but— nope, her hips are too wide, she gets stuck!"

"Sounds sizzling hot."

"It was."

"You remember *Gentlemen Prefer Blondes*, when Marilyn Monroe tries to squeeze through a porthole on a ship, but her hips are too wide?"

"I *don't* remember that. I better rent that."

"It would be funny if Tinker Bell inspired old Marilyn," she said. "You know, I found the Disney *Peter Pan* vaguely sexual, too."

"Well, yeah—J. M. Barrie was a fudgepacker from way back, and clearly some of that forbiddenness sneaks into every version."

"The girl floats around in her nightgown," she said.

"That interested me quite a bit. And she's *too old* to live in the room with the littler kids—I remember that. I must have been about twelve. I saw it with my friend Pamela, who I think has turned out to be a lesbian, bless her soul. We used to build tents in her bedroom and eat Saltines and read the medical encyclopedia together. It showed the dotted lines where the surgeon would cut cartilage from the ears if you were having an operation to make your ears flare out less. And at the end of each entry it would say, it was done in a question-and-answer format, it would say, 'When can marital relations be resumed?' And the answer always was four to six weeks. No matter where the dotted lines were, it seemed you could always resume marital relations after four to six weeks. I used to read the articles aloud to her. And once she read a whole romance novel aloud to me in one night. I fell asleep somewhere in the middle and woke up again later—Pamela was a little hoarse, but she was still reading. And once, maybe it was that same night, I told her a sexual fantasy I'd had a few times, in which I'm at a place where I'm told I have to take off all my clothes and get into this tube."

"Sorry, get into what?"

"This tube, a long tube," she said. "I slide in, feet first, and I begin moving down this very long tube, on some sort of slow current of oil. I'm sure you remember those water slides that you set up on the lawn, that destroyed the grass? This was not as fast-moving as that, much slower-moving, but no friction, and in a luminous tube. As I went along these pairs of hands would enter the tube a little ahead of me, waving around blindly, looking for something to feel, and then my feet would brush under them, and they would try to grasp my ankles, but their fingers were dripping with oil, and as I moved forward they slid up my legs, holding me quite hard, but without friction because of the oil, and then they pressed down as my stomach went under them, and then they sort of turned to encounter my breasts, the two thumbs were almost touching, and they slid very slowly over my breasts, pushing them up, and believe me, in this fantasy I had very large heavy breasts, it took a long time for the hands to slide over them."

"Wow! What did old Pamela say when you told her that?"

"I finished describing it, and I asked her if she had thoughts like that and she said 'No!' in quite a shocked voice. She said, 'No! Tell me another.' You think maybe my tube was what turned her into a lesbian?"

"Well, it certainly would have turned me into a lesbian. But now—can you clarify one thing for me? Do you right now have the light on or off in the room you're in, the combination living room dining room?"

"I have it on. It's a table lamp. I could turn it off if you'd like."

"Perhaps that, perhaps that would . . ."

"Listen." There was a click.

"Now your silverware is glinting in the moonlight, right?" he said.

"I can't see it."

"Have you noticed that little juncture in movies, or I guess it's more in TV shows, when somebody has some pensive thought, or peaceful thought, close-up of her face, and then she reaches over and turns out the bed-side light, click, but of course this is a movie set, with elaborate lights all over the place, so her turning that little switch has to coincide with the shutting off of major flows of current, *kashoonk*, and the problem then is that movie film doesn't work in the dark, so there has to be quite a high light level but with the impression of dark-ness, and so at the same instant the big imitation incan-descent lamp lights are turned off, the imitation moonlight or streetlight lights have to come on outside the window, and yet there is often a problem, there is often a tiny millisecond delay while the filaments of the moonlight lights heat up and reach their peak, and so in this changeover you can see the second set of lights that are supposed to mean 'dark peaceful room' spread over the bed and the walls? Have you noticed that?"

"No," she said. "But it sounds very interesting and I promise I will look for it next time I watch TV."

"Do," he said. "Meanwhile you'll be glad to know that the real streetlight outside my window is beginning to come on. It's the most amazing effect. It doesn't come on all at once, it's nothing like what I just described. It

comes on very very gradually, over about twenty minutes. It starts off in a very deep orange phase. I very
seldom have *time* to watch it, of course, with my hectic
schedule. But when I do, it really is quite beautiful. It's
so gradual that you're not quite sure whether it's the light
coming on and shining a little more brightly, or if the sky
has darkened—of course it's both, but you can't tell
which is overtaking the other, and then there's this moment, about five minutes from now, when the streetlight
is exactly the same color as the sky, I mean exactly the
same green-violet-yellow whatever, so that it seems as if
there's a *hole* in the middle of the tree across the street,
in the branches, where the sky, which is really the light
on this side of the street, shows through."

There was a pause.

"Listen," she said. "This is getting expensive, at a
dollar a minute or whatever it is."

"Ninety-five cents per half minute, I think."

"So give me your number and I'll call you back," she
said.

"All right. But."

"Yes?"

"But then you'll have to turn your light on again to
write my number down," he said.

"What do you mean? I have a good memory for numbers."

"Oh, I'm sure it's much better than mine. But what if
in this one isolated case the number slips your mind?"

"Okay, to be safe I'll turn on the light and write it down."

"But what if you write it down wrong, just because this is such an unusual sort of occasion, and you reverse two numbers, the first time you've ever done it?"

"Sexual dyslexia."

"Right! Or what if you hang up and you get another Diet Coke and then you decide, no, this is crazy, I don't want to call him back? How do I know you won't just not call?"

"I'm going to call you back," she said. "I'm *enjoying* this. I'm going to call."

"Okay, but what if you do call, but because of the break, even that one-minute break, when we aren't connected, what if fate shifts, and we're suddenly awkward with each other, and we're never quite able to resume the intimacy that we seemed to hit so easily the first time?"

"All right, you convinced me. Don't give me your number."

"Really I think two dollars a minute is *cheap* for this. I need this. I'd spend twenty dollars a minute for this. And there isn't a time limit on this line, either—at least my ad says NO TIME LIMIT in big letters."

"Okay," she said.

"Okay, and in return for your indulgence, I'm going to try to do something with your heirlooms there, on your dining-room table. Let me see. All right, once there was a guy who had a big party, a big dinner party for a dozen people, which really wasn't his style, but he did it anyway, and when all of his friends had left, he began cleaning up, feeling slightly depressed. He took the plates in, the glasses in, the cutlery in, man, he'd never seen the basket in his dishwasher so *stuffed* with silverware. He jammed the last fork in, but in his impatience to close the dishwasher door and go to bed, he didn't check that the fork was all the way in the basket, and as it happened it was not, because the forks were so tightly squeezed in there that he would have really had to work it down for it to stay put. This was one of the older-style dishwashers, and when that fork was tossed aloft by the first powerful spray of water up from the impeller, it fell, and it happened to fall so that it was caught dangling somehow between a plate and the little loop on the handle of a saucepan, with the points up, and the handle dangling far enough down that the sprayer in the bottom swung into it at full speed and notched it, and made it swing up again but not completely out of the way, and so it swung down into the path of the sprayer thing again and again, and got very messed up, and by the time this guy was able to get back to the kitchen and turn off the dishwasher, which sounded awful, the fork was badly injured. He dried the fork with a paper towel, and the rough places on the fork tore the paper, and that was too much for him, he almost felt like throwing the fork away, and he went to bed very dejected, wondering what the point of it all was. Okay? Now in this same city there was a jewelry store, that some might say was a little bit too trendy, but that was still a very nice place—they didn't sell diamonds or emeralds or conventional big-ticket items like that, in fact it was called 'Harvey's Semi-Precious,' after Harvey, the owner—and mostly it sold artisan stuff and collectibles. And *you* got a job there."

"I did?" she said.

"What happened was, you went to a program in a university, and you got a masters in silversmithing, with some postgraduate work in pendant mounting and bead drilling, and you found that you had a very good eye, and you really were able to make bracelets and earrings and especially necklaces that looked good on people, not that looked good in the display case, in fact sometimes your work even looked a little strange, a little knobby and unsure of itself in the display case, but on the human form—divine. So you graduate from the program and it's time to make a living, and you take your best work around to various jewelry places, and you get a mixed reaction, frankly, the world isn't quite ready for you, and finally you take it to Harvey's Semi-Precious, which you've avoided because in a way it's a little down-market—it started as a head shop in fact, and Harvey's this fairly old guy now with a big collection of fancy cigarette cases from the twenties that you find saddens you, and he's got what you might call an old-world smell, but you interview with him, and he seems nice, and he's very encouraging about your work, and you decide what the hay. But the only stipulation is, if you work for Harvey, you have to work in the store, in this small glass enclosure that kind of projects from one of the windows so that people walking by on the street can watch you work. You're a little hesitant about that, but he draws the curtain open, tells you to take a seat, and it's this nice little room, with many many small wooden drawers that are handy on either side, and a whole set of silversmithing tools that are mounted on little spring clips, and a nice flame there, a nice blue flame, with a yellow tip, and it really seems very cozy, and yet of course visible from the street, and so you start work. And Harvey could not be nicer—he treats you with kindly irony, and when you make a piece he especially likes, he is very appreciative. He sets up a special display case for just your work in the store, and he doesn't mind when you come in a little late. And over the first few months you start doing this series of bracelets, simple elegant silver bracelets, which Harvey puts in the case. Naturally many of the customers who wander into the store are young men buying jewelry for women they love, and they're uncertain, they want to be sure they're right to buy that particular piece, and so Harvey gets in the habit of poking his head through the curtain and asking you, very hesitantly and politely, if you might want to come out and show the prospective buyer what the bracelet looks like on a real woman. And you find this a trifle embarrassing, because, after all, you made the piece, but you take off your welder's glasses and you run your hands through your hair and there you are walking out into the store toward smiling Harvey and the open display case with the key in it, and this nervous man who's in a hurry to get something for his wife or mistress is standing there, and you extend your arm, and Harvey puts on the bracelet, and the man's mouth moves, and his checkbook falls open, and there, so easy, it's sold. You sell about ten, fifteen bracelets this way, and with this success, you start to get ambitious, and you design and make a necklace, a very simple necklace, but with three stones that Harvey's procured for you, a tiny chrysolite in the center, and then, on either side, two lovely lustrous pieces of unpolished strumulite, which are, as you know, fossilized drops of dinosaur ejaculate. Nothing could be more tasteful—you surprise yourself with how well it turns out—nothing you did in school equals this necklace. Harvey is in rapture—he holds it draped over his fingers, which are all dry and discolored from silver polish, and he just shakes his head, and you feel very happy, happy at having found your metier, and happy at having found as good a person to work for as Harvey. Well, so, the necklace is hung up in the display case, not in as prominent a position as you think it ought to be, perhaps, and Harvey insists on putting a very high price on it, too high to sell, you think, but Harvey is, for once, adamant. Some weeks go by, and you sell several other small pieces, a ring, some earrings, but the necklace does not sell. You're curious, you peep through the curtain and watch Harvey taking customers over to your case, and you notice that he seems to be avoiding calling attention to the very fine piece, he's distracting buyers when they comment on it. You realize, not without a certain pleasure, that Harvey is probably somewhat in love with you, though he's too gentle ever to raise the issue. He now averts his gaze whenever you extend your wrist to put on one of your bracelets for a customer. And you begin to sense that he doesn't want to sell the glorious strumulite necklace you made because he is afraid that when he does he's going to lose you. And you feel that he's probably right. He's started asking you if you're happy, if you have all the tools you need. There have been other jeweleresses in the window of Harvey's Semi-Precious in days gone by, of course, and they have all gone on to bigger things, bigger commissions, but none of them has gotten to Harvey the way you have, you suspect."

"I'm a little full of myself, aren't I?" she said.

"You are, yes, and yet you're uncertain too. And so one morning, you're in your glass enclosure working away, and you look up and there's this guy standing quite close to the glass, peering in at you. You nod, you're used to this, and he nods. He's wearing a suit, and he's carrying what looks to be a fork, wrapped in a piece of paper towel. He looks up at the sign over the shop and you hear him go in and you hear him talking to Harvey. Harvey sounds a bit testy. You hear him say, 'She can't take her time up with uncreative work like that.' Then the guy says something, a note of urgency in his voice. Harvey says, 'No, I'm not kidding, really, no.' And you pop your head out of the curtain. The two men look at you. Harvey goes, 'I'm trying to tell this gentleman that you're an artist and you are not able to do something like repair his fork. He doesn't want me to do the repair, he wants you to do it.' The guy in the suit looks embarrassed, he holds up his hands. You walk out into the shop. You take off your insulated soldering gloves and put them carelessly down on a display of rare campaign buttons. You're wearing a shirt with small green and black stars on it, and black pants, and black sneakers. You hold out your hand for the fork, the guy gives it to you. You say, 'An incident with the dishwasher?' and he nods yes. And you say, 'Harvey, it won't take me a second.' Harvey goes, 'Fine! Go ahead!' and sits down near the register, staring straight ahead. He's pissed. You say to the guy, 'I'll have it for you by noon.' And you go back into your area in the window. You take up the piece you've been working on. It's some kind of brooch, and it isn't turning out very well. You've lost your inspiration to some degree, since Harvey hasn't sold your best effort. You look at the fork sitting there, and then you become conscious of a presence outside the window, and you look up, and it's the same guy. You give him a questioning expression, and he moves his arms to say, 'Don't mind me.' But he doesn't walk away. You look down at the brooch again, but you don't like it, you don't want Mr. Fork to see it and think of it as representative of your work. And so you set it aside and you clamp the injured fork in several delicate vises, and you put on your insulated gloves, and you start playing the flame of the torch over the nicked parts. Repair is Harvey's area, so you don't get much of a chance to do this, but you find now that in small doses it's a very satisfying and soothing activity. Naturally you can't restore the fork to mint condition—you melt the roughnesses until they subside, and what you're left with is a lovely irregular mottled very shiny surface. You're glad you have your dark welder's goggles on: you look up covertly, with just your eyes, not lifting your head, and you see the fork man standing there sort of *slumped*, looking at you do those things to his fork. He's melting, he's smitten, he's silversmitten. You plunge the fork into a tray of water. He smiles. He goes back into the shop. You come out of your enclosure. Harvey looks up. You hand the fork to Harvey and Harvey looks at it and says, 'Twelve dollars.' Mr. Fork pays the twelve dollars and takes the repair job and says thank-you to Harvey. Then he says, 'I was just curious how it was done. I'm sorry to have taken up her time.' And then he asks, 'You say she's an artist. Can you show me some things she's done?' Slowly, slowly Harvey walks over to the display case, unlocks it, sighs. The guy leans very close to the jewelry, his head is practically *in* the case. You're watching all this. You notice for the first time that he's got his hair in a kind of ponytail. And then he points to the necklace and he says, 'May I take a look at that?' Harvey looks at you, he's got this almost pleading look, but you don't say anything. So Harvey seems to decide something, and he says sadly, 'That's the best thing in the store.' And he unhooks it from its little mounts and he hands it to Mr. Forkman, who again looks closely at it, holds it up in the air. Harvey says, 'For a fiancée or something? What's her complexion, dark or light?' And Forkman vagues out, saying, 'I don't really know who it's for.' Again Harvey looks at you, and you don't say anything, and so Harvey swallows and he says, he almost whispers, 'Really you can't get a good sense of it unless you see it worn.' And the fork guy says, 'Gee, yeah, too bad.' And he asks what the stones are and Harvey tells him and the guy just nods. Finally Harvey, almost in exasperation, says, 'Look, *she* made it, she knows all about it, she'll tell you everything you want to know, I'm going to get a bite to eat.' He turns to you and says, 'Show him the piece, all right?' He grabs his jacket and goes out, pulling the door shut with unusual force, so that the sign saying OPEN flips down to say CLOSED. And so . . ."

"Mm-hmm?"

"No, that's it, I shot my wad getting the two of you face-to-face."

"No! You're bailing out right there? Did you really shoot your wad, or you mean figuratively?"

53

"At the moment, my true wad could not be farther from shooting. It is *work* getting the two of you together. I feel that any second I'm going to misstep in telling this. It's very stressful."

"Now listen," she said. "Harvey leaves, slamming the door, so the sign says CLOSED, and I, me, I am left, abandoned right in the middle of things by Harvey, and I'm standing there in the shop with the taciturn and very rich guy Forky, Forky Pigtail, who's holding the necklace that I made in his big knuckly fingers. He sits down on a step stool, he looks down at the necklace, looks up at me. *What does he do?*"

"He says, 'I really do have to see what it looks like on someone before I know whether it's something I want.' And you look down at your shirt with the green and black stars and you sort of pluck at it and smile and say, 'I'm sorry, I'm not wearing the clothes for that piece. It's really an evening piece, for a low-cut dress.' With your finger you trace the ideal curve of the neckline of the dress. And Fork says, 'Then unbutton your shirt.' Well, what can you do? You unbutton the top three buttons of your shirt. With each button, you feel the fabric shift slightly against your collarbone. Fork stands up, letting the necklace dangle from his left hand, and, to your astonishment, he begins unbuttoning the buttons of his fly. Because of course he's a button-fly kind of guy. He unbuttons three buttons. The two of you are still about ten feet apart. You fold your shirt down, trying to make it follow the line of the dress that you should be wearing to wear the necklace, but looking down at yourself you see that you really need to undo one more button, and you dart a glance at him—has he reached the same conclusion? Oh no, he has! He is shaking his head. He says, 'I think really you'll need to go down one more in order to wear your necklace.' So you unbutton one more button, and he responds by unbuttoning the last button of his fly. He doesn't do anything, he doesn't reach in, you almost couldn't tell that his fly was undone, if it weren't for the fact that you've just seen him undo it. Oh, he is a bold bastard! What is he up to? He takes the necklace in both his hands, by both ends, and he shakes it, indicating for you to walk toward him, which you do. When you are standing close to him, he says, 'I think it'll be easier if you turn around. Then I'll be able to see the clasp.' So you turn around, and you see this necklace, your own handiwork, descend very slowly in front of your face, and you feel the dangly elements just touch your skin and you try to hold your shirt so it doesn't get in the way, but instead of doing the clasp, he lowers the necklace further and lets it accommodate itself to your breasts, and you hear him say, thoughtfully, 'Hmm, no, I really think the shirt has to come off entirely before I can evaluate this necklace. The green and black stars clash with the stones.' So you unbutton the shirt completely and let it fall off your arms. You're wearing a black cotton undershirty thing, with very thin shoulder straps. Very gently he drags your piece of jewelry up again, against you, and then finally he fastens it, holding the ends away from your neck so that his hands hardly touch you. You look down at it. It's hard to tell, but you think it looks kind of beautiful. Your nipples are visible through the black material. He's silent behind you. You say, 'Don't you want to see it now?' But he says, 'Wait, let me just do something.' And you hear a slight scrape of the step stool against the floor, and you hear his shoes on the steps, and then you hear some rustling, and then a very soft rhythmic sound, the sound of the sleeve of his suit jacket making repeated contact with one side of the jacket itself, and, as the speed of the rhythm increases slightly, you hear every once in a while a little sort of *plick* or *click*, a wet little sound, and you know exactly what he's doing, and you hear his voice, with a bit of strain in it, say, 'I think I'm ready to see it now.' And you turn, and there he is, on the top step of this little stool, with his cock and both balls pulled out of his pants, and with each pull he makes on his cock you can see the skin pull up slightly on his balls. I mean is this guy for real? And you touch your shoulders with your hands, and you pull the straps of your black undershirt down, and you pull it down around your waist, so your breasts are right there, out, and now you take hold of your breasts, your frans, and you lift them, so that each of the two side stones of your necklace touches a nipple, and by moving your breasts back and forth, you move your nipples, which are hard, back and forth under the two cool dangly stones, and you see him stroking faster and faster, he's starting to get the about-to-come expression, and you smile at him and move a step closer, so your breasts and your silver necklace and your collarbone are ready for him, and then you look straight at him and you say, 'Well, what do you think? Do you like it? As you see, it's really an evening piece.' And then, stroking very fast, he bends his legs slightly and then straightens them and he goes 'Ooh!' and then he comes in a hot mess all over your art."

There was a pause. She said, "Does he buy the necklace or does he just take his fixed fork and go home?"

"I don't know. I assume he takes the paper towel that he'd wrapped his fork in and uses it to wipe you off and wipe off your necklace and then he buys it and gives it to you."

"That's good. He sounds like an honorable sort. A bit precipitate maybe. Um—would you excuse me for a second?"

"Sure."

"I just—my mouth's dry—I want to get some more—"

"Sure," he said.

There was a long pause. She returned.

"It's funny that you cast me as an arts-and-craftsy type," she said.

"Not aggressively arts-and-craftsy. Are you?"

"Well, no. I'm really not, I don't think. Do you have a ponytail?" she asked.

"No."

"Then do you have an old-world smell?"

"I don't think that would be the word for it."

"I wonder what your smell is."

"I've been told I smell like a Conté crayon," he said. "Hm."

"Or I guess it was that I smelled like what a Conté crayon would smell like if it had a smell."

"Well, that's good to know," she said. "Of course I have no idea what you're talking about. But no, you know what your story reminded me of, when I was in the kitchen just now?"

"What?"

"I was in a museum in Rome with my mother, and we passed a statue that had all these discolorations on it, a nice statue of a woman, and my mother pointed to a sort of mottled area and she shook her head and said, 'You see? It's so realistic that men feel they have to . . .' She didn't explain. And I don't know now if she was serious or not. I was—I guess I was eighteen. I thought, oh, okay, in churches in Italy, people wear down the toes of the statues of popes by touching them so much, and in museums in Italy, men come on the statues of women."

"Yes," he said, "I think I do remember coming on that statue. It's all a blur, though. There were so many statues in those years."

"Do you, as they say, like to travel?" she asked.

"You mean get in a plane and fly somewhere for rec-

reation? No. I've never been to Rome. I spend my vacation money in more important ways."

"Like this call."

"That's right. Now tell me, though, really, when your
mother pointed out that statue, was it faintly arousing?"

"I don't think it really was," she said. "It was just
interesting, an interesting sexual fact, like something in
Ripley's. I'm not, by the way, to get back to *your* story for
a second, I'm not wearing a black undershirt under my
shirt."

"What are you wearing under your shirt?"

"A bra."

"What kind of bra?"

"A nothing bra. A normal, white bra bra."

"Oooo!"

"It's shrunk slightly in the wash but it was my last
clean one."

"It's always impressive to me that bras have to be
washed like other clothes. Does it clip on the front or on
the back?"

"The back."

"Shouldn't it come off?"

"I don't think so," she said.

"Oh, I can hear in your voice the sound of you frowning and pulling in your chin to look down at them! Oh
boy."

"Hah hah!"

"The idea of women looking down at their own breasts

drives me *nutso*. They do it while they're walking. Some walk with their arms sort of hovering in front of their breasts, or awkwardly crossed in front of them, or they pretend to hold the strap of their pocketbook so their hands are bent in front of them, or they pretend to be adjusting their watch, or their bracelets, and the fact that even fully clothed the helpless obviousness of their breasts is embarrassing to them drives me absolutely *nutso*."

"They see you staring, with your eyes sproinging out of your skull, of course they're embarrassed."

"No, I'm very discreet. And this is only in certain moods, of course. Once I got into a wild state just standing at a bus stop. It was rush hour, and there were all these women driving to work, and they would drive by, and I would get this flash, this briefest of glimpses, of the wide shoulder strap of their safety belt crossing their breasts. That thick, densely woven material, pulling itself tight right between them. That's all I could see, hundreds of times, different colors of dresses, shirts, blouses, over and over, every bra size and Lycra-cotton balance imaginable, like frames of a movie. By the time the bus came, I was literally unsteady, I could barely get the fare in the machine. What's that noise?"

"Nothing. I was just changing the phone to the other ear."

"Oh," he said. "Did you see that thing about the Chinese kid who suffered an episode of spontaneous human combustion?"

"No."

"You really missed something. It was originally in one of the tabloids, I think, but I heard about it on the radio. You know about spontaneous human combustion, right?"

"I'm familiar with the general concept."

"All right, well this kid apparently spontaneously human combusted, but the combustion was confined to his genitals. Boom! He was very uncomfortable. But see, I understand perfectly how that could happen. I fear for my own genitals sometimes. I get so fricking horny . . . now there's another inadequate word . . . so porny, so gorny, so yorny . . . I get so *yorny* that I look down at my cock-and-balls unit, and it's like I could take the whole rigid assembly and start unscrewing it, around and around, and it would come off as one solid thing, like a cotterless crank on a bicycle, and I would hand it over to you to use as a dildo."

"Okay then, hand it over. Although I've never cottoned to dildos particularly. I used one once, to oblige someone, and I got a yeast infection. I think it was called a 'Mighty Mini Brute.' "

"That's a fair description of my . . . crank."

"I know what you mean, though. Sometimes I get the same way, so worked up. My clit gets hard and it feels like this discrete wedge item, like a piece of candy corn, and I feel as if I should put it in a little wooden box for safekeeping. I usually like to come in the shower."

"Mm! Shouldn't that bra come off, really?"

"No it really should not, and I'll tell you why. When I dither myself off . . . . no, I don't want to tell you."

"Please, yes you do, please tell me, yes you do, please, right now."

"When I masturbate and I'm not in the shower, I need my breasts to be tended to, but, boo-hoo, there's nobody to tend to them, so what I *do* is I pull my bra down so that the edge of it catches under my nipples, and then they're all taken care of, and I can use both hands to tend to matters below."

"This is a miracle," he said.

"It's just a telephone conversation."

"It's a telephone conversation I want to have. I *love* the telephone."

"Well, I like it too," she said. "There's a power it has. My sister's little babe has a toy phone, which is white, with horses and pigs and ducks on the dial, and a blue receiver that has no weight to it at all, and I find there is an astonishing feeling of power when you pretend to be talking to someone on it. You cover the mouthpiece with your hand and you say in this dramatic whisper, 'Stevie, it's *Horton the Elephant* on the phone. He wants to speak to you!' and you hand it over to Stevie and his eyes get big and you and he both for that second believe that Horton the Elephant really is on the phone. And then you get *two* phones going. Stevie's on the white phone with the ducks and pigs, and I'm on the yellow phone with the wheels and the eyes that move when you pull it along the floor, and I ask how Stevie's doing and have a little conversation with him and then I say, 'Stevie, would you like to speak to *Paul?*' And Stevie says yes. Paul is a relative—this happened last time I was back home—and Paul, who's sitting right there, gets this startled look, his hand automatically flies up to take the tiny plastic phone that I'm handing to him, he interrupts whatever real conversation he's been having and he says, 'Hello?' and his smile is very complicated—he *almost believes.*"

"That's right!" he said. "And here I am talking to you, and you truly are somewhere on the East Coast, and you're wearing a bra!"

"Amazing as it may seem. What other words do you have for the things I'm looking down at right now and admiring?"

"Other words for breasts? Frans is the main one. Sometimes . . . frannies. Frans, nans, and Kleins. And I never thought 'ass' fit. Sometimes I think of a woman's ass as a 'tock.' "

"So then it follows that she has a 'tockhole' as well?"

"I never pushed it that far."

"Kleins is strange. 'I'm squeezing my big fleshy Kleins'? You sure?"

"I don't know, I think Patsy Cline is a sexy name. I don't even know who she is."

"She's a singer."

"I know that much. Once I looked down the list of

Kleins in the phone book and found one with a woman's name spelled out, and God, it was everything I could not to call that number. In fact, I did call the number, and she answered, and I said, 'Oh gosh, I must have the wrong number.' And yet the Kleins I've known in real life haven't been surrounded by a mysterious sexual power."

"It's that telephone."

"Your last name isn't Klein?"

"No," she said. "But I will tell you something."

"What? What? What?"

"Occasionally when I'm just about to reach an orgasm I . . . I think of it as a 'Delgado.' "

"Think of what as a Delgado?" he asked.

"The erect male cock."

"Oh, oh. Sorry."

"It's because I was infatuated with a boy named Delgado in high school. So when you said something about, something about your 'sperm-dowel' earlier, I misheard for a second, and I felt this *rush* of blood—I thought you were using my secret word."

"Now see that is what I live for, for someone to tell me something like that. I need that to happen to me every minute, every second."

"That's an impossibility."

"I will feast on that revelation for weeks to come."

"It's a secret, though, so . . ."

"*Up*, it doesn't go beyond this conversation. Out here

we say everything, but in our lives, nothing. Out here you can tell me, just *request* me, to pull on the knot of my bathrobe until it falls open."

"What kind of bathrobe is it?"

"White terry cloth. And you can just tell me, you can just say, 'Jim, please lift the waistband of your gray underpants up to its extreme limit of stretch so that it clears your erection and then bring it around and hook it under your balls, and then take that *Juggs* magazine and use it to fan your overheated pop stand.' And you know what? I would do it."

"Well, yes, I could tell you to do all that, but I don't know, those are important decisions you maybe ought to make for yourself."

"And I could probably ask you to tell me anything about yourself and you will tell me."

"Maybe," she said.

"You told me the secret word you have for the adult male cock, anyway. Not for my cock, leave me out of it. For the one you think about *on your own*. See, see, this is what I need. I need to know secrets and have secrets and keep secrets. I need to be confided in. Each time you come alone and you don't tell anybody, that's a sexual secret. The event has taken place and only you know about it and you have ministered to yourself in exactly the way you wanted to and thought of exactly what you wanted to think about. And each of these thousands of times you have come alone constitutes a perfectly unique moment, with precisely this order of images and that fold of yourself being moved by your middle finger in just that way and that biting of lower lip with exactly that degree of force, all entirely private. I almost think that each one of the times a woman comes in private in her life has to continue to exist as a kind of sphere, a foot-and-a-half-wide sphere, in some ideal dimension, sort of like all the ovums you've got queued up in you, except these are . . . ovums of past orgasms, weird as that sounds, and I am this one viable spermazoid lurking around among them, and I would happily spend my life floating up to one after another of these unique orgasm-spheres and looking inside and I'd be able to watch you make yourself come that one time."

"I bet each one of these mystical spheres has a little window in it with a little Levelor blind that's down almost but not quite all the way, right, that you creep up to and peer into, am I right?"

"Exactly, as if it's a stylized cartoon bubble with a curved window drawn on it, and you're naked in there, strumming like there's no tomorrow. But no, actually it isn't like simple voyeurism, I don't think—it's holier or more reverent than that, because when I'm in that mood I don't want to exist. I don't mean I want to kill myself, I mean that I'm a man and a man is a watcher and a watcher disturbs the purity of the event, so I don't want to exist, I want to be faded away to almost nothing. And of course all other men are completely foreign, they aren't allowed in this at all. When I'm very aroused I almost hate all other men. Sometimes when there's a kissing scene in a movie, and the camera shows the actor and actress chomping away on each other's gums, *moyong, moyong*, and then there's this sudden folded-up piece of shaven male jaw skin, I feel a wave of disgust— what the fuck is he doing there, get him off the set! That's not even to mention the bestial idiots in porn movies: this nice woman donating her perfect self to these horrible lascivious dumbfucks, with their suggestive evil laughs, and their intent lustful expressions, and their singlemindedness, and their constant diverting of the conversation around to sex. Get *rid* of them. One time I was in a store at the dirty-magazine rack and it was a little congested there and I reached sort of over this guy's shoulder to get a copy of the magazine I wanted to look at—*E-Cup* or something—didn't touch him, just reached over him, and the guy half turned his head and said in this psychopathic voice, but very soft, he said, 'Stay away from me or I'll cut you up.' I said, 'Sorry, sorry, I was *just* trying to get the magazine!' And he said, 'Well just stay the fuck away from me, okay?' Now I'd never say that or threaten that but that guy's reaction, when you're at the magazine rack and you want to be the only one there, among all these lovely kindly wonderful naked women, is a reaction I can at least understand. These groups of buddies who go out and drink beer together at strip clubs—it's totally mystifying to me that they would want to do that, have male company."

"But women *like* men from time to time."

"I know that, I realize that, and that's how I trick myself into accepting men's existence: women often imagine men when they come, so men have a reason to exist. In fact, this secondary deductive twist allows me to get aroused by stuff that doesn't really arouse me, like for instance when you went into that catalog thing earlier about the row of male models in the warehouse with their cream horns popping out of their shorts, I could think to myself, okay, her arousal is supremely arousing to me, and this image she's describing is the source or current expression of her arousal, and I could imagine your face thinking of those images, and therefore I was able to make them somewhat arousing to me. Like the religious nut who embraces the devil because it shows his utter humility before God—except I don't go that far. Oh! I know what I meant to tell you."

"What?"

"You know you mentioned that friend of yours reading you a romance novel all night? Okay, this is a good example of what I'm talking about. I went into this used bookstore one time, just to browse around, called Bonnie's Books. But it wasn't really the kind of place I thought it was going to be, it had hardly any old books, what it had was recently published pre-enjoyed books. A de-facto library. Shelf after shelf of these things, big thick historical romances, super neatly shelved, sometimes five or six copies of the same book side by side, *Love's Hurry*, *Love's Eager Trial*, *Love's Tender Fender Bender*, all that kind of material, but even though there were multiple copies of these books, they weren't identical, because every one of them had been read. They looked *handled*. *All* of their pages were turned. And turned by whom? Turned by women. My heart started going. I had entered this enchanted glade. I took a historical romance off the shelf, and I felt as if I were lifting a towel that was still damp from a woman's shower. The intimacy of it! But it was long—no way I could ever read a book that long. So I put it back. There was a woman at the counter, maybe thirty-eight or forty, perhaps Bonnie herself. She'd read some of these books! I think I was the only one in the store—I knew she was aware of me—I'd smiled at her when I went in. I wanted her to *see me* looking at the historical romances. And then I went a little further up this one aisle, and I came to a huge trove of romance novels—hundreds and hundreds of them—all organized by the specific subseries, some of which are slightly softer core or harder core, you know, in some they're allowed to say 'he frisked his tongue over her navel' and some they can't. And I got to this set of red books, only about maybe fifty of them, called the Silhouette Desire series, and 'desire' is written in this luscious sloppy longhand, in a diagonal—*Desire*. Alarm bells started going off in my head, and I thought of going over to Bonnie and saying, 'Um, do you know those Silhouette Desire books? Can you tell me which title in that series is the most arousing of all of them, in your judgment?' But I could never have done that. And it didn't matter anyway, because hundreds of female orgasms could be *inferred* from the books themselves—you didn't need to harass any particular woman, you didn't need to invade anybody's privacy, you could just hold any copy and think of a woman holding it open with one hand, with her thumb and little finger. It was all there in the pliability and the thumbedness of the book itself—it practically shouted at you, 'I have been near a clit as it underwent two orgasms.' "

"So did you buy one of these Silhouette Desire books?" she asked. "*Love's Tender Gender Bender?*"

"Can you hold on for just a second? I have to get it."

"I guess so, sure."

There was a pause.

"It's called *Beginner's Luck*," he said, "by Dixie Browning, and it's singled out by the publisher as a quote 'Man of the Month' volume. *Not only* is it heavily thumbed, but the woman who owned it before I did spilled water or gin or something on it, so that it's all wavy. It's got a permanent wave. You can imagine."

"Whew."

"As I was driving home I was so stiff from owning this pre-enjoyed book that once when I was stopped at a stoplight and I saw a woman in my rearview mirror I made a very small clit-circling motion with my fingers on the roof of my car, despite the bird droppings up there— the idea that she might notice and understand what this motion meant made me feel faint with excitement—but

70

she was expressionless. Anyway, I took the book home and read it, and you know what? It was good! Not only did it give me a partial erection on two occasions, I actually got tears in my eyes toward the end! It's about a man and a woman in a cabin in the woods. He's a klutzy scientist, she helps him get less klutzy and finally gets him to shave off his beard and it turns out that when he's cleaned up he's irresistible and despite being unschooled in the ways of love he is successful in bringing her to a fever pitch. Good stuff. I mean I probably won't reread it very soon, but when you think of some of the stuff that passes for highbrow these days, you've got to admire it for hanging back so humbly in the genre category. But never mind that. I finished the book, and I pictured the woman who owned the book finishing the book, with her normal flannel nightgown on—she switches out the light, she closes her eyes, she switches on the alarm—and then I turned the last page of the book, and there were more pages, there were four or five pages of promotion, up-coming titles, etcetera, and I turned to this one page. You ready? I'm going to read it to you. It says, 'You'll flip . . . your pages won't! Read paperbacks *hands-free* with BOOK MATE I. The perfect "mate" for all your ro-mance paperbacks. Traveling, vacationing, at work, in bed, studying, cooking, eating.' Did you hear that 'in bed' in the middle there? It's squirreled away in a non-sexual list, legitimized, like those gigantic massager wands that are always accompanied by catalog copy that talks about relieving aching muscles and lower back pain, when what we're all really talking about is women making themselves come in bed. What this Book Mate is is this rigid-backed thing to which you *strap* the book using this quote 'see-through strap.' There's nothing the book can do, it's powerless—it's strapped wide open—open for all the hungry eyes of the world to admire. The ad says, 'This wonderful invention makes reading a pure pleasure! Ingenious design holds paperback books OPEN and FLAT so even wind can't ruffle pages—leaves your hands free to do other things.' And *that*'s the page of this book *Beginner's Luck* that I finally masturbated to: the thought of a woman reading that this invention will leave her hands free to do other things, and the thought of her ordering it and then maybe holding the strapped-open book between her bent knees so she can read the crucial page of pleasure while she goes to town down there . . . needing to have both her hands free *to do other things* . . . ho God! The problem is, though, that you yourself almost certainly don't find any of this arousing."

"No, well," she said, "I find it mildly arousing, for the very reason you already said—it's something that's arousing to you."

"But there's the thing," he said. "If you only find it mildly arousing because I found it exceedingly arousing, then I have to cancel my strong arousal and replace it with mild arousal, since the degree of your arousal is the primary source of my arousal. And then, the problem is, you'll find it only infinitesimally arousing and I'll then have to discard it as a total turnoff. That's the problem."

"We have to find a middle way," she said.

"The middle way is for you to tell me the last thing you thought of that made you pay some attention to your candy corn."

"I liked the story you told about the jeweler pretty well."

"No no, before tonight. Whenever the last time was you made yourself come."

"Last night. I really don't remember. These are fleeting things."

"Oh, you *do* remember."

"I was in the shower."

"Wait a second. Okay. You were in the shower."

"What did you just do?" she asked.

"Nothing. My underpants were starting to bug me. Go on."

"I was in the shower, which is almost always the place I come best. In college there were very nice marble showers, with high showerheads, and the water, the shape of each *drop* of water, was exactly right, fat soothing generous drops, but billions of them. I came many many times in those showers."

"Public showers, you mean?"

"No no, private," she said. "This little high marble box, with a marble foyer. It was very loud, and sometimes when the water collected and flowed together down my arm and between my legs and then fell from there it made this almost *clacking* noise on the tile. The dorms were coed, so potentially there was a man from my hall in the next shower over, but that didn't interest me. I used to take showers at odd times of the day anyway, when the bathrooms were deserted. One-thirty in the afternoon. I'd go to class, and I'd start drawing in the margin of my notebook, and I'd draw a little curve, and I'd think, hm, a curve, and then I'd turn it into a breast, and I'd make it a bit larger, and then I'd make another one, and then I'd draw a pair of hands holding the breasts from behind—that was always an idea that interested me, that I'd be sitting in some class or auditorium, dimly lit, an architectural history lecture, with slides, and a person sitting behind me would reach his hands forward and take hold of my breasts, pulling me back against the chair. So by the time I'd drawn those hands and those large breasts I really had to come, and I'd walk briskly back to my brown marble shower. I read something about river gods that excited me, too. Really, back then I'd put out for any body of water at all—a pool or a bath or a pond, or an ocean. We rented a house on the Carolina coast for several summers, this was when I was in junior high school, and I'd go swimming in the ocean, and as soon as I was in the water I'd want to dither, I'd swim far out and I'd think of the tons and tons of water underneath my legs, but of course I couldn't because there were lots of people swimming, so I'd come in the shower—oh, and that was an especially good kind of shower too because it was outdoors, in this wooden shed, and I had this freezing cold bathing suit on, which I would take off *in the shower*, and because the suit was cold my nipples were erect, as in your wet T-shirt contest, and I was stripping in the warm shower water, I'd slowly strip off this cold bathing suit, *very* pleasant to have the warm mingle with the cold, so that sometimes I could feel cold rinsing down my legs and sometimes warm, and I could hold the suit open and let the water fill it so that warm was just pouring out around my legs, that was nice, so my skin was all confused and very aware of itself, with the steam rising—oh, and there was a little metal mirror, I guess it was a shaving mirror, in this shower enclosure, which would get steamed up, even though I was outside. It was on the left wall as you faced the showerhead, which in this case was quite low. And after I'd taken off my swimsuit I'd hang it up on the nail next to the shaving mirror, and the sight of it all crumpled and dangling there was exciting, because it implied my complete full nudity, and when the shaving mirror got steamed up, I used to draw a pair of breasts on it in the fog with my fingers. The glass was cold. I wanted to press my breasts against the mirror, but it was too high for that, but I imagined myself pressing my breasts against this little mirror, so first squeezing them together and then pressing them against the mirror, and I'd just seen something on TV about one-way mirrors, so I thought of men in the garden being able to see my breasts stuffed flat against the foggy mirror. Once I even brought in some lip gloss after my swim and spent a long time putting lip gloss around my nipples and soaping it off."

"God, car washes must have driven you wild."

"Car washes. I did like that one part at the end, where the felt flappers drag over you, but no, not really—it was very rare that my family took the car to the car wash. Almost never. Oh, but I do remember one thing I used to imagine—I imagined that I shared a ride back home from college with someone I didn't know, and we get caught in a terrible tropical monsoon of some kind, and his windshield wipers don't work, and so I have to go out on the hood of the car and take off my top and kneel there and hold on to the antenna and kind of sop my breasts over the windshield just so he can drive. Actually, that wasn't something I thought of very much, that was just a one-shot deal."

"There are strong evolutionary pressures on fantasies, aren't there?" he said. "If it doesn't work, and if it doesn't metamorphose itself into something that does work, it doesn't survive."

"Yeah, even in the buildup to one orgasm, it's a kind of bake-off. You think: two cocks, each one poking from under one of my armpits, sperm squirting from them? Yes or no. No. I'm a geometry teacher measuring boys' penis length? Yes or no. No. Am I a nurse at a fertility clinic and my job is to strip for clients who have difficulty coming and then suck their cocks and let their sperm drip from my tongue into a test tube? No. I'm in a dressing room and some native-Hawaiian security guard is watching me try on blue jeans over the video monitor? Ooh, maybe yes. In fact it's kind of like getting dressed for a party, and being unsure of what to wear right up to the last minute, and frantically trying on one image after another like clothes, not knowing which combination looks really *good*, and it's getting later and later, and then finally you pull out this wonderful dress, with some rich pattern, and you slip it on, and ah, you can come."

"Jesus. But what about if you're reading and the images are not under your control? Say maybe with a Book Mate thing holding the book open?"

"Hah hah! You mean with my hands free to *do other things?*"

"For instance, yes."

"Well, I have a whole system if I'm reading."

"Say you're reading your copy of *Forum*," he said.

"Right, what I do is I read a little of it, whatever it is, the story or the letter or the novel, to see whether it's something I do want to masturbate to or not. If it's something that looks promising, I read it all through very fast, to find out exactly what happens and locate the spot in it where I'm going to want to be coming, and what spots I'll want to skip because they're whatever—violent or boring or somehow irrelevant. Then I go back, not always to the beginning, but I backtrack, and the distance I backtrack

77

from the point where I've scheduled my orgasm I have to gauge exactly, depending on how close to coming I think I am—so if I'm very close to coming I only go back a paragraph, but if it looks like it'll be a while I may even read the whole scene or the whole letter that's *before* the letter I'm interested in and then go on and read the letter I'm interested in. And sometimes I misjudge, and I start to get close to coming when the big moment of the story is still on the next page, and I have to race ahead looking for the words I need, or sometimes the opposite happens and I'm crowding up to the big moment of the story and my orgasm is dawdling, not all the precincts are reporting yet, and so I have to read the chosen come-sentence very slowly, syllable by syllable, 'up . . . and . . . down . . . on . . . his . . . fuck . . . pole . . .' "

"So if you walked into a room," he said, "and there was an armchair, and a table, and on one end of the table was a TV and a VCR and an X-rated tape, and at the other end of the table was some book of Victorian pornography, what would you choose?"

"The Victorian pornography, no question."

"That's incredible to me."

"You'd choose the tape, right?" she asked.

"That or possibly the armchair itself. Not the book."

"The classic opposition," she said.

"True, but no—actually, it's interesting. Because I've heard for so long about those studies that say that women like stories and men like pictures I've started to feel lately that stories *represent* women and are therefore sexually charged for me, and in fact that's what got me so hot at Bonnie's Books that time, the idea that I was peeping in on a women's preserve. I think I *am* slowly starting to understand why in general people would prefer written porn. It gives your brain a vaginal orgasm rather than a clitoral orgasm, so to speak, whatever that means. I read one story in some men's magazine once, years ago, in the first person, written by a woman, or probably not, but written at least with the pretense that a woman was telling the story, about a sixteen-year-old girl who goes swimming in a neighbor's pool and of course her frans are still somewhat new and unfamiliar to her, and she'd forgotten that her top from last year was flimsy and inadequate to the demands that were made on it, and presto it comes off after she's swum a lap, and she's *so* embarrassed and apologetic, but Mr. Grunthole reassures her that she needn't be ashamed, he doesn't mind if she swims without her top, and so on and so on, and even though it was a totally conventional and undistinguished story, the fact that it was written in the voice of this girl, so I could peep in on her mixed feelings when her top came off, did give me a huge . . . an unexpectedly large return on my investment. I guess insofar as verbal pornography records thoughts rather than exclusively images, or at least surrounds all images with thoughts, or something, it can be the hottest medium of all. Telepathy on a budget. But still honestly I need the images. For instance of you there in the shower. I mean, when you come are your legs slightly apart?"

"Yes."

"And do you have one of those legendary Water Pik shower-massage showerheads?"

"I do, but I don't use it with any of the special settings. It was installed already when I moved in. It's useful for cleaning the tub. But when I'm—I don't hold it or put it between my legs or anything, I just treat it as a regular showerhead. What I do is . . ."

"Yes?"

"When I start to come?"

"Yes?"

"I—"

"Yes?"

"I open my mouth and let it fill with water. The feeling of the water overflowing my mouth . . . You there?"

"Don't stop talking."

"But that's all," she said.

"You were in the shower, yesterday night, and the water was coursing onto your face and falling down from one part of you to another, like balls in a pinball machine, and your eyes were closed. What was in your mind? Oh I'd like to . . ."

"Excuse me? You're murmuring."

"I said I'd like to *clk*," he said.

"What?"

"Sorry, I occasionally have a problem with involuntary swallowing. I said I'd like to . . . put my hands on your thighs, very high up, and hold them apart and cover your whole mound with my mouth and just breathe on you, through the fabric of your underpants."

"Ooch."

"Are your legs apart right now?"

"They're crossed at the ankle on the coffee table."

"That will have to do," he said. "Tell me what was in your mind in the shower last night."

"I honestly don't think I remember. And anyway the things I think of go by so fast. And it's not like all I do is come and come. Very often in the shower I remember some embarrassing moment, or some dumb thing I've said, and I curse it out, I say, 'Get away from me, stinker.' For instance, I might remember this time after I'd come back from a party when I was quite drunk, so drunk that I started to feel that I was going to be sick, but this person was in my bathroom, washing their face, brushing their teeth, humming happily away, and I moaned, I was leaning against the door, I knocked politely, I made these feeble scrabbling sounds, but this person had used the hook and eye on the inside because the latch didn't work on that door, and he was just too pleased with the world to hear me, or thought I was joking, saying hello by knocking, and so I was sick on my own bathroom door."

"Oh, terrible."

"Sorry to be gross. Fortunately it was just the usual fruit punch. He was very nice, he cleaned me up, he

cleaned my door up, he took off my clothes and put me in a nightgown. Then of course later he drops me abruptly because I tell him to put his pen in his back pocket. But so, in the shower, the memory of that kind of thing will hit me and I swear at it to make it go away."

"I understand completely. 'Git out of my shower! Go on!' "

"Yeah, yeah. And I wash, too, in the shower. And I think of all the things I have to do. So the coming is just one item on the list. It's not as if my life is wholly absorbed with it."

"Oh yeah, oh no, *I* know that. But—do you wash your hair before or after you come?"

"Usually I get the nuts and bolts out of the way, and then I test the waters to see whether I do want to come."

"What color is your hair?" he asked.

"It's a light brown. It's wavy. But it's fairly short. What color is yours?"

"It's black," he said. "So now tell me the things you have to do that you remembered last night in the shower."

"Oh, work things. Letters I should write—I should be writing them right now."

"No you should not."

"And I need to repaint the hall in my apartment. Ah, now I remember one of my sexual images from yesterday. The people before me put up this dreadful wallpaper, a kind of metallic wallpaper, with a design of a tree and a split-rail fence with a wagon wheel leaning on it, repeating over and over. *Bad*."

"Doesn't sound good."

"So I painted it when I moved in," she said. "I painted it a color called Paper Lantern—and I put on two coats. Someone said, 'You *know* that you're painting over metallic wallpaper, that's going to come through-hoo,' but I just couldn't make myself steam off all that old paper— the design would imprint itself in my psyche if I did that, it would rise up when I'm eighty years old, on my death bed. So I just painted it over, with two heavy coats. And the first year it was fine. But then we had that killer summer, and somehow the humidity sweated the metallic pattern back out, so that now you can make out the split-rail fence and the wagon wheel. But it's very faint. Now in fact I kind of like it. But I really should repaint it. So in the shower I had this image of painting the hall wall with a roller. What a waste of time. And then I thought, wait, I have the money, this time I'll hire people to paint it for me. And so three painters materialized, and then suddenly there was a large *hole* in the wall, about three feet off the floor, big enough so that I could fit through so that my legs were standing in the front hall and yet my head and upper body were in the living room. The hole was finished off and lined with sheepskin. I had nothing on. My hands were resting on two full paint cans. But the strange thing was the cans of paint were *warm*. There was one painter doing the living room, and the other two were doing the hall, where my lower body was. The painter I could see didn't seem to notice me. He was painting a wall with his back to me. The painters in the hall were using rollers, but they were those little detail rollers that you use for trim work, that are about three inches wide, the darlingest little rollers, that can go *everywhere*. Somehow I knew that one of these hall painters was mistakenly using the wrong color, it's a color I used in the living room, called Opulent Opal— apparently he'd taken the wrong can of paint from his truck. *Very* careless. The other one was more conscientious—he was using the glossy Paper Lantern on the trim. These are Sherwin Williams's paint names, not mine, by the way. Anyway I called out, 'Ah, people, sirs? Please be sure to use the right color! There is a potential for confusion!' But they were talking and they didn't hear me. I could hear their sticky little rollers moving over that wall, *ssshp, ssshp, ssshp*, and they were having an idle conversation about the chick they saw on the lake that weekend riding in the back of an inboard motorboat in a pair of overalls with no top, so her tits flopped around behind the fasteners on the top flap, and then they made reference to the time on one job when one of them evidently quote 'ate out' the woman whose house they were painting and then she jerked him off onto a cracked slate hearthstone because she was paranoid about hurting the finish on the antique pine floors, and again I called out, as nicely as I could, 'Guys, please, make

sure you're painting the right colors!' and this time, instead of answering, one of them simply took his little
roller and got it very heavy with the semi-gloss Paper
Lantern and touched it to the right side, you know, the
. . . cheek, of my ass, and then I could feel him rolling
a stripe of paint right down my leg, over my calf, right
down to my Achilles tendon, and then rolling right back
up again. Like the seam of a pre-war stocking, except
wide. Then he worked the roller a little on the tray,
loading it up again, and he started on my other asscheek,
and went very deliberately down and up again. At first he
pressed quite lightly, so I could just barely feel the sodden fluff touching my skin on my upper thigh, and the
roller barely rolled, but then as he traveled down he
pressed harder, and some of the paint was squeezed from
the roller and dripped down my leg ahead of it. It was so
surprisingly warm. They'd had the paint cans in the back
of their truck, which was parked in the sun. When the
roller traveled over the backs of each of my knees it felt
very very nice. I felt myself arching myself up slightly,
like a cat who's being stroked. Meanwhile the third
painter, who was in the room that my head and my
upper self were in, was still blithely painting away, with
his back to me, so at least part of the job was moving
steadily forward. And I expected that the two of them in
the hall would now get back to work. But instead I felt a
pair of hands on each leg, and I was lifted for a moment,
and a paint can was slid under each of my feet. This was

not a particularly comfortable position. The rims of the paint cans hurt the balls of my feet slightly, and my legs were farther apart than I was used to standing, and the small of my back was pressing against the sheepskin lining of the hole in the wall. Not comfortable, but tolerable. And then I felt knuckles brush against the inside of my thighs—and I knew that the first hall roller was now beginning to paint a stripe of Paper Lantern that started just at the top of my pubic hair and rolled very slowly over my clit and the rest of it, like some heavy steady piece of road equipment, and then back over my clit. And at the same time, the other hall painter had loaded his roller with *the wrong paint*, the Opulent Opal, and he'd turned his roller sideways and he was now pushing a horizontal stripe over my ass, at first a light stripe, and then, on the return, a harder stripe, and then he rolled down in between, and I called out, 'No no, I'm telling you that's the wrong paint!' but he was very deliberately working the roller in the region of my, what shall we call it, my 'tockhole,' without seeming to hear me. Nontoxic paint, of course. And then I heard him put down the roller and he planted his hands high on my ass, holding my hips, and then he did an amazing thing. I felt his whole weight go on his hands, and on my back too, and he was apparently supporting himself like a gymnast, entirely on his hands, with his knees bent and his legs apart, and then a second later I felt this burning blunt nub press against my Opulent Opal tockhole, and then kind of urge itself a little ways in. I went, 'Yew!' and the painter in the living room turned in surprise and registered my existence for the first time. My hands were still planted on the cans of paint. And back in the hall, while the one gymnast painter was sinking himself unapologetically deep into my ass, I felt the other, the one who'd responsibly used the right kind of paint all along, now use his thumbs to hold my real . . . self open, my lips, and then I felt him slide slowly up my real hole. I said, 'Vvoo!' The living-room painter's eyes got big, and he studied my face with this look, like, 'What exercise tape has *this* lady been using?' I'm afraid that by now I was curling my upper lip with pleasure. My expression in fact was exactly the one I would have had if I had been biting open a condom packet with my teeth, that gnashy look, but the thing was—*there was no condom packet*. My painter loaded up his roller with wall paint, this was a warm neutral gray, and I mean warm, and he came over and he lay down on the floor underneath me, in the opposite direction, with his head touching the baseboard, so I could see his face and his paint-spattered glasses between my breasts, and he touched the roller to one of my nipples, and then rolled up between my breasts and down and over the other nipple, and as he was doing that he used his foot to pull another paint can into position, and then, still lying on his back, he lifted his hips up in the air with both boots resting on the can of paint sort of like a circus elephant on one of those little stools, you know? And he brought out his cock. The hall ass painter took this moment to remove his hands from my back, so that all his weight was directed through his thigh muscles and his cock into my ass, while at the same time the leg painter, who was standing, pulled almost all the way out of me and then he slid himself all the way back in so that I could feel the muscles of his legs hit against me, and I opened my mouth to say, 'Hooh!' which is I think almost certainly what I would say if all that was going on in my front hall, but of course as soon as I opened my mouth the cock of the man underneath me slid right inside, so all I could do was hum, and then all three of them came in me, one right after another, first the one in my mouth, surprisingly enough, then the one in my pussy, then finally the one in my ass.''

"My *gracious*," he said. "And that's what you came to in the shower?"

"One of the things. I mean—it takes a while to describe it, but it was just a quick succession of images, among many. It takes me a good long time to come."

"Tell me others."

"Well, hm. The idea I actually finally came to was—it was really two ideas. Excuse me for a second."

There was a pause.

"What did you do?" he asked.

"I just got a towel so that I can have it whenever I need it to mop myself up. I don't want to come yet, and I seem to be getting awfully wet."

"Does that mean you've taken *off* your black pants and your sneakers?" he asked.

"Yes."

"Underpants?"

"No."

"And what color is the towel?"

"Green," she said.

"Where is it?"

"It's bunched in my hand, held in my unders where I need it. Now I've put it aside."

"Why don't you want to come yet? I won't object, you know."

"Because if I do, I'll crash, I'll want to stop talking to you this way, and I like talking to you this way. My clitoris is duplicitous: it always tries to trick me when I'm with someone, or when I'm alone, even—it says, 'Go on and come, Abby, no problem, you can come a second time in a few minutes, this feels real good, come on, don't be so conservative, I'm good for three or four!' But I know better. I'm not a multiple-orgasm sort of person. The *second* after I've come, no matter how foaming and frothing my level of arousal was, that's it, my clit is already starting to creep back into its clit-cloister and I'm thinking about other things. Two or three hours after that generally I'll top myself off in the shower, but not before."

"I see. Well then by all means keep that towel handy. I'm in for the long pull."

"Good. Where were we?"

"You were just about to tell me the exact thing that was in your mind when you came in the shower yesterday evening."

"Right, but do you mean the image that made me come, or do you mean the image that I had in my head *when* I came?"

"I—don't know."

"There's a big difference," she said. "I mean, the actual images that I have when I'm coming are things like, I don't know, elephant seals dozing on rocks, a carousel selection of greeting cards, a painting tightly wrapped in canvas, porch furniture—my brain is going so wild that there's no way to predict what sort of oddment will be there when all the flashbulbs go off. They're almost never sexual images. But before that, when I'm getting close, you mean, right?"

"I guess, yes."

"Yesterday I think there were two ideas, combined. I'm embarrassed."

"You're *embarrassed*, after just telling me about a triple-cock blowout?"

"But that's nothing, that's just a picture. The thing that made me come, I've acted on, to a degree, indirectly."

"I told you about buying the romance novel, didn't I?" he said. "I even told you about making obscene fingerings on the roof of my car. I've let my hair down!"

"Tell me what you look like erect."

"You mean from memory?"

"No."

"You mean undo my bathrobe etcetera?"

"Yes."

There was a pause.

"Welp. Um. What can I tell you?"

"Is it hard?"

"Yes."

"Was it already hard, or did you just make it hard?"

"It was somewhat hard, I just made it somewhat harder."

"Talk to me about it. Look at it and talk to me about it."

"Well, it's this thing. I don't know. Gee."

"Are you stroking it?"

"I'm—truthfully?"

"Yes."

"I'm pinching the underpeening skin in the fingers of my right hand, and I'm jostling my balls nervously with my left hand."

"Stroke it now, slowly," she said.

"All right. God, each time I pull on it, its muscle clenches. I mean, of course it's always done that, but now, with you telling me to look at it, this seems the most noteworthy feature, this clench."

"Go faster."

"Just for a second, though, right?"

"Right, no spontaneous human combustion yet."

"Right. Eee, that feels pretty good."

"I can hear your strumming in your voice, you nasty boy."

"Nastybation. I don't want to come, though. I'm going to stop."

"Prudent."

"Funny," he said. "When I was going fast, I pictured something that I've pictured for years and yet never noticed. I pictured doing an impossible thing—I thought that if I got too close to coming, I could somehow angle my leg and contort it so that I caught hold of my cock in my bent knee and squeezed it like a nut in a nutcracker until it stopped wanting to come."

"You're a strange case," she said. "It was fun getting imperious with you for a moment, though."

"Hah! Frightening, too. There are different rules on the telephone. You want to know what I actually thought of when you asked me to quote 'talk' to you about my cock? After the thrill and the terror had passed?"

"What?"

"This time I had a crush on a woman at work," he said. "She had beautiful long arms, of which she was very proud. I don't think she had a single dress with full sleeves. She had a hopeless thing for a man named Lee, who was a smugly flirtatious married guy, whom I personally disliked intensely. This woman knew I had a crush on her, in fact I used to send her a memo with a single asterisk in the middle of the page on the day after any night I'd masturbated thinking mainly about her. I don't know if she thought this was charming or not. On the whole I think it pleased her. I was not completely serious myself anyway. One time she even held her arms out in perplexity and said, 'What, no asterisk today?' She knew I loved her arms. I tried to get her to send me a memo with a pound sign on it the day after any night she had masturbated thinking about Lee, but she never did. One night I was working late and I started to need to jerk off. The place was absolutely deserted, it was a holiday weekend. I went past this woman's door, her name was Emily, and it was like I was passing a huge vulva, so big it had a desk inside, and I decided that what I should do is make an actual photocopy of my dick, in fact two copies, one before coming, one after, and leave these, along with an asterisk memo, on her desk."

"What did you hope to accomplish by doing that?"

"Well, I was very interested in having her *see* my cock, but of course I wasn't ever going to just flip it out in front of her, I needed some . . . distancing step, so that ho ho ho yes we're civilized adults here, it's all on paper. Well it's harder than you may think to make a copy of your dick. I know it's done in offices all the time, but I found it to be quite a project. Maybe if I'd been able to do some kind of *planche*, like your painter friend did on your . . . back, it would have been easy, but what I had to do was first try to get something akin to an erection standing at the copier of a deserted office on a holiday, I had to think of her seeing the copy of my cock on Monday, I had to think of her first thinking, Golly, what a nut, and then finding she had to stare uncontrollably at the specific image of my cock, *boyoing*, had to file that image away in a secret file folder where she filed away all my asterisk memos, and that some night, working late, she'd reach her long arms down to that drawer and bring out the asterisk file and go through the pages, asterisk after asterisk, until she found my cock. So I got hard, that was one hurdle. Then I had to place my cock down on the glass, but the way this copier is designed—I disliked this copier, by the way, that place is too cheap to lease a decent brand of copier—the way it's designed is that a normal eight-and-a-half-by-eleven piece of paper is oriented sideways in the middle of the glass between two marks, you know how that works, right?"

"Yes."

"So the problem then is that only a little sliver of the tip of my cock was going to make it in range of the footprint of a normal eight-and-a-half-by-eleven copy. There were ways I could straddle the machine, but this just seemed ludicrous. Finally I made a seventy-percent reduction copy of my dick, because the highest reduction setting used the whole area of the glass that my dick could reach, and so I captured something vaguely obscene-looking, even if the total overall scale was reduced. It looked like a little Quonset hut, halfway up the right side of the page. I wrote 70% REDUCTION on the copy. But obviously my plan to strum off hastily and then make the second copy had to be abandoned, because my dick wouldn't even begin to reach over the plastic strip between me and where the glass started when it was soft. But by now I was crazed with the idea of doing something for this woman that retained some shred of playfulness to it, so she could think to herself, All in fun, all in fun, and yet which conveyed the full force of the idea that I had been alone in that office that weekend with a huge erection, thinking of her. How do I give her that sense? Actually come *onto* the asterisk memo? That seemed crude. Do you think that would have crossed the line?"

"I think, yeah."

"I thought so. So instead what I did was—you remember making outlines of your hands in kindergarten? You held your hand still on the page and you traced around each finger, and all the little contours of your finger joints were captured, and you would go around a few times, and each time the pencil was at a slightly different angle, so you got this *aura* of your hand, that was so much more accurate than you could ever draw, and all you had to do was put in the fingernails and the little wrinkles on the backs of your fingers and you really had something? Once this girl traced my hand and I traced hers at the same time—I went very slowly, which triggered her ticklishness, and she laughed hard every time my pencil made it to the place between two of her fingers, but she was brave, she stayed put. Her name was Martha. I'm pleased to have remembered that! A teacher showed us how to make a turkey, using two hands superimposed. But that wasn't interesting, that was just a trick. It's the same with shadows: the beautiful thing isn't the alligators or bats you can make with your hands, the beautiful thing is the way the shadow image allows you to see so precisely what the outer contour of your own hand really looks like, those little bunches of flesh under each bent finger joint. Obviously this was what I had to do. So I closed the top of the copier and I took a blank piece of paper and again I concentrated on the idea of this woman's surprise and then transfixion when she saw my memo until I was hard again. I traced around my dick with a pen, holding myself in place with a finger and holding the pen straight up and down, and it was a very interesting sensation, not pleasurable, but very interesting, this cold pen. I went around about five times. And the great thing was, on paper, my dick looked really impressive. It looked like a *big dick*. Because of course the image you get is bigger all the way around by what, two pen radii, or one full pen diameter, so a good quarter of an inch. Much better than the copy, which as I said was this miniature sideways thatched farmhouse there in the right margin. So I wrote FULL-SCALE COCK TRACING, you know, 11:43 P.M., SUNDAY, NOVEMBER 24TH or whatever the date was. And I put the memo and the two pieces of artwork in her in box."

"You're kidding! Did somebody find them?"

"No no. I plucked them back out just before I left."

"Ah, okay."

"And I didn't send her any asterisk memos at all for about a month after that, which was highly unusual. She started giving me quizzical looks. Then one afternoon she came by and she asked me what was up. She said I wasn't my usual buoyant self. And I griped to her about a certain person at work, I lamented the fact that we were a second-rate company when we could be a first-rate company, the usual junk. And then I said, 'And there's something else.' She said, 'Well, what is it?' She knew it was about her. So, with this weird combination of reluctance and eagerness, I confessed to her that I'd made a copy of my cock and a cock tracing and that I'd put them in her in box late one night and then thought better of it. She said, 'Well, do you still have them?' I said, 'Gee, I think I do!'"

"You'd *kept* them? In a little file of your own?"

"Of course," he said. "After all that trouble? Plus this was in some way part of the whole thing, that I'd blurt out what I'd done and she'd ask to see and I'd have it on hand to show her."

"What did she say?"

"She said that the copied cock looked like a sonogram."

"That's it?"

"I'm telling you, she had it very bad for this Lee guy. I suggested that she could take the two pages if she wanted, for her reference. She said no thanks. We had lunch a week or so after that. She moaned about Lee, I listened sympathetically. Then I asked her, I couldn't help it, I asked her, I said, 'Never mind the photocopy,' I said, 'let me just ask you, was the cock tracing I showed you in any slight way arousing? Not right then in my office, to be sure, but later? Did you feel the slightest smidgin of arousal later?' And she gave me an indulgent look and she said, 'I'm really sorry, the pictures made me feel tender feelings for you, but they just really did *not* arouse me.' So that seemed conclusive."

"I would say so," she said.

"Yep. Yep. It wasn't. More happened."

"You mean you and she ended up getting together? What was her name?"

"Emily."

"That's right, you told me that. Well?"

"Well, we did spend an evening in my apartment," he said.

"The usual? You draped your best cummerbund over the lamp shade? She toasted you with the Koromex tube?"

"Something like that. But anyway, that was what I thought of when you asked me to look straight at my cock and talk about it. I have to say, that was one of the more unsettling questions I've been asked in my life."

"Would you like to know whether I would find a tracing of your cock arousing?"

"I would be curious about that, yes."

"I suppose it would depend on my mood. I might like to perform the tracing. If you traced my whole body, I might in exchange trace your pale Ramone . . . This mouthpiece I'm talking into? Of the telephone?"

"Yes?"

"It's like a sieve. It's like those little filters you put over the bathtub drain. Sometimes I think with the telephone that if I concentrate enough I could pour myself into it and I'd be turned into a mist and I would rematerialize in the room of the person I'm talking to. Is that too odd for you?"

"No, I think that sometimes," he said.

"But the interesting part," she said, "is that the trip itself would take a while. I think a lot about what it would feel like to be turned into some kind of conscious vapor. You know those trucks that come around on streets and grind up the brush on the curb? Those droning trucks? The guy throws a branch in, and it goes mmmmn-*yooonnnng*-mmmmmm, and all these tiny chips fly out of a high pipe? I think of that, except of course it wouldn't be painful—I think of the part where I'm just this spume of wood chips and pieces of leaves. Or you know what else? You remember those birds that were getting sucked into the jet engines? Sometimes I lie in bed at three or four in the morning and I imagine myself flying miles above the earth, very cold, and one of those black secret spy planes is up there with the huge round engines with the spinning blades in it, the blades that look like the underside of mushrooms? The black plane's going very fast and I'm going very fast in the opposite direction and we intersect, and I fly right through one of those jet engines, and I exit as this long fog of blood. I'm miles long, and, because it's so cold, I'm crystalline. *Very* long arms, you'll be pleased to hear. And then I recondense in bed, *sshhp,* as my short warm self. It must have something to do with my estrogen level. But that's what telephone travel would be like out there, I think. What am I saying, that's what it *is* like."

"Ooh, I love you, you tell me everything."

"I do seem to, don't I? It's very unlike me."

"It is?" he said. "God, I'm a compulsive confessor. But it's rare for me to cast my bread on the waters and have it return tenfold like this."

"Tell me the rest of what happened with your friend Emily."

"Why? No, no, it'll make me seem like too much of a type."

"You *are* a type," she said.

"You're right, I am."

"Don't feel bad about it—I am too. I just want to know what you're like when you're physically holding a woman. As opposed to calling up catalogs and strangers named Klein and that sort of thing, worthwhile pursuits though they may be. What did you and Emily end up doing?"

"I never actually held her, that's the first thing I'll say. So it's certainly going to disappoint you. It's a very common story, really, and I'm starting to want to impress you a little."

"Impress me with your candor—that seems to be your style."

"Well here's what happened, anyway," he said. "After I showed her my cock tracing and all that, it marked some kind of conclusion, and we were more reserved with each other. After all, what was there to say? I'd laid it right out on the table and she'd basically rejected me. But then there was a big good-bye party for somebody, and at it Lee flirted with her in his perky cool way. Boy I dislike the way he funnels peanuts into his mouth. He'll never see forty-eight again, and yet he throws his whole head back after he's been asked a question, drops in a hopperful of nuts, and then he answers the question while he's crunching. He tries to be sardonic eating peanuts! This is some TV convention that has gotten people in its clutches. Of course there are times when you are so full of something you want to say that you talk with your mouth full, I have no problem with that. What I find fault with is when you are deliberately using the act of talking with your mouth full to demonstrate just how totally relaxed and spontaneous you really are as a conversationalist. It's from growing up watching all those salted-snack commercials. Bugles. So I hate him, clearly, and he's at the party, and midway through, something bad happens between Emily and him, basically it's just that he makes it clear that he likes flirting with her but forget it, he's married. She tells me about it in the parking lot, she's near tears, and then she squats and holds on to the side mirror of my car and looks in it and she says, 'Well well—*I* look convincingly haggard.' That was her best line—in fact it probably makes her seem more vulnerable and lovable than she really is. That's not fair—she's very nice. So anyway, for the next full week I talked with her about Lee and talked with her about Lee, every possible angle on the situation, though I avoided telling her that I found him repulsive and childish, but otherwise we ventilated the topic fully. Finally I couldn't stand to talk about him anymore, and I said, 'Look, I have to ask your advice.' Because what she obviously needed was to have her mind off her own troubles. It was six, we were again leaving work. And somehow, by pure luck, this was the perfect exact *second* to ask her advice: she just about crumpled with relief and helpfulness, and she pointed to a café across the street and she said, 'Why don't we go in there?' So over a pair of up-signal caffè lattes, I told her the problem. I pulled out a piece of newspaper, and I unfolded it, and I looked at it, and I looked at her, and then I looked at it again, and then I told her that I was thinking of running a personals ad requesting something *very* specific. And she was politely curious about this, so I said, 'This is what I was thinking of saying,' and I handed it to her. It was the personals ad form, which I'd filled out. The ad went—this is going to disappoint you, though."

"I fully expect to be disappointed."

"Good. It said something like, 'You and me are sitting side by side on my couch, watching X-vid, not touching. You are short or tall, etc., you want me to see pleasure transform your features. I am SWM, 29.' "

"Was this an ad you really planned on running?"

"I think so, possibly. No, I probably never would have. I'd carried it around in my pocket for a while, it was starting to get that folded-for-a-long-time look."

"How did she react?"

"Emily said, 'Well, you can try, but I seriously doubt anyone's going to respond to that.' Which was quite true."

"Oh, I don't know."

"Even if she was wrong, I don't think I really wanted what I said I wanted. Meeting strangers, the awkwardness. It would take such a huge effort of will to get over the pure chit-chat socialness of the context. My erection would never survive it. What I really wanted was to hand that folded piece of newsprint to *Emily* and watch her read it. I said, 'What about if I took out the lame line about pleasure transforming their features?' And she said, 'But that's the only thing in it that's any good.' So I asked her, if she were me—I said, 'I know you're not me, but if you were me and you wanted to achieve this objective, how would you word it?' She said, 'Well, tell me what your objective really is, in your own words, so I get a better sense of it.' So I told her that I, well er um, I was interested, you know, in sitting on my couch, next to a woman, with an X-rated tape on, and the woman's looking only at the movie and I'm looking only at the movie, and she's well, um, masturbating, and as she starts to come she says, 'Look at my face,' and I look at her face, and she looks at the TV, and we both come. So she says, Emily says, 'All right, good, now we have something to work from.' She takes out a pen and starts drafting the ad on the place mat, she writes, 'You and me are sitting,' and she goes, 'Good, okay so far, nice colloquial note, that's fine.' I think she was really delighted not to be talking about Lee. And then she taps the pen on the place mat and she looks up at me and she says, 'No, look, you need to make the situation a lot clearer. You need to make her feel that it's all right. You need to talk about some kind of a blanket.' Out of the blue, a blanket! No, wait, I know what she said, *before* the blanket, she said something like, 'You need to make the woman reading it understand that some sense of what is right and fitting coexists alongside your depravities.' Not those exact words, but close to that. You believe it? *Then* she brings up this blanket. This was a whole new side to her. I said, 'All righty, what kind of blanket? You think we should specify the actual kind of blanket?' And she nods and goes, 'Yes, absolutely, the specific kind of blanket, the size, the thickness, the color, that's all they have to go on.' I said, 'Okay, well, what do you think? Army surplus green blanket, Mormon quilt, what?' She thought for a second, and then she said, she said, 'I think you should mention a blanket with a fringe.' I said, 'But I do not *have* a blanket with a fringe.' And she said, 'You're right, that's a problem.' And then she starts hitting me with all these questions. She goes, 'How far is the TV from the couch?' She'd never been to my apartment, of course. I said, 'Well it's on a rolling table, so there's no fixed distance, but then, the cable cord limits the range, so I guess it's probably about six feet from the couch.' She noted this down and she goes, 'Because the woman skimming these personals may need to know that. That little fact might be of the highest importance. Now, is the couch two pillows wide or three pillows wide or four pillows wide?' I said it was three pillows wide. She said, 'Like this?' and on the place mat she started drawing a couch and a TV, so I said, 'No no, like this,' and I sketched the layout of the room. Just the couch, the walls, the doors, the electrical outlets. I drew two stick figures with two arrows to indicate where they'd be sitting on the couch. She looked at this, and nodded, and said, 'Okay, now, the other thing is, you can't just say "X-vid." What tape will actually be playing when this is happening?' I said 'Wulp, it would be a pornographic movie of some sort, I guess I'd rent a bunch before she showed up, six or ten, and there'd be some trial and error.' She said, 'Well I just don't think you'll get a response with that kind of vagueness. You have to *commit* yourself to a situation.' And I said, 'But you know there are thousands upon thousands of dirty tapes.' She said, 'That's just it. Is it a classic that she may well have seen, or will it be something she probably hasn't seen? Will it be new to you or not? These little distinctions are *crucial*.' And she said, 'And also—if you specify a certain tape, then, you see, she reads the ad and she rents the tape and while she's watching it, the ad may become more and more interesting to her.' So I said, 'Golly, you're absolutely right. I do have to say which tape.' But I said, 'But I don't know which it should be. I know what tapes I like, but I don't know which particular tape would potentially be interesting to her.' And much to my surprise, she had a suggestion. She said, 'Let me make a suggestion. A dubbed tape. A foreign dubbed tape.' And she explained why. She said it's because you've got more layers—you've got the graphic stuff going on, but you've got mouths saying Italian sex words or French sex words, and then American actors going ooh and ah, and usually the American actors who do the dubbing are somewhat better than the American actors who've got to both have sex *and* act. And no L.A. boudoir interiors, no L.A. fireplaces reflected in L.A. wineglasses, no Ron Jeremy. Again, that's not exactly what she said, but that was what she was getting at. And then she said, still in a very pragmatic way, she said, 'For instance, Atom Home Video distributes a few good dubbed ones.' So I clanked down my coffee and I said, 'Okay. I accept everything you say. I'll specify the couch size, I'll specify high-end dubbed Italian-import porno, but still I just don't trust myself to *buy the right blanket*. That's what worries me. And I see now that I really need the right blanket to complete this. Will you help me pick out a blanket?' And she said, 'Tonight?' And I said, 'Yeah it *has* to be tonight, it really does, because tomorrow I'll want to send in the ad, and as you say I have got to include the size, the color, everything, if I want this to work. I *need* your help with this.' And she said okay."

"What kind of blanket did you get?"

"We went to this discount place, kind of a seedy place, blinding fluorescence, in a strip right near where we work, and we went to the blanket department, and there were all these big blankets stuffed into clear plastic containers with snaps, some awful-looking, but some not so bad, and it was very strange, it was as if the two of us were a real couple shopping for a blanket. She poked around, looking at this and that, and I'd go, 'What about this?' and she'd feel it, make a judicious face, nod. But then, when she'd covered both aisles, she said, 'No, I just don't see any blanket with a fringe, I mean a real *fringe*. I think I better get back.' I said, 'No, we'll go to another store!' and she said, 'Nah, the good stores will be closing by the time we get there. If there'd been a decent fringe available here, I could have helped you with the selection, but I think you're on your own now.' I went nuts. I started really hunting through those blankets, I was ready to call the manager over and have him go in the back. And god damn it if I didn't find this little acrylic blanket, jammed behind on a high shelf, kind of a standard green-and-blue plaid thing, no beauty, let me tell you, but with a long thick twisted fringe. She looked at it, she touched it, and she blushed, and she said, 'This one will do.' So I marched right over to the register and bought it. There was a cardboard insert saying, you know, SEEDYCREST FIRST QUALITY ACRYLIC BLANKET, and there was this stock picture of a woman smilingly asleep under a blanket, and as we're waiting for the woman to enter in the SKU number Emily and I both looked at this picture, and I'm telling you, nothing, anywhere, was as obscene as that picture on the blanket insert."

"How much was it?"

"Ten bucks, something like that, I can't remember. On an impulse, I bought a *People* magazine, too. So then we went back to the car, and the great lucky thing was, I'd been able to park craftily not right in front of the discount store, but to one side, a little ways down—we were driving in my car—and I'd parked almost directly in front of this video spot. The place hadn't been too noticeable when we'd driven in, but now that it was darker it had the flashing lights on, video video video, it was the brightest thing in the whole mall. So I opened the door for her, and she got in, and I handed her the blanket in this enormous bag, and I said, 'Hang on, I'll be right back,' and I darted into the video place and went to the adult section that they had sequestered away and I started looking over the boxes. I was out of breath, and my senses were so hyper-alert, I was scanning the boxes for 'Atom' 'Atom' 'Atom.' I knew I had to get only one single film, the right film, which seemed impossible, but I could feel myself surging forward on this irresistible surge of luck, and I found a couple of 'Atom' productions among all the Caballero Controls and the Cal Vistas and all the other little companies, and I rented this thing called *Pleasure So Deep*. I mean the title *reeked* of translation, it was perfect. I signed up for membership, rented the movie, was back in the car in five minutes. Emily was there leafing calmly through the *People* magazine. She said, 'What did you get?' and I said, 'It's called *Pleasure So Deep*.' She made this little 'Oh!' and she said, 'And you're going to watch that tonight?' I said, 'Yes, I have to, I need to commit myself to a situation, you've totally convinced me.' And she said, 'Tell me again, so I have it clear in my mind. What you're advertising for is a woman who wants to sit on the couch next to you and watch this movie and masturbate, right?' She put her hand lightly on the box holding the tape. I said 'Yep' and she said, 'Just that, nothing else, only that, nothing beside that, right?' And I said, 'Yes, just that. And I think I really have a shot at formulating the ad that will find someone who wants to do that, thanks to you. You helped me pick out the right blanket, and I think now I've got the right tape . . .' Then I hesitated, and I said, 'I *think* I've got the right tape, but still—that's worrying me now. How will I know that the tape is really right, and which specific scenes on it are the ones . . . ?' By this time we'd pulled in the company parking lot right behind her car. She was either going to get out or not get out. I said, 'Look, I'm at sea. I don't know anything about imported sex movies. I really need your advice on this. I won't be able to judge on my own. I won't be certain.' And I looked at her, and she looked at me, and, remember, I'd spent *hours* listening to her think out loud about Lee, and she said, 'Okay.' So we went to my apartment."

"Was it a good movie?" she asked. "Were there any statues?"

"Statues? Ah, you mean *statues*? I don't know if it was set in Rome or not. It was about this woman who seemed to be managing some kind of counterfeiting operation that stored the fake money in caskets. In one scene she has sex with this guy who has a huge clownish yellow tie on with a U.S. dollar sign on it. Pointless, silly—but never mind, Emily was right, the fact that it was dubbed was outstandingly erotic. And the breasts really looked European somehow: not quite so corn-fed and symmetrical, but again maybe that was an illusion of the sound track."

"So you watched the movie, or you watched Emily? What was Emily wearing, by the way?"

"She was wearing a skirt, and a short-sleeved sweatery thing, I think it was dark red, some kind of dark red with thin vertical gold stripes. Lovely small, proud, elegant breasts—I mean in the sweater."

"And you were in a jacket and tie?"

"Yes. I let her into the apartment, and the way my apartment is laid out, there is a very short entryway with a kitchen that opens on the left, and then you're immediately in the living room—so she walked ahead of me into the living room, and even though I was careful not to turn on any lights in there, still, *there* was the couch against one wall and *there* was the VCR on a table against another wall, and it was as if there was this phosphorescent dotted line connecting the two things, they were linked, nothing else in the room counted, and I saw her turn quickly toward me so as not to face the living room quite yet, and she put down the bag with the blanket— oh, I forgot one other important thing that happened in the car. I parked the car in back of my apartment building, and I went around and opened the door for her, and she handed me the bag with the blanket and *People* magazine in it, and then she got out, and then—and for some reason this seemed exactly right—she held her arms out for me to hand her the blanket bag again. It had become somehow hers to carry. I held the tape, she held the blanket. Anyway, she put the bag down in the middle of the living room, and she said, 'So, will you give me the *grand tour*?' And the conventionality of 'grand tour'" showed how nervous she was, but she was one of those people who are improved by being nervous, you know?—who are nervous in a way that makes your detection of their nervousness seem like a privilege. So I showed her the kitchen, the bedroom, the bathroom—she nodded knowingly at the magnets on my refrigerator—beautifully nervous. I listed off what I could offer her to drink, and she said she wanted orange herb tea and she went in the bathroom. So I put two cups of orange herb tea in the microwave. Normally I make only one cup, of course, and I put it on two minutes, but I figured four minutes to handle the extra volume of water, but it was a bit too long, and the water was very hot. I walked out with the two teas and saw her again in the living room, with her back to me: she had been looking at the TV—it's just a dinky Malaysian TV, somehow everybody still thinks that if you have a VCR, that means you've got to have a TV worthy of it—but I don't know, I think maybe even the smallness was right for that evening. But anyway she slid her purse off her arm and put it on the rug next to an armchair on the wall farthest away from the couch, and took off her shoes and put them next to her purse—establishing a little separate non-couch locus for herself. I went into the bathroom for a second, and when I came out, she was sitting on the couch leafing through *People* in the dim light coming from the kitchen. I still hadn't turned on any of the lights in the living room, because it would have been so uncomfortable to have to turn them off later. She half pretended to be startled out of reading an article when I clicked the TV on, with no volume, and she said something about Arsenio Hall. But the irrelevance of what she said made her smile, because she was sitting on the couch, and now the TV was on, and that tiny super high-pitched sound of electrically charged picture-tube glass, that sound that you can sometimes hear even if you're walking along the street, if windows are open, that is the TV giving itself away, declaring itself, even with the volume off, that sound that your ear seems to be able to hear better and better in the evening, or appreciate better, that means privacy and at-homeness and closed curtains and secrecy too, because it's like when you snuck downstairs at six in the morning to watch *The Three Stooges* and kept the sound extremely low so your parents wouldn't detect it, but you always worried that even though super high-pitched sounds don't carry well at all, you thought it might travel upstairs and the knowledge that you were up and watching *The Three Stooges* would trouble their dreams—*that* sound was in the room with me and Emily, and even though it was just faces at a press conference on C-SPAN, we knew what it really meant. She pointed at her tea and she said, 'On second thought, could you maybe plop a little bourbon or something in this?' So I did. I put the tape in, and the VCR made its little swallowing sound, and I turned the sound up, and then there was, without even an FBI warning or anything, there was the logo, this blue word

ATOM, with this wow-wow-wow-wow sine-wave kind of music that focused in on a note while the word ATOM focused too. There was a little stylized spirograph atom even—it was kind of moving to see this symbol which once meant progress and science fiction and chemistry and then the evils of radiation, and now it just means 'Hey, you're going to have to take this sex film very seriously, as seriously as anything that requires a linear accelerator to discover, I mean you can pretend to laugh, and think how funny and ridiculous, but you aren't really going to laugh, because no matter how many times you see X-rated filmed sex in your apartment, just by renting a tape, it still will have the power to shock you a little bit, it's still always miraculous, always a blessing.' And then there was a preview. I handed her the controller and I said, 'Fast-forward anytime something bores you.' I'd forgotten about previews—all that fast editing, without any progression, and the sudden jolt of bouncing frans, then a sudden come-shot. I remember once going to an arty movie with Richard Dreyfuss in it, I think, a long time ago, called *Inserts*, that had an X rating, and wasn't very good, by the way, full of the grimness that films get into when they try to make art out of porn, so uncheerful, but the thing about the experience was that it was a legitimate movie, but because of the X rating, it was playing in a porn theater, this was sometime in the seventies, and I remember seeing a man and a woman walking up the slight slope from the ticket booth ahead of me, holding containers of popcorn, because the popcorn stand, which normally was completely shut down, had been reopened in honor of this legit, name-star film, and the couple went through the opening so they could hear the bad electronic music, and they turned the corner, and then bang, they were in the darkness of the theater looking out over all those seats during the previews, which were of course previews of standard porn films, five or six of them, so on the screen there was this gigantic shot of somebody like Brigitte Monet sucking a huge horizontal cock, with loud squelching noises, and electronic octaves thumping away, and I saw the woman stop and flinch and grab her date's arm and look at him pleadingly—'You told me it wasn't going to *be* this kind of thing!'—and her date made this awful horrified 'I'm sorry' face, and behind them I went 'Tut tut tut' in refined disapproval at what was on the screen, because I wanted both of them not to think they'd made a terrible mistake, I wanted her to still like him, I wanted women then, this was when I was maybe eighteen, to see why X-rated films were so wonderful, I still do in some ways, and it has happened, over the last fifteen years, with video, to a limited extent, though as you say you would still reach for the Victorian paperback if given the choice, and probably you are right—but I wanted to reassure this woman that it was okay, people like me were showing up at this theater, nonviolent normal intelligent men, it wasn't the end of civilization—I made the disapproving

sound even though the sight of the cocksucking wouldn't
have bothered *me* in the slightest if it were just me seeing
it: I felt her tentativeness, and I wanted, sort of like a real
estate agent who takes a special route to the house he's
showing that goes through the nicer, fancier streets, I
wanted her to be squired gently toward the graphic image
of a come-shot, and to have a good experience here, not
to leave disturbed by male tastes, the same feeling I have
sometimes when I see foreign tourists in some city I know
walking around bewildered in some downtown area, and
I can tell that they're disappointed, and I want to go up
to them and say, 'I know this is the standard guidebook
thing you are doing, but forget it, this isn't our city really,
go see this neighborhood and that neighborhood'—I
wanted chivalrously to save that woman from the giant
crude cock of the coming attraction, just the same way I
used to think when I was little of swimming up toward
the surface holding a woman in trouble and letting her
use my scuba mouthpiece, and carrying her up on the
boat and taking off her wet cold wetsuit and toweling her
off as she got her breath and shook her head at her close
call."

" 'Oh, thank you, Popeye, for saving me from that
large low-born cock!' "

"Exactly. Anyway—do you still want to hear this?"

"Yes."

"Okay. Anyway, there was the preview, which was for
some terrible-looking post-*Caligula* post-*Devil in Miss*

Jones kind of movie, with lots of gratuitous grotesquerie, stuff I hate, torchlit sets, dwarves, but in the midst of that stuff of course there were, bang, these shocking pure normal sex scenes, whose abruptness I felt through Emily, because Emily was my guest on my couch watching them. Then the preview was over, and the ATOM logo came on and focused itself again, and I looked over at her. She was looking straight at the TV—the light from the kitchen was behind her profile—and she had her legs crossed, and one of her forearms was resting on her stomach, and her tea was in her left hand. Her skirt was pleated. She looked so exceedingly *clothed*. She lifted the mug, and I could see her lips meet it—the water was still too hot, so she had to do one of those long inward sips that makes the liquid lift off from the surface into a tea aerosol, and her eyes narrowed when she felt the fine hot spray of it touch the tip of her tongue. And then the movie began—*Pleasure So Deep*. It starts with a maid who hears a tinkling bell and takes something on a tray to a man and they talk for a second and then she walks away."

"Have you rented this movie since then?" she asked.

"Twice. It's also one of the three I rented tonight, which I'm probably not going to watch. Much more fun telling it to you. Anyway, the maid walks away, and then this thin Europop electronic sex-music starts going, and then instantly: cut to half-naked woman and man with cock, with dubbed moans. The woman is in her late

117

thirties maybe, very attractive, with her hair pinned back. Emily watched this for maybe a minute, and then she looked over at the windows and she said, 'Are you sure people can't see in?' I do have curtains, but I honestly wasn't sure if people could possibly see in or not, and my apartment is on the first floor, on the side of the building, so it was a legitimate concern, so I hopped up again and got my keys and said I'd be back in a second, and I went outside and tried to look in my windows, and it was surprisingly secure: not only could you not see Emily or anything in the room, you couldn't even tell the TV set was on, I guess because it's a small set. So I went back in and sat down, slightly out of breath, and told her that you couldn't see a *thing* from outside. She said, 'Great, thanks.' I said, 'What's happened so far?' and she said, in a slightly unnatural voice, 'The woman and her lover have been fucking in various ways.' It was the same scene, in fact—this Italian guy, whose name turns out to be Mario, has his amazingly long cock between her breasts—I remember seeing that image and immediately turning to Emily and watching her eyes: every time there was a cut, I could see her eyes make a tiny movement to find the center of gravity of the next image. Porn movies are almost always done with very repetitive cuts back and forth between two or three camera positions, so I knew what the images were and yet I could watch Emily's eyes: say the alternation was between a close-in shot of the woman's head bobbing as she was sucking the cock, and then a farther-back shot showing that she was kneeling on the bed holding her hair out of the way of the camera and he was lying on his back, A B A B, and I could *see* the mixture of colors change on Emily's iris, and I could see it make these exact little adjustments. The miracle of sight. She had an expression of very alert frowning amused distaste. When that scene was over, I said, 'What do you think so far?' I just wanted to hear her voice. And she said, 'As it happens, I've seen this movie before, about a year ago.' Then we watched maybe three sex scenes silently. Maybe more. Once I asked some question like 'Is that one of the counterfeiters?' And she said, 'Yes.' Otherwise we were totally silent, while these hard-working Europeans struggled and jacked and sucked and moaned and came in English in front of us. The men came, anyway. It's still a rarity to see a woman really come on a video, as opposed to thrashing around. There was more of the dimensionless electronic Europop music. After one giant come-shot Emily put her tea down and took a deep breath and puffed out her cheeks and smiled. I laughed with relief. I said, 'Is it as you remembered it?' And she said, 'I'm a little chilly.' So I unsnapped the plastic cover of the blanket and unfolded this big acrylic plaid thing and put it over her, but I did it wrong, evidently, because she said, 'Could you turn it this way?' and she showed me how she wanted it. So I tucked her in with the fringe of the blanket running under her neck. Then I sat down again, focused on the

movie, and again there was the jolt—you have a moment
of two fully clothed work friends in a living room adjusting a blanket, and I'm stuffing two of its corners behind
her shoulders, probably the first time I'd ever touched
both of Emily's shoulders at the same time, absolute
coziness, we should have been talking about the very first
birthday we could remember or something, and then we
turn to the TV and there are tits swinging around and a
woman's hairdo swinging around while she rises up and
down on some expressionless Eurodick and we're hearing
'Oh Mario Mario!' After a little while there were some
movings around under the blanket, and then it started to
shake, sort of. She didn't say anything, she didn't even
change her breathing, she was keeping it very steady. Her
mouth was closed. She said, 'Could you do me a favor
and hold the blanket for a second so it doesn't slide
down?' So I held it in place while she lifted her hips and
moved around some more, frowning. Her face was fairly
close to mine but we didn't have eye contact. Then her
panty hose appeared from under the bottom of the blanket, with her underpants still nested in it, and then her
feet disappeared again. She said, 'Thanks,' and took hold
of the top of the blanket. Again the slight fast movement
underneath. Her mouth opened slightly, and I could see
her tongue pushing against her lower teeth, and she made
these very subtle little movements with her lip—not
twitches, that sounds too obvious and uncontrolled, just
these very controlled barely perceptible sudden move-

ments, as if several times she were on the verge of saying something that began with the word 'you.' On the TV a woman was making her fist go up and down on a cock with her mouth slack. When a sex scene ended, Emily's blanket would stop. We got to the scene where the guy with the wide yellow tie with a dollar sign on it has sex with the heroine. She says something like, 'Don't play around, just fuck me,' and so he does. This scene really got to Emily, and she took the blanket in her teeth so she could have both hands free and yet have it over her, so now there were these loomings as her left hand moved back and forth between breasts, and the little circling rhythm was slightly less constrained."

"What were you doing?"

"Whenever we were in a sex scene, I mean in the middle of watching one, I would slip my hand under my belt and press on myself, through my underpants. When the sex scene was over, I took my hand out and rested it decorously on my leg. Anyway, this scene with the man with the yellow tie with the dollar signs really aroused her, and when it was over she took the blanket out of her teeth and wiped her mouth with the back of her right hand, spitting out some of the blanket fuzz, and in the TV light I could see that her two fingers were all shiny from stroking herself. We waited through the filler stuff, we didn't care about dialogue or cars driving or any of that, now we both wanted to see fucking, period. The next scene was two women and a man. Halfway through,

it threatened to be a lesbo scene, and I saw Emily's
blanket vibrate with less conviction and then stop. She
needed to see cocks at work. Fortunately it didn't turn
out to be a lesbo scene—one of the women was content
to strum quietly on the sidelines. Emily's blanket began
moving fast. But this time she didn't have it in her teeth,
it was loose over her, so her movements began to pull it
down. I watched the fringe say good-bye to her throat,
and began to travel slowly over her bunched-up sweater,
and over the bunched-up bra under that, and then the
individual fringe things fanned out and conformed to her
breasts and slipped off them. The slow descent finally
stopped at the waist of her skirt. I was a little hesitant to
watch her directly now; I watched her more out of the
corner of my eye: I saw her squeeze one nipple with a
finger-do-the-walking kind of movement, and then her
hand moved to the other breast. This was her left hand.
And no oohs and ahs, everything quiet, just breathing,
sometimes her mouth open slightly, sometimes closed.
Once she pressed her lips together and bit them. Certain
signs also made me think that at times she was biting the
insides of both her cheeks. I could tell now exactly how
her legs were positioned—they were somewhat apart, the
blanket drooped between them, and the back of her hand
was making the blanket move freely—but that wasn't the
thing that got me. What got me was, her whole arm was
now visible, her whole right arm, and the fringe inter-
sected with it just at the wrist, which was arched, reach-

ing down, circling, and the thing was that I could see her long beautiful forearm tendon pulling and pulling, controlling her fingers. I just kept watching this. Then the scene ended; I pulled my hand out of my pants, Emily crossed her arms over her breasts. She whistled a little, mock casually. Three wet fingers rested on her arm. We waited. More filler. The heroine goes into an office with two men we haven't seen before, both in business clothes. They think she is charging them with cheating her in the payment for the counterfeit money. She says something like 'Gentlemen, I'm talking about my own needs.' And suddenly two men with ties on are standing on either side of her, and she's sitting in a straight-back chair wearing white stockings, and she's sucking one and then the other. Emily whispered, *'That's it,'* and her hands both now slid under the fringe. And then she whispered, 'Do you want some blanket?' I said, 'Yes,' so she held on to her half so that it didn't slide off her any more and I pulled some of it over me, so we were both covered from the waist down. I undid my belt and pants and pushed off my clothes. We were both stroking ourselves, and I could feel against the back of my hand the blanket pulling with her little movements as I made mine. I sort of clamped the blanket against the top of my cock with my thumb so that I'd stay decent and yet have my left hand free, and I looked over at Emily's face, and watched her eyes traveling over those double-cock images, and I looked down at her breasts. I wanted to touch them, but I knew this would complicate things, it would have been a mistake. I could have come anytime. But suddenly the scene ended—one man suddenly comes on the woman's face and breasts, the other pulls out and comes on her bush, with strikingly white sperm. Emily wasn't fazed. She said, 'Do you mind if I rewind a little?' I said no, so she rewound it and replayed some of the two cocks. When it started playing, she said, kind of softly, 'I think I want to come to this scene.' I said, 'Okay.' But again the scene ended too quickly for her, and she had to rewind it a third time. This time, I just looked at her, she was flushed, her cheeks were shiny, she looked so trans-formed and sexual and elegant, and I looked down and both her hands were converging under the blanket, both wrists arched, so that her arms sort of pushed her breasts in from the sides, and I said, 'Can I touch your arm?' and she nodded, and I put my fingertips very lightly on the inside of her forearm, just above her wrist, and I felt her tendon going and going as she stroked herself, and this indirect feeling of being able to take the pulse of her masturbating was too much, I said, 'I think I'm going to come,' and I started to come into the blanket, and when the first guy in the movie came on the heroine, Emily closed her legs and started to come herself, and when the second guy came on the heroine, Emily was still com-ing, but not with any thrashing around, very focused, but I could hear the shaking of her legs slightly in her breath-ing. It was really a wonderful experience. She picked up her panty hose and after I'd stowed myself away she wrapped the blanket around herself and I escorted her to the bathroom, holding the spermy corner like a footman so that it wouldn't fall against her skirt. Then I drove her back to her car. We kissed ceremonially, and she said, 'Thanks, Mario.' I sent her an asterisk memo the next day. And that was it. A perfect evening, perfect."

"Not to be repeated, or to be repeated?"

"Not to be. A work friendship probably can't handle more than one evening of parallel blanket masturbation without things flying out of control. I think that's what Miss Manners would say, anyway. She did get over Lee—in fact, maybe *Pleasure So Deep* was what finally did it. She's now going out with an academic and seems very happy. I haven't told her that I've rented the movie twice since then on my own and relived that buildup. I was surprised to find that we'd actually only watched about half of it. And I also found, when I watched it through to the end, that it wasn't as good later on—the movie was only good because she'd seen it, so the parts she hadn't seen seemed flat. Well, not *flat*, there was some hot stuff, but I rewound and came to the scene where the woman says, 'I'm talking about my own needs' to the two men. Since we're being truthful with each other, since we're being truthful, I'll tell you that that evening with Emily was probably the best sexual experience I've had, or at least one of the elite few. The sound of her breathing while she was biting the inside of her cheeks! God! And the sight of that blanket slowly sliding off her. And when she put her knees together. And it's not like I haven't done normal stuff here and there. But I don't know, you slip inside, and that first moment is paradise, incomparable, but then you're there working away, and you can't *see* the clitoris properly, you can't really concentrate on what it feels like to hold her breasts, what they look like when they move, you're distracted, your brain is moving your hips, moving your torso, holding her soft hips—hey, it sounds good! But you know? When I come inside it feels mystical but muffled—it's as if I don't feel the perimeter of my cock anymore, because that's merged with her, it's melted away and all I feel is the technical interior conduit structure of the thing and the bulb of come swelling and all that—I lose a sense of outer boundaries. You know? Or do you prefer the physical presence of a cock?"

"Well," she said, "I mean, if one is in there, I'm not going to tell it to go away. But actually, it's funny, it's another little bit of clit-trickery. As I'm starting to get close to coming, and I'm with a man, I get this intense wish at a certain point to have him in me, but if I pull him up from what he's doing and guide him in, that first moment is great, but then my whole area becomes, as you say, distracted—my clitoris is suddenly in close conference with my vagina, and I'm out of the loop. I like to *think* about cocks in me, though. Also, yeah, I do unfortunately tend to get yeast complications from real sex, inside sex, the friction seems to cause them."

"Exactly! See that? Who cares about my cock? It'll fend for itself. We're talking about your orgasm. We're talking about your strummed orgasm, the joy of it, the triumph of it, the greatness of it. I think of that moment you described of you coming in the shower after swimming, with the hot and cold water, and it's like I can hold out my hands and something tremendous and valuable is being dropped in my arms to hold."

"A folded blanket," she said.

"That's it!"

"I think it's fair to say that you are interested in women masturbating," she said.

"Any woman masturbates anywhere, I want to know about it. No woman is anything but beautiful when she is masturbating. Any plainness or overweightness or boniness or even a character flaw, an ungenerousness or something, everything is part of the recipe of her particular transfiguration, everything bad is pressed out of her when she shuts her eyes tight and comes. There used to be a tiny ad that ran in a lot of men's magazines, a half-inch-high ad, that had a shot of a woman lying back with what seemed to be, and it was very hard to tell at that scale, but what seemed to be her two middle fingers inside herself, and the headline was, I LOVE TO MASTURBATE. I probably came fifty times to that little ad. I'd look through at the full-page shots, but then when I was almost there, I would find this ad. You were supposed to send money to Mrs. Somebody in Van Nuys, and she would send you six hot photos and a pair of panties.

Right, sure—I never sent off for them. But the ad was a tiny window onto something, onto an idea: because there *is* a Mrs. Somebody in Van Nuys, California, who *does* love to masturbate, there are lots of Mrs. Somebodys in fact, and she is not advertising herself in men's magazines, she isn't wasting her time with that, she is simply masturbating, right now, and that idea fills me with energy, it's all I need from life, the notion that women are masturbating, and I don't know when or where, but it's going on. One time I drove all night back from college my sophomore year, and I shared the ride with this girl who was on my hall in the dorm who had a car, and it started to *rain* this mysterious warm rain . . . no, but I really did share a ride with her, totally uneventful, but just this past year, ten years later, we had a sort of reunion of the people who'd been on that hall that year, because it had been kind of a funny nice group, and this same woman sat next to me at dinner and told me in a low voice at one point that on that all-night trip, at six in the morning, while I was driving, and she was supposed to be fast asleep, that she'd made herself 'comfortable' in the back seat, just as we were going past the big GE plant in Syracuse. I said, Thank you, thank you, thank you for telling me. Ten fucking *years* that secret orgasm of hers was accumulating interest. Sometimes I think of myself up in a satellite, and I'm looking down at America, or anywhere, really, but I usually imagine America, and all these little lights are blinking on and off, and each one represents a woman's orgasm. That's what 'simultaneous orgasm' should really mean—the awareness of all those women's orgasms simultaneously going on. Maybe the women who are reading while they come create a slightly different flare of infrared color than the ones who are imagining something or coming in their sleep. I see them all. There is the woman who put the anchovies on my pizza tonight, there is Jill at work, who I got the tights for, there is an overweight rural woman with greasy hair and a missing front tooth, but she doesn't care about keeping her lip down over the gap, it feels too good to care, there's nobody to feel self-conscious in front of and therefore she's beautiful, and there is the thruway woman who hands you your ticket, and there's Blair Brown coming, and Elizabeth McGovern, and that woman in the John Hughes movies, what's her name, with the lovely mouth, and Jeane Kirkpatrick, and the porn stars too, but off-camera, Keisha and Christy Canyon—all these flares. Maybe it's not a satellite, maybe it's really a big black spy plane I'm in, and what's this, you're up here too, flying toward my fan-jet, surprise surprise."

"All that is somewhat indiscriminate of you, you know. You're using me as a proxy for all women who are masturbating at this very moment."

"Well, that may have been the original motive for calling this number, but I have never *talked* like this to any woman before. You're right, though, I can see that the idea of me suspended ten miles up over a dark twinkling continent, taking in the totality of female orgasms, might seem a bit indiscriminate. The fact is, I *am* indiscriminate. If I had called this number, and there had been a woman of extremely limited intelligence who responded to my voice, like say that one woman, Carla, who was on the line after you first came on, and she and I had entered our private code numbers and been transferred together into this 'back room,' and if she'd come, if I could have talked her through coming, that would have been a wonderful privilege and I would have come too and I would have hung up after twenty minutes feeling great. But that's why talking to you seems like such a miraculous once-in-a-lifetime thing, because you are smart and funny and aroused and delightful—you are *not* representative. We're actually talking! If you come on this phone with me, it will be, as far as I'm concerned, it will be the top item on *Washington Week in Review*, it will be bigger than anything your bearded friend who eats the meatball subs has ever experienced, it will be really *something*, because you get it, you understand, you have a complicated response to things, and, I mean, an orgasm in a complicated mind is always more interesting than one in a simple mind—maybe that's not true, maybe sometimes a simple mind is made subtler and finer as it comes, since that's the most mental activity that's gone on in there for a while—but I mean an orgasm in an intelligent woman is like a volcano in a mountain with a city built on the slope—you feel the alternative opportunity cost of her orgasm, you feel the force of all the other perceptive things she could be thinking at that moment and is not thinking because she is coming, and they enrich it. You still there?"

"I'm just trying to feel my wrist tendon," she said, "to see what it might have felt like for you. Actually, you know, there is a little muscle high up on the *outside* of my forearm that is moving, almost at my elbow. That's the one that's more visible in my case. Feels kind of interesting."

"Ooh, don't say that or I'll shoot."

"Hah hah! I like a man who knows what he likes. Do you want to hear what I thought about when I came in the shower yesterday?"

"Yes."

"I'll tell you. No, I know what I'll tell you. First I'm going to tell you something else. First I'm going to tell you about how I masturbated in front of somebody. It's short."

"By all means, tell me."

"Shall I tell you every nasty thing that comes into my head?"

"Yes."

"I will then," she said. "We went to the circus. It's funny, it excites me quite a bit just to tell you that I'm going to tell you. Doing that is probably the best part. It's just like that moment when you're lumbering around on the bed to get into opposite directions to do sixty-nine, that feeling of parting my legs over a man's face, *before* you put your hands on my back and pull me down, and my legs remember the feeling from the last time, the feeling of being locked into a preset position that is right for human bodies to be in, like putting a different lens on a camera, turning it until it clicks."

"And I," he said, "would feel the mattress change its slope, first on one side of my head, and then the other, as the weight of one of your knees and then the other pressed into it, and I'd look up at you and open my mouth and I'd slide my hands over your ass with my fingers splayed and hold your ass and pull you down to my tongue."

"Kha."

There was a pause.

"You there?" he asked.

"Yes."

"Tell me about the circus."

"Okay. Excuse me. I'm going to have to get a fresh towel pretty soon. This guy took me to the circus."

"The guy with the fancy stereo?"

"Another guy," she said. "It wasn't Ringling Brothers, it was some smaller-scale South American circus, with lots of elephants, and lots of women in spangles riding the elephants. It was incredibly hot in the tent, and everything had this reddish tint, because the sun was bright enough outside to make it through some of the tent seams, and I was wearing shorts and a T-shirt but I was soaked, and so was Lawrence, who was also wearing shorts and a T-shirt, and so was everyone around us, including the performers. There was some Venezuelan act in which a woman spun hard balls around very fast on long strings while two men played percussion behind her, and the balls smacked against the floorboards in interesting rhythms around her legs, and she was *streaming* with sweat, and quite beautiful, but in a way that I thought was vaguely like me, and suddenly the two men would stop hitting the drums and she would freeze and make this kind of trilling scream, a beautiful strange wild sound. She was just covered with sweat, she looked really wild, and the two men behind her were exceedingly good-looking, wearing wide-brimmed black hats with chin straps, and I momentarily wanted to be her, and while they were taking their bows I adapted my time-tested striptease fantasy, and I thought that I was this woman in the black spangles, and I was spinning these balls very fast, faster than she could, so they were a blur, so fast that somehow, like in a cartoon fight when it's just a blur from which things, pieces of clothing, fly outward, somehow my whole outfit was torn in pieces from my body, and flung out into the audience, so that when the drumming stopped and I froze suddenly and made my trilling scream, I was totally naked, and all these pieces of my costume were still floating aloft in all directions, and each man who caught some damp shred of costume was overpowered and took his place in line to fuck me, and the two percussionists played the drums the whole time, and then they stopped drumming and naturally they fucked me too. But that's just an aside. The elephant acts were what were interesting. I've ridden on an elephant once or twice in my life, when I was small, and I remember touching the big lobes of its head, and let me tell you, the skin is not smooth, it's warm and dry and quite bristly—that's how I remember it, anyway. And these were not little elephants, these were big old elephants, with big tusks. Well, these women were sliding down the side of the elephants, riding on the elephants heads, with their legs between the elephants' eyes, and repeatedly pivoting around on their bottoms on the elephants' backs, and they were wearing flesh-colored stockings, or tights, so it was not skin to skin, but even so, those little leotards are cut extremely high in the back, and I really started to be concerned about their bottoms, about whether they were more uncomfortable than their smiles let on, and I started thinking about whether if *I* were dressed in a very high-cut leotard I would like the sensation of the elephant's dry living skin on my bottom, and then, during the beginning of the very last big elephant promenade, one of the women was riding on the elephant's back with one leg in the air, and as the elephant turned I saw this woman's bottom, and even through the tights I could see that it was in fact red! She was the main elephant woman, I think. Anyhow, for the big finale she rode around on this elephant's tusks for a minute or two, sat on his trunk, fine fine, all gracefully executed but surprisingly suggestive, and then she did this thing that really shocked me. She took hold of one of the tusks and one of the ears, or somehow swung herself up, and then she lifted one of her knees so that it went right *into* the elephant's mouth, and she waited for a second for the elephant to clamp on to it, and then she threw her head back, and arched her back, and spread her arms wide, so she was held in the air supported entirely by her knee, which was stuffed in the elephant's mouth! I mean, think about the saliva! Think about those elephant molars that are gently but firmly taking hold of your upper calf and your mid-thigh, while this elephant tongue is there lounging with its giant taste-buds against your knee! The elephant did a full turn while she was swooning like this. Then she got down and took a bow and patted the elephant under his eye."

"Wow, that's better than *King Kong*."

"Well *I* was impressed. Lawrence had come up with the idea of going to the circus—this was our very first time out, by the way, though I'd known him for a while—so he was careful not to be too impressed. While we were walking out to the car he said, 'I guess those elephants really respond to training.' He thought the elephant wasn't biting the woman's leg, but rather that its tongue was actually hooked under her knee. I was dubious, but it was an interesting idea. It was touching to see how pleased Lawrence was that I'd liked the circus. We were standing out by my car in the parking lot, just drenched with sweat, he was plucking at his shirt and squinting at me, and we were supposed to go to this clam-shack place and have an early dinner on a picnic table outside, and I just didn't want to do that. So I thought what the hell, and I said, 'You look hot. Why don't you come back to my apartment and you'll have a shower, and I'll have a shower and then I'll make some dinner and we'll do the clam shack another time, okay?' He agreed instantly—he was delighted to have the responsibility for the success of this date taken out of his hands. So he had a shower, and I happened to have a pair of very baggy shorts with an elastic waistband that fit him fine, and a big T-shirt, and then I had a shower, and I put on a pair of shorts and a dark red T-shirt, and everything was fine."

"But separate showers, no nudity."

"No, very chaste," she said.

"What was he doing when you got out of the shower?"

"He was peering inside a Venetian paperweight."

"Classic. He'd obviously heard your shower turn off, and then he'd stood there, holding the paperweight to his face for ten minutes, so that you would be sure to discover him in that casual pose, appreciating your trinket."

"Quite possible. Anyhow, he sat in the kitchen and we talked rather formally while I made a spiral kind of pasta and microwaved a packet of creamed chipped beef—this is a great dish, incidentally, Stouffer's creamed chipped beef over any kind of pasta noodles—I have it about once a week. Lawrence made an elaborate pretense of being impressed by this super easy recipe, and when I poured the spirals from the drainer into a bowl he came over to where I was standing and he said, 'I have to see this.' I was going to simply slice the packet of creamed chipped open and dump it over the spirals, which is what I normally do, but I was feeling sneaky, I'd just had a shower, and you know about me and showers, but I hadn't dithered, despite the *major* striptease fantasy I'd had at the circus, because obviously I couldn't, since a man was in my apartment, so I was feeling devious, and so I got out some olive oil and poured a little of it on the spirals, and he—he was definitely not in the know about cooking, and I'm certainly not much of a cook myself—but he said, 'So *that's* how you keep them from sticking and clumping.' I stirred them up, and they made an embarrassingly luscious sexy sound, and I just decided, fuck it, I've dressed this person, I'm feeding this person, I'm going to seduce this person, right now, today, so I said, I said, 'How very strange,' I said, 'I just remembered something I haven't thought of in years. I just remembered this kid in my junior high—you remind me of him in some ways—I just remembered his commenting that a certain girl must have used olive oil to put on her jeans.' Well, I saw Lawrence's little eyeballs roll at this. He said something obvious about extra virgin cold pressed and he snuffled out a nervous laugh and I thought, yes,

I am in charge here, I am going to see this person's penis get hard, and even though I have a smoldering yeast problem and so can't really have full-fledged sex I am going to have my way with this person somehow. It was probably that Venezuelan ball-twirling screamer that put me in that mood, now that I think back. I mean, I felt powerful and shrewd and effortlessly in control and everything else I usually don't feel. I cut open the packet of creamed chipped and I said, musingly, 'My grandmother was very careful about money—she always used to say that she was as tight as the bark on a tree. And I used to think about what that really would feel like, whether bark does feel tight to the inner wood of the tree. I used to put on my jeans and take them off, thinking about that.' Lawrence said, 'Really!' I said, 'Yeah, although actually I didn't like my jeans to be at all tight, even then. I liked them loose. The appeal was the rough fabric, and the rough stitching, very barklike, the appeal was of being in this sort of complete male embrace, but then when you took them off, being all smooth and curved.' Lawrence nodded seriously. So I said, making the leap, I said, 'And when I started getting my legs waxed, which is quite an expensive little procedure, I also thought of that phrase, *as tight as the bark on a tree*, when Leona, my waxer, began putting the little warm wax strips on my legs and letting them solidify for an instant and ripping them off.' I said, 'In fact, I just had my legs waxed yesterday.' Lawrence said, 'Is that right?' and I said, 'Yes, it's amazing how much freer you feel after your legs are waxed—it's almost as if you've become physically more limber—you want to leap around, and make high kicks, cavort.' I waited for that to sink in and then I said, 'Leona's a tiny Ukrainian woman, and she makes this growly sound as she rips the strips of muslin and wax off, *rrr*, and when she's done both my legs and there's no more hurting, she rubs lotion into them, and it's a surprisingly sensual experience.' Lawrence was silent for a second and then he said, 'I'm inexperienced with depilatory techniques. I've never known anyone who had her legs waxed.' I said, 'Let's have dinner.' "

"What a tactician!"

"Not really. Anyhow, we had dinner, which was pretty tame. Lawrence had many virtues, he had a kind of bony broad-shoulderedness, and a deliberate way of blinking and looking at you when you spoke, and he was quite smart—he was a patent lawyer."

"Ah. Patent in*fringe*ment?"

"Yes indeed. But he had no conversational skills at all. He was putty in my hands. No, I'm actually making myself seem more completely sure of my powers than I felt—but still, I was pretty much in control. I started asking him how electrical things worked—you know, like what shortwave radio was, and how cordless telephones worked, and why it is that at drive-ins now you can hear the movie on the FM radio in your car. And he was full of interesting information, once you jump-started him that way. But the thing was, I kept a faint racy undertone going in the conversation. For instance, I'd say, 'What do you think those ham-radio buffs really talked about? Do you think some of them were secretly gay, and they left their wives asleep and crept down to their finished basements in the middle of the night to have long conversations with *friends* in New Zealand or wherever?' He said, 'I suppose it's a possibility.' And about the drive-ins I said things like, 'It must be much more comfortable and *private* in drive-ins now, because you can close the window completely, you don't have that metal thing hanging there with the tinny sound, covered with yellow chipped paint, like a chaperone, you're not attached to anything around you, it's much more like being in a car on the expressway.' He said he didn't know exactly how drive-ins supplied the FM sound, because he hadn't been to a drive-in since he was eight years old, but he said that technically speaking it was an easy problem to solve, for instance there was a thing advertised in the back of *Popular Science* that picks up any sound in the room and broadcasts it to FM radios within several hundred yards, it's called a Bionic Mike Transmitter. I said, 'Ooo, a Bionic Mike Transmitter!' He said, 'Oh sure, it's this device that you can leave in this room, for instance, and it will broadcast any sound in the room to any nearby FM radio, if it's correctly tuned.' He said, 'Of course it's advertised with a big warning about how it's not meant for illegal surveillance. But probably that's what it's used for.' I said, 'You mean that whatever I did, whatever intimate private activity I engaged in, would be heard by the people swooshing by in the cars on the expressway?' He said, 'If they were tuned correctly, yes.' I said, 'Hmmm.' You see, my living room is on the second floor, about three hundred feet from a raised part of the expressway."

"In some eastern city," he said.

"That's right," she said.

"So what did Lawrence do when you expressed a keen interest in his description of the Bionic Mike Transducer?"

"Transmitter. He asked if he could have a fourth helping of creamed chipped beef. Then we were finished and I started to clear the table and he said, 'I'll wash up.' I said, 'No, forget it, I'll do it later,' but he said, 'No no really, I like washing up.' So I said fine, and he cleaned the kitchen, quite efficiently, while I told him the plot of *Dial M for Murder*, really lingering over the hot letter that's found on the body of the man with the pair of scissors in his back. You know? Lawrence listened carefully—he'd never seen the movie, if you can believe it. He said he didn't like black-and-white movies. I said, 'Fine, don't like them, *Dial M for Murder* is in color.' He said, 'Oh.' And then he said, 'Well, I think Hitchcock was a fairly sick individual anyway.' I said, 'You're probably right.' Then he dried his hands with a paper towel and turned toward me holding the glass bottle of olive oil and he said, 'Now, where does this go?' I said, 'Well, where would you like it to go?' And he said, 'I don't know.' So I said, 'Well sometimes, after I get my legs waxed, the day after, they're still a little tender, and I've found that olive oil really helps them feel better.' Which wasn't true, they feel fine the day after, but anyway."

"Erotic license."

"Exactly. He said, 'But that would be terribly messy!' I said, 'So I'll stand in the bathtub.' And he said, 'But won't it be cold and clammy?' So I turned the bottle of oil on its side and put it in the microwave for twenty seconds. He felt it and he shook his head and said, 'I think it needs a full minute.' So we leaned on the counter, looking at the microwave, while it heated the oil. When the five beeps beeped, Lawrence took it out, and we went to the bathroom together. I stood in the bathtub and pulled my shorts up high on my legs, and very solemnly he poured a little pool of olive oil on his fingers and rubbed it just above my knee."

"He was kneeling himself?"

"Yes. The bathtub wasn't really wet anymore—I mean it was still humid from both the showers, but we didn't have the water running or anything. He said, 'You're very smooth.' I said, 'Thank you.' A rather powerful smell of olive oil surrounded us, and I began to feel quite Mediterranean and Bacchic, and honestly somewhat like a mushroom being lightly sautéed. He stared at his hand going over my skin, blinking at it. I pulled the sides of my shorts up higher so he could do more of my thighs, and I said, 'Leona is very thorough. No follicle is left unmolested.' Then, whoops, I wondered whether that was maybe too kinky for him and whether he might think that I was trying to give him the idea that Leona had gone over the edge and waxed off all my pubic hair, horrifying thought, so I said, 'I mean, within limits.' He just kept on dolloping oil on his fingers and rubbing it in. After a while I turned around and held on to the showerhead and he did the backs of my legs. He wasn't artful at all, he didn't know how to knead the deep muscles, but I could feel the intelligence and interest in his fingers when they came to each new dry curve. His hands went right up underneath the bagginess of my shorts. I liked that. He didn't say anything. Once I think he cleared his throat. Finally he said, 'Okay, I think that's everything.' I turned around and looked down at him: he was sitting with his legs crossed, looking at my legs, very closely, really letting his eyes travel over them. He had curly hair—he needed a haircut, in fact. He had the top of the olive oil in one hand and the bottle in the other, and before he stood up he pressed the circle of the plastic top back and forth up the inside of both my legs, in a zigzag. Then he stood up and handed me the bottle. He was blushing. I smiled at him and I said, 'Are you suffering from any sticking or clumping?' And he said, 'Yeah, some.' So I pulled on the waistband of his shorts and poured about a tablespoonful of oil in there."

"No kidding!"

"Yes, well, he looked at me with shock. And I know I wouldn't have been able to do it if they hadn't really been my *own* shorts that I'd lent him. I said, 'I'm awfully sorry, I don't know what I was thinking. Take those off and I'll see if I have another pair.' So he marched that peculiar march that men do as they are taking off their pants. He was not erect by any means, but he wasn't dormant either. I said, 'Did the olive oil feel warm?' And he said, 'Yes.' So I said, 'Would you like some more?' and he said, 'Maybe.' So I held the mouth of the bottle right where his pubic hair bushed out, high on his cock, I mean near the base, not near the tip, because he was still drooping down, and I tipped it as if to pour it over him, but I didn't actually let any come out. I just held it there. And the expectation of the warmth of the oil made his cock rise a little. I tipped the bottle even more, so that the olive oil was right in the neck, ready to pour out, but still I didn't actually pour it. And his erection rose a little more, wanting the oil. It was like some kind of stage levitation. His hands were in little boyish fists at his sides. When he was almost horizontal, but still angling slightly downward, suddenly I poured the entire rest of the bottle over him, just *glug glug glug glug glug*, so that it flowed down its full cock length and fell with a buzzing sound onto the bathtub. And this was not a trivial amount of oil, this was about maybe a third of the bottle. The waste was itself exciting. It was like covering him in some amber glaze. He hurriedly moved his legs farther apart so he wouldn't get oil spatter on his feet. By the time there were only a few last drips falling from the bottle, he was totally, I mean totally, hard. And of course with this success I had second thoughts. I almost wanted him to leave right then so that I could come in the shower by myself. I stepped out of the tub and I said, 'Sorry, I got carried away. And the problem is, I have this darn yeast situation, so I can't really do anything with that magnificent thing, much as I'd like to.' He said, 'Ah, that's all right, I'll just go home and take care of that myself, that's no problem,' he said, 'but your *tub*, on the other hand, is a mess. Ask me to clean it and I will.' I said, 'Oh don't worry about that, it's just oil, it's nothing.' But he was on his own private trajectory, and he said, 'That's right, it's oil, plus I have to say the tub is not terribly clean to begin with.' I said, 'No no no, don't even think of it, really.' He picked up an old dry Rescue pad that was in a corner and he held it up and he said, 'Look, tell me to clean your tub.' He's standing there, a pantless patent lawyer, semi-erect, wearing my Danger Mouse T-shirt, holding the tiny curled-up green Rescue pad with a fierce expression. *He wanted to clean my tub*. I said, 'Well, great. Please do. Sure.' He asked for some Ajax, so I brought some from the kitchen, along with a folding chair so I could sit and watch. Well, this Lawrence turned out to be some kind of demon scrub-wizard. He hands me my bottles of shampoo, one by one. My tub is now naked! He squats in it, so that his testicles are practically gamboling in the giant teardrop of oil that's on the bottom, and he takes the Ajax and he taps its rim against the edge of the tub, all the way around, so that these *curtains* of pale blue powder fall down the sides, kind of an aurora borealis effect, and then he moistens his Rescue pad and he starts scrubbing and scrubbing, every curve, every seam, talk about circling motions, my lord! He did the place where the shampoo bottles had been, that I'd simply defined as a safe haven for mildew, he was in there, *grrr, grrrr,* twisting and jamming that little sponge. Not that my tub is filthy, it isn't, it's just not sparkling, and there *is* a faint rich smell of mildew or something vaguely biological, which I kind of like, because it's so closely associated by now with my private shower activity. But here I was watching this guy *in* my shower! He took down the Wa- ter Pik massage head and he rinsed off the parts he'd done, and he began to herd all the oil down the drain with hot water, and the oil and the Ajax had mixed and formed this awful stuff, like a *roux* first, and then when the water mixed in it became this yellow sort of foam, which didn't daunt him, he took care of it. And then he started scrubbing his way toward the fittings, using liberal amounts of Ajax alternating with hot water. He said, 'You don't worry about scratching, do you?' I said I didn't. So he gnarled around the cold-water tap and he gnarled around the hot-water tap and he circled fiercely around the clitty thing that controls the drain, and then when the whole rest of the tub was absolutely *gleaming*, he went to the drain itself—he set aside the filter thing, and he reached two fingers way in, and he pulled out this revolting slime locket and splapped it against the side of the tub, and then he really went to work on that drain, around and around the rim of chrome, and deeper, right down to those dark crossbars, that I'd never gotten to, he worked the scrubber sponge in there, *grrr*, more Ajax, more circling, more hot water. I mean I was in a transport!"

"I bet."

"Then I held out the trash can, and he threw out the drain slime and the Rescue pad, and he rinsed his hands, and he stood, and in the midst of this newly cleaned tub he started to rinse off his cock and his legs, where a little oil had fallen, and I watched the water go over him, I watched the way the even spray of the showerhead in his hand made all the hairs on his legs into these perfect perfect rows, like some ideal crop, and he was quite hairy, and so I slipped off my shorts and unders and sat on the far end of the bathtub and propped my left foot against a washcloth handle and I hung my right leg out over the edge of the bathtub, so I was wide open, and I said, 'I'm a bit rank, too, do me,' so he started playing the water over my legs and then directly on my . . . femalia, and I held my lips open so that he could see my inner

wishbone, and the drops of water exploding on it, and as
he sprayed me, he began to get hard again. But I can't
come with just water, so I started strumming myself,
while he sprayed my hand, which was a lovely feeling,
and I held out my left hand and he maneuvered closer to
me and I took hold of his cock and tried to begin to jerk
it off, but I didn't do very well, because my own finger on
my clit felt so good, and I couldn't seem to keep the two
kinds of masturbating motion going with my left and
right hand independently, I was making big odd circles
with his cock, so instead I took the showerhead from him
and I said, 'You're on your own,' and I sprayed his cock
and some of his Danger Mouse T-shirt, that is, *my* Danger Mouse T-shirt, while he began stroking away, staring
at my legs and my pussy, and I liked spraying him quite
a lot, I liked aiming the water at his fist, I liked the sight
of his wet T-shirt, and he had, this is rather bad of me to
say, but he had a kind of gruesome-looking cock, a real
monster, and the relief of not having that girth in me was
itself almost enough to put me over the top, and it looked
quite a bit more distinguished through the glint of the
spray. But I also wanted the water on me—I wanted to
spray him, but I wanted the water flowing on me as
well—and suddenly it seemed like the most natural thing
in the world, I remembered the elephant woman lifting
her knee, and so I reached forward and pulled his hips
toward me so that his legs straddled my left leg, and I
lifted my knee, and he clamped his thighs around it, and

I let my other leg sprawl so that I was absolutely wide open, and now, when I sprayed his cock and his hand the water streamed down his thighs and then down my thigh and on me. And it was exactly what I wanted, and it started to feel so good, and I said so, and suddenly he started stroking himself incredibly fast, it was this blur, like a *sewing* machine, and he produced this major jet of sperm at a diagonal right into the circular spray of the water, so that it fought against all the drops and was sort of torn apart by them, and he was clamping my leg, my smooth leg, extremely tight with those perfectly water-groomed thighs, and I shifted adroitly so that the poached sperm and hot-water runoff wouldn't pour directly into me and possibly cause trouble, but so that it still poured over me. And then he took the showerhead again, and still holding his cock and still clamping my knee very tight, he sprayed slowly across my hand and my thighs very close with the water until I closed my eyes and came, imagining I was in front of a circus audience. So that was nice."

"God of mercy, I am so jealous!"

"Don't be," she said. "I think my offhand talk of yeast unnerved him, and his subservient streak unnerved *me*. Anyway, the point is, that story is connected to this very call between you and me, because when I was in the shower yesterday, and close to coming—"

"Thinking about the three painters."

"No, *after* the three painters, when I was very close to

coming, I was thinking of that time with Lawrence, as I occasionally do, I imagine him handing me my bottles of shampoo with a serious expression, or some fragment of it, anyway yesterday I thought of the Bionic Mike Transmitter that he'd described, and I started to make these very theatrical moans, like 'oh yeah, oh yeah baby, ooh yeah, pump it deep, pump it deep, oooh yeah' and I imagined that someone had left a Bionic Mike Transmitter in my bathroom and that random men on the expressway were driving by with their radios scanning the stations and suddenly they would pick me up, they'd hear me moaning exaggeratedly in the shower. I started to feel myself beginning to come, and I filled my mouth with water, and I thought of the men on the expressway hearing my mouth fill with water, and as I started to come I pushed the water from my mouth so that it poured from my chin over me, which is what I usually do, and I said, and this was not theatrical, this was heartfelt, I said, '*Oh, shoot it, shoot it, you cocksuckers!*' I guess that in my ecstasy I was a trifle confused."

"Perfectly understandable. So then you called to-night . . ."

"I called tonight I think out of the same impulse, the idea that five or six men would hear me come, as if my voice was this *thing*, this disembodied body, out there, and as they moaned they would be overlaying their moans onto it, and, in a way, coming onto it, and the idea appealed to me, but then, when I actually made the call, the reality of it was that the men were so irritating, either passive, wanting me to entertain them, or full of what-are-your-measurements questions, and so I was silent for a while, and then I heard your voice and liked it."

"Thank you. Yours is nice, too, you know. Very smooth."

"Thanks. I just had it waxed yesterday. Shall we, do you think, should we perhaps come soon?"

"Yes. You're absolutely right. Are you naked?"

"Wait a sec. Yes, I am now officially naked, except for the bra."

"Are your legs apart?"

"My toes are holding on to the edge of the coffee table."

"Is your right hand touching your clitoris?"

"How impertinent! But yes, the answer is yes. My clitoris is in fact squeezed between my two index fingers, left and right, which are on either side of it."

"All right. You do whatever you want with those index fingers, and I'll tell you about a kind of sensing device that I own. What it does, it doesn't eavesdrop, it doesn't pick up sounds, it simply senses the presence nearby of any intelligent strumming woman. It looks like an antique pocket watch, it's gold, with a cover, but when you open it, instead of the dial, there is this mysterious fluid, this very special fluid in there that glows in several colors when the right conditions are met, for reasons

that are not clear, except that of course a woman masturbating is so important an event in the physical uni-
verse that elemental relations in matter are affected as it
occurs, and there are these sort of currents in the fluid
that slowly move in a certain direction, like lines of force,
which give you some sense of where the masturbation
signals are coming from, although it takes years of practice, and of course a great deal of native skill as well, to
learn how to read the fluid correctly. It's called the Bionic
Mmmm-Detector, as you might suspect. Well, I'm driving down the expressway of an eastern city one evening
around ten o'clock, in town on business, in my rented
midsize car, my Ford Topaz, with the radio going, a
classics oldie station, playing 'Ain't Nobody,' and I'm
just driving along, and as usual I have my Mmmm-
Detector open on the seat beside me, but the fluid is
dark, and then I start curving through this residential
area, very close to the buildings on either side, and I
glance down at the seat beside me, and my God, I'm
getting a very strong signal, I'm getting wave patterns I've
never seen before, from very near and to my right, and
craning my neck I catch sight of a lighted window, and
I know that behind it you are in process, you are beginning. My years of practice in reading the flux patterns in
the watch tells me this is something very special, something I cannot pass by, and so I palm the steering wheel
around suddenly and veer onto the off ramp and scoot
back through the narrow streets, swearing at all the one-
way signs, and when I come to the door where the

Mmmm-forces are flowing from, I park in a place that is sure to get me a ticket, and I leave my flashers on, and I go into the foyer. There's a row of buttons with names beside them: I hold the detector to each one until one, the third one down, makes the Mmmm-Detector glow with strange colors, and I hesitate, I know that I am interrupting you, and I don't want to do that, that's the last thing I want to do, but it seems so clear to me, reading the force waves, that there is a strong possibility that you would want me to interrupt you, if you knew me, and the conviction that this is true grows in me, and my finger trembles at your button, and there is a huge interior war between reticence and attraction, between the fear that I will inspire fear and the certainty that I should not inspire fear and that we would like each other if I could simply push that button, and I look down at the Mmmm-Detector and I see that you are going to come in less than four minutes if you keep on at that rate, you're really moving, the colors are increasingly intense, and I'm trembling, I'm shivering, but I'm compelled, and I push the button, *bzzzzt*. You're on your bed, and you're wearing a blue long-sleeved pullover sort of shirt, and black pants and black sneakers, but your black pants are around your ankles, and you've got that tattered, disintegrating issue of *Forum* in your left hand, and you're reading about a job interview in which the woman interviewer is sucking the interviewee's cock, and you're right in the middle of things, when *bzzzzt*, the doorbell. Who could that be?"

"So I do up my pants and I go to the speaker and I say, 'Hello?' "

"And I say, 'Hi, this is Jim. I know it's late, but I wonder if I could use your phone. My car's engine has seized up, and all the oil lights on the dash are glowing, and I don't dare drive it any further, and the pay phone down the street isn't working.' "

"I say, 'Why did you buzz my apartment?' "

"And I say, 'The others don't answer. You're right to be hesitant, but this isn't a normal situation, this is urgent, I've got to get back to my hotel, I've got a whole day of appointments tomorrow, I just *have* to get seven and a half hours of sleep or I won't function, and I need to use your phone, and I assure you that I'm reasonably sane and peaceable, and I would not normally do this, invade your privacy, but I'm telling you nothing could be more important than this. *Please.*' And you hear the conviction in my voice, and you buzz me in."

"Well, no, first I hold the talk button in and to my empty apartment I call out, 'Jeff? *Jeff!* Enough with the weights! Do you and Mojo Cartilage-Popper mind if someone comes up to use the phone for a second?' *Then* I buzz you in downstairs, knowing that I can look at you through the peephole in my door, and call Bobby the super if you look strange."

"Exactly. I run up to the second floor, and I find your door, and before I stand right in front of it, I check the Mmmm-Sensor and find that your arousal has suffered some decline, you are now ten or more minutes away from an orgasm, though the glow faintly persists. I knock, and I begin pacing back and forth in front of the door, distractedly, like a guy impatient to make a phone call. You look through the peephole and you see this guy, middle height, black hair, not bad-looking, somewhat frazzled, pacing back and forth in front of your door, checking a pocket watch. You let me in. And I introduce myself, I apologize for bothering you, I smile at you, and immediately I can sense the alertness and intelligence in your face, and I see that we understand each other, and I know my Mmmm-Sensor hasn't misled me. Ah, but I've lied my way into your apartment, which is a problem."

"It is, because if I knew!"

"Curtains. So you bring me the phone, and I sit on the edge of a dining-room chair, and I call my answering machine, and I start telling it about the oil lights on my dashboard, I really have to have someone take care of it, I need the number of a cab company, etcetera, and then all of a sudden I stop, in midsentence, and I click off the phone and I say, 'Nah, I can't.' "

" 'You can't what?' "

" 'I can't do it. I can't pretend.' And I confess to you that I've lied, that my car is fine, that I was driving on the expressway, and I got this highly unusual, if not unique, reading on my Mmmm-Sensor, or Mmmm-Detector, whatever I'm calling it, and I pull it out of my pocket and open the finely scratched gold top and show it to you, and I explain, hesitantly, that it, um, picks up the flux currents from intelligent, um, masturbating women, and I show you how it glows, and I point out the wavy flow lines as they move in your direction, and I say, 'They're somewhat fainter now, but they're definitely still there, and they really look great. Now, let's see what happens if I do this.' And I stand next to you, so you can see the Mmmm-Detector as I hold it a foot or so from your face, and then I lower it and slowly pass it a few inches in front of each breast, and the pattern makes these complicated shifts. And I say, 'But as you may be able to see, I'm getting other readings, interference fringes,' and I hold the thing up and I walk slowly to the walls of your hall, where there is a faint rural pattern showing through the paint, and I say, 'For instance, the walls, very curious,' and I shake my head in perplexity, and then I follow the flow lines to a drawer in the kitchen, filled with silverware—very odd—and I follow it into the bathroom, and you follow me in, and I lean into the shower and move the Mmmm-Detector past the fixtures, the drain, the shampoo bottles—beautiful color changes and convergences of flow waves—and I shake my head and I say, 'Gosh, I've never seen anything as rich as this,' and I follow its lead into the bedroom, and you follow me, and I say, 'Wow, *very* high flux levels in here,' and I pass it over your chenille bedspread and I say, 'Your feet must have been here and here,' pointing to two places quite far apart on the bed, and I know that everything I'm doing is forward, is really inexcusable, but in a way you're curious, and I'm just relaying facts, and I sense your willingness to have this happen, and I push the Mmmm-Detector into the pillow and then reach under it and find your disintegrating copy of *Forum*, and I sit down on the bed and page through it slowly, holding the device to each page, until I reach a certain page, and I peer very closely at the sensor, and then I hold it close to the button on your pants, and I inspect it again, and I look up smiling, and I hold the magazine out to you, pointing at something on the page, and I say, 'You were reading this sentence, this phrase right here in this sentence, when I buzzed your apartment.' "

"And," she said, "I take the *Forum* and read what you're pointing at, and you're pretty close, it's not exactly the right phrase, but you've found the right paragraph, anyway. And I don't know quite what to do. I probably should be calling the cops, because you seem to know all this stuff about me, but on the other hand, there you are, and I am still feeling all puffy down below, and you have a certain amount of charm, and an intriguing pocket watch, and so I offer you a, a what? A dry Vermouth on the rocks. And you accept."

"I do, you're right," he said, "and now I'm sitting on an armchair when you come toward me with the drinks, a low sort of armchair, and I have my legs sprawled open in a fairly innocent way, and I just dust off the area of the armchair that's between my legs, indicating that if you want to, you could sit there with no problem and lean back against me, and you do turn and sit there, but you don't lean back, you're leaning forward, and so I have this warm back, covered in loose blue shirt material, in front of me, this miracle of a back, and I take a sip of the drink, and put it down on the table, on a napkin, so it won't leave a ring, and I reach up and click off the table lamp so it's a bit darker, and I close my eyes and find your shoulders with my hands and you ask where I found the Mmmm-Detector and I describe the table of junk I found it on in a flea market in Anaheim, a hundred and forty bucks, without any manual, and how I taught myself over several years what it was for and how to read it, and as I'm telling you this I'm moving my thumbs in two little arcs back and forth above your shoulder blades, which is as much of a back rub as I can handle, because the notion of something called a *back rub* tires my mind out instantly, and I can't do anything that has to do with that, even though your back and my hands are interested in each other. What interests me is your bra, quite honestly, and so I relax my left hand and let it slide down the middle of your back, just let the fingers slide very lightly down over the material of your shirt, until I come to the place where your bra is fastened, and with my eyes closed, and with your ass warm between my legs, but still innocently there, I feel the three possible places for the hooks on the little fastener to hook, and that you've used the third setting, because of shrinkage probably, and I take my fingers and I follow the upward curving edge of the bra as it rises toward your shoulders, and I ride this curve up a little way over your shoulders and then back down your back and in to the middle again. It's like driving over the Bay Bridge. Then I follow the bottom edge horizontally around, under your arms, until I just reach the seam where a cup begins, and you feel all this somewhat dimly, because it's through your shirt and through the bra, but you are more aware now of the shape of the bra that you're wearing, and then I go back to the fastener and I make that time-honored pinching move and release the hooks through your shirt, and each side pulls away, and now I feel that I have this perfect central stretch with no interruption, and I press my left palm between your shoulder blades and slide slowly down, moving your shirt, feeling wrinkles in it form and pass, and I can feel some slight bumps of your backbone—what a beautiful back, so warm. I want very much to feel your skin. So I put both hands on your hips and hook my two thumbs and index fingers under the bottom edge of your shirt, or no, I grab hold of it on either side and pull it, because it was tucked into your pants, and I pull it out, and then I hook my hands underneath, and I can feel your skin move slightly as my fingers first touch it, just above your hips, and I run my fingers back along the inside of your waistband, and I can feel the warmth of your ass, and then I flatten my hands against your back and slide them up under your shirt, ah, all the way up so the fingers come out and go a little way along the nape of your neck into your hair before subsiding. It's a loose shirt, don't worry. Am I going too slow for you?"

"No no, keep going, that's fine."

"Oh, I love moving my hands over you under your loose shirt, I love that. I'd slide my hands around over your stomach, so that my fingertips met, and feel it pull in, and slide up slowly along your ribs, and when I got to where the curves of your breasts started, I would trace them around, out to the sides, back to the middle, and I would pass just my fingertips up between your breasts, up along your breastbone, pushing under the loose bra, and then one finger even higher, along your voice box, to where your chin starts, and you'd lean your head back and I would be able to smell your hair, and then I'd pull back down, deliberately avoiding your breasts."

"And I would stand up," she said, "and turn around so I'm facing you, with my shins touching the armchair, and I'd undo the button of my pants."

"And I would reach out," he said, "and take hold of your zipper and push it slowly down, so that I'm pushing against your mound with it, not at your clitoris, but above it, and I'd slide my fingers under your waistband and guide your pants off over your hips and ass, and when they fell to your knees I'd put my foot on the inside of the crotch so you could step out of them easily, and I'd smell how wet you are, and I'd slide my hands up your legs and slip my fingers under the waistband of your underpants, and pull them down a little, and then I'd roll them under my palms, so the fabric just rolled up, and they fell and you stepped easily out of them, too. And then . . ."

"And then," she said, "you'd undo your belt and the top button of your pants, and the clink of your belt buckle would be like the little bell signaling the start of something serious, and I would slowly move the zipper over the high lump of your erection, and you'd lift your hips and I'd pull your pants off, but not your underpants, and then I'd slide one knee on the cushion of the armchair, between your legs, against your balls, and the other outside your legs, and I'd let my weight settle on your thigh, so we're close but facing each other."

"And first," he said, "my leg would feel the roughness of your pubic hair, I'd feel it scratching against itself, and then I'd feel you open and I'd feel this wet oval of heat on the muscle of my thigh, and I'd look down at your folded legs straddling my leg, and run my hands up them, and scoop up your shirt again, and this time I'd lift it with me as my hands moved up, and I'd watch them, I watch your shirt rising, the seam of your shirt is over my wrists, and then I reach your breasts and I lift your shirt and your loose bra up just a little more, and, ah, there they are your nipples, finally, and you see my hands reveal them, and I see your breasts moving slightly as you breathe, and

I sit up and bend toward them, and then on second thought straighten and lick my lips and kiss you, and your tongue is very warm and very friendly."

"Whoo!"

"And I bend back down toward one of your breasts, and I open my mouth, which now finally remembers how to kiss from just kissing you, and I just breathe on your nipple, and the shirt starts to fall down over it, and I nudge it aside with my tongue and then hold it out of the way with my hand, and now I have your breast entirely surrounded with both my palms, and you feel your breast held this way, completely under my care, and I just touch the tip of my tongue once to the almost flat top of your nipple, which is hard, and then I open my mouth quite wide, and draw my tongue way back, and you arch your back slightly, and so my lips make contact with your breast, surrounding your nipple but *not* touching it, and I suck on it without touching it also, so that you feel the pulling as it's being drawn into my mouth, and even becoming soft, or losing its definition, from being drawn in that way, and wanting to be directly touched, and then you feel the tip of my tongue just touch the base of your nipple and then paint a warm vertical stripe up over it, and then back down, and then my whole tongue, much wider and fatter, pushes and moves against your nipple, and then I hold my mouth and tongue still and a little looser and with my hands I move your whole breast in circles and back and forth under them, so that you feel its whole size in my hands, ho, I'm sucking on your breasts . . ."

"And I'd hold on to your head as you sucked my breasts, and feel your tongue doing all those nice things to me through your cheeks. I am so *wet*."

"Oh, and I'd tighten my thigh muscle where your pussy was pressing down on it and feel your wetness slide against me, and I'd look up at you and kiss you again, and slide my hands down to your hips and push down, so that there was more pressure still against your notch, and I'd feel your hips move slightly, adjusting themselves so that it felt best . . ."

"And while we were kissing I'd reach down and catch my fingers under one leg hole of your underpants and pull it up and over your cock and balls and then I'd hold your balls in my hand for a second and then I'd bring my hand up and squeeze the head of your cock in my fist and kind of pull and push on it while I was squeezing it tightly."

"And you'd feel my lips making an *oh* shape while we were kissing, with the pleasure of your hand doing that, and, ho, I'd need to suck your clit soon, because I'd feel the come in me starting to want to spurt out, and so we'd shift positions so that you were sitting on the armchair and I was kneeling on the floor, and you'd scoot your hips forward so that your ass was just at the edge of the pillow, and when you glanced down you could see your own breasts, and your pubic hair, and your knees held together, with my hands on them, and you'd see the glossy wet place on my thigh, and then I'd encircle your legs with one arm, holding them together, and bend toward your bush and breathe on it, the little of it I can see, and I run my fingers just down the long place where the insides of your thighs touch, all the way to your knees, and then I'd let go of your legs, and they'd fall slightly apart, and as my hands started to move up inside them, with my fingers splayed wide, they'd move farther and farther apart, and then I'd lift your knees and hook them over the arms of the armchair, so that you were wide open for me, and in the darkness your bush would still be indistinct, and I'd look up at you, and I'd move on my knees so I'm closer, so I could slide my cock in you if I wanted, and I touch your shoulders with my hands, and pass my fingertips all the way down over your breasts and over your stomach and just lightly over your bush, just to feel the hair, and then I say, 'I'm going to lick you now,' and I lick both your nipples once very briefly good-bye, and I breathe my way down, and I pass over your bush this time with my mouth, and I see where the tan stops, and where the hair begins, and I keep going, and your legs are spread wide, and so I kiss inside one knee, and then across to the other, and up, back and forth, and at the end of each kiss I give a little upward lick with my tongue, up lick, lick, lick, back and forth, moving closer and closer to where your thighs meet. And then the last time I turn my head, there's nothing I can do, my mouth is just buried in your pubic hair, and I breathe through it, I fill it with warmth, and I open my mouth more, and I bring my tongue out, and I start low, and the underside of my tongue is touching my lower teeth, and I lick slowly upwards, until I reach the place where the skin is more folded, and I find that beautiful clitoris, and I move over it with my tongue, and then when I've found it I close my mouth and sort of burrow my way into you so that all your pubic hair is away from my mouth, and my mouth is entirely around your clit, and I hold my hands very high on the insides of your thighs, feeling those stretched tendons, so you feel how wide apart you are, and I suck the skin around your clitoris into my mouth, like I did with your nipple, so that you feel it drawn into my mouth, and when you feel it drawn in I take my tongue, very high, right at the base of your clitoris, where I can feel that little ridge beginning, and I start to go back and forth over it, back and forth slowly over it, and you feel the tip of my tongue traveling down toward the part where it's hotter, and then I reach the very full part of your clitoris, and you pull your hips in slightly and re-adjust to that feeling, and I cup my hands under your ass and lift you into my mouth and just *suck* on you, and I shake my whole head back and forth very fast, as if I'm saying, no, no, no, but I'm saying yes to your clit with my tongue."

"Oh, I'm going to come soon. Put your cock in me, I want to think about your cock in me."

"Are your legs spread apart?"

"Yes."

"Oh, and you're stroking that clit?"

"Yes."

"Okay, so I'd take one last long up-lick on your pussy and then I'd straighten up, and I'd still be cupping your ass in my hands, and you'd be completely visible by now, wide open, sopping wet, and I'd take my cock in one hand and kind of vibrate it over your clit, and you'd slide your hands down and hold your lips apart with your fingers, and then I'd push my cock down and I'd feel how hot you were and I'd have to slide myself slowly all the way in, and then I'd pull almost all the way out again and slide in, into that nice nasturtium, and each time I pulled out I'd be able to see your hand circling your clit, and I'd slide in until my pubic bone thumped against you, and I'd watch your breasts move each time I reached this limit, and we would be fucking, sliding in and out . . ."

"Oh!"

"And your finger would be flying over your clit, your hand would be lifted and your finger would be flying back and forth, and I'd have your asscheeks cupped in both my hands, so you could feel a pulling on your asshole, and I would be sliding with long strokes out, and in, and out, and in, and I'd see your tits moving each time . . ."

"Oh! *Oh!*"

"Oh, I'm starting to come for you, my cock is pumping inside you . . ."

"*Oh!* Nnnnnnnn! Nnn! Nnn! Nnn! Nnn! Nnn! Nnn!"

"It's spurting out! I can't help it! Ah! Ah! Oooooo."
There was a pause.

"Oh man," she said. "Wow. You there?"

"I think so." He swallowed. "Let me catch my breath."

"That was—that was—*man*," she said. "I saw the great seal of the Commonwealth of Massachusetts when I came."

"I heard you come and I came," he said.

"Whoo! How long have we been talking?"

"Hours and hours."

"Hours and hours and hours," she said. "My mouth is chapped. Too much making out."

"Is your voice sore?"

"It really is. Whoo! Gee, I'm going to have to call in sick *again*. I'll sleep all day, mm, sounds delightful. The hiss on the phone is very loud now, isn't it? That companionable hiss. It's always louder at the end of conversations."

"Oh, is it the end already?" he said. "Couldn't we just fade out somehow, talking and talking? I can't think of a better way to invest my life savings. Not that I'm much of a saver."

"You're quite a telephoner, though."

"You are too! I mean it! I think really this is one of the nicest conversations I've ever had."

"I liked it too," she said. "I don't know, though—do you think we talked enough about sex?"

"Not nearly enough. I—"

"Yes?" she said.

"Do you think our . . . wires will cross again?"

"I don't know. I don't know. What do you think?"

"I could give you my number," he said. "I mean if you still want it. I'll avoid a possibly awkward moment by not asking for yours. Or we could meet out here again, if you'd rather do that."

"Out here under the stars? I can't afford it. Where's a pencil? Ah, a nice blunt pencil. Tell me your number."

He told her. She read it back to him.

"Call me soon," he said. "In fact, call me in a few hours, after you've topped yourself off in the shower."

"You know me too well."

"I like you a lot."

"I wonder what you look like," she said.

"Surprisingly normal. Maybe someday you'll know."

"It's a possibility."

"We'd probably be a little nervous at first, if we met. But then . . ."

"Then we'd start masturbating like ferrets," she said, "and that would quickly break the ice."

"That's right. I hope you will call. You remember I have this pair of cotton pointelle tights. Unopened."

"Size small?"

"Size small. In faun. Put Leona to work, get those legs waxed, I'm on my way. No. But call me soon. Soon soon soon. I hope you will."

"All right," she said. "Let me think about things. Let me absorb the strangeness."

"What's strange?"

"Nothing," she said. "I guess nothing. I think I should probably sign off now, though. I have to put a load of towels in the laundry."

"Certainly. Okay. Thank you for calling this number."

"Thank *you*. Bye Jim."

"Bye Abby. Bye."

They hung up.

'My heart is still **beating furiously**'

'Ben Hope is **a thinking Jack Reacher**'

'**Fast and furious** as ever'

'**Action-packed** and forward-thinking **suspense** and **thrills**
throughout . . . great for technology, history and action fans
and those looking for a comfortable and **intelligent** read'

THE FORGOTTEN HOLOCAUST

Scott Mariani is the author of the worldwide-acclaimed action-adventure thriller series featuring ex-SAS hero Ben Hope, which has sold over a million copies in Scott's native UK alone and is also translated into over 20 languages. His books have been described as 'James Bond meets Jason Bourne, with a historical twist.' The first Ben Hope book, THE ALCHEMIST'S SECRET, spent six straight weeks at #1 on Amazon's Kindle chart, and all the others have been Sunday Times bestsellers.

Scott was born in Scotland, studied in Oxford and now lives and writes in a remote setting in rural west Wales. When not writing, he can be found bouncing about the country lanes in an ancient Land Rover, wild camping in the Brecon Beacons or engrossed in his hobbies of astronomy, photography and target shooting (no dead animals involved!).

You can find out more about Scott and his work, and **sign up to his exclusive newsletter**, on his official website:

www.scottmariani.com

By the same author

Ben Hope series
The Alchemist's Secret
The Mozart Conspiracy
The Doomsday Prophecy
The Heretic's Treasure
The Shadow Project
The Lost Relic
The Sacred Sword
The Armada Legacy
The Nemesis Program

To find out more visit **www.scottmariani.com**

SCOTT MARIANI

The Forgotten Holocaust

AVON

AVON
A division of HarperCollins*Publishers*
1 London Bridge Street,
London SE1 9GF

www.harpercollins.co.uk

A Paperback Original 2015

2

A catalogue record for this book is
available from the British Library

ISBN-13: 978-0-00-748617-5

Set in Minion by Palimpsest Book Production Limited,
Falkirk, Stirlingshire

Printed and bound in Great Britain by
Clays Ltd, St Ives plc

MIX
Paper from
responsible sources
FSC® C007454

FSC™ is a non-profit international organisation established to promote
the responsible management of the world's forests. Products carrying the
FSC label are independently certified to assure consumers that they come
from forests that are managed to meet the social, economic and
ecological needs of present and future generations,
and other controlled sources.

Find out more about HarperCollins and the environment at
www.harpercollins.co.uk/green

Acknowledgments

Of the various historical sources I was fortunate enough to be able to make use of in writing this novel, there is none to which I am more indebted than the late Thomas Gallagher's 1982 book on the great Irish famine, *Paddy's Lament.* This is a book that moved and inspired me many years ago, and *The Forgotten Holocaust* would not have been written otherwise. Thanks, Thomas.

'*They are going! They are going! The Irish are going with a vengeance! Soon a Celt will be as rare on the banks of the Liffey as a red man on the banks of the Hudson.*'
The London Times, *1847*

'*Could not anyone blow up that horrible island with dynamite and carry it off in pieces – a long way off?*'
Alfred Lord Tennyson

Prologue

County Cork, Ireland
May 29th, 1846

It had been raining all morning, but now the sun shone brightly over the fields. Other than the gentle breeze that rustled the crops, all was still and silent. Beyond the rickety wooden fence, the country road was empty, except for two men approaching on horseback.

Any local observing the pair of riders would have been able to tell at a glance that they weren't simple peasants. They made an odd couple. The younger of the two was a tall, broad, self-assured man with a certain air, whose high-bred chestnut hunter was worth far more than any Irish farmer could have afforded – the Penal Laws had made it illegal for many years for an Irish Catholic to own a horse worth over £5. His older companion, a smaller, much slighter bespectacled fellow jolting uncomfortably along beside him astride a bay mare, had the look of a parson or a schoolmaster, and certainly not one from these parts.

What no observer could have guessed, though, was the deadly secret nature and equally deadly purpose of their mission. A mission that had taken many months to engineer, and was now about to become complete.

1

Although they knew each other very well, few words had passed between them during the ride. The older man seemed ill at ease in the saddle and kept nervously checking his silver pocket watch and twisting round to glance over his shoulder, as if he expected to spot someone following. All he saw was the deserted road snaking away for miles behind them until it disappeared into the green hills.

He wanted to say something. The words were right on the tip of his tongue: 'Edgar, this plan . . . I have terrible misgivings. I'm just no longer sure that we're doing the right thing.'

But he swallowed his words, kept silent. He knew what the reply would be. He couldn't afford for his commitment to come into doubt. Things had advanced much too far for that.

The younger man halted his hunter by a rickety gate and glanced around him. 'Here,' was all he said to his companion. They dismounted, led their horses to the gate and tethered them up where they could munch at the long roadside grass.

The younger man reached into his saddlebag and took out a box-shaped object wrapped in cloth. Handling it with care, he passed it to the older man, who clutched it anxiously as he waited for his companion to vault over the gate into the field beyond and then handed it back to him.

The time to express any last-minute doubts was definitely past.

The older man awkwardly clambered over the gate and scurried to join the other, who was already striding purposefully towards the middle of the field with the cloth-wrapped box under his arm.

All around them the leafy plants were springing up in the regularly spaced furrows the Irish called 'lazy beds', full of the same vitality and vigour that could be seen across the whole countryside. Even in the miserable patches of land sown by the poorest tenant farmers, the dark green leaves and purple blossoms were healthy and erect. The men walked in silence to the middle of the field, the older one having to trot to keep up. He was out of breath by the time they halted.

The younger one gazed back at the road. There was still not a soul in sight. Silence, except for the soft breeze. The horses were grazing contentedly in the distance.

'Let's get it done,' he said.

The two of them crouched among the plants, so that nobody could have watched them from the road even if the landscape hadn't been deserted as far as the eye could see. The younger man unwrapped his package to reveal a small casket made of varnished oak with brass fittings. He set it carefully on the ground and opened its lid. Inside, protected by the red velvet lining, was a row of small glass phials containing the precious substance.

Each phial held just a few fluid drachms. That was all that was needed.

He picked one out of the velvet folds, holding it gingerly so as not to crush the thin glass. For such a large, powerful man, his movements were surprisingly delicate and exact. He carefully removed the cork stopper from the phial, keeping it well away from his nose.

The thick, glutinous substance inside looked faecal, and smelled worse. The older man looked on with a frown as his companion emptied the contents of the phial into the ground, scattering it among the bases of the crop stalks where it quickly soaked into the moist earth. He restoppered the empty phial, replaced it in the box with the others.

That done, he closed the lid, wrapped the box back up in its cloth and stood up with the package under his arm and a look of grim satisfaction.

The older man's expression was quite different as he got stiffly to his feet. He couldn't take his eyes off the ground where

3

they'd poured out the substance. He'd broken out into a sweat that wasn't caused by the warm sun. He felt a sudden chill and nervously thrust his trembling hands into his waistcoat pockets.

'And so it begins,' he muttered solemnly. 'May God forgive us, Edgar.'

'You talk too much, Fitzwilliam. Let's go. We have a lot more work to do.'

They walked in silence back towards the gate.

Chapter One

Oologah Lake
25 miles from Tulsa, Oklahoma
The present day

The August sun was still high above the trees by the time Erin reached the cabin. The driver pulled the Cadillac Escalade to a halt, got out and opened the back door for her.

'Thanks, Joe,' Erin said brightly, stepping down from the car with her small backpack, which was all the luggage she'd brought.

'You have yourself a great weekend, Miss Hayes,' Joe replied. 'You got the number, right? Just call me whenever you want, and I'll come right away to take you home.' With a final smile, he got back behind the wheel, and she watched the car disappear down the track that was the only access to this remote spot.

'So here we are,' Erin said to herself, gazing around her once she was alone.

Angela hadn't been kidding about the beauty of the place. So this was how the wealthy folks lived. And for just a couple of days, humble charity worker Erin Hayes was to have it all to herself. Everyone should have an employer this generous.

Oologah Lake. The name came from the Cherokee word

for 'dark cloud'. This northern corner of Oklahoma was known for its fearsome windstorms. Today, though, the lake was as still as glass, visible through the trees with the sunlight glittering across its vastness and gleaming off the windows of the boathouse by the little jetty. The cabin itself was long and low, surrounded by a whitewood veranda complete with rocking chair and beautiful old lanterns. The nearest neighbours were about a mile away through the woods, or so she'd been told.

The solitude didn't bother Erin a bit. It was Friday, the end of a long week, and she had nothing on her mind other than the peaceful weekend ahead. She let herself inside and quickly entered the alarm code on the keypad panel near the door.

Angela might call it a cabin, but the place seemed three times the size of Erin's miniscule house in Tulsa's Crosbie Heights district. The furnishings were predictably expensive. The walls and floor were burnished oak and walnut, gleaming with a thousand coats of varnish. Some architect must have got paid a packet to come up with the design. The right blend of traditional and modern, with a high ceiling framed all the way around by a galleried landing that overlooked the open-plan living space below. Four bedrooms radiated off the landing, east, south, north and west. She spent a while exploring, then carried her backpack upstairs to the room she'd decided would be hers for the weekend. The east bedroom, so she'd be woken by the rising sun in the morning. She dumped her stuff on the bed and then changed into her running shoes, trotted back downstairs and headed outside to discover the tracks Angela had said wound for miles through the woods.

Erin was in training for that November's Route 66 Marathon, which she'd entered to help raise funds for the

Desert Rose Trust, the youth education charity she worked for and of which Angela was president. As she jogged along the sun-dappled track that skirted the lake, she thought about the employer who'd become her friend. Angela had never really confided in her, but Erin got the impression that she and her husband lived somewhat separate lives. They were rich, of course – unimaginably rich, at least by Erin's standards, with a fabulous mansion in north Tulsa. But even rich folks had their problems. Angela's husband was often off somewhere or other on 'business'; Erin wondered whether Angela might be seeing someone else on the side, someone who could make her laugh and treat her with a little more warmth. There had only ever been tiny hints, but women noticed these things.

Erin enjoyed her long run through the lakeside woodlands. At thirty-three, she was in the best shape of her life, an achievement that made her feel proud. Returning to the cabin as the sunlight was fading, she showered, changed into soft lounging-around clothes and then spent the evening doing just that. Angela had said to help herself to whatever was in the fridge, but Erin ignored the well-stocked drinks cabinet.

After a light meal and a couple of hours' reading and exploring the CD collection, she turned on the alarm system the way Angela had instructed, then padded contentedly upstairs to bed. She fell asleep gazing at the moonlight through the trees and listening to the soft noises of the woods in serene anticipation of the weekend ahead.

She was deep in a pleasant dream when she awoke suddenly. It wasn't the rising sun on her face, greeting her at the start of a fine new day.

It was the sound of voices. The room was still dark. It was still night. She checked her watch. Nine minutes to two

7

in the morning. She sat rigidly upright in the bed, suddenly alert, heart beating fast. She strained to listen.

She hadn't imagined it.

The voices were coming from *inside* the cabin. From downstairs.

Frightened but quickly gathering her wits, Erin scrabbled out of bed and reached into her backpack for the compact Springfield nine-millimetre that her daddy had given her: one of the former security guard's two gifts to his only daughter before he'd died. His comfort as he left this world had been that she would always be able to look after herself. *Always have a backup*, was the motto he'd drummed into her from when she was a little girl. Erin had honoured that by learning to use the pistol effectively and safely and keeping it near her, always loaded.

Clutching it now, she sneaked out of the bedroom and onto the landing, crouching to peer through the wooden railing. She shrank herself down as small as possible, almost too afraid to look. Her heart was thumping so loudly, she was scared it would give her away to whoever had entered the cabin.

The open-plan space below was all lit up. From her vantage point in the shadows, Erin had a clear view of the whole living area, as well as the open doorway leading out onto the veranda.

There were four men inside the cabin. One was standing with his back to her. He was tall and broad and silver-haired, wearing a tan sports jacket, chinos, loafers. The second and third were standing by the window. Younger men, maybe late thirties, lean and serious-looking, one with dark hair cropped military-style and the other with a thin blonde ponytail. Both wore jeans and T-shirts.

The fourth man Erin could see was short and heavy, with

8

black curly hair and a beard. He'd made himself comfortable in one of the cabin's plush armchairs.

What was happening? How had they got past the alarm system? If they were burglars, Erin thought, they were pretty damn relaxed about it. The large silver-haired man had already served out cut-crystal glasses of liquor from a decanter and was heading back towards the sideboard to pour one for himself.

It was as he turned round that Erin recognised his face.

She heaved a sigh of relief and her fingers relaxed on the grip of her handgun.

It was Angela's husband. Of course! She should have known that large, imposing figure anywhere. He and his guests were talking business, but Erin couldn't make out much of the conversation. She was suddenly too busy worrying about what the hell she was going to say to explain her presence here at the cabin. Angela obviously hadn't told him it was being used by one of her employees. What would his reaction be? Embarrassment, probably. Irritation. Annoyance. Perhaps outright anger. But she couldn't very well just hide up here out of sight in the man's home.

She was about to make her presence known – come what may – when the situation downstairs suddenly changed.

Angela's husband abruptly set down his glass and signalled to the two younger men by the window. Instantly, without a word, they also put down their drinks and stepped quickly over to where the bearded man was sitting. Before he could stop them, they'd grabbed his arms and turfed him out of his armchair. He sprawled on the rug. Then it got worse. Calmly, almost casually and out of nowhere, the two produced expandable batons, the kind the cops used, that telescoped out to full length at the flick of a wrist. The bearded man's cries and protests were swiftly silenced as they began raining brutal blows on his head and body.

9

'Not here,' Angela's husband said. 'Get him outside.'

Erin watched in growing horror as the two hard-faced men dragged their bleeding victim to the door and out onto the moonlit veranda. The bearded man tried to struggle to his feet.

That was when it got worse again. She almost let out a scream as she saw the short-haired one take out a pistol from a concealed holster. Two loud stunning blasts filled the cabin as he shot the bearded man in the left knee, then in the right. The boom of the gunshots was followed by a howl as the victim crumpled and rolled in agony on the veranda.

The silver-haired man simply watched impassively.

Erin couldn't believe what she was seeing. This was *Angela's husband!*

Nobody would ever believe her . . . unless . . .

Erin scrambled back through the shadows into the bedroom. Grabbing her phone with a trembling hand, she activated the video recording function and crept back out onto the landing. If they saw her, they'd kill her. Even armed, she wouldn't stand a chance against these men.

The bearded man was dragging himself across the veranda away from them, wailing in pain and terror as he clawed his way forward, one hand behind the other. Angela's husband continued to watch, the way someone would watch a bug crawl across the floor. At his signal, the ponytailed man stepped up alongside the victim, took out a pistol and fired a deafening shot through one of his hands.

The wailing became a tortured screech. The other three men began to laugh. The other one shot him now, this time through the thigh. Then once more, blowing fingers off his other hand. The screaming became continuous.

Erin could hardly keep the tiny video camera steady in her shaking hands.

'Hell with this,' Angela's husband said. 'I'm tired of this prick's hollering.' He reached under his jacket and came out with a large shiny revolver that glittered in the moonlight. He thumbed back the hammer, aimed at the back of the bearded man's head and pulled the trigger.

The blast and flame were far greater than the other gunshots. The crawling man was thrown forward on his face in an explosion of blood, twitched violently and then lay still.

Angela's husband twirled the revolver theatrically around his trigger finger, like a movie cowboy, and then thrust it back in its holster. 'All right,' he said to the others. 'Stick this piece of garbage in the van. You can chop his ass up and get rid of it later.'

'Okay, boss.'

'Ah, shit, I got blood on my goddamn brogues.'

'Sorry, boss.'

'What the hell. Gonna take a leak,' Angela's husband announced.

Erin watched, quaking, as the body was dragged down the veranda steps and away towards the trees. All three of the men had moved away from the cabin. This was her one and only chance to get out of here. She turned off the phone, stumbled back inside the bedroom and snatched her backpack. She threw the phone into it. Some of her other things were strewn about the room, but there just wasn't time to retrieve them.

With the pack on her shoulder and the pistol held out in front of her, she scurried barefoot down the stairs. She felt naked and vulnerable under the lights of the main room. One of the men had only to turn and glance back at the cabin, and she'd be spotted right away. If that happened, she knew the exchange of gunfire would be very brief – and that she wouldn't survive it.

She almost retched as she picked a path around the blood-slick on the veranda and the broad trail of it down the steps. Just a few yards, and she would be in the shadow of the trees. Her legs were shaking so badly, she was terrified she'd fall over.

Angela's husband had strolled casually over to a tree and was urinating against it with his feet braced apart and his back to her, left hand on his hip, whistling to himself. She passed within twenty feet of him, close enough to hear the patter of his stream on the ground. The other two had carried the body to a white van that was parked across from the cabin, just a pale outline under the shadows of the trees. She could hear their low voices. They were turning. Heading back. They were going to see her.

She ducked into the dark bushes just in time and crouched there, holding her breath, petrified that the slightest rustle would betray her presence. One of the men walked by so close that she could smell the minty odour on his breath, like gum. It was the one with the ponytail. He paused, seemed to stiffen like an animal when it senses something. Through the leaves she could see his face half-lit by the moon and the glow from the cabin. The gleam of his eyes.

'What is it, Billy Bob?' the other one said.

The one called Billy Bob stood still, so close that Erin could have reached out of the bushes and touched him.

'Nuthin',' Billy Bob said, and walked on.

Angela's husband had zipped himself up and was strolling back towards the cabin, complaining in a loud voice about the goddamn mess. The other two exchanged glances. The one called Billy Bob grinned. They followed him back inside.

And Erin clambered out of her hiding place in the bushes and ran like she'd never run before.

Chapter Two

The Galway coast
Republic of Ireland
Two days later

It was cold for the time of year, and the steady breeze from the sea made him turn up the collar of his old leather jacket. The pale early evening sun was beginning to drop lower over the Atlantic horizon, casting his shadow long and dark over the empty, pebbly beach as he walked.

Ben Hope was alone out here, and glad to be. He walked slowly, because he had nowhere in particular to go. He didn't even know why he'd come to this place. Now and then he paused in his step to stare out to sea, as if somehow the iron-grey ocean would give him the answers he was looking for.

He had lived here once. Spent many hours standing in this very spot, watching the waves roll in and crash against the rocks. It seemed a long time ago now. Just as he had in the old days, he bent and scooped up a handful of pebbles from the stony beach to fling into the surf. He watched them disappear one by one in the hissing foam.

'Fuck it,' he muttered to himself after the last pebble was gone. He turned his back on the water and started making his way towards the big house.

13

As he got closer, he paused again and gazed at it. The Victorian building stood perched on rock overlooking the long, curved stretch of its own private beach. He knew the house very well indeed, as it had once belonged to him. But he'd been away long enough to have forgotten just how large and imposing it looked.

It'd always been too big for him, just one guy rattling around with only his elderly, harried, ever-fussing housekeeper for company. In any case, he'd been away so often that it had felt more like a base than a proper home. The roving, spartan existence of a freelance kidnap rescue specialist had often seemed hard to distinguish from the harsh military life he'd known before that.

The house looked different now, and even though he'd expected it to, it gave him a strange pang to see how it had changed.

Funny, he thought: when the place had been his, he hadn't cared much for it, never thinking about it on his frequent travels around the world; but now he could feel a creeping sense of nostalgia.

Stupid. What am I doing here? he asked himself once again.

Where the pebbly beach ended, stone steps led up towards the back of the house. The iron safety railing was new. Health and safety regulations, he guessed. So was the large conservatory that the new owners had added where the sea-facing terrace used to be. The dropping sun reflected in its glass panes.

Ben walked around the side of the house, along a neat path that hadn't been there during his time. At the front of the house, he stopped and looked up. Of all the unfamiliar additions to his former home, the most striking was the sign over the front door that said 'Pebble Beach Guesthouse'. It was a strange feeling, looking at it. Like something telling him definitively 'this is no longer yours'. *You no longer belong here.*

Final. Irreversible.

So where did he belong? He didn't know any more.

He was just about to turn away, feeling defeated and sad, when he heard a voice.

'Mr Hope?'

He turned to see a hefty woman in her late fifties smiling at him. Dressed in a baggy black dress, her grey-flecked hair wrenched back into a bun, there was a matronly look about her. Unlike the house, she didn't seem to have changed since he'd last seen her, the day the sale had gone through. Maybe a little thicker about the hips, but it was hard to tell. She'd probably been built like a sideboard since the age of twenty.

'Mrs Henry,' he said, forcing a smile. 'It's good to see you again.'

'And you,' she said, smiling back.

'How's business?' he asked, for want of anything better to ask.

'Can't complain. What brings you back out to Galway? On holiday?'

'Something like that,' he said. 'Is Mr Henry well?'

'Much better since the hip operation, thank you. He's out on the golf course today. Won't be home until later. He'll be sorry he missed seeing you.'

'Likewise,' Ben said, quietly relieved that he wouldn't have to get dragged into a conversation about the absurd game of golf, which he recalled seemed to be all Bryan Henry could talk about with any enthusiasm, other than his gammy hip. How the man even managed to hit the ball straight with eyes like that was anybody's guess. The right one looked *at* you, the left one looked *for* you.

'Come inside and have a drink,' Mrs Henry said brightly. 'We've just had the new bar put in.'

Ben followed her inside. More strange memories struck

15

him everywhere he looked. The dark period woodwork of the entrance hall had been stripped out to create a bright modern reception area. Full of pride, Mrs Henry led him down the passage to what had once been his living and dining rooms, the wall between them knocked down. He inwardly winced at the floral wallpaper and tacky paintings. Through an archway that hadn't been there before, he could see into the new conservatory, filled with tables neatly set for Sunday dinner. On the other side of the room was the bar, and beyond that a lounge area where a couple of septuagenarian guests were sitting placidly reading in the silence.

A young woman sat in an armchair by the window. Ben glanced at her just long enough to see that she was in her early thirties or thereabouts, with sandy hair cut short, giving her an elfin kind of look. She was wearing light blue jeans and a white T-shirt. There was a mini laptop open on a low table in front of her, next to a half-finished glass of red wine and a small, square jotter from which she seemed to be busily copying handwritten notes into the computer. Someone was obviously having a working vacation.

Ben looked back at Mrs Henry to see she was watching him expectantly. 'Well?' she prompted him at last. 'What do you think?'

'Love what you've done with the place,' he forced himself to say.

'Really? I'm so glad.' Mrs Henry wedged herself in behind the bar and picked up a glass. 'What can I get you, Mr Hope? On the house, naturally.'

Lies and flattery could get you anywhere. 'Thanks. I'll have a Guinness.'

As she was finishing pouring it for him – the proper touch with the shamrock on top – the bell rang in reception and she hurried off to attend to business. Left on his own, Ben perched himself on a bar stool and sipped the cold Guinness. He thought about all the times he'd got drunk in this room and poor old long-suffering Winnie had had to bring him strong black coffee to help sober him up.

He sighed quietly to himself and shook his head. He'd been a screw-up then, and he was one now. What a mess he'd made of his life. The woman he loved despised him. His own son, Jude, would barely speak to him. His sister, Ruth, thought he was a lowlife.

Nice job. Well done.

It was two months since Ben had walked out on his fiancée, Brooke Marcel, virtually on the eve of their wedding. The way he'd seen it, he'd had no choice but to help a friend in need. The way Brooke had seen it, the friend in need was a very attractive old flame who'd mesmerised him into running off with her to get involved in yet another of the crazy, high-risk adventures that littered his past life.

When Ben had returned to England two weeks after they'd been due to get married, he'd been hoping he could pick up the pieces with her, try to make her understand why he'd needed to do what he'd done. Then, fix a new wedding date and get back on with the life they'd planned together. But it hadn't worked out that way. The house in Oxford was empty. Brooke was no longer there, and had taken all her things with her: everything except the little neck chain he'd once bought as a gift for her. It was lying on the bedside table, snapped in half. Next to it had been a handwritten note. Just four scribbled words.

Don't look for me.

Brooke knew all about Ben, his past, his skills. She knew about the kidnap victims he'd retrieved from the most cunning hiding places their captors could have kept them in, and brought them home safe.

She knew he could find anyone.

But she didn't want him to even try to find her. It was the most painful thing she could have said to him.

He couldn't let go that easily. He had to try. Had to see her. Thinking she might have returned to her former place in Richmond, he'd called only to find that a new tenant had moved in. Next, Ben had tried calling Brooke's friend and former upstairs neighbour, Amal.

When they'd last spoken, Amal had been warm and friendly. Not any more.

'She isn't here.'

'I know that already. But do you know where she went? I really need to speak to her.'

'I don't know where she is,' Amal said in the same cold tone. 'But if I did, Ben, you'd be the last person I'd tell.' Then he hung up before Ben could say more.

After that, Ben had tried calling Jude on his mobile. It had taken two days of trying, and when he'd finally got through, his twenty-year-old son had given him the same frosty reception as Amal. 'I'm not surprised she's gone off. She cried for a solid week after you left and you never called once to ask how she was. Basically, you've been a real shit to her.'

'I would never have hurt her on purpose.'

'You walked out on her! I was there, remember? How did you think that would make her feel?'

'I need to talk to her. Explain things. If she calls you, tell her—'

'Forget it, I'm not going to tell her anything,' Jude interrupted him. 'And take my advice: don't go chasing after her. We all know you were in the SAS and can track anyone anywhere on the planet, and all that stuff. But Brooke doesn't want to see you. Leave her alone. Come to that, leave me alone too, okay?'

'Jude, listen—'

'Oh, just fuck off, *Dad*.'

Lastly, Ruth. 'What do you expect, Ben? You let her down. You let us all down. And what about my plane? The insurers are going wild.'

These days, Ben's younger sister was the CEO of the huge corporation she'd inherited from her adoptive father, Swiss billionaire Maximilian Steiner. The plane she was talking about was a Steiner Industries prototype turboprop that Ben had borrowed. Ostensibly, he'd only wanted it for the short trip from Oxfordshire to northern France and back. Ruth was having trouble understanding how her two-million-euro baby had ended up at the bottom of Lake Toba in Indonesia.

'I've told you, I'm really sorry about the plane,' he'd said. 'Things got complicated.'

'Like they always do with you, Ben.'

And once more, he'd found himself on the end of a dead line.

In the end, Ben had realised that if he pushed on with his search for Brooke and caught up with her, as he surely would, he'd only alienate her even more. Giving up the search was one of the hardest things he'd ever done.

So here he was, sitting in the barely recognisable surroundings of what had once been his home, feeling lost. He'd no clear idea what had made him drift back here to the Galway coast. Maybe he hadn't let go of that part of his past as completely as he'd thought he had. Or maybe he just wanted to punish himself by rubbing salt into his own wounds. All he knew was that after two months of drifting aimlessly from place to place, squandering his cash on hotel rooms, drinking far too much and spending most days in a trance-like state of numbness and regret, he'd found himself heading back to Ireland and renting a cottage on the beach less than half a mile from the large house that had once been his home.

Mrs Henry returned, interrupting his thoughts. Noticing that Ben's glass was almost empty she said, 'Ready for a top-up?'

'I'm always ready for a top-up.'

'See that nice-looking young lady over there?' Mrs Henry said, lowering her voice and nodding towards the window as she refilled Ben's glass. 'She's a famous writer.'

'Uh-huh?' Ben glanced back over his shoulder, feigning interest for the sake of politeness. The sandy-haired woman was still bent intently over her small laptop, tapping keys, very deeply absorbed by whatever she was working on. Finished with whatever was in her notebook, she paused to slip it into a slim leather pouch, then zipped the pouch shut and dropped it into the cloth bag at her feet before going back to her typing.

'I wonder what she's writing,' Mrs Henry whispered, with a glimmer of excitement. 'Perhaps she's writing about this place. That'd really put us on the map.'

'Murder at Pebble Beach?' Ben said.

'Oh, you are a one,' Mrs Henry laughed, nudging him playfully. Then she bustled off again, leaving him alone at the bar.

Chapter Three

Some time later, Ben left the guesthouse and wandered back down the private beach towards the water to sit on the big, flat barnacled rock he'd often sat on in the past. At high tide it overhung the surf and he'd spent many hours gazing at the water, smoking, thinking, alone. With three pints of Mrs Henry's Guinness inside him, he was feeling a little more mellow than he had earlier. The booze helped to take the edge off his raw emotions, but he was acutely conscious of having been overdoing it lately, as well as of being somewhat out of condition after these weeks of neglecting his fitness. It didn't take long at all for self-discipline to slip and bad habits to begin to shoot up like weeds.

He hated himself for letting it happen. In all the years since qualifying for 22 SAS, he'd kept up virtually the same disciplined, even punishing, regime and now here he was, by his own strict standards, intolerably slack, lazy and listless.

As he watched the waves, he made himself a promise that tomorrow morning, rain or shine, he'd be up with the sunrise and out running on the beach. He didn't expect to be able to jump right back into his routine with the usual five miles followed by a hundred or so press-ups and sit-ups. But you had to start somewhere.

Meanwhile, there wasn't much to do but let the time slip

idly by. Reaching into the pocket of his leather jacket he took out his rumpled blue pack of Gauloises and Zippo lighter. He lit up the thirteenth – or was it the fourteenth? – cigarette of the day and gazed at the steel-coloured horizon. Those dark clouds over there in the west, somewhere over the Aran Islands, were gathering and sweeping in fast towards the mainland. A rainstorm was coming.

The crunch of approaching footsteps on the pebbles made him turn to see someone crossing the beach towards his rock. He recognised her at once: the sandy-haired woman who'd been sitting in the guesthouse earlier. She'd put a lightweight fleece on over her T-shirt and had her cloth bag slung over her shoulder.

As she came closer, she smiled at him. 'Hello,' she said. She had blue-grey eyes, which she shielded from the sun. The sea breeze gently ruffled her short hair.

Ben smiled back, but his smile was a little forced. He'd have preferred to have been left alone. When this had been his own private stretch of beach he'd been used to having it to himself. It seemed odd to have uninvited company here.

'Mind if I join you?'

'Be my guest,' he replied.

She smoothed her hand along the rock and found a place to sit. 'Nice here, isn't it?'

He nodded. 'Certainly is.'

'I'm Kristen. Kristen Hall.' Her accent was English, Home Counties maybe.

'Ben.' He held out his hand. Her grip felt soft but firm in his.

'I know,' she said. 'Ben Hope.'

He stared at her for a moment.

'Mrs Henry told me who you were,' she said, laughing at his surprised look. 'She said the place used to belong to you.'

22

'It's true.'

'It's so lovely. You must miss it.'

This wasn't a topic he wanted to dwell on. 'So I hear you're a writer,' he said instead.

Kristen grinned. 'Mrs Henry does like to blabber, doesn't she?'

'Certainly does. She's all excited that you might include the guesthouse in your novel.'

'She's going to be disappointed. I'm not a novelist.'

'Oh,' Ben said, nodded, and looked back out to sea again.

'More of a glorified journalist, really,' she added.

Ben fell silent. He didn't have much to say, about books or journalism or anything else.

'I'm sorry,' she said. 'I can tell I'm disturbing you. I'd better go.'

He felt a stab of remorse. 'Not at all.'

'It's okay.' She smiled. 'I know what it's like to want to be left alone.'

'It's me who should be sorry. I'm being rude.' He paused. 'Look, I was going to take a walk along the beach before the weather closes in. Maybe you'd like to join me?'

She hesitated, looked at her watch. 'There's something I have to do later, but I have some time. All right, then. I'd love to. Being as you're a former resident, you can show me the sights.'

Leaving the rock and setting out with her along the beach, he said, 'There's not much to it. What you see is what you get.' He pointed ahead, to the north. 'See the big rock over there, where the road turns away inland? That's where my bit . . . I mean, the bit of beach belonging to the guesthouse ends. Just out of sight on the other side is where the cottage is that I'm renting. The coastal path takes you all the way around the headland.'

'Nice to have my own guide.'

'My pleasure.'

They walked along the beach, leaving the guesthouse behind in the distance. 'So, are you here with your family, Ben?'

'I'm on my own.'

'Business or pleasure?'

'Neither.'

A broad shadow passed over them as they walked. Kristen looked up. A large gull swooped overhead, banked out to sea and glided high on its wide wings. 'I've never seen such big gulls.'

'We get all sorts here,' he said. 'That one's a great black-backed gull. If you think he was big, you should see an albatross. They come inshore now and then.'

Kristen paused and breathed in the fresh sea air. 'It's so peaceful here. I can see why you came back. What on earth made you leave?'

'I went to live in France for a while. Place called Le Val. An old farm in Normandy.' He didn't add that the facility he'd founded there, under his management, had operated as one of Europe's key specialised training centres for tactical raid and hostage rescue teams. Certain aspects of his past, most of it in fact, were subjects he generally wouldn't, couldn't, discuss with people.

'You certainly pick nice places to live.' She pulled a face. 'I live in Newbury. Hardly the most romantic spot on earth. So where's home for you now?'

'Wherever. Nothing permanent.'

'A rolling stone.'

'Not by choice,' he replied. 'That's just the way it is.'

'So where to after this?'

'No plans. Sooner or later, I'll move on. Don't know where.'

They walked a little further. Kristen seemed about to say something, then reached for her bag. 'Excuse me a moment. I really need to check my messages.' She dug in the bag, and Ben got a glimpse of the small laptop inside.

'You carry that thing around with you everywhere?' he observed with a smile.

'Never know when the muse might strike.' She took out the slim leather pouch that she kept her notebook in and unzipped a little pocket on the front. Inside were two mobile phones. She took one out, gave it a quick check and then tutted to herself and shook her head as though disappointed. 'Damn it,' she muttered, zipping the phone back inside the pouch and replacing it in her bag.

'Something important?' Ben asked.

'Oh, it's just about my research,' Kristen said quickly, and he thought there was a slight evasive tone in her voice, as well as a momentary nervousness in her expression. 'Someone I was hoping to hear back from.' She shrugged. 'Never mind.'

'Is that what brings you to Galway, research?'

She nodded. 'I've been travelling around a few places, the last ten days. Killarney, Limerick, Athlone, all over really.'

'Useful trip?'

'Oh yes. Very much indeed. And in ways I couldn't have imagined.'

'I won't ask.'

She smiled. 'And I won't tell. Trade secrets. Don't take it personally.'

'Never,' he said.

The wind from the sea was rising. Ben looked at the sky. Those dark clouds were nearing ominously. 'We might have to make a run for it. Weather's coming in faster than I thought.'

'Hardly feels like August, does it?'

'Must be the global warming they keep promising us,' he said.

'Yeah, right.'

'So what's the book about? Or is that part of the trade secret?'

'No, the book I can talk about. Historical stuff. A biography.'

'Someone I might have heard of?'

'Lady Elizabeth Stamford. Nineteenth-century diarist, novelist, poet, educator, considered one of the first feminists. I won't be surprised if you haven't heard of her.'

'I can't say I have,' Ben said. 'But from the name and the fact that you came here for your research, I'm guessing she was married to Lord Stamford, owner of the Glenfell Estate that covered about a million acres near Ballinasloe, just a few miles away.'

'Ten out of ten. Nothing like local knowledge.'

'More like local legend. You still hear the old story of the tyrannical English lord who went mad and burned his own house down with himself inside. But that doesn't make me an expert. So Lady Stamford's the subject of your book?'

'Yeah . . . she is.' She gave a non-committal kind of shrug.

'You don't sound too sure.'

She looked at him. 'Don't I? I suppose not. That's because . . . well, the fact is that I don't really know that I'll be writing it any more. Something else has come along in the last couple of days that makes me think . . .' Her voice trailed off and she frowned up at the clouds. They were directly overhead now and more threatening than ever.

'Here it comes,' Ben said. Moments later, the first heavy raindrops began to spatter down, quickly gathering force.

Kristen drew her fleece more tightly around her. 'Christ. We're going to get soaked.'

He glanced back over his shoulder. They'd walked quite a distance from the flat rock. 'Listen, we're closer to my place than we are to the guesthouse. If you want to shelter from the storm . . .'

'Lead on,' she said, nodding.

Chapter Four

They ran. The rain was pelting down now, carried in gusts by the wind, as the path led them away from the pebbly beach and between the rocks to the cottage. Ben creaked open the gate in the little picket fence, and they hurried to the door. He unlocked it and showed her inside.

Kristen stood shivering and dripping on the bare floorboards. 'I'm like a drowned rat.' She took off her fleecy top, which was wet through. Her bare arms were mottled with cold.

'Here,' Ben said, pulling a wooden chair out from the table. He hung the fleece over the back of it. 'This'll dry off fine once I get the fire going.' He'd prepared it earlier, split logs and kindling sticks on a bed of balled-up newspaper.

Kristen checked inside her bag. 'Thank God, my stuff didn't get wet.' As she slung the bag over the back of the chair, Ben motioned towards the narrow wooden staircase. 'You'd best get yourself dried off. There's towels and a hair dryer in the bathroom.'

As Kristen trotted upstairs, he knelt by the fireplace and used his Zippo to light the paper and kindling. By the time she returned a few minutes later, her short hair frizzy from the dryer, he had a crackling blaze going and the cottage was already filling with a glow of warmth.

'What a lovely little place,' she said, now that she could admire it.

'Back when I had the big house, this was just a derelict fisherman's bothy, no more than four walls and half a roof. I used to shelter in it sometimes when I was out running and it began to rain. Good to see it all done up.' He walked over to the old oak dresser by the window and picked up a half-finished bottle of whisky. 'Would you like a drink? Afraid all I have is this stuff.'

'Laphroaig single malt, ten years old. Very nice,' Kristen commented. Then, noticing the case of identical bottles sitting on the floor next to the dresser, she added, 'You must be a bit of a connoisseur.'

'That's a nice way of putting it,' he said with a sour chuckle, and poured out two measures in a pair of chunky cut-glass tumblers.

'I shouldn't. Whisky always goes right to my head. But what the hell.'

'That's the spirit,' he said. 'This will warm the cockles of your heart.'

'I always wondered which bit of the human heart the cockles were,' she mused, accepting the tumbler. 'Next time I meet a cardiologist, I must remember to ask. Cheers.'

'Cheers.' They clinked. The fireplace had a brass surround with a single padded seat on either side. They sat opposite one another, in the glow of the crackling flames.

At her first sip, Kristen spluttered. 'Jesus.'

'It's cask strength,' he said. 'Fifty-five per cent proof.'

'The strong stuff.'

'You get used to it.'

'I wouldn't want to get too used to it,' she laughed, then took another sip. 'I can feel those cockles warming up already.'

Ben was beginning to appreciate the company now. It felt good to have someone to relate to again after long weeks of being very alone. He was glad he hadn't turned Kristen away when she'd approached him on the beach.

'So what is it you do, Ben?'

'Right now, nothing.'

'You certainly are the mysterious one. No family, no home, no future plans, and now no occupation either.'

It was his instinct to be evasive when being questioned. 'Let's just say I'm kind of between things,' he said. 'Considering my options.'

'What did you do before? Or would I be prying?'

He knew there was a limit to the whole Mr Mystery bit. Any more, and he risked putting out alarming signals. He didn't want to come over as a weirdo or a serial killer. It was time to open up a little with her. 'I was in the military for a while. Then I left to start up in business for myself.'

'You don't strike me as the businessman type,' she said, laughing.

'It was a particular kind of business.' His tumbler was empty again. He refilled it once more and topped hers up too. She was drinking much less quickly than he was.

'Now you really have me intrigued. Remember you're dealing with a nosy journalist.' She grinned, pointing a jokey finger at him. 'I can get information out of a stone.'

'Really?'

'Famous for it.'

'Fair enough. I helped people.'

'People?'

'People in trouble. And people whose loved ones were in trouble.'

'Now we're really getting somewhere. Helped them how?'

'By bringing the loved ones home safely,' he replied.

30

'You're talking about missing persons?'

'Kidnap cases, mostly.'

'Wouldn't the police normally deal with that kind of thing?'

'In theory,' he said. 'But when clients begin to see how badly things can get botched up by going down that road, they'll often turn to the freelancers.'

'That's what you were, a freelancer?'

'The term was "crisis response consultant". I worked alone.'

'And did what exactly?'

'Whatever was required,' he said.

She sipped a little more whisky, getting acclimatised to the burn now, staring at him intently over the rim of her glass. 'Sounds like a risky business.'

'It had its moments. I was trained for it.' He reached for another log from the neat stack by the fire, and lobbed it into the flames. The blaze crackled up with a shower of orange sparks.

'Sounds like you enjoyed the danger,' Kristen said. 'Some people are attracted to it. Even thrive on it.'

'Funny. That's what Brooke said, too.'

'Brooke?'

'My fiancée. I should say, ex-fiancée. We split up a couple of months ago.'

'Oh. I'm sorry.'

'It's okay,' he said. 'Well, no, it isn't.'

'I know how it goes, believe me.'

'You too?'

She nodded. 'We'd been together three years. I thought it would last forever, you know?'

'That's what I thought, too,' he said. 'That Brooke and I were for life. Sometimes things just don't work out the way you planned.'

'You never know what life's going to set in your path,' she said, with a one-sided smile.

'I miss her. There's not an hour I don't think about her.'

'What's she like?' Kristen asked.

Ben paused a long time before replying. 'What can I say? She was the morning of my day.'

'My God,' Kristen coughed.

He looked at her. 'What?'

'I can only wish that, one day, a man will say something that beautiful about me. I think I just met the last of the real romantics.'

He smiled darkly. 'I've been called a lot of things, but that's a new one.'

'Here, give me another drop of that stuff, will you?' she said, proffering her empty glass.

Ben found it strange that he should be confiding like this in a stranger. Whisky and loneliness made for a powerful cocktail. A little too powerful. He hadn't eaten much that day, and with all the Guinness inside him already, he was feeling uncharacteristically light-headed. He poured another measure for Kristen. He knew he needed to stop topping up his own drink, but topped it up anyway.

'So what about this book of yours that you're thinking of giving up on?' he asked.

She shrugged. 'Seemed like a good idea at the time. Nobody's ever done a proper biography of Lady Stamford before. I've spent the last eight months travelling back and forth researching everything about her life, both here in Ireland and after she returned to England. Which is what I'll be doing myself tomorrow.'

Ben looked at her and found himself smiling. She was attractive, she was warm and engaging. Under any other circumstances, a man might have felt a pang of disappointment that she'd be gone the next day. A new female attachment was the last thing Ben was looking for at this point in his life, but he was still sorry that he was going to lose an interesting companion. He shoved all those thoughts to the back of his mind.

'Eight months is a lot of time to spend on research, just to give up on it,' he said. 'What happened, did you lose interest?'

'Not at all. Lady Stamford's is a fascinating story.'

'Tell me some of it.'

'You really want to know?'

'I wouldn't ask if I didn't.'

Kristen shrugged. 'She was born Elizabeth Manners in Bath in 1824. Just turned nineteen when she met her soon-to-be husband, Lord Edgar Stamford. He was only two years older than her, but already well known as a botanist and chemist. He'd inherited the family fortune very young. Massively rich, dashing and handsome, whisked her off her feet and brought her to Ireland. It wasn't exactly the happiest of marriages. She soon found out that Stamford was a controlling despot of a man who treated everyone around him like filth.'

'That's what they say.'

'They're not wrong. Total bastard wouldn't be too much of an understatement. As lord of the manor he was also a Justice of the Peace, which in rural Ireland in the mid-nineteenth century basically allowed him to play God with the peasant farmers who worked on his lands. They had a pretty rough existence under his rule. Then when the Great Famine struck the land hard in 1847, things got worse for them. A lot worse.'

Ben was no historian, but he had a fairly clear idea of what Kristen was talking about. It wasn't possible to live in

Ireland for any length of time, or for that matter to have had an Irish mother, without picking up a few of the key facts about one of the defining moments, and quite possibly the darkest hour, of the country's history.

'Bad time,' he said. 'About a million dead from starvation. They'd become too dependent on the potato for food. When the blight wiped out the crop, they didn't stand much of a chance.'

'More like anything up to two million, by some estimates,' Kristen corrected him. 'That's out of an overall population at the time of just eight million. Compare those figures to the famine in Darfur in 2003: a hundred thousand dead out of a population of twenty-seven million. We tend to forget nowadays how bad things got here. Irish people died like flies. Heaped in mass graves, sometimes while they were still alive but too weak from starvation to protest. Starvation was everywhere. Yet if Lord Stamford caught one of his hungry tenants stealing so much as an apple to feed their children, he'd have them strung up.'

'Sounds like a nice guy to be married to.'

'It was a wretched time for her. Women couldn't just walk away from an abusive relationship in those days. Husbands had complete control over everything. Marital rape was legal; men could basically do what they wanted. I'm sure Edgar Stamford exploited that freedom to the nines, though I can't prove it without the journals.'

'Journals?'

'She kept a private diary during her years in Ireland, several volumes long. They'd have been a key resource for me, if I'd been able to get hold of them.'

'They were lost?' Ben asked.

Kristen shook her head. 'I finally tracked them down to this former academic who has them now, a private collector

34

specialising in Irish history. Tried to persuade him to let me view them, but I'm still waiting for him to get back to me.'

'Pity.'

'Anyway,' Kristen said, 'we know a lot about her married life from her later writings and personal letters, some of which I managed to get hold of.'

'Did she leave Ireland after her husband died?'

'No, he died later. She had eight years of hell with him and then managed to escape back to England with a little help from sympathisers. That was when her life really began. She campaigned for women's rights, published a couple of volumes of poetry and a successful novel, and founded a school to help educate underprivileged girls and young women.'

'Sounds like a happy ending, for her at least,' Ben said.

'Sadly not. The good times didn't last long. I've got some of her personal letters that suggest she got herself mired in some kind of legal action in the late summer of 1851, though it's all a bit of a mystery. From what I managed to piece together, Elizabeth made contact with one Sir Abraham Barnstable, who was one of the very top lawyers in London at the time and a bit of a shadowy figure.'

'Shadowy how?'

She shrugged. 'Government connections. Some have said he was a spy. What she was in touch with him for, nobody knows, because then the Gilbert Drummond thing happened and—'

'You're losing me completely.'

'Sorry. Gilbert Drummond was a new teacher Elizabeth had hired to work at her school that July. He was twenty-six, handsome, dashing, but volatile. The story goes that he fell obsessively in love with her, and in September he finally declared his passion for her. When Elizabeth rejected him, he became convinced she was in love with someone else, went off in a rage and got a horse pistol . . . and you can guess the rest.'

Chapter Five

'He shot her,' Ben said.

Kristen made the shape of a gun with her index finger and thumb, aimed it and clicked her tongue. 'Single slug to the heart.'

'So that was the end of that.'

'Except there's a mystery to it,' Kristen said.

'Even more mystery?'

'I told you, I can get information out of a stone. I'm the only researcher I know of who's found out that Gilbert Drummond couldn't have fallen in love with her at all. He was actually gay, and his conviction for murder was a complete set-up. The real killer knew that Drummond wouldn't bring shame and public scandal on his family by revealing the truth about himself, even though he was facing the gallows for a crime he didn't commit.'

'Very noble. So who did it?'

'A paid assassin called William Briggs. As for who employed him, well, I'm still working on that one. Or . . . *was*.'

'1851,' Ben said. 'Wasn't that the same year old Stamford torched his house and killed himself?'

'Actually, it wasn't just the same year – they died in the same month. Just two weeks apart, Elizabeth on September sixth, her former husband on the twentieth.'

'Maybe he did it out of grief for her,' Ben said.

Kristen wrinkled her nose. 'Seems a bit out of character, don't you think?'

Ben pondered for a few moments. 'Anyway, I don't know much about writing books. But it sounds to me like you've got a great thing going here. Drama, murder, injustice, scandal, intrigue – why give up on it?'

Kristen hesitated, as if uncertain what, or how much, to tell him. 'It's like I said. Because something else came up.'

Ben could see the shadow of anxiety, intermingled with excitement, that had entered her face. The nervous light that had come into her eyes was similar to the expression she'd worn earlier when checking her messages. 'You told me that this research trip had thrown up something unexpected,' he said. 'Are we getting to those trade secrets now?'

She nodded. 'You see, a few days ago I . . . I *found* something.'

'Found something?'

'Yes. Something that changes everything. The reason I'm stopping with the book. If my hunch is right and this comes off, I might never have to write another book again.'

'You didn't find the leprechauns' gold, did you?' Ben said with a dry smile.

'No, I found something very real. Information that nobody else knows, that's been kept a secret for a very long time. Just stumbled on it in the middle of my research, totally by chance, almost like it was sitting there waiting for me. Something big, and I mean *big*. I can't say more than that. No offence.'

'None taken,' Ben said. 'But I'm curious. Earlier on you didn't want to tell me anything at all about your secret. Why tell me this much now?'

'Because of what you told me,' she said. 'About how you helped people. People who might be in trouble.'

'I said I used to. What's the connection?'

'Would you . . . I mean, would you still . . .?'

He looked at her. 'Go on.'

'Just that . . . this *thing* I found out . . . there's, well, a potential risk involved. Quite a bit of risk, if I'm honest.'

'How big a risk are we talking about?'

'Let's just say it stands to upset some people. Some fairly powerful and important people. I might need someone.'

'Someone?'

'You know, like a bodyguard, or something.'

Ben looked at her. 'Come on.'

'I'm serious. You said you were at a loose end, so I was just thinking . . .'

'That you'd hire the services of some guy like me?'

'It crossed my mind.'

'You only just met me.'

'You've got an honest face.'

'I was never a bodyguard,' Ben said. 'Besides—'

'I understand perfectly,' Kristen replied, making an effort to look jovial. 'You're in between things. Last thing you need is me messing with your life. Forget I mentioned it. Stupid idea.' She blinked and shook her head. Her unfinished drink was cradled in her lap. 'Oof. I've had a little too much of this stuff. My head's spinning. Jesus, look at the bottle. We've almost polished off the lot.'

'I think that was mostly me,' Ben said, quite truthfully. 'Listen, if you need help, I know people in the business. I could make a call.'

'Really?'

'But first you'd have to tell me more about this situation you're in. You said this has something to do with your research.'

'Let's just say it's connected.'

Ben frowned. His own mind was becoming a little fogged from the Scotch, and he struggled to make full sense of what she was telling him. 'How does the history of a dead woman stand to cause trouble for you a hundred and fifty years after the fact? Who might be threatening you? Why?'

Kristen was about to reply when she suddenly seemed to remember something, looked at her watch and let out a sharp gasp. 'I didn't realise we'd been talking so long. I've absolutely got to make this business call at ten o'clock. Just got time to get back to the guesthouse.'

Sunday evening seemed to Ben like a funny time to make a business call. 'Use the phone here, if you like,' he said.

'Thanks, but . . .' Kristen glanced out of the window. It had stopped raining and the sun was shining over the beach in a last orange-gold blaze before it plunged into the horizon and dusk fell. 'Better if I go back. The call might take a while, and it's, well, a little delicate. But I'd still like to take you up on that offer, if I can. And I promise I'll tell you everything. Give me your number. I'll call you.'

'How about telling me in person tomorrow morning?' he suggested. 'Meet me on the flat rock.'

She sighed. 'Can't. Taxi's coming at seven thirty to take me to the airport.'

'Forget the taxi,' Ben said, jerking his thumb in the direction of the little lane behind the cottage, where his rented BMW was parked. 'I'll drive you. We can talk on the way.'

Kristen seemed genuinely pleased and relieved. 'If you're sure . . .? It seems like an imposition.'

'It seems important.'

'It's really kind of you.' She glanced again at her watch. 'Shit. I really have to go. I don't want to miss this call.'

She got up from the fireside seat and moved towards the nearby table to set down her whisky tumbler. A little unsteady on her feet, she lost balance for a moment and stumbled against the wooden chair over which she'd hung her fleece and her cloth bag. It toppled over. Nearly falling with it, Kristen reached out for Ben's arm to steady herself, and in the process let her tumbler slip out of her fingers. It fell to the floor and smashed, glass fragments bursting in all directions across the bare floorboards.

'Look what I've done,' she exclaimed. 'Oh, I'm so sorry.'

'Don't worry about it. My fault.' Ben bent down and picked up the fallen chair. 'I don't think your computer's damaged.' But some of her other things had spilled out over the floor. Hairbrush, make-up, perfume. To someone like Ben, who travelled light everywhere he went, the quantity of assorted paraphernalia the average modern woman toted about with her was mystifying. Brooke had somehow always been the exception.

Kristen was apologetic and flustered as she stooped down to retrieve her fallen things. 'If you have a dustpan and brush, I'll clear up the broken glass.'

'Leave it,' he said. 'You'd best be heading back. Your phone call, remember?' He thought she still looked a little unsteady as she stood up again, and reached a hand out to help her. 'Are you okay? Sure you don't want me to walk you back?'

'I'm not completely plastered,' she laughed. 'I'll be fine.'

'See you in the morning, then,' he said. 'Say seven o'clock, outside the guesthouse? Then we'll have more time to talk.'

'I really appreciate this, Ben.' She touched his hand. 'Seven o'clock it is.'

Then she was gone. Ben watched from the doorway as she hurried off. He closed the door and went back to his drink.

'Now that,' he said to the empty room, 'was one of the strangest conversations of my life.'

Chapter Six

Kristen kept glancing at her watch as she headed quickly back towards the guesthouse, leaving the cottage out of sight behind the tall rocks. She felt giddy and light-headed from the rocket-fuel whisky. *Sober up. Sober up. You have work to do.* Just twelve minutes to get back, close herself in her room and get on the phone. She'd make it, just.

She had to. There was a hell of a lot riding on this.

If she hadn't been in such a rush, she'd have paused to admire the sunset. This really was a beautiful spot. And so tranquil, not a soul in sight. Apart from the waves and the birds, the only movement was the faraway car she could see, a black Range Rover or something like it, tracking slowly along the lane running parallel with the beach in the distance.

She hoped that Ben hadn't thought that she'd made up her pressing business call as a pretext to get away. The fact was, the call really was every bit as important as the need for discretion. It was a chance that wouldn't come again, and she needed to stick to her plan.

Yet, she regretted having had to break away from Ben so soon. She'd gladly have stayed with him all evening. She pictured his face. A nice face. Not too craggy or butch. Thick blonde hair, blue eyes. Seemed a bit sad and lonely, which maybe accounted for the drinking.

Single, too. And not gay, apparently.

She was definitely interested. Question was, was he?

She wished she could have hung around here for a few more days rather than have to rush back to Newbury. She might have got to know him better. The thought was exciting. But again, business was business. Right now was no time for amorous distractions. Maybe – just maybe – those could come later.

Get your head straight, Kristen.

She cleared all thoughts of Ben Hope from her mind and focused instead on the other man in her life right now, who was sitting by the phone half the world away, just waiting for her to call at the appointed time.

This would be the second contact. The first, thirty-six hours ago, seemed to have gone perfectly according to plan. She'd had the element of surprise, had heard the total amazement in the man's voice when she'd called him like that out of the blue.

So far, so good. The sum of money involved made her ears pop. She tried to imagine it all sitting there in front of her, a mountain of cash. She couldn't. But if all went smoothly, she wouldn't have to imagine it. It would be there, real, all hers.

This second call was even more critically important to carry off right than the first. By now his shock and surprise would have worn off. He'd be ready to talk business. There was a lot riding on this for him, too.

He might even be so eager to talk business that he'd tried calling her while she'd been with Ben. There'd been no message from him earlier – but there might be one now. As she strode over the pebbles, she dipped her hand in her bag for the leather pouch in which she kept her personal BlackBerry and the untraceable, cheap prepaid Samsung she'd bought especially for her plan.

She stopped.

The pouch wasn't there.

'No! No!' She rummaged urgently in the bag. Definitely gone. Where the hell was it?

Only one place it could be. Ben's cottage, still lying there on the floor.

She remembered picking up the items that had fallen from her bag. Make-up, mirror, hairbrush, purse. What about the pouch? Now that she thought about it, she'd no recollection of picking it up. That's what you get for drinking all that whisky, she thought angrily. It must have slipped under the sofa or something, and her wits had been too astray to notice.

Kristen looked at her watch. Damn it. Nine minutes to ten. She had time to make it back to the cottage, but there was no way she'd reach the privacy of her room at the guesthouse in time to make the call.

She'd have to make it from Ben's place after all. Maybe she could lock herself in the bathroom, get him to put some music on so he wouldn't overhear her conversation. This phone call was definitely not one she wanted anyone else to listen in on, even accidentally.

But she had no choice, and nobody to blame but herself. She turned and started heading impatiently back in the direction of the cottage. She hadn't gone far before she noticed the black Range Rover again.

It had been driving slowly along the empty lane in the distance, in the same direction she was walking. Kind of meandering along, as if the driver were taking their time to drink in the sea view. Or as if they were lost and looking for someone to ask for help. Now that she'd doubled back the opposite way, it had U-turned, pulled right off the tarmac and was bouncing diagonally in her direction across the uneven grassy ground between the lane and the beach. The sinking sun reflected on its shiny black metal.

She turned to peer back at it as she walked. There was no question that the Range Rover was following her. Should she stop? She couldn't help them, not being local. And she was in too much of a hurry. In any case, some instinct told her to keep walking, told her something about the vehicle wasn't quite right. A frisson of worry went down her back.

The Range Rover kept coming, constantly correcting its course across the grass, as if tracking her, just thirty yards behind and catching up rapidly. As it reached the edge of the grass and began crunching over the pebbly beach, Kristen really began to worry. She suddenly felt quite sober.

Something's wrong here, she told herself. *Something is very wrong.*

The driver's intentions were clear. They meant to cut her off before she could get to the cottage. Her heart began to race in panic. What did they want from her? Thoughts of abduction, rape, or worse, flew through her mind. She broke into a run.

Ben's cottage was almost in sight up ahead.

The Range Rover's engine growled and it accelerated after her, its tyres crunching, spitting pebbles left and right. Kristen reached the rocky part of the path. She tripped over a boulder and nearly fell. Swore and ran on. Behind her, the Range Rover lurched to a sudden halt. Its front doors swung open and two men got out. She threw a frightened glance at them over her shoulder and saw they were both staring right at her. They left the vehicle doors open and started striding quickly, purposefully, after her.

Kristen had once got away from a man who was pestering her with a lucky kick in the groin. But this situation was something else. There was no chance she could fight them

45

off if they caught her. They were both big, powerful-looking men. One was wearing a hooded top, the other a baseball cap. Their faces looked hard and determined.

And whatever they wanted from her, she could be certain it wasn't directions.

This was for real. She was in serious trouble.

She ran faster. Her cloth bag kept slipping down her shoulder and the computer inside slapped against her leg as she ran. She let it fall. Glanced back and let out a whimper of fear as she saw the men's pace quicken.

Suddenly they were sprinting after her. Without slackening his pace, one of the men bent and scooped up her fallen bag. What did they want from her? They split up, taking different lines over the rocks, one to head her off and the other to block her retreat. Hunting her like two dogs after a rabbit. If she didn't make it to the cottage before them, the only place she could run was right into the sea.

She raced on, her mind a blank, too terrified even to dread what they'd do if they caught her.

The cottage was almost in sight.

Chapter Seven

As Ben swept fragments of broken glass into the dustpan, he was considering the wisdom of pouring himself another drink. In fact, he was contemplating opening another bottle after the remnants of this one, and keeping it company for the rest of the evening. It seemed like a very inviting prospect.

You've had plenty enough already, said one part of him.

Don't know about that, said another.

'What the hell,' he muttered out loud. He carried the remnants of the smashed tumbler through into the kitchen, dumped it in the recycling bin with the collection of empty bottles he'd already accumulated, chucked the dustpan and brush back in the cupboard and headed back into the living room with the thought of another generous measure of cask-strength Laphroaig looming large in his mind.

The night was young. He was just getting started.

He reached for the bottle and poured himself the last of its contents. He put the tumbler to his lips.

That was when he heard the sound outside.

A woman's scream.

He slammed the bottle and tumbler down on the dresser and hurried over to the window. His movements weren't perfectly coordinated and he bumped his hip against the corner of the table as he went, making a lamp sway on its pedestal. He stared out of the window and saw a figure, eighty or so yards from the cottage, running towards it for all she was worth.

Kristen.

Behind her, chasing her across the rocks, were two men. Both white, both fit and lean, both around Ben's age or a little younger. One had dark hair shaved into a military-style buzz cut and wore a navy-blue jacket; the other was in a green hooded top. They were running fast. The one with the blue jacket had a distinctive cloth bag over his shoulder that Ben recognised as Kristen's.

Ben blinked. For an instant he just stood there, unable to react or move.

Kristen screamed again, calling his name. Her voice was hoarse with fear. 'Ben! Help me!'

Suddenly spurred into action, Ben raced to the door and burst outside. Kristen was just fifty yards away now, but the men had almost caught up with her.

He ran down the path towards the front gate, crashed it open and went bounding over the rocks towards her. He tripped on a boulder and almost went sprawling on his face. *You bloody idiot*, he seethed inside. Whatever the hell was happening here, this was the wrong time to be pissed.

The men caught up with Kristen. If they'd noticed Ben racing towards the scene, it didn't seem to put them off. The one in the navy jacket grabbed her by the shoulder and spun her violently around, then shoved her harshly to the ground. She cried out as she fell.

Ben sprinted faster. His heart pounded and his breathing rasped in his ears. He saw Kristen trying to struggle to her feet and tear herself away from her attackers. Saw the second man, the one in the green hoodie, kick her brutally back down.

48

But now Ben was on them. He ran straight into the hoodie without slowing down, twisting slightly to ram his shoulder into the guy's chest. Ben heard the grunt as the impact drove the wind out of him. Up close, he smelled a minty smell on the man's breath. The man staggered but stayed on his feet. He reached behind him to draw a stubby black cylindrical object from his belt. Clutching it at one end, he gave it a sharp flick and the extending law-enforcement baton whipped out to its full length: an impact weapon prohibited from civilian use in most countries and capable of belting a man's brains to jelly with a well-aimed strike.

Ben had been in dozens of fights against multiple armed attackers. In situations like these, gaining control of the weapon was always the first priority. He shouldered his way inside the arc of the coming blow and made a grab for the hand clutching the baton. But while years of training had sharpened his instincts to a fine edge, weeks and months of drinking and self-neglect had dulled them back down. Not all the way down to the defenceless, vulnerable level of Joe Public, but enough to make the difference when up against two men like these.

They were quick and determined. They weren't afraid of him. They'd done this before.

Ben's lunge for the weapon was too slow. The man side-stepped him and came back with a downward baton strike that hissed through the air an inch from Ben's face.

He ducked back. Suddenly he was on the defensive. The other man was coming at him from the side, ripping an identical baton from his jacket and extending it with a prac-tised flick of the wrist. Ben skipped backwards over the rocks, dodging a blow that would have smashed his collarbone. But as he moved, his heel caught a rock behind him and he fell. He rolled, twisted, ready to spring back to his feet.

Too slow again. A boot lashed out at him and his vision exploded white as the hard kick caught him in the side of the head. Pain bursting inside his skull, he managed to get upright just in time to see the guy in the navy jacket make another move at him. He was lucky this time. His right fist closed on the guy's wrist. Yanked it sideways and downwards while he twisted the elbow upwards with a rising blow from the heel of his left hand. The man cried out and dropped the baton. Without letting go of his opponent's wrist, Ben threw a kick and caught him in the belly. But it was a bad kick with not enough drive and power behind it, and failed to bring him down.

The next thing, it was Ben's arm that was being trapped. He twisted his body around to wrench it free. The man had a strong grip. Ben punched him in the face and saw blood.

But now the other one was rushing back into the fight, and Ben didn't react in time. The baton flashed towards him in a dark blur that his senses were too blunted to block quickly enough, and connected hard with his cheekbone.

Ben went straight down, blinded by agony.

Then the baton hit him a second time, and a third, and the lights went out.

Chapter Eight

From out of the dark depths, Ben felt himself rising. It was a long, slow swim to the surface. Sounds were faraway, all blended into a roar of meaningless noise that filled his head and made it feel about to explode with pain. He blinked, rubbed his eyes. The left one felt strange. It wouldn't open at all. What little he could see through the right one was blurry and dancing with flashes and strobes of light. He couldn't think straight or stand up. His head was pounding badly.

Slowly, things began to focus.

The twilit beach and the rocks were illuminated by a glow of swirling blue. Radios fizzed. Someone was helping him to sit up. He felt cold. He winced as another searing stab of pain pierced his head. He still couldn't quite see straight, but could make out figures of people around him. Shapes that he made out to be a police car and an ambulance were parked a little way off, at the edge of the beach. No, two ambulances. Why were there two?

'Let me go,' he mumbled to the person who was helping him, brushing them away. Looking up, he saw the person was a woman. She was wearing overalls like a paramedic, and her voice was gentle and reassuring even though he couldn't make out the words she was saying. He tried to stand up so he could see past the crowd of people and find out what was happening, but pain and dizziness made it impossible. The paramedic helped him patiently over to a rock, where he sat and bowed his aching head between his hands. He felt the wetness of his palms and stared at them in the flashing blue light. They were slick with blood. He touched his face and realised where the blood was coming from. It was all down the front of his T-shirt and spotted over the blanket that someone had draped around his shoulders. He put his fingers to his blind eye.

'Try not to touch it,' said the paramedic, her words sounding clearer now. His cheek felt swollen and hurt badly to the touch. He wiped the blood from his eye, and found he could make out blurry images with it again. He remembered that he'd been hit there. Hit very hard. He remembered the baton. Recalled the man holding it.

'Kristen,' he mumbled, his voice coming out garbled and indistinct. He looked around. 'Where's Kristen?'

A policewoman appeared out of the confusion and spoke to the paramedic. Ben heard her say, 'We need to ask him some questions.' The paramedic replied, 'He's got to be seen to first.' And something about a hospital. It didn't feel as if they were talking about him.

'Where's Kristen?' Ben repeated. 'I have to help her.'

The paramedic said something that sounded like, 'You can't help her.'

'Those men . . . they were attacking her,' he protested. But nobody seemed to pay any heed to what he was saying. Couldn't they understand?

Finally he stopped trying to speak, as his voice was slurring and his eyes wouldn't stay open. He felt himself being lifted and laid down on a stretcher.

Time seemed to drift. Then there was the sound of doors

slamming and an engine, and he could sense he was in a moving vehicle. Someone was with him, maybe the same gentle female paramedic. Maybe someone else. He was somewhere very far away. He floated off and felt numb.

Then suddenly he was in a new environment, hard white light dazzling him, walls rushing past either side of him. Faces peering down. He realised he was lying on his back on a gurney being wheeled through a white corridor.

'I'm okay,' he tried to protest. 'I just need to find Kristen . . .' Then he passed out again.

The next several hours were a blur. How he got from the gurney to the couch in the curtained cubicle, his bloodied clothes replaced by a hospital robe, seemed to pass him by. He was half-conscious of the activity that milled around him. People came, people went. More faces looking down at him, as if he was some kind of specimen under observation. The nip of a needle, followed by a tickling sensation, he realised was the gash in his scalp being stitched. He vaguely remembered all the occasions in the past when he'd been sewn back together. This was nothing. Twice he tried to tell them so and get up, but dizziness overcame him and he slumped down against the couch.

His eyelids felt heavy, but they wouldn't let him sleep. 'I feel much better already,' he kept saying. Still, he'd been through this routine enough times to know that was the procedure in suspected concussion cases. A grey-haired consultant named Dr Prendergast, sporting a florid bow tie and an ironic sense of humour to match, shone a light in his eyes and asked him a lot of questions about his headache, his vision, whether he felt any weakness down one side of his body, which he didn't. Nor was he showing other telltale symptoms – he wasn't vomiting, his skin wasn't pale, his speech was no longer slurred and he didn't have one pupil dilated larger than the other.

But Dr Prendergast seemed concerned about the severity of the headache and the dizziness. Ben was wheeled off to have his head X-rayed to check for a skull fracture before being taken back to the cubicle, where they still wouldn't let him sleep, plied him with pills and as gently as possible refused to answer his questions about what had happened to Kristen, where she was, whether she was all right. He clearly remembered seeing two ambulances at the scene. Had she been in the other? Either they didn't know, or they wouldn't say.

Every hour, a different nurse returned to do a neuro check on him. 'It was just a bang on the head,' he told each one in turn. 'If I was going to drop dead, I'd have done it by now.'

After half the night seemed to have dragged tortuously by and they finally seemed satisfied that he hadn't suffered a major concussion and wouldn't fall into a permanent coma the moment he shut his eyes, he was moved to a ward and allowed to sleep. He didn't have much choice in the matter, because whatever cocktail of stuff they'd pumped him full of made him woozy. He laid his head on the pillow and was instantly floating.

But it was an uneasy sleep. He kept seeing Kristen in his mind, snatches of their conversation drifting through his consciousness but meaning little. Then his dream turned darker and he replayed the images of the two men chasing her along the beach. The fight. The baton held up in the air and then flashing down towards him—

He woke with a start. Blinked. Focused. White ceiling. Sunlight streaming through blinds. It was morning. He'd slept right through the night.

He craned his head to the side and saw that his bed was at the end of a ward. Most of the other beds were occupied by much older men. One of them couldn't stop hacking and coughing. A large, intimidating matron was doing the rounds. A clock on the far wall read just after ten past eight.

Ben was feeling a little stronger, less hazy, but his headache was still thumping painfully. It was partly thanks to the smart couple of blows his skull had received, partly a hangover from the Laphroaig. He missed his Gauloises and wanted another drink.

He drew his hand up from under the crisp sheet and touched the thick dressing on his brow. It hurt, and so did the bruises on the rest of his body from the fight. But what really pained him was that he'd failed to protect someone who was vulnerable, who needed his help.

He'd never failed like that before. He lay restlessly in the bed, haunted by self-blame, tormented with questions. Where was Kristen? Was she okay? When could he see her?

The ward clock was showing eight thirty by the time Ben finally decided he needed to get out of here and find some answers before he went insane. He was just about to throw back the bedcovers and get up when a hospital orderly, an ancient man with wizened arms protruding from his blue smock, who looked like he should be in one of the beds himself, appeared with a trolley and brought Ben his meagre, tasteless breakfast. Ben told him he didn't want anything and turned the tray away, inquiring urgently about Kristen. The old guy just blinked at him and tried to urge him to eat. Ben told him to go away.

The exchange drew the matron to his bedside. Up close, she was a veritable bison of a woman, who berated him for skipping breakfast and thrust some painkillers at him. After he'd grudgingly washed them down, he asked her the same questions, thought he saw a look flash through her eyes and wondered what it meant.

'Where is she?' he repeated. 'Is she all right? Tell me. I need to know.'

'I can't tell you.'

'Then I'll find someone who can,' he said, flipping back the sheet.

'You can't just wander about the place,' she said fiercely, drawing herself up so that she looked even larger.

'Where are my clothes?' he demanded, getting out of the bed and eyeing the matron with a look of savage intent that made her back off a step.

'I see our patient is feeling sprightlier this morning,' said a voice. Ben turned to see Dr Prendergast walk in. His paisley bow tie was even more garish than the one he'd been wearing last night – but what instantly caught Ben's eye instead were the grim-looking pair who had followed him into the ward. They certainly didn't look like medical personnel.

'You have visitors,' the doctor said.

Chapter Nine

Oklahoma

It was 2.30 a.m. and Erin Hayes couldn't sleep. She stood at the window of her dark motel room, gazing blankly out. There was nothing to see out there but the blinking neon sign that said 'Western Capri Motel' and the lights of the occasional passing vehicle on West Skelly Drive beyond. But even if there had been, Erin would barely have registered it. Her mind was focused inward on what she'd witnessed just two nights ago at the cabin by the lake.

Thinking back to it was like trying to recall the fragments of a nightmare. Some things her memory seemed to be trying to blank out, as if to protect her from the horror of what had happened; other things she remembered as vividly as if they were happening to her right this moment. She pictured herself running, running through the woods, stumbling over the uneven ground, thorny undergrowth biting at her bare feet, branches lashing at her face. Reaching the road, her aching soles pounding on the hard surface as she willed herself to get far away, the breath tearing out of her lungs. Glancing back in terror every few seconds in case they were chasing her.

The lights of the car coming up behind had almost

stopped her heart with fear. She'd wanted to leap off the road and run back into the trees, but it was too late. They'd seen her. The car had slowed as it came near. The window had wound down.

And a woman's voice had called from the driver's seat, 'Are you in trouble, honey?'

Erin had quickly thrust the gun out of sight into her backpack. Saved! For now.

Maggie was a waitress returning home after her shift at the all-night bar where she worked outside the town of Foyil, a few miles east. She'd been only too happy to give Erin a ride back into Tulsa, joining Route 66 and heading southwest through sleepy Claremore and Catoosa. She'd kept asking if Erin was okay, and so Erin had made up a story about having had a terrible bust-up with her boyfriend. A few years ago, with Darryl, that might've been true enough. A veteran of four stormy marriages, Maggie could empathise. She kind-heartedly insisted on driving all the way across town to Crosbie Heights and dropping Erin off right outside her door.

It had been late when Erin had finally run up the porch steps of the tiny two-bedroomed house and let herself inside, triple-locking the door behind her. In the bathroom, she'd nursed the tender, inflamed soles of her bare feet before padding downstairs in fresh socks and pouring herself a stiff drink. Quickly followed by another, it had done little to settle her nerves as she wondered what to do.

Nothing else for it, she'd thought. *I have to call the cops. Angela's family will be torn apart. The Desert Rose Trust won't survive the scandal. I'll lose my job. I'll lose everything. But I have to call the cops anyway.*

The evidence, she'd remembered. The evidence was in her backpack. She fumbled the phone out of the bag and

58

replayed the video she'd taken. With luck, she was just going crazy and she'd simply imagined the whole thing.

To her horror, the video playback confirmed that she hadn't imagined any of it. Worse, the quality of the footage was terrible. You could hardly see a thing except grainy shadows and overexposed glare. Quickly searching out a USB cable, she'd connected the phone to the computer in the little room she used as an office and downloaded the video onto that, but it hardly looked any better on the larger screen. For just one moment, there was a clear glimpse of Angela's husband standing there, but he'd been facing away from the camera and only his outline and the back of his head could be made out. Even the sound was garbled and booming and virtually incomprehensible.

Her first thought had been *Shit! How can I go to the cops with this? Nobody will believe me.*

She'd been standing there, frozen in indecision, when the sudden ringing of the phone on her desk had made her jump. Who would be calling her at this time of night? She'd hesitated, shaking, then picked up the handset.

'Hello?'

No reply. The caller had just hung up without a word.

Erin had dialled to check their number, but it had been withheld. It could have been anything. It could have been a wrong number.

Or it could have been *them*.

What if they'd discovered the things she'd had to leave behind in the cabin? What if there was something among them to identify her? Or else, what if Angela had innocently mentioned Erin's visit to the cabin to her husband? Or what if Joe, the driver, had said something? There were any number of ways that her presence there could be found out.

59

They know where I live, she'd thought. *And that was them calling. Now they know I'm home.*

Convinced that it wasn't safe to stay put another minute, she'd acted fast. The video evidence wasn't great, but nonetheless she'd quickly burned it onto two blank DVDs. Like Daddy had said: *always have a backup.* Then she'd hurried upstairs to pull on an old pair of running shoes from her wardrobe. Stuffed a few more things into her backpack. Unlocked the steel ammo cabinet under her bed, taken out all three of the ready-loaded Springfield magazines she kept in there, and dropped them into the zippered side pocket of her backpack together with the pistol itself. There was a can of Mace in a bedside drawer, put there as a last defensive resort in case of a home invasion when she didn't have her gun to hand. She tossed the Mace in the pack, too. Now she was ready.

Outside, the sleeping street had been empty. No suspicious-looking cars were parked nearby, no sinister watchers spying on the house. Hobbling slightly on her tender feet, she'd left the house at an awkward jog that quickly became a run.

And she hadn't been back there since.

Now here she was holed up in this motel, two nights later and eleven miles outside the city, unable to sleep, barely venturing outside except when hunger drove her the quarter-mile to the greasy diner the other side of the highway. She was still racking her brains night and day as to how to deal with what she'd witnessed, and going nowhere.

All she knew was that she daren't return home right now. There was nobody else she could go to, either. Darryl, her ex? Forget it. Her friends? How could she burden them with this? Her mother? No chance. Now she'd hooked up with her new man – was that the fourth since Daddy died, or the fifth? – she spent her days in the trailer they called home, steadily obliterating what was left of her brains with cheap liquor. They hardly even spoke any more, and Erin was damned if she was going to turn up there looking for help or shelter.

Maybe she should just take off. Hit the road in Daddy's old car and keep going, get as far away from Oklahoma as she could and find a place to begin again.

It wouldn't be the first time she'd had to start a whole new life.

Chapter Ten

After a quick check, the doctor determined that Ben was in a fit state to receive the visitors. The police detectives sat either side of the bed and a screen was pulled around the three of them to serve as a flimsy shield against the curiosity of the old guys on the ward.

The male officer, who introduced himself as Detective Inspector Healy, was a nervous, sallow little man in his fifties, with eyes that wouldn't stay still and never seemed to blink. Ben took an instant dislike to him, but there was nothing so unusual about that. His female sidekick, Detective Sergeant Nash, was about twenty years younger and looked a little more human.

Ben knew why she was there. Send a woman officer in for the gentle touch when there's bad news to break. Just in case the weaker ones break down.

'Let's have it,' he said to them before they could state the nature of their visit. 'Was she killed or was she kidnapped?'

'Why would you think she'd been kidnapped?' Healy said with a curious look.

'We'll get to that,' Ben said. 'Talk to me.'

'I'm afraid Miss Hall was dead when we arrived on the scene,' said Nash, as gently as it could be said. 'She suffered very extensive wounding. It wouldn't have been possible to save her. Next of kin have been informed and family members are on their way. I'm very sorry.'

Ben took a deep breath. He remained silent for a long moment as he absorbed the news. So now he knew. His worst fears were confirmed. He'd let her down, and now she was dead as a result. If he'd had all his wits about him and hadn't been rat-arsed on Scotch, weak and unfit and softened up by weeks of wallowing in self-pity, the two killers wouldn't have had a chance. Not if there'd been three of them, or even four. Kristen Hall would still be alive now.

'What kind of extensive wounding?' he asked, and saw DS Nash almost flinch at the question. When he looked at Healy, he could see the sudden pallor in the man's face. He knew right away that they'd both personally seen the body; and that whatever injuries Kristen had sustained were like nothing either police officer had seen before.

Nash began, 'Mr Hope, I think it would be best if we didn't—'

'I want to know.'

'Miss Hall suffered, ah, multiple stab wounds to every major organ,' Nash said with difficulty, after a pause. 'Extensive lacerations to the face. They . . . they—' She stopped, as if she couldn't bring herself to say it. She looked pale, almost ready to throw up.

'They punctured her eyes and slit her throat,' Healy finished grimly. 'The cut was so deep it almost severed her head. We don't know whether she was still alive by that point.'

Ben felt something rip in his hands, and realised he'd been gripping the hospital bed sheet so tightly that he'd torn it. Now he understood why Nash looked so sick. He thought about Kristen, saw her face in his mind, heard her voice, her laugh. He wanted to be sick too. He swallowed hard and steeled himself.

Healy cleared his throat and went on, 'We have two witnesses, a couple on holiday from Antwerp who are staying at Pebble Beach Guesthouse and observed a pair of men get out of a vehicle and pursue Miss Hall along the beach. They witnessed the whole thing: the attack, your intervention, you being struck over the head and knocked to the ground, after which one of the attackers produced a bladed weapon. The male witness got a detailed view of it all through binoculars. He's, uh, what do you call it?'

'An ornithologist,' Nash filled in.

'So he saw the stabbing take place?' Ben asked.

Nash nodded. 'Moments later, the two suspects retreated to a vehicle that had been reported stolen from Ballyvaughan earlier in the day.'

'The car was found abandoned and on fire late last night, down the coast near Lahinch,' Healy said. 'A local saw the blaze and called the Garda.'

'And no sign of the two men.' Ben wasn't asking.

'Everything is being done to trace their whereabouts,' Healy replied insistently. It was the usual line, designed to make it sound as though the authorities were in full control of the situation.

'Doesn't sound to me as if you have a lot to go on,' Ben said. 'They've covered their tracks pretty well so far.'

'We're hoping you can help us there,' Nash said.

'Meaning I'm the only one who saw them up close and personal. The only one alive, that is.'

'Would you recognise them?'

'I'd know their faces.'

'Can you describe them?'

Ben shrugged. 'Both white. Not young, not old. Maybe around my age, late thirties, early forties. Both physically fit, lean build, able to handle themselves. Neither of them spoke a word, so no telling if they're Irish, or English, or what. One a little taller than the other, say six foot. Short hair, military style. Navy jacket, synthetic, maybe nylon.'

Nash had taken out a pad and was rapidly scribbling notes.

'The other had a hoodie on,' Ben continued. 'It was green, a couple of shades darker than olive. I didn't get such a good look at his face. He's left-handed.'

'How do you know that?' Healy asked.

Ben looked at him. 'It's not rocket science, detective. That's the hand he was holding the baton in. Both of them were wearing boots. Steel toecaps. I know *that* because I can still feel them.'

'This is good information,' Nash said.

'You think?'

'Anything else?' Healy asked.

'The one with the green hoodie smelled of mint,' Ben said.

Nash paused in her scribbling. 'Mint?'

'Gum. But not ordinary gum. Particular smell.'

'Particular how?' Healy said, narrowing his eyes.

'Nicotine gum,' Ben said. 'You know what that is, detective? The disgusting stuff people chew on when they want to give up smoking.'

'You're sure?'

'I tried it once. You don't forget.'

'Okay,' Nash said, resuming her note-taking. 'Anything else?'

'Just general impressions,' Ben said. 'These men are no strangers to violence. They know what they're doing.'

'And you'd know that because . . .?'

'Because I'm no stranger to violence either. You might be dealing with a couple of psychopaths here, but they're trained, professional psychopaths. By trained I mean army trained. I recognise one when I see one.'

Nash and Healy glanced at one another. 'We're aware of your background,' Nash said.

'Only what you'd be allowed to know.'

'Then perhaps you could fill in the blanks for us,' Healy said.

Ben shook his head. 'I wouldn't consider that appropriate. Neither would the Ministry of Defence. With respect, detective, that information is way above your pay grade.'

'I see,' Healy said, clearly stung. 'You're on file as being the director of something called the Le Val Tactical Training Centre. In France, I believe.'

Ben nodded. That part of his history was open record. 'Normandy. I don't work there any longer.'

'And what is it you do now?'

'Nothing,' Ben said.

'Nothing,' Healy repeated, with an eyebrow raised. 'But we can assume that you yourself are highly trained in certain, ah, skills?'

The question hurt. 'I used to be.'

'I thought training like that stayed with a man forever.'

'I drink,' Ben said. 'I'd been drinking when the attack happened. It slowed me down. Otherwise, you'd have had two dead men to clear up off the beach instead of one dead woman.'

Nash stared at him. 'You'd have killed them, is that what you're saying?'

'You'd have had to pick them out from between the cracks in the rocks.'

'See, now, that's the kind of talk we don't like,' Healy said, staring at him closely.

Ben stared back. 'Join the club. I'm not wild about your

line of questioning, detective. It sounds as if you're trying to connect me with the attack.'

'That's not what we're saying,' Nash cut in, with an anxious glance at her superior.

But Healy was on a roll. 'And let me tell you how seriously concerned we are when members of the public take it upon themselves to "do something".'

'You think it would be a better society if people stood by and did nothing?' Ben said.

'I think nothing good ever comes of citizens intervening with undue force in situations that can all too easily become aggravated.'

'Undue force,' Ben repeated. 'You think that's what I used? Kristen is dead.'

Healy nodded. 'Absolutely. Under different circumstances, this incident might not have escalated into a life-threatening situation. What may start as a minor crime can sometimes get out of hand. Especially when there's alcohol involved.'

'It looked a little out of hand before I got there,' Ben said. 'And I didn't see any of your goons stepping in to save her, either. They'd have run a mile.'

'Seems to me you have a bad attitude, Mr Hope,' Healy said.

'You have no idea,' Ben said.

Healy glowered. Ben glowered back. The cop would never know how close he'd come to having his teeth smashed down his throat that morning.

'Let's talk about your relationship to Miss Hall,' Nash said, very deliberately changing the subject with another nervous glance at Healy. 'You and she were seen on the beach together some time before the incident.'

Ben let his gaze slowly trail away from Healy. 'No relationship to speak of. We'd only just met. I'm sure Mrs Henry at the guesthouse has already confirmed that.'

'So you didn't know her previously.'

'We'll be here an awfully long time if I have to say everything twice,' Ben said.

Nash pursed her lips. 'According to the eyewitness account, the killers took a bag from Miss Hall. Can you tell us anything about that?'

'It was a cloth shoulder bag,' Ben said. 'It was colourful, red and yellow. Ethnic kind of style. She had a computer inside, a small laptop, along with a notebook, couple of mobile phones, and some personal items like a hairbrush, make-up, and so on. That's all I can tell you.'

'You seem to know a lot about the victim's personal effects,' Healy cut in.

'I'm observant,' Ben said. 'You should try it some time.'

'We're just trying to put together a picture here, Mr Hope,' Nash said.

'That's a start,' Ben said. 'That's what I'd be doing, too. I'd be trying to figure out why a crime like this happened on my turf when there hasn't been a murder here for over thirty years. I know, I lived here. Most of the local Gardaí spend their days snoozing in their patrol cars or sitting in the pub. Which is where the talents of DI Healy here would be much better employed, rather than sitting here on his arse making veiled accusations against someone like me to hide the fact that he can't do his job.'

'Now listen—' Healy began, pointing a finger.

'No, Healy, how about you listen?' Ben said, staring him down. 'If it was me, I'd be thinking that two professional crooks didn't go to all the trouble of arming themselves with a pair of illegal batons, then steal a top-of-the-range car and cruise out to the arsehole of nowhere just on the off chance of finding some solitary easy victim they could mug and rob before cutting her to pieces for the fun of it. I'd be thinking about a motive for what's very obviously a planned killing, and I'd be looking into the connection with Kristen's work.'

Healy lowered his finger and slumped a little deeper in his chair, visibly fuming.

Nash was frowning, thinking hard. 'Her work?' She glanced at her notes. 'According to her self-employment records, she was a writer. The proprietor of the guesthouse says she was working on a novel. No clear motive there, is there?'

'She wasn't that kind of writer,' Ben said. 'She was doing historical research here in Ireland.'

'So?'

'So, in the course of that research, she said she'd accidentally discovered something. Information. Secrets. She believed that discovery had placed her at risk.'

Nash frowned. 'What kind of risk?'

'We didn't have the chance to go into that.'

'And why would she confide all this to you, if you'd only just met and hardly knew each other?' Healy asked.

'Because she wanted my help.'

'Why?'

'Because I'd told her a little about my past.'

'I thought that was "classified",' Healy said sarcastically, making inverted commas with his fingers.

'I worked in the personal security industry after leaving the military,' Ben said.

'As what, a bodyguard?' Healy said, not doing much to hide his contempt.

'Kidnap and ransom negotiator,' Ben replied. It was the only aspect of his former profession that sounded remotely legit. 'Close protection wasn't my main speciality.'

'That's why you asked if she'd been kidnapped,' Nash said.

Ben nodded. 'It was either one or the other. Kristen was clearly right to be anxious about the level of risk she'd become exposed to. She said she wanted protection. I told her I knew people in the business. We'd agreed to talk more about it this morning when I drove her to the airport.'

'Why you? Why not go to the police?'

Ben almost smiled at that. 'I can't imagine.'

'And you have no idea why, or more importantly from whom, she needed to be protected?' Nash asked.

'I told you, it wasn't discussed. Maybe it would have been, if we'd had the opportunity, but as things stand I don't know the answer to that. What I do know is that this was no random attack. She wasn't in the wrong place at the wrong time. The killers didn't just stumble on a lone woman on the beach. And no amount of intervention on my part, short of putting them in the morgue where they belong, was going to make any difference to that.'

'I think there are enough bodies in the morgue already, don't you?' said Nash. 'These men will be brought to justice.'

'Not by you guys,' Ben said. 'You're not in their league.'

'That may be so,' Healy said. 'But then, it seems, neither are you.'

'I wasn't ready for them,' Ben said. 'Next time, I will be.'

'That's our job,' Nash said.

'You'll never even come close.'

'And where do you suppose you're going to find them?' Healy sneered.

'Not anywhere nearby,' Ben said. 'They're getting further away every second we sit here wasting.'

'We'll find them,' Healy said. 'Make no mistake about that.'

'Healy, you couldn't find your own arsehole in the dark,' Ben said. 'But maybe you'll be able to find the hospital exit. Or do I have to call the matron to escort you out?'

The detectives stood up. Healy's cheeks were flushed red and Nash was looking at the floor. Healy said something about needing to speak to Ben again as the inquiry progressed.

Ben said nothing more to them. Healy pulled open a gap in the screen around the bed, and through it Ben watched them file out of the ward.

He sat for a while, thinking about Kristen. It was only now that he was left alone that the reality of her death properly sank in. He gritted his teeth tightly at the thought of what those men had done to her. Kept picturing her lying there with blood oozing from the stab wounds all over her body. Bloody holes where her blue-grey eyes had been. Her throat gashed wide open, windpipe severed. Blood pooling on the stones, seeping into the ground.

He couldn't bear it any longer.

He called for the nurse.

Fifteen minutes later, he was dressed and ready to check himself out of the hospital, despite Dr Prendergast's protests that they should keep him under observation for at least twenty-hour hours. 'If I drop dead of a brain haemorrhage in the hospital car park, you can tell me you told me so,' he said to Dr Prendergast.

In a bathroom off the ward, he peeled the dressing away from his brow and quickly inspected the stitched-up gash under the hairline.

He'd live.

'Fuck it,' he said to the mirror. 'Let's get out of here.'

Chapter Eleven

Ben didn't return to the cottage for a few hours. The bus he took back from the hospital wound its unhurried way back through several villages and finally dropped him on the main road, quarter of a mile from Pebble Beach. From there, avoiding the guesthouse, he cut across a patch of wasteground and down a rocky slope that joined the coastal path where it curved around the headland. A short way further on was a little cove he'd discovered years ago. It was a place he knew he'd be alone, and solitude was what he needed.

He found a place to sit among a cluster of rocks overhanging the water, and took out his cigarettes. He lit one mechanically, shielding the Zippo flame from the wind with a cupped hand. He stared out to sea, watched the hissing foam boil around the foot of the rocks. The cigarette didn't taste of anything much. He plucked it from his lips and tossed it into the surf where it fizzed briefly and then was gone.

He barely noticed the grey swell. All he could see was the choice that now lay in front of him.

It was a simple matter of two options. Left, or right. Black, or white.

The first option was to step back, yield to the police and

trust them to deal with this. He'd meet with Kristen's family, offer condolences and support. He'd hang around here for as long as necessary, do whatever he could to assist the authorities, but remain firmly in the background. He could be passive, patient and calm. Take a back seat and stay there.

But as he sat there, he knew in his heart that could never happen. He'd never been passive in his life, let alone supportive towards the authorities – two ingrained habits that right now didn't seem a good time to start trying to break. That led him to the second option.

He thought again about Kristen, replayed one more time in his mind the brief period they'd spent together, and the way it had ended. He'd barely known her, and yet he couldn't have felt the responsibility more heavily. Maybe it was because he felt so powerless to fix other things in his life that this pressed on him so much. He didn't know why, and he didn't care to ponder the reasons too closely. He just knew what felt right to him. In fact, he realised, there never had been a choice. This had to be finished his way, the way he'd always done things. The only way he really knew. No matter how hard he tried to stay off that road, it kept calling him back. Maybe it always would.

From the cove, he walked back along the beach. It was after lunchtime but he wasn't hungry. He passed his cottage at a distance and barely glanced at it. He passed the crime scene, saw the police tape flapping in the wind and the Garda Land Rover parked on the shingle. Nearby, a pair of chunky, unfit-looking cops were scratching slowly about for whatever clues bare rocks could yield up. He had no doubt that pretty soon, they'd retire empty-handed to their vehicle and go trundling back to the comfort of the police canteen for their pie and chips.

Ben walked on towards the guesthouse. Inside, he found the reception desk unoccupied. While nobody was about, he grabbed the register and flipped it around on the desk to check for the names of the Belgian guests Healy had said had witnessed the attack. They weren't hard to find. Monsieur and Madame Goudier had been staying for most of the week and were scheduled to leave tomorrow.

'Room five,' Ben said to himself as he headed for the stairs. Before he got there, what had once been the door to his office, now with a sign that said 'STAFF ONLY', swung open and Mrs Henry appeared in the passage. Her eyes were red and puffy. She stopped dead when she saw him, took one look at his battered face and instantly broke out blubbering.

I don't need this now, Ben thought as the tears flowed and the words flowed faster.

'That poor girl,' Mrs Henry repeated over and over, though Ben got the impression that she was generally more concerned with the impact this would have on bookings. The media hadn't stopped pestering her all morning, she complained, and they were whipping up a storm that their poor fragile business could surely never weather. What kind of reputation would they have now that it wasn't safe to walk the beach with all these maniacs and killers lurking about the place? If things got any worse, Bryan might have to give up his golf club membership. It would be the end of him.

Ben briefly expressed his sympathies for Bryan's imperilled sporting career. He pointed up the stairs. 'Which is room five?'

'That'd be the Goodyears',' Mrs Henry sniffed, mopping the corner of her eye with another tissue. 'They're in the conservatory, finishing their lunch. Though they could hardly eat a thing, poor souls, after the shock they've had.' It didn't seem to occur to her to ask why Ben wanted to speak to them, and he didn't feel the need to explain. As quickly as he could, he detached himself from her and headed for the conservatory.

A gloomy pall seemed to have descended on the guest-house, and the few guests having lunch in the conservatory were eating quietly, just a murmur of occasional conversation and the clinking of cutlery. Ben spotted the middle-aged couple from the unmistakably European way they were dressed. They were both lean, as if they did a lot of sports or hiking. The man's hair was silvery and swept back from his high forehead, while his wife's was an expensively coif-fured bottle-blonde. They were sitting in silence at a table in the corner, drinking an after-lunch pot of coffee. Even at a distance, they looked obviously upset and shaken by the horror of what they'd witnessed yesterday. They didn't notice Ben walk up to them.

'Monsieur and Madame Goudier?' he said.

They looked up at him, startled. 'I am Bernard Goudier,' the man said in accented English. 'This is my wife Joelle. And you are . . .?'

'Hope, Ben Hope. I'm sorry to interrupt your coffee,' Ben said, switching to French. In the amazed silence, he motioned at the empty chair at their table. 'May I join you for a moment? This won't take long.'

'What won't take long?'

'I'd like to talk to you about yesterday,' Ben said. 'A few questions, and I'll leave you in peace.'

The Goudiers both stared, too taken aback to say no as he pulled out the empty chair and sat down. 'You're not from the police,' Joelle Goudier said. She had perfect teeth and smelled of Chanel.

'No, I'm the man you witnessed trying to stop the attack.'

'I see you were hurt,' Bernard Goudier said, glancing at Ben's cut.

'I'll survive. But as you might have noticed, I didn't get to see all that happened. I'm just trying to flesh out the picture.'

The Belgian gave a dry smile. 'Is it normal in Ireland for civilians to conduct their own inquiry?'

'It's not normal for a young woman to be murdered on this beach, either. You're the only witnesses. Please. Is there anything else you can remember about the incident?'

'We told the police everything,' said Joelle Goudier. 'Bernard and I had spent the afternoon walking and we were returning towards the guesthouse when we heard an engine revving loudly, and turned to see a big, black car—'

'A Range Rover V6 Sport,' her husband filled in for her.

'—veer off the road and drive very fast towards the beach. We soon realised who they were chasing. The poor woman began to run as they got out of the car and chased her. She dropped the bag she was carrying, and one of the attackers picked it up. For a moment I thought that would be the end, that they would leave her alone now that they had stolen from her. But no, they continued chasing her. Then we saw you come to help her. You were very brave, Monsieur.'

'I have an interest in birdwatching,' Bernard Goudier explained, 'and I'd been hoping to get a close sighting of a sandwich tern that afternoon, as they're around at this time of year. I use excellent binoculars, Zeiss Victory HT ten-by-fifties, which is why, even though the sun was setting, I had a very good view of the man who took out the knife.'

'Was it the one in the green hooded top, or the one in the navy jacket?' Ben asked.

'Jacket. I thought he looked like a soldier. And it was a military-issue knife.'

Ben looked at him. 'May I ask how you would know that?'

'It happens that another of my interests is collecting militaria,' Goudier said. 'Insignia, medals, also items such as bayonets and knives. The weapon used was a United States Marine Corps fighting and utility knife. Seven-inch blackened blade, clip point, leather handle.'

'A Ka-Bar,' Ben said, and the Belgian nodded. 'You told the police these details?' Ben asked him.

'Naturally,' Goudier said. 'Anyhow, when the man produced the weapon, the woman was in extreme terror and tried to get away from him. That was when she disappeared out of my sight, behind a large rock. The man in the navy jacket stepped after her with the knife in his hand. He seemed very calm, deliberate. I soon lost sight of him too, but I could see the other man, the one in green, watching. I knew what was happening. It was sickening. The man was smiling.'

'Smiling,' Ben said, his fists tightening.

'As if he was enjoying the spectacle of the woman being butchered. As if it was just an amusing game for them. And I could do nothing but watch. I was so shocked that I was simply paralysed for several moments.'

Goudier looked as if he could spit into his coffee. 'Then the man in the navy jacket reappeared. He still looked very calm, like someone who does this every day. He began to walk towards where you were lying unconscious, and I knew that his intention was to kill you too, in cold blood. That was when I regained my wits. I had to do something, so I started running towards them, waving my arms like a lunatic and shouting at the top of my voice. The men saw me and ran back to their car.'

'Then I have you to thank for saving my life,' Ben said. 'But you risked your own. You might have regretted it.'

'What I regret is that I didn't act sooner,' Goudier said. 'I won't ever forget the look on that poor girl's face.'

Joelle Goudier reached across and clutched her husband's hand. 'Then we called the police,' she said. 'But of course it was too late. What a terrible, horrible thing to happen.'

'And I apologise to you both for making you relive it,' Ben said, getting up.

'Can we buy you a drink, Monsieur Hope?' Bernard Goudier asked.

'No, thanks. Have a safe journey home.'

Chapter Twelve

As Ben walked back along the beach, the wind blew more dark clouds in from the sea and the gusting curtains of rain soaked him to the core. He didn't try to hurry out of the weather. He was too busy thinking about the knife.

Bernard Goudier seemed to be a man who paid attention to details. The exact type of Range Rover. The precise model and magnification of Zeiss optics. Maybe he was a little anal-retentive. But maybe that wasn't always a bad thing. In this case, it meant Ben could be fairly certain the Belgian was being accurate when he'd said that the killing tool had been a USMC Ka-Bar.

Which might possibly be a significant detail. It was a weapon Ben had come across many times, and personally used on several occasions to do things he didn't really want to remember. Light and handy at just over a pound in weight, with a murderous seven-inch Bowie-style blade and grippy handle made of stacked, hard-lacquered leather washers, the American-made knife had been in military service since World War II. Along with the British Fairbairn-Sykes commando dagger, it was one of the most famous and recognisable pieces of edged weaponry of all time, used in every modern American war from Vietnam to Iraq.

Assuming that Detective Inspector Healy had the wits to

understand what Goudier had told him, the cop was most likely supposing that a type of weapon so easily available from a thousand mail-order outfits to anybody over eighteen wasn't a key indicator in this case. Ben could see two problems with that:

One, Healy's stamping ground was a place with the lowest violent crime rate in the whole of the British Isles.

Two, the guy was an idiot.

An *inexperienced* idiot, who'd probably never dealt with a single stabbing before and wouldn't stop to think that the vast majority of knives used in crime were kitchen knives. Ubiquitous, cheap to obtain, not a big deal to throw away after the dirty was done.

The Ka-Bar, on the other hand, was an expensive and sought-after specialist tool. Which instantly set this case apart. No low-end thug would contemplate kitting themselves out with such a high-end item to butcher somebody, only to have to chuck it away afterwards. But a trained killer, someone used to handling such weapons and proficient in their use . . . that person might.

Ben was building a profile in his mind. A profile of two men who'd done this kind of work before and knew the kind of gear that suited them for the job. Men who had no problem taking the risk of carrying a piece of concealed military hardware about with them in public. Who'd come through an extensive and rigorous training, possibly several years long over the course of a military career – and not at the spit-and-polish, square-bashing level of a simple squaddie either. Which meant that, in the darker corners of the civilian world where they could find employment, their deadly skills wouldn't come cheap.

No matter how much they enjoyed using them.

Now the question was where the money came from, and

why. Who was financing these guys? Someone with contacts and resources, who also had some reason to feel threatened by whatever it was that Kristen Hall had dug up in the course of her research travels in Ireland. The wrong kind of knowledge had killed more people than bullets. There was no question in Ben's mind that Kristen had been one of that kind of casualty.

Knowledge of what? Find the answer, reveal the motive. Find the motive, and the money trail would lead right back to source.

Only one problem there. Ben had nothing to go on.

By the time he reached the cottage, he was drenched and his head had begun to ache badly again now that the last dose of painkillers he'd taken at the hospital was wearing off. He felt suddenly weak, almost despairing. Something had to take the edge off. Something.

The whisky bottle and tumbler stood on the dresser where he'd left them yesterday evening. Before he'd even thought about drying himself off and getting out of his damp clothes, he impulsively made a beeline for the booze. The bottle was empty, but there was still a couple of inches in the tumbler.

He reached out to snatch it up – then stopped as the realisation hit him, full force, that this was the same glass of whisky he'd been about to gulp down at the very moment Kristen was being attacked. He drew his hand back and stood for a moment staring at the tumbler.

What the hell are you doing?

He reached out again, picked the glass up together with the empty bottle and marched into the kitchen. He tossed the bottle in the recycling bin, then resolutely poured the contents of the glass down the sink. Then he marched back into the other room, grabbed the box containing the rest of

81

his whisky stash and carried it, jinking and clinking, to the kitchen sink. He dumped it heavily on the draining board. Thrust his hand inside the box and yanked out the first bottle by the neck, like a chicken about to be placed on the block for slaughter. For an instant of terrible weakness, he gazed at the familiar label and the warm caramel-hued liquid inside the clear glass. He sighed, then ripped open the foil, plucked out the cork and upended the bottle over the sink.

Seven bottles, over one gallon of ten-year-old cask-strength Islay single malt. By the time the last of it had washed down the plughole, Ben's eyes and nose were full of the fumes and the small kitchen reeked like a distillery.

'There,' he said fiercely.

The afternoon rain was falling steadily outside, streaming down the windows. His head was aching worse. But he didn't care. He kicked off his shoes and went digging in his luggage for the pair of trainers he remembered having packed but hadn't worn in weeks. The moment he'd finished lacing them up, he launched himself out of the cottage door and into the rain.

Once upon a time, he'd run this beach every day. End to end, taking in the whole curve of shingle from beyond his former home all around the headland, there was a five-mile stretch that had been his regular morning exercise, to which he'd added the punishing regimen of press-ups, sit-ups and crunches that had kept him at peak fitness. He could spend hours at it without getting out of breath. Damned if he wasn't going to prove to himself he could get back into that condition again.

The pain and breathlessness were already on him after the first mile, but he just gritted his teeth and kept on through the rain, letting his anger and remorse push him harder. His feet pounded over the rocks, every step jarring his aching head. His muscles screamed. His lungs felt raw as he gasped in as much rainwater as air. On and on, willing himself to keep moving by reciting inside his head the motivational lines from the James Elroy Flecker poem, *The Golden Road to Samarkand*, that had for many years been an unofficial motto of his old regiment and were inscribed on the clock tower at the SAS headquarters in Hereford:

> *We are the pilgrims, master; we shall go*
> *Always a little further: it may be*
> *Beyond the last blue mountain barred with snow,*
> *Across that angry or that glimmering sea.*

When he eventually staggered back inside the cottage, he could barely stand. He left a wet trail across the varnished living room floorboards before collapsing in an armchair near the dresser. His legs and calves were inflamed beyond pain. Groaning, he lifted his right leg to rest his ankle on his other knee, unlaced his wet, dirty trainer, peeled it off along with the wet sock and flung it carelessly across the room. He let his bare right foot flop down to the floor like a dead piece of meat, then went to remove his left shoe.

As the sole of his bare left foot slapped heavily to the floorboards, a lancing pain jolted all up his leg. He winced loudly and bent down to inspect the sole of his foot, then swore as he saw the thin, triangular shard of glass stuck into the flesh. He grasped the shard between finger and thumb and plucked it out. A trickle of blood ran down his foot and dripped to the floor. The cut wasn't bad, but now he was even more annoyed with himself that he couldn't manage to sweep up a bit of broken glass without leaving half of it lying about.

Cursing, he got down on his hands and knees to search

for more fragments that might have found their way under the armchair, an accident waiting to happen. He grabbed the bottom edge of the armchair's frame and tipped it up a few inches to reveal a dusty square patch on the floorboards. There were no more shards of broken glass under there.

But there was something else.

He reached underneath the armchair and retrieved it.

It was a black leather pouch. And it wasn't his.

Chapter Thirteen

Ben sat back on the floor and inspected the pouch with a growing frown on his face, trying to think how it had got there. So much had happened since, but now he remembered how Kristen's bag had been hanging over the back of the wooden chair to dry out. When, a little tipsy from the Laphroaig, she'd upset the chair and the bag had dropped to the floor, the pouch must have spilled out along with the other items. He could only guess that when she'd stumbled and reached out for his arm to stop herself from falling, it'd been accidentally kicked out of sight under the armchair. He'd picked up the fallen chair, her fleece and her bag. She'd stooped down to snatch up her personal items. Neither of them had noticed the pouch still lying there.

He wondered whether she'd missed it on her way back towards the guesthouse. Had that been why she'd been running towards the cottage as the men chased her?

The pouch was about four inches by five, soft black lambskin with a larger main compartment and a smaller zippered pocket on its front. He already knew what she kept inside. He hesitated a moment, thinking that perhaps he ought to turn this stuff over to the police as possible evidence.

The idea didn't linger long in his mind. Opening up the main compartment, he found her notebook. He flicked quickly through it and saw pages of notes, names of places

85

she'd visited on her travels about Ireland during her stay. Laying the notebook aside for the moment, he unzipped the front pocket. There were her two phones, a well-worn BlackBerry and a much less expensive Samsung pay-as-you-go type of device that still had the protective plastic over the screen and the glossy look of a recent purchase.

Ben thought hard, casting his mind back to when he'd first met Kristen and had been walking along the beach. She'd taken the leather pouch from her bag, removed one of the two phones and checked it for messages, and then seemed frustrated when there hadn't been any. She'd said she'd been hoping to hear back from someone, and that it was something to do with her research. He remembered how she'd seemed a touch anxious, not wanting to say too much about it.

At the time, it had meant nothing. Now, just maybe, it meant a great deal.

Which phone had she been using? He gazed at the two side by side, and his memory told him it had been the cheap Samsung. He turned it on. The first thing to check was her list of contacts, as an important caller might be among them. But the contact list was empty: either all entries had been deleted, or there had been none to begin with. He pressed the 'back' key and then, following a hunch, went into the SMS messages menu.

He wasn't surprised to find nothing other than a 'welcome, new user' message from the service provider, dated three days earlier. As he'd suspected, this was a brand-new phone, barely used and so fresh from the box that Kristen might even have bought it here in Ireland, in the middle of her research trip.

Why had she felt the need for a second phone? he wondered. Could it have anything to do with the discovery she'd claimed to have made 'a few days ago'? Ben pondered the possibility and its implications.

Leaving the messages menu, he checked her call history. As expected, she hadn't used the phone a great deal. In fact she'd made exactly three calls with it, all on the same day as the received text from the service provider, which was to say the day she'd bought it. The first call had been to an overseas landline number, with the international prefix for the USA. Kristen had called it at 3.04 p.m., local time, speaking for just a few seconds. The second call had been made less than ten minutes later, at 3.12. It was to another landline, this time in London, and had lasted seven minutes.

Some time later, at 5.22 p.m., she'd made her third and final call, this time to a mobile number, again in the USA. It was the longest in duration, at thirteen minutes. There was a growing American connection here – but what did it signify? If indeed it meant anything at all, he thought.

Checking the received calls, Ben found just one. It had come in at 5.18 p.m. the same day as the others, and it was from the same London number she'd dialled a little over two hours earlier. Whoever had called her obviously hadn't had much to say, keeping her on the line for less than two minutes. Almost immediately afterwards, she'd called that US mobile number. No traffic either way since.

Ben returned to the landline call Kristen had made to America, pressed 'options' and called the number again while glancing at his watch. It was after three here, morning there. A woman's voice came on the line. 'Tulsa City Hall. Mayor's office. May I help you?' She spoke with a nice southern twang.

Mayor's office? Surprised, Ben had to think fast. Morning, this is Ronnie Galloway in London. I'm following up the call to your office from my colleague, Kristen Hall, three days ago.'

'Uh-huh. What's it regarding?' the woman asked curtly.

'I'd need to speak to the mayor about that,' Ben said.

'And you work for . . .?'

'Marshall Kite Enterprises,' Ben replied. Marshall Kite was Brooke's investment banker brother-in-law. Ben had no compunction about using his name. Sensing the woman's reticence, he pressed on in a brisk tone. 'Listen, we have an issue here that I need to get cleared up as a matter of priority. Can I confirm that my colleague Ms Hall contacted your office three days ago?'

His bluff threw her a little. 'Uh, hold on, let me check.' Pause. 'Uh, yes, I'm showing a call from a Kristen Hall for the mayor on that date. But—'

'Did she speak to the mayor personally?' Ben asked, interrupting.

'No, he wasn't available. Can I ask—'

'She didn't say what she wanted to talk to him about, did she?' Ben said, cutting her short again. This conversation was getting crazier by the second, but he had nothing to lose by pushing.

'Who is this?' the receptionist snapped.

And with that, Ben knew he'd got all he could out of her. 'Thanks. Have a nice day,' he said, and ended the call.

What the hell was Kristen doing calling the mayor of Tulsa? Ben racked his brains pointlessly for a few moments, then moved quickly on to the next number on his list, the call she'd made to London. There was no reply, and no answering service, so he immediately followed up by trying the American mobile she'd called.

Another dead end. Whoever it belonged to had it switched off.

Ben turned to Kristen's other phone. As he'd suspected from its appearance, the BlackBerry had had a lot more use and was crammed with numbers, many of them personal calls to her parents and the other friends and family members

88

in her busy address book. He couldn't find anything of interest connected to her work, and after a few minutes was beginning to feel bad for snooping into the dead woman's personal business.

He slipped both phones into his pocket.

With his options running low, Ben examined the notebook. On closer inspection, it was a composite of a notebook and a diary, with enough space for a few notes on any given daily entry. Kristen had been one of those researchers who liked to keep records of where she'd been and who she'd met along the way. But while her mind was tidy, her handwriting was anything but. Flipping through to August, Ben quickly found the section of pages devoted to her most recent Irish research trip, and spent a while deciphering them. She'd done a few miles in the last couple of weeks, and her scribbled notes mentioned locations she'd visited all around rural Ireland. Among them were the ruins of the old Stamford mansion, and several villages in its vicinity that had once belonged to the sprawling Glenfell Estate. One of her notes read:

Spoke to Father Flanagan, St Malachy's church
Looked at records NOT ONLINE
PADRAIG BORN 1809
→107!!!! HOW POSSIBLE?????

The names, dates and numbers meant nothing to Ben, but now it seemed to him as if he needed to get out and cover a few miles himself, retracing her steps.

Only then might he begin to find out what the hell was going on.

He closed the notebook, sprang to his feet and went to grab the BMW keys. It felt good to get moving.

Chapter Fourteen

Oklahoma

Before nine a.m., and already the sun was burning the concrete outside. Even in the relative coolness of the lock-up garage, the air was stifling.

Erin carefully shut the trunk of the old car, locked it and pulled the tarpaulin back down over the smooth, waxed bodywork. *Always have a backup*, her daddy's voice echoed once more in her head.

She stepped away from the covered car, moving quietly in the shadows as if her every move was being watched and listened to by unseen eyes and ears. After two days of hiding, she was jumpy as hell. But now, at least, she'd made a decision. It was the right thing to do. The only thing.

A strip of sunlight shone from the gap beneath the garage's steel rolldown shutter door. Erin dropped to her knees and slid out under it, blinking in the strong light. She peered left and right with her hand shielding her eyes, to make sure nobody was following her. The weed-strewn, graffiti-walled yard between the rows of lock-ups was deserted.

So far, so good. Her spirits brightened at the thought that the killers might not even have the slightest idea that there was a witness to their actions on Friday night. If that was the case, then they were about to find out. The hard way.

She hurried away from the lock-ups and towards the street, where the taxicab was waiting for her with the meter running. 'Where to now, missy?' the driver wanted to know.

'Downtown,' she said. 'Police Department Headquarters.'

'It's a done thing,' the driver said, and took off as she shut herself in the back. Erin leaned against the seat and closed her eyes, thinking about what she was going to say, about the DVD and phone in her backpack. And about Angela's husband.

At the downtown police building, she walked up to the main desk and cleared her throat to get the attention of the grizzled duty sergeant. He looked up at her, unsmiling. He was in a dark blue shirt with short sleeves and the shield that bore the cityscape logo with the legend 'TULSA POLICE'.

'My name is Erin Hayes,' she said. 'I want to speak to a detective. The most senior one you've got. And right away.'

Whether it was the look in her eye or the tone of her voice, something appeared to make the cops take her seriously. Within five minutes she was met in the reception lobby by a tired-eyed though pleasant-looking plainclothes officer about the same age as her, who introduced himself as Detective Topher Morrell and led her to a small office away from the hubbub. He waved her to a chair, where she sat clutching her backpack on her lap, and perched himself on the corner of a desk with one leg dangling casually, as if he didn't expect this interruption to last more than a minute or two before he could return to the many more pressing matters littering his desk. 'Now, uh, Miss—'

'Hayes. Erin Hayes.'

'Right. You told the duty officer this was serious.'

'I doubt you'll get anything more serious come in this week,' she said.

'Then talk to me.'

'I'll need to start from the beginning, okay?' she said, and Morrell frowned as if stabbed by an internal pain. 'I work for the Desert Rose Trust,' she went on determinedly. 'We're a charitable organisation that provides resources to help the underprivileged young Catholics of Oklahoma to get an education.'

'Yeah, I know what the Desert Rose Trust is,' Morrell said, bored already, and flicked a downward glance at his watch.

'Then you'll know who its director is,' Erin said.

'Uh-huh. Sure. Everyone in Tulsa knows that.'

'I'm her personal assistant. I answer directly to her. It's a rewarding job, but I have a lot of responsibility and it gets stressful sometimes.'

Get in line, Morrell's expression was saying.

'My boss and her husband own a cabin out on the east shore of Oologah Lake,' Erin went on. 'Three days ago . . .'

He listened as she went on with her story. It wasn't long before his look of boredom vanished completely. He wasn't looking at his watch any more. The leg stopped swinging. He shifted into a more alert posture, watching her intently and the crease in his brow deepening. He looked as if he was having trouble keeping his jaw from gaping open. By the time she'd told the whole story, he was off the desk and pacing the room in agitation. 'You're sure?' he kept asking her.

'If you don't believe me, watch the video,' she said, placing a hand on the backpack. 'It's all here. Everything I just told you.'

Morrell stared at her for several intense seconds, then held up a hand. 'Wait here and don't move. I'll be right

92

back.' He strode hurriedly out of the room, shutting the door hard behind him.

Erin waited in the empty room for a couple of minutes before the door burst open again. She looked up to see a large, square-shouldered man enter the room, with Morrell in his wake. He was several inches taller than the detective, and twenty years older, with thinning silver hair and a severe, granite face. His cheeks were flushed red with broken veins and his nose looked as if it had been broken at least twice in his life. He wore no jacket. A large black revolver hung heavily from the tan leather shoulder holster strapped over his shirt. Old-time cop, old-time six-gun. His sleeves were rolled up to expose the thick, gnarled forearms of a lumberjack. He planted himself in front of Erin and scrutinised her coldly.

'I'm Chief O'Rourke,' he said in a gravelly voice. 'I want you to repeat to me what you just told Detective Morrell here.'

Feeling small in her chair, Erin peered up at his intimidating bulk. 'You want me to start over from the beginning?'

'Just from where your employer said you could use the cabin on Oologah Lake. Why was that?'

'Why did she let me use it?' Erin shrugged. 'Because she's a nice person and we get along, I guess.'

'Heart-warming. Keep going.'

'I'd been complaining about feeling tired, and she said I could use it to get away for a weekend, unwind. She said the place would be empty, her husband was away in Boston on business, their son Sean was canoeing in Canada with friends and their daughter Amy was in Paris studying at this fancy cookery school. When I said my car was having problems, she offered for the family driver, Joe, to take me there in the Cadillac. So off I went, all happy with myself, looking forward to doing some running. I already told all this to Detective Morrell.'

'Running?' O'Rourke asked, as if this gave him grounds for deep suspicion.

'Came fourth in the Tulsa city marathon last year, and I'm meaning to better that this November, to help raise funds for the Desert Rose Trust. But that's not what you want to hear, is it?'

'No, I want to hear what happened next, every detail.'

'What happened next was I hung around there all evening, didn't do a lot, went to bed. I woke up hearing voices. I snuck out of bed, thinking it was intruders. I had my handgun with me and—'

'You have a carry permit for that?' Chief O'Rourke interrupted.

Erin frowned. 'Is this about them or about me?' she wanted to snap at him. She kept her voice level and asked instead, 'You want to see it?'

'Later. Go on.'

'But it wasn't intruders. They'd let themselves in the door with a key, and a few moments later I realised why. Angela's husband wasn't in Boston, he was there using the place to entertain a bunch of business associates. Or so I thought. One of them was a man with a beard. Caucasian, dark hair, forties.'

'The victim,' Morrell explained.

'You didn't get a name?' O'Rourke asked Erin without glancing back at his colleague.

'I never heard it mentioned. There wasn't exactly a lot of conversation going on from the point I joined the party, you know? Then soon afterwards, an argument broke out. They grabbed hold of this bearded man and threw him on the floor and—'

'Hold on,' O'Rourke cut in. '*They?*'

'The two goons. I don't know what you'd call them. Heavies. Henchmen. They started beating the crap out of the guy with batons, like the ones that cops and security guards use. Then he ordered them to take him outside.'

'*He?*' O'Rourke cut in again.

Erin nodded. 'Yes, *he*. Angela's husband. He said, "Not here", like he didn't want blood on the rug or something. So these two thugs, they got hold of the bearded man and kind of dragged him out the door to the veranda. That's where they shot him.'

'How many shots were fired?' O'Rourke asked.

'I can't say for sure. Three, four. They didn't kill him at first. It was like they were playing with him. Torturing him, just for the fun of it. *He* was watching the whole time. Then he took out a gun. It was a big old revolver, like that one.' Erin pointed at the weapon in O'Rourke's shoulder holster. 'Maybe a forty-four. Except it was bright, not blued. Stainless steel or nickel, I can't say for sure.'

'Know your hardware, Miss Hayes,' O'Rourke said, looking at her penetratingly, and so intently that his pale grey eyes never seemed to blink.

'My daddy taught me to shoot,' she replied.

'You like your weaponry, huh?'

Erin looked at him. What was O'Rourke doing, trying to paint her up as a gun nut? 'I'm a woman in the modern world,' she said. 'One who'd rather not wind up a victim.'

'All right, all right,' O'Rourke said, waving his hand impatiently. 'Save it. What happened next?'

'Next? He aimed it at the guy and fired.'

O'Rourke gravely pursed his lips. 'You're saying he personally shot the guy. Pulled the trigger himself. Deliberately.'

'It couldn't have been more deliberate,' Erin said. 'He shot the guy right in the back of the head from just a couple of feet away. Then he ordered the other two guys to take the body away, cut it up and get rid of it.'

'Cut it up? He said that?'

She thought for a moment. 'You know what, he might have said "chop his ass up". If you want an exact quote.'

O'Rourke caught the pointed tone of her words and gave a snort. 'Okay. And how did he sound when he was instructing them to do that?'

'He sounded just like himself.'

'Sober?'

'Stone cold.'

'Calm and rational?'

'Like he did it every day,' Erin said. 'The way you'd ask the help to carry out the trash.'

'So you're saying he was in charge of this whole deal.'

Erin understood that O'Rourke was being extremely careful to confirm every detail of her story. Under the circumstances, she'd have done the same. But did he believe her? She tried to read his expression and could see only a severe glower. She nodded vehemently. 'Absolutely. The whole time. Everything that happened, happened because he ordered it. No question.'

'And you'd testify to that?'

'So would the video,' she replied. 'It'll prove everything I just told you.'

O'Rourke exhaled noisily through his nose. Stepped away from Erin and exchanged a quick glance with Morrell. 'And you haven't told anyone else about this?' he asked her after a moment's heavy silence.

'Nobody, not even my boss. I just spent the last two days hiding in a goddamn motel room wondering whether to call her. I decided against it. Now I'm here.'

'You understand the seriousness of this allegation, Miss Hayes?' O'Rourke said.

'Look, I'm not an idiot,' Erin replied, fighting to contain her frustration. 'I know what it means. I know how bad it sounds and what the implications are for this whole city. But I also know what I saw. The man I witnessed ordering the beating and shooting of this other man, and then blowing the guy's brains out himself, personally, of his own volition and free will or whatever the hell the law calls it, is the husband of my boss, Angela McCrory.'

The cops were silent, staring.

Erin said, 'He's Finn McCrory, the mayor of Tulsa.'

Chapter Fifteen

Ben's first glimpse of the derelict mansion was the craggy remnants of its east wing that appeared over the brow of the hill as he approached along the lonely country road. The mid-afternoon sun was bright and hot now that the rain had passed over, and he drove fast with the windows open, catching the scent of heather and the distant salt tang of the sea. As the car sped over the top of the hill and began the winding descent towards Glenfell House, the full extent of the place's ruined state came into view.

He had driven by this lonely spot once or twice before, during the time he'd lived in Ireland. And he'd heard the age-old legends from the leathery, salty grey-bearded old men who hunched over whiskies and pints of the black stuff in the back rooms of pubs, fixing their glittering eye like Coleridge's ancient mariner on anyone who'd listen, and not leaving much choice to those who wouldn't.

From one generation to the next, nobody had ever known for sure who'd really started the fire of September 1851 that had gutted the west wing and brought down part of the roof: the most enduring tale was that it had been Lord Edgar Stamford himself, gone mad and intent on burning the place to the ground and himself with it.

If that was true, then the suicidal part of his plan had

succeeded, even if Stamford hadn't been much of an arsonist and the fire had burnt itself out before it could claim the whole house. According to the more colourful legends, all that had remained of the burly six-foot-six hulk of the much-disliked lord was a half-roasted corpse identifiable only by the gold family ring on one blackened, claw-like hand and the engraved pocket watch they'd found in a charred waistcoat pocket. So the story went, the reason that nothing had ever been done to save the gutted mansion from falling into total ruin was the legacy of its association with Stamford's harsh and despotic rule over the peasant tenants who'd worked his land, and died on it like flies during the Great Famine of '47. Memories like that would take another five hundred years to die.

Glenfell House itself was dying much faster, as Ben was reminded when he rolled the BMW up outside and got out to wander about the grounds. Over a hundred and sixty years of decay had reduced the place to a melancholy shell. It was common knowledge locally that much of its crumbling stonework and more than a few roofing slates had found their way into the construction of a good many of the county's farmhouses, cottages and outbuildings during the twentieth century. The endlessly cycling seasons had done the rest. Autumn and spring rains had rotted the timbers to black stumps, winter frosts had driven deep cracks into the stone floors, from which the summer sun had coaxed thick growths of nettles and brambles that encircled the ruins like barbed wire. They hadn't kept everyone out, though, judging by the empty spirits bottles and beer cans rolling in the dirt and the remnants of a fire. What the roofless mansion lacked in shelter for the vagrants who loitered here, it made up for in privacy. Nobody else ever came near the place any more.

Ben wandered about the desolate site for a few more

minutes, kicking a can around in the dust and thinking about Kristen's notebook in his pocket. Then he walked back to the car, fired up the engine and spun it around in the opposite direction, heading for the small market town of Glenfell, two miles west.

Back in the heyday of Lord Stamford's little empire, the town had been surrounded by a plethora of even tinier hamlets and primitive rack-rent smallholdings, now mostly swallowed up by its expanding outskirts. To say it had been a poor area back then was no understatement. Among its older greystone buildings was the former workhouse, where during the famine years forty or more orphaned children a week died from malnutrition or disease, the living and the dead often hard to tell apart and lying together in the same beds for days at a time. Ben had heard all the stories, unforgotten scars on the history of this and so many other towns and villages across Ireland.

As if to symbolise happier times, the grim old stone workhouse had long ago been turned into a thriving country store where farmers' pickup trucks came and went, and its yard was now a car park where Ben left the BMW as he went off in search of St Malachy's church. On his way there, he passed the town's famine memorial, a marble slab that had been erected nearly a hundred and twenty years after the tragedy it commemorated. Ben paused to gaze at it, then walked on.

It was just after five as he entered the coolness of the church. It wasn't big, and it wasn't especially pretty either, but there was a still, echoey serenity to the place that Ben found familiar and comforting. He tried to remember the last time he'd been inside a church, and realised how long it had been: a painful little reminder of how lapsed a Christian he was. But he could at least console himself, from a glance at the empty pews, that he wasn't the only one around here who'd been neglecting God.

The sound of his footsteps drifted up to the high ceiling as he paced slowly around, pausing for a moment to look at the plaque on one wall dedicated to the 8,348 men, women and children whose skeletons had been unearthed from the mass famine grave discovered outside Glenfell in 1922.

Walking away from the plaque, he went over to sit in a pew facing the altar, bowed his head and tried to summon up devout thoughts. None in particular came to him, so he just said the words that were in his heart.

'Here we go again, Lord. It's been a while, I realise that. I don't try and talk to you as often as I should. Maybe that's why you keep putting trouble in my path, when all I ever wanted was a life of peace. I don't know why else you would. I only know I didn't ask for this. So please don't judge me for the things I have to do, and please give me the strength I need to do them well. That's all I can ask of you now.'

He broke off as he heard the sound of footsteps behind him, and glanced round to see the priest walking in. He was old and stooped, with a kindly smile appearing as he saw Ben sitting there. As if not wanting to disturb one of the faithful at their prayer, he began to turn away.

'Father Flanagan?' Ben said, getting up.

The old priest paused in his step and looked at Ben, still smiling. 'I'm Father Flanagan. I didn't wish to interrupt you. That sounded like a very heartfelt prayer.'

'I've been saying it a long time,' Ben said. 'I sometimes don't think he listens.'

'He always listens,' the priest said, putting his hand on Ben's arm.

'In any case, it's you I came to talk to,' Ben said. 'If you have a moment.'

'Of course. How may I help you?'

Ben couldn't bring himself to give a false name this time, but his piety didn't extend to telling the whole truth, or much of it at all. He told the priest that he worked for a research foundation that was doing a project on the history of the Great Famine, and was taking over from his colleague who'd suddenly been taken ill.

'She was here a few days ago and I'm trying to pick up the pieces. I think you saw her, spoke to her?'

The priest took in Ben's description of Kristen, and nodded. 'Yes, she was asking to see the old parish registers. Struck me as a very meticulous young lady. Asked me if the records were accurate. I replied, as far as I know they are. Why shouldn't they be? But, oh dear, did you say she'd fallen ill? Nothing too serious, I hope.'

'Pretty serious, I'm afraid,' Ben said.

'What a pity. What a terrible pity. Such a sweet child. So what is it I can do for you, Mr . . . Hope, was it?'

'If it's not imposing, father, perhaps if I could view the same records she did, it might help me make sense of her notes. I'd ask her myself, but . . .'

'I understand, of course. Dear me, what a shame. Imposition? Not at all, not at all. Come with me, my son.'

Leading him around a crunchy gravel path to the back of the church, Father Flanagan took a large iron key from his pocket, unlocked a peeling old door and showed Ben into an office that was like taking a step back into history. The place looked as if it had been gathering dust since about 1750, and it probably had. A powerful odour of damp hung in the air.

'This is where all the old records are still kept,' the priest said with a regretful look, waving an arm at stacks of ancient, yellowed registers on sagging shelves. 'Births, deaths, marriages, even emigration records dating back to the century before last. Nowadays a lot of parish records are going online, but I'm afraid that'll be my successor's job. I'm not one for all this new technology. Don't even have a television, can you believe that?' He gave a sad, wizened smile, then seemed to catch his mind wandering and snapped himself back to the present. 'Now then, the records. I can barely remember the last time anybody wanted to look at them. Now I get two come along in a week. Such are the mysteries of life. What was it you were after?'

'The information my colleague left me was pretty incomplete,' Ben said. 'She was interested in the life history of a particular member of the parish here.'

'I do remember her saying so,' Father Flanagan said, scratching his white head. 'But sure, for the life of me, I can't recall the details. What was this person's year of birth?'

'1809,' Ben said.

'Hmm. That *is* a long way back. If it's here, you may have to dig for it. What was the name?'

'Padraig someone,' Ben said.

Father Flanagan looked at him. 'That's all you have, Padraig someone who was born in 1809? My son, have you *any* idea how many Padraigs have lived in this parish over the centuries? You're talking to one of them.' He shrugged. 'Anyhow. All yours, and good luck. Take as long as you need, and bring me back the key when you're done.'

'Thanks, father.'

'Oh, just to make life even more interesting for you, you'll find some of the records were written in Latin. One day someone will organise it all, but it'll be a nightmare, God help them.'

Left alone in the cramped office, Ben began searching through the old records. If Kristen had been here just two days ago, he shouldn't have to dig too deep to find what he was looking for. He ran his eye along the disorganised stacks until he spotted it sitting right at the top of one of the piles: parish birth records from January 1805 to December 1809. Lifting it down, he saw the fingermarks that Kristen had made in the dust, and had to fight back another vision of her lying dead, covered in blood.

Laying the register down on the tiny table in the corner of the office, he flipped pages and more dust clouded the air. The entries were all done in the beautifully calligraphed handwriting of a bygone era. The ink was faded with age and scarcely legible in places, and mouse nibbles and mildew had taken their toll on some of the pages. Towards the back of the register, Ben found the birth records starting January 1809. All he knew about that month in history was that the British had defeated the French at the Battle of Corunna during the Peninsular War. Now he could see that while that had been going on, an awful lot of baby boys named Padraig were being born here in Glenfell and the surrounding villages. As he tracked on through the following months, flipping more pages and peering through the dust clouds at the ancient writing, he quickly lost count and realised Father Flanagan had been right. There were hundreds of Padraigs. Without a surname, he might as well give up.

Soon afterwards, he did.

'Did you find what you were looking for?' the priest asked when Ben found him in the church and gave him back the old key.

'I might have, if I knew what it was.'

'If it's the famine period you're interested in, you should visit the museum.'

'Museum?'

'Oh, it's not exactly on a grand scale. But the impact of

the Great Hunger upon this and every other rural community of Ireland cannot be overstated.'

'I'll do that. Thanks again for your help.' Ben shook his hand. He felt real warmth towards the old man.

'I hope your friend gets better,' Father Flanagan called after him as he walked away.

'That'll take more than a prayer, father,' Ben replied, but not loudly enough for the priest to hear him.

Chapter Sixteen

With no more clues to play with than he'd had when he arrived in Glenfell, Ben stepped inside the Famine Museum. It was as empty as the church, just one room that might have been a village post office or shop at one time. Exhibits and glass-fronted cabinets lined the walls.

Ben walked slowly around the room, pausing now and then to gaze and read. In one display unit, preserved in jars of clear fluid, sat a dismal assortment of rotted, lumpy-looking potatoes: victims of the *Phytophthora infestans* outbreak that had destroyed the food supply of millions of rural Irish and swept death and starvation wholesale across the country. As he walked on, he came to a gallery section featuring contemporary ink drawings and sketches of starving peasants mourning their lost loved ones. The sense of their misery was palpable, and even more so in a collection of early sepia-toned photographs depicting huddled, ragged people, of a level of poverty inconceivable to the modern western mind, sitting outside their tumbledown homes with the blighted fields in the background. Ben looked at their hollow faces and ghastly sunken eyes, and wondered how so many of these folks had ended up stacked like sandbags on the death carts that had routinely patrolled Ireland's roads during that dark era.

A slightly more recent and less grainy black-and-white photo hung, framed, nearby. It showed the grisly scene of the 1922 unearthing of the huge mass grave that was referred to on the memorial plaque in the church. Work-hardened, wiry men in flat caps and shirtsleeves leaned on their shovels to pose grimly inside the vast hole they'd dug out, while a solemn crowd of spectators clustered around the edge. The sombre picture was accompanied by various smaller close-up photographs of their discovery, the most poignant of which showed a child's skeleton, pathetically twisted as if it had died in agony.

In a little caption beneath the photographs, Ben read that the Glenfell mass grave had been just one of hundreds discovered across Ireland, together containing as many as 1.9 million bodies of the famine's victims. One famine grave at Skibbereen in west Cork alone had yielded up some 12,000 heaped corpses. Kristen hadn't exaggerated the numbers. And for all anybody knew, beneath the lush green land of southern Ireland were many more of the same forlorn caches waiting to be unearthed over the decades and centuries to come.

A display cabinet nearby showed another angle to those miserable years of starvation. In starchy, officious tones, a landlord's eviction notice informed some poor tenant farmer that he and his family were about to be turfed out into the arctic winter of 1847 for non-payment of rent: effectively a death sentence for poor souls already clinging desperately to what little life was left in them. Ben shook his head and felt angry for their plight.

On another stand were displayed a set of primitive, almost medieval hand tools once belonging to an Irish peasant labourer of the mid-nineteenth century. Ben noticed how the wooden shafts had been worn thin by his hands.

Wondering at the thought of the sweat and blood that must have seeped into the wood, he walked on to gaze at a scale model of one of the American sailing ships that had carried the thousands of refugees west from Ireland to the New World during the 1840s and the decades that followed. They'd been the lucky ones.

Less lucky, according to the blurb next to the model vessel, had been the Irish voyagers crammed below decks on board the British 'coffin ships', where conditions were brutally squalid, disease was rife and murder and rape were common occurrences. The only consolation for the many who died on the Atlantic crossing was that it was a slightly better death than they'd have faced back home.

As Father Flanagan had said, the museum was hardly on a grand scale, but it was effective at painting a deeply compelling picture of misery. Ben left the place feeling low with an indelible impression of the terrible suffering of all those starving millions of people. At the same time, he was racking his brains to understand what it could have been that Kristen had found in the course of her research, and what she'd been looking for in the records at St Malachy's church.

He walked as he thought, wandering down the winding main street of the little market town. He didn't know where he was heading or what he was looking for, other than illumination.

Then he stopped. Turned and did a double take. Retraced his steps a few yards back to the shop window he'd just passed. The sign above the door was old and chipped and said 'Murphy's Surplus'. In the window, behind a taped-on cardboard notice that read 'OPEN LAITE', was an untidy heap of pre-used army rucksacks and haversacks, everything from modern British army bergens to ancient American and West German issue kit from the fifties and sixties.

'I'll be damned,' Ben muttered aloud. Right in the middle of the window was a bag exactly like the one he'd carried with him for many years on adventures all over the world and finally lost, not so long ago, in a tsunami in Indonesia. It had been nasty and tatty, much repaired with coarse green thread, but he'd been attached to it and missed it.

He walked straight into the shop and smelled that old familiar smell of musty canvas, wax oil and slightly rancid ex-issue high-leg boots. Everything from folding shovels to tent poles to plastic imitation assault rifles dangled from the walls.

'Closing up,' grumbled the old guy behind the counter, who Ben presumed was Murphy. The bulldoggish look in his eye vanished as Ben fanned out a couple of twenty-euro notes in front of him.

'Let me take a look at that bag.'

On closer inspection, the bag had certainly seen a lot of action. And it was going to see some more before Ben was done with it. He let Murphy hang on to his forty euros and walked out of the shop feeling strangely more complete with his new acquisition over his shoulder. It was well after six now, and he was thirsty from the heat. A few doors down from the army store, a pub was gradually filling up with customers.

At the bar, Ben ran his eye along the row of upside-down bottles of Irish whisky, then along the line of beer taps.

'What'll it be?' the barman asked with a welcoming smile.

'Mineral water,' Ben said with an effort.

The barman looked disappointed. 'You want ice or lemon in that?'

'Just as it comes.'

He carried his drink outside into the beer garden, laid his new green bag on a vacant slatted wooden table and sat

109

on the weathered bench next to it to take in the last of the evening sun and think about what his next move should be. He was running out of options, and it wasn't a good feeling.

As he sat slowly sipping the water and containing his frustration, an argument brewing at another table across the beer garden kept breaking into his thoughts. He glanced across. It was a typical enough scenario. Two guys in their twenties were sitting with a couple of girls, and judging by the number of empty pint glasses on the table they'd been there for a while. One of the guys, a big steamed-up oaf with the neck and shoulders of an Angus bull, was doing all the loud talking. Whatever he was ranting about at the skinny blonde across the table from him, it was enough to make her shrink timidly away from him.

This was exactly the kind of bully boy Ben most disliked. *Leave it alone*, he thought, and turning back to his own business, he took out Kristen's phones. From the prepaid Samsung he redialled the London number on which he'd got no reply earlier. This time, after six rings, a man's voice answered: 'Chris Ingram.'

Ben turned his back slightly to the other tables, so as not to be overheard. 'Mr Ingram, I'm calling on behalf of Kristen Hall.'

The voice on the line sounded taken aback and suspicious. 'Uhhh . . . okay . . . what's it about?'

'You do know Kristen?' Ben asked him.

'Uhhh, yes. Yes, I know Kristen. Excuse me, who's—?'

'My name's Jarrett. Don Jarrett. I was a friend of Kristen's.'

'How'd you mean *was*?'

'She's dead,' Ben said, and sensed the man's shock. 'Don't hang up. This is not a prank call. Kristen was murdered yesterday in Galway. You mustn't have been watching the news, Chris. Go and see for yourself online.'

Ingram's reaction was enough to convince Ben that he was genuinely horrified by the news. 'Oh, my God. I can't believe it. I was talking to her just—'

'Just two days before, I know. What were you talking to her about?'

'Who did you say you were? Are you the police?'

'I'm just someone who cares what happened to her, Chris. And I care what happens to you, too, so don't hang up. You could be in danger, too.'

'What danger?' Ingram said, sounding alarmed.

'You and she talked twice on the phone the same day. She called you at 3.12 p.m., and you phoned back just over two hours later. You spoke for less than a minute, but I need to know what it was about. Talk to me, Chris. It could save your life.'

'She called me for information,' Ingram blurted out. His tone of alarm had turned to real fear now. 'I called her back to pass it on. I do . . . did . . . that for her sometimes. When she was researching stuff. That was all it was, I swear.'

'So you're in the information business?' Ben said. 'What kind of information?'

'She needed a number, that's all.'

'What number?'

'A mobile number.'

'In the US?'

'Yeah. Tulsa, Oklahoma.'

'You're doing well, Chris. Keep talking. Whose number?'

'I can't really divulge—'

'It's an easy question,' Ben said. 'Whose number?'

Ingram hesitated, then reluctantly said, 'Finn McCrory.'

'Who's Finn McCrory?'

'The mayor of Tulsa.'

The mayor of Tulsa again, Ben thought. 'She paid you to get his number? How much?'

'A grand,' Ingram said after another hesitation. 'I had to pull a couple of strings to get it. That puts the price up.'

'You're obviously an expert,' Ben said. 'Now tell me, Chris, why someone like Kristen Hall would pay someone like you a thousand quid for the personal mobile number of the mayor of Tulsa. Whatever she wanted with him, it must have been pretty important.'

'Look, she didn't say, all right? She never tells . . . never *told* me her reasons. No questions. That was our business relationship.' Ingram was breathing nervously. 'Jesus. Listen, I've said far too much already. I've got nothing more to say. I'm sorry about Kristen. She was a good client. Goodbye. Please don't call this number again.'

The moment Ingram hung up, Ben checked the phone's call history again and looked at the mobile number to which Kristen had made that final thirteen-minute call at 5.22 p.m. two days before her death. Oklahoma time was six hours behind. If Ingram was to be believed – and in Ben's experience, very frightened and shocked people more often than not told the truth – then Kristen's conversation that day had been with this McCrory.

Thirteen minutes?

You're Finn McCrory, the mayor of an important city. A busy man with a lot on his plate. Late one morning out of the blue, this British journalist calls you on your personal number. Why don't you tell her to take a hike and hang up, like any other high-ranking official would without a second thought? What've you got to talk about with this total stranger from another country that would keep you on the line for nearly quarter of an hour?

Wheels ground against wheels in Ben's mind. Stamford. Ireland. McCrory. Tulsa. He searched for a connection. Found none.

That was when his thoughts were interrupted once more by the dispute at the other table. He sighed. Turned slowly round to look. The big bully with the thick neck was even redder in the face and his voice had risen as he ranted on at his shrinking girlfriend. His beefy fists rested like a couple of pineapples on the table. 'Stupid bitch,' he was saying. 'Stupid useless fucking bitch. Someone needs to slap a bit of sense into you.' He lifted one balled fist from the table, clumsy from the beer.

Two things happened. First, his girlfriend flinched as if he was going to hit her. Second, with the back of his hand he accidentally swept his half-full pint glass off the table, along with the iPhone that had been lying next to it.

'Now look what you made me do,' he said, glaring down at the iPhone in the puddle of spilled beer. 'Pick that up. It better not be broken.'

'Pick it up yourself,' the girl retorted, finally talking back, and Ben thought, *Good for you.*

Bully boy's face flushed scarlet. He reached a big arm across the table, grabbed a fistful of her hair and twisted it, trying to force her off the bench. 'I said pick that up!'

The girl was yelping in pain. The other girl at the table started yelling at Bully boy to let her go. Her own boyfriend snapped, 'Shut your hole.' Bully boy grinned and twisted the girl's hair harder.

Ben took a sip of water. Then he quietly put down his glass, stood up and walked over to them.

'Enjoying yourself?' he said to Bully boy. He didn't wait for an answer. Instead he raised his right foot and brought it down on the fallen iPhone, dashing it to bits with his heel. Then he twisted his foot from side to side, grinding the remnants of the phone into the spilled beer and broken glass.

'You can let her go now,' he said. 'There's nothing to pick up any more.'

Bully boy stared up at Ben, still clutching the girl's hair. She was whimpering now. 'What the fuck did you do?' he growled at Ben.

'Ended your dispute,' Ben said, looking steadily back into the big guy's eyes. 'So now let her go. You're hurting her. I'm not going to tell you a third time.'

Other people in the beer garden were beginning to turn and stare. Kristen's BlackBerry suddenly started ringing on Ben's table. This wasn't a good time to take the call.

'I'll fucking cripple you, you bastard!' Bully boy shouted. Enraged, he untangled his beefy fingers from the girl's hair and hauled himself up to his feet. He was two inches taller than Ben. His friend got up with him. Hostile stares, balled fists. The usual routine. Too much beer, too much confidence.

Bully boy was used to hitting people, Ben could tell. Women, mostly. Then again, Ben had known a few women who could have kicked the guy's arse so hard he'd be wearing it as a hat. He'd just been lucky this far.

The big meaty fist clenched tight, like a rolled gammon joint. The fleshy elbow came up. The arm rotated back. The lips rolled away from the tombstone teeth. The chest puffed out, sucking in air for the one and only punch that would be required to crush this worm. All in slow motion, or that was how it seemed to Ben.

Then the wrecking-ball fist began to accelerate his way. Heading for the bridge of his nose. It was about as fast as Bully boy could move, but to Ben it was like catching a beach ball tossed to him by a child.

With barely a movement, he plucked it out of the air. Next, he twisted it in a direction it wasn't supposed to twist. There was an audible crackling of cartilage, quickly followed

114

by a shrill scream. Then Bully boy's face plunged downward as if it had been hooked up to a plummeting iron weight, and crashed into the top of the table. Not with enough force to shatter his nose and teeth, but plenty hard enough to make a very satisfying thud and leave stripe marks from the wooden slats across his features for a few weeks.

Ben held him there for a moment until he felt the fight go out of him. He let go. The fleshy mass slithered off the table to the ground.

The second guy gawked at his crumpled pal, then at Ben, then at his girlfriend, and then turned and ran away.

'You okay?' Ben said to the girl. She nodded timidly.

'You can do better than this moron,' Ben told her, pointing down at the groaning, blubbering heap. 'Same goes for your friend. Find a couple of decent guys, all right?'

More people were turning and staring, and a few had come out of the pub to check out the commotion. With a nod to the girls, Ben walked back to his table, picked up Kristen's phones, shouldered his bag and drank the last gulp of his mineral water. The crowd parted to make way for him as he left before the Garda turned up.

He was feeling a bit better now.

Chapter Seventeen

Police headquarters
Tulsa, Oklahoma

It was still just the three of them, Erin, Detective Topher Morrell and the intimidating shape of Chief O'Rourke. They'd moved from the little office to a larger room deeper inside the headquarters building. At the end of a long table flanked by plastic chairs was a stand with a DVD player and a large screen.

'Is this the only copy?' Chief O'Rourke growled in his gravelly voice as Erin handed him the disc from her backpack.

'That's the only one,' she lied.

'What about the phone itself?'

'Right here,' she said, pointing at her backpack.

'I'll need that as evidence, too,' O'Rourke said, and took it from her. He motioned for her to sit, and she perched on the edge of one of the plastic chairs. Morrell sat near her, saying nothing. Erin's mouth was dry and her neck and shoulders felt tense.

The police chief fed the disc into the machine, grabbed a remote control from the stand and sat heavily across the table from Erin. 'Now let's see for ourselves,' he growled, pointing the remote like a gun at the screen and pressing the play button.

The screen popped into life with the opening moments of Erin's video. She'd revisualised the scene so often in her mind during the last two days that she'd forgotten how poor the quality of the playback was. It was jerky and grainy, and where it wasn't overexposed with the glare of the cabin lights, the murky shadows made it almost impossible to see what was happening.

And on it went, for over two full and very long minutes during which Erin sat and dug her teeth into her lip and didn't dare to glance at either of the two cops. She could sense Detective Morrell shifting about uncomfortably next to her, and wondered what he was thinking.

Through a confusion of light and shadow, the horror on the veranda played out. For Erin, it was like reliving the scene yet again. But she wondered how much actually having been there was colouring her interpretation of the shockingly poor footage. What would someone make of it, seeing it for the first time? As for the sound, it seemed to her even more muffled and boomy as when she'd played it on her computer at home. The blasting gunshots had overwhelmed the phone's tiny, sensitive mike, reducing nearly all the voices to a drowned garble.

The video clip was reaching its climactic moment now, but it was a long way from what it had been in real life. The squirming shape of the victim on the veranda was just a blur. His executioner could be made out, but only just, and his features were still very unclear. As he fired the coup de grâce that had flattened his struggling victim to the floor for good, the bright muzzle flash and detonation of the huge revolver obscured everything else. In the second or two it took for the camera's automatic exposure to readjust, it was barely possible to see the killer do that cowboy gun-twirl whose nonchalance had so chilled Erin at the time.

'Stick this . . . in the . . . his . . . later,' said the badly muffled voice. The three shadows moved away from the shadow on the floor. Next, a flurry of movement as Erin had scrambled away on her knees and elbows. Then the clip was over and the screen blacked out.

There was a moment's silence in the room. Slowly, Chief O'Rourke laid down the remote and turned his heavy gaze on Erin.

'That's it?' he said.

She shrugged. 'That's it.'

'Then we have a problem,' O'Rourke said. 'I can't see Mayor McCrory in this video.'

Erin reached across the table and grabbed the remote before he could snatch it away. She pressed the rewind button, and the screen lit up again with the playback in high-speed reverse until it returned to just before McCrory had shot the bearded man on the veranda. From her vantage point at the top of the stairs, she'd got the mayor framed right in the doorway. Between his feet, the victim's face and part of his body were visible as he crawled on his belly, his mouth open in a scream that sounded distorted and inhuman through the speaker. She hit play, then pause, and the image froze right where she wanted it to. She pointed. 'What are you talking about, you can't see him? That's him right there.'

O'Rourke glanced at the screen, then turned back to face her. 'All I see is a big guy in what might be a suit, with hair that could be any shade from blonde to white. You want me to arrest everyone in Tulsa who answers that description, then I'd have to arrest myself.' He grinned at his own joke, but there was no humour in his eyes.

'It's not exactly Oscar material,' Detective Morrell said, speaking for the first time. 'Frankly, it's pretty disappointing.'

'But you can see enough, right?' Erin protested. 'And even if you can't see his face that well, that's the McCrorys' cabin. His own place. Doesn't that count for something?'

O'Rourke was unmoved. 'Could be anybody.'

'Sure, with a key. And who knew the alarm code,' Erin said, feeling her temper rising.

'Miss Hayes, we deal with a hundred cases like this every year,' O'Rourke said in an attempt at a reasonable tone that just sounded patronising. 'Someone wants to get into a place, they'll get in. Criminals adapt. They're becoming more sophisticated all the time.'

'Don't give me this crap,' she said. 'The victim was invited to the place. McCrory set up a business meeting of some kind as a pretext, but it's obvious that he meant to kill him there, because it was out of the way and he thought it'd be empty. How would some opportunist criminal have known that?'

She turned to Detective Morrell, but he was shaking his head. 'There might be a way our forensic techs can clean up the video—' he began.

'But for the moment, there's nothing here to support your story, Miss Hayes,' O'Rourke finished for him. The reasonable tone was gone again.

'But you do agree that a murder was committed there, right? Surely there's evidence at the scene?'

'That footage could have been shot anywhere,' O'Rourke said flatly. 'I don't see any goddamn thing that convinces me otherwise and we're not making a move until we know better.'

'But I witnessed it happening right there!' Erin yelled, banging on the table.

'Calm down, please,' Morrell said.

'Call Angela McCrory and ask if she didn't give me the key to the place.'

O'Rourke actually laughed. 'Beautiful. You want me to call the first lady of Tulsa to ask if her husband, our city mayor, popped some guy in their lake cabin. Sure, I'd like to see that on *Oklahoma's Own*.'

'So what happens now?' Erin asked, shocked. 'Nothing?'

'Let's start with the video,' Morrell said. 'One step at a time. It might clean up. The technical folks can work wonders.'

'What about me?' she said. 'I just put my neck on the block. These people are murderers. Don't I have a right to police protection, or something?'

'It's a little early for that,' Morrell said. 'No formal charges have even been made. If it comes to it, you'll be entitled to full witness protection.'

'*If* it comes to it?'

O'Rourke stood up, towering over the table and looking down at her with hard eyes. He handed her a card from his pocket. 'My number's there. Call me if you need to.'

'That's it?' she said, amazed this could be over so soon. Her situation remained exactly the same as before.

'Go home, Miss Hayes. Speak to no one. Don't leave town. We'll be in touch.'

Chapter Eighteen

On his way back to the car, Ben checked Kristen's BlackBerry for the missed call, and found a new voice message in the inbox.

The man spoke hesitantly. Very educated-sounding, very crisp, more than a little guarded. There was a faint trace of an Irish accent mixed into those upper-class tones. 'This is a message for, ah, Kristen Hall. Gray Brennan here, responding to your enquiry some time ago about Lady Stamford's journals. I'm sorry I haven't replied sooner, but I've been, ah, busy.'

Ben thought, *who was this guy?*

'Regarding the journals,' Brennan's message continued, 'I fully appreciate your interest in viewing them for the purposes of researching your book, and they do indeed contain hitherto unseen material that I'm sure would be of, ah, significant interest to you. As a matter of fact, some of their revelations could be highly explosive to say the least . . . However, ah, I'm afraid that's all the more reason why I'm reluctant to share them with anyone, least of all a writer – *unless* I could be fully persuaded that certain extremely sensitive information would be, ah, appropriately handled. Anyway, that's my response. Contact me again if you so desire. Goodbye.'

Bit of an odd-bod, Ben thought. He listened to the message once more as he walked towards the car, then saved it and slipped the phone back in his pocket. A Garda patrol car sliced by in the opposite direction, two uniforms up front, one of them talking on the radio.

Ben got back in the BMW and sped out of Glenfell, thinking about what Kristen had said about the private journals documenting Lady Stamford's years in Ireland, and the historian in whose possession they were now. He'd been trying to figure out what could be so hot about her research; now here was this Brennan acting all cautious and secretive over 'explosive' material. What the hell was this about?

Back at the cottage that evening, Ben used his own smart-phone to go online and check the guy out. There was very little to be gleaned about the man, other than the fact that until about twelve years ago he'd been Emeritus Professor of History at Trinity College, Dublin. A photo in the university's archives showed a thin, jaunty-looking man with combed-over greying hair and little wire glasses. Taking the number from Kristen's BlackBerry, Ben dialled from his own phone.

The same voice he'd heard in the message answered after a few rings. 'Brennan.'

'Professor Brennan, you don't know me. My name's Hope, Ben Hope. I'm returning your call on behalf of Kristen Hall.'

'About the Stamford journals?' Brennan said. 'Yes, she left me a phone message a couple of weeks ago. But I don't understand. Why are you calling on her behalf? Is something wrong?'

'You might say that. Kristen can't return your message personally, because she's dead. She was murdered the day before last.'

There was a pause on the line. 'Oh, no. *Murdered?* Are you . . . were you a friend? A relative?'

'She wasn't my friend. I hardly knew her. We'd only just met. But I liked her and she didn't deserve to die.'

'This is awful. Just awful.'

'Professor Brennan, I'm not going to beat about the bush. I think Kristen was killed because of something she discovered about Elizabeth Stamford. You said in your message that the Stamford journals were explosive. Your words. I need to know more.'

'Aren't the police investigating?'

'They're doing what they do,' Ben said. 'I'm doing what I do. Call it a parallel inquiry. Professor, apart from the men who butchered Kristen and cut her throat, I was the last person to see her alive. I mean to find out what happened and I'm asking for your help, because I think you know something about all this.'

'I wouldn't be so sure of that,' Brennan replied. 'Lady Stamford's journals were lost for over a century, until they were rediscovered among the ruins of Glenfell House. They've been part of my personal collection for sixteen years, going back to when I worked in Ireland. Now they're locked in a safe here in my home. I live alone, and I don't share my collections freely. Nobody but me in all that time has seen Lady Stamford's journals or had any inkling of the revelations in them. So I can't see how it's possible that they'd have anything to do with this terrible tragedy.'

'Someone knows,' Ben said. 'Someone who knew Kristen was on the trail and is prepared to do anything to keep whatever it is a secret. The best chance I've got of finding out who, is to know what's in those journals. Which means that right now you, Professor Brennan, are the best chance anyone has of catching Kristen's killers.'

A pause. Then, 'What did you say your name was?'

'Ben Hope.'

'Benjamin?'

'Benedict,' Ben said, fighting his impatience. 'Can you help me, or not? Say no, and I promise you won't hear from me again. Say yes, and I'll meet you wherever you want. Please trust me.'

There was more silence as Brennan thought about it. Ben gripped the phone tightly and held his breath, waiting.

'Very well,' Brennan said at last. 'I'll meet with you and show you the journals. But you'll have to come to me. I don't leave the island any more.'

'What island would that be?' Ben asked.

'Madeira.'

'Give me your address,' Ben said. 'I'll be there.'

Chapter Nineteen

The quickest and earliest flight Ben could find to Madeira was direct to the island's capital, Funchal, leaving at just after seven the following morning. But the flight departed from Dublin, meaning a two-hour drive eastwards across Ireland, coast to coast.

By nine that evening it was booked and Ben was packing a few spare clothes into his green bag. After grabbing a couple of hours' sleep, he jumped into the BMW and raced away from the cottage under a pitch-black starry sky.

Hours later, as he sat in the departure lounge at Dublin sipping scalding coffee, he wondered what he was going to find in Madeira. After giving him the address and directions to his countryside villa, Brennan's last words on the phone had been something strange. 'Don't arrive before dark. I can't meet people during daylight.'

Either the guy was a vampire, or he was more than a little weird. It wouldn't be the first time that Ben had had dealings with an eccentric recluse, but that didn't make it any less frustrating that most of the day would have to be wasted before they could meet. Nightfall wouldn't be until around ten.

By mid-morning, Ben was one and a half thousand miles away from Dublin, exchanging the hard, cool, unpredictable beauty of Ireland for the vibrant lushness of the Portuguese archipelago they called the Garden of the Atlantic. The plane overflew clear blue ocean and pristine beaches. Black volcanic cliffs rose sharply up from the sea, their craggy base rimmed with the foam of breakers visible even from afar. Thousands of boats crammed the island's main port, dwarfed by giant pearly-white cruise liners that crawled majestically in and out of the sun-spangled harbour waters.

Beyond, Ben gazed from the aircraft window across a landscape of towering mist-shrouded mountains and sweeping forested valleys of a near-tropical verdant green. Crowded by sheer cliffs on one side and the ocean on the other, Madeira's airport was famed for being one of the most dangerous for even skilled pilots to land at, despite – or maybe partly because of – the extended runway that stretched precariously over the water on massive concrete pillars.

Still alive forty-five minutes later, Ben stepped out into the heat haze from the small single airport terminal and found a Europcar rental place where he picked out a black VW Touareg four-wheel-drive. When they handed him the key, he flicked the rental agreement casually onto the front passenger seat, flung his leather jacket and bag in the back, cranked the air conditioning to beer chiller levels and sped northwards. He skirted Funchal, heading towards the island's forested and mountainous heartland, according to the directions Brennan had given him.

It was a spectacular landscape, but Ben was too pre-occupied to enjoy it as he wound his way deeper into the countryside, increasingly irritated at the delay caused by the man's strange insistence that they couldn't meet during daylight hours. Stopping at a village nestling up in the hills, he found a quiet little restaurant with a shaded, flowery garden high over the valley, where he hungrily refuelled himself on grilled limpets followed by a dish of the local speciality *espetada*, chunks of beef roasted over wood chips. Instead of wine, he drank a jug of iced water. Dessert was four Gauloises end to end, which he lingered over for as long as he could, letting the smoke trickle from his lips as he gazed down across the lush valley below. He'd sworn off drink for as long as he needed to get the job done. In the meantime, he'd just have to smoke twice as much.

Back in the Touareg, he meandered along empty, winding roads thickly overhung by trees and listened to a jazz station that played a lot of Art Blakey and McCoy Tyner until, at last, the day began to cool and evening started to fall. In the purple-blue haze of twilight, Ben was finally able to home in on his target and drive the last of the way to Brennan's secluded villa.

The place was four kilometres from the nearest village, encircled by a high white stone wall spilling over with foliage. He drove slowly around the perimeter, searching for the way in, until he came to a tall gateway framed by stone pillars.

The gate was closed. As he got out of the car he could see no latch or handle to open it, but there was an intercom box on one of the pillars. He pressed a button and announced his arrival into the metal grid. There was no reply. He was beginning to wonder if the intercom was working when there was a click and the gates whirred open.

Driving into the courtyard in front of the villa, even in the falling light it was plain to see that the place was well beyond the means of the average retired university professor. Evidently, its owner was not only independently wealthy but highly security-conscious, too. As soon as Ben was inside, the gates whirred and clicked shut behind him.

He stepped back out of the VW. The temperature had

fallen sharply with the onset of evening. He grabbed his leather jacket from the back seat and slipped it on. Slung his bag over his shoulder and walked towards the house. Within seconds he'd counted four cameras trained on him from their discreet positions among the foliage. The villa was long and low, surrounded by creeping plants and tumbling flowers. To reach it, Ben had to pass a pair of large dog kennels from which two enormous bull mastiffs emerged at his approach, growling and showing their teeth. Ben didn't make eye contact and walked coolly by them, but he felt acutely defenceless under their hostile gaze and was grateful to reach the front steps of the house without getting mauled.

There was another intercom box by the door, and from it came the same Irish-tinged voice Ben had heard on the phone. 'The door's open,' it said. 'Come in.'

Ben pushed through the door and found himself in a large hallway with a mosaic stone floor. Long drapes dimmed out the moonlight from the high windows. Off the hallway, a wide corridor, flanked by huge leafy indoor plants and paintings on the walls that could barely be made out in the shadows, led deeper into the house. He followed the dark corridor until he came to a bend and saw a door hanging half-open.

The faint glow of a light shone from inside.

'In here,' said the voice he'd heard first on the phone and then just now on the intercom. 'Close the door behind you, will you?'

Chapter Twenty

Ben entered and clicked the door softly shut. The room was lit only by a single lamp on a large desk to one side. In its glow he could see the tall bookcases that covered three of the walls and the antique furnishings that gave the impression of a gentlemen's club of yesteryear. In the shadows on the far side of the room, turned away from the door so that its back was to him, was a huge leather wing chair.

'I see you found the place all right,' Brennan said from the chair. 'Glad you could make it.'

'Thanks for the invitation,' Ben said.

Brennan gripped the chair's arms and hoisted himself slowly to his feet. He was still in shadow and Ben could see no more than a silhouette of him. 'It's nice to have some company for a change. You see, Mr Hope, it's not out of choice that I live like a recluse. And I say that quite *without wax*.'

It took a second for Ben to understand. '*Sine cera*,' he said. 'Sincerely.'

'Please forgive me. Old classicist's joke,' Brennan said with a chuckle. 'So you speak Latin, I gather?'

'Theology. Long time ago.'

'An educated man. Whose unquenchable thirst for knowledge now brings him all the way to my humble home. Welcome to Madeira, Mr Hope.'

Brennan took a step into the light, and for the first time Ben saw his face. He was the same man whose photograph was on Trinity College's website, but then again he wasn't the same. Ben had seen a lot of mutilation and disfigurement in the years he'd spent fighting wars all over the world. He'd thought he was used to it. But his eyes narrowed involuntarily and he felt his jaw tighten at the sight of what Professor Gray Brennan had become.

'Please don't be too alarmed by my appearance,' the historian said, catching Ben's expression. 'It's been some time since I could bring myself to look into a mirror.'

His face was livid with glistening sores and patches of raw flesh. The tip of his nose was gone, nothing but bubbling exposed meat where it looked as if an animal had bitten it off. The skin around his eyes and over most of his scalp seemed to have atrophied and was tattered and peeling horribly right down to the bone. Ben saw the hand resting on the back of the wing chair. It looked like a bloody claw.

'Skin cancer,' Brennan said. 'That's the reason I no longer leave this place. Not fit to be seen in public any more, you see. Call me vain. It's also the reason it took me so long to reply to Miss Hall's phone message. I have good weeks and bad; when it's bad I can't really do anything at all. Luckily for you, this is a good week, but I can't stand the sunlight. Hence the lateness of the hour, for which I can only apologise.'

'I'm sorry,' Ben said. 'Is it treatable?'

'Not without irradiating me until my bones glow in my grave,' Brennan chuckled. 'Either way, you're looking at a condemned man. So if you're here to kill me, you're welcome. Just make it quick and painless, there's a good fellow.'

'Why would I be here to kill you?'

Brennan smiled. 'It just crossed my mind. I imagine you

probably could, though, pretty easily, if you were inclined. I looked you up, you know.'

'Thought you might,' Ben said, remembering the way Brennan had probed on the phone to get his name.

'The Internet is my only window on the world these days. Not many Benedict Hopes in the world.'

'Just the one,' Ben said. 'Not a bad thing.'

'How is Normandy these days? Le Val? Tactical training? What is that?'

'The past,' Ben said.

'From what little your extremely brief, carefully worded professional profile reveals about you, you seem to have a *lot* of past, Mr Hope. Or should I say, Major?'

'I prefer Mr,' Ben said. 'I retired from the military a long time ago, as you know if you've read my résumé.'

'Oh, I have, and with great interest. It leaves plenty to the imagination. *Crisis response consultant?* That would be a neat little euphemism for . . .?'

'When people went missing, I tried to find them.'

'Quite a step from that to a murder investigation, I'd say?'

'There's no chance of bringing the victim home again to her loved ones,' Ben said. 'Apart from that, it's pretty much the same thing. But I didn't come here to talk about me.'

'Of course. Tell me, have the police made any progress in finding out who did this terrible thing to Miss Hall?'

'I'm not holding my breath,' Ben said.

'What a world we live in,' Brennan said sadly. He shook his head, sighed. 'Drink? Help yourself. There's whisky, brandy, vodka . . .'

'No, thanks,' Ben said.

'Suit yourself. You won't mind getting one for me, will you? Scotch. Fill 'er right up.'

Ben laid down his bag and went to the cabinet, found the

amber whisky in a cut-crystal decanter and glugged some into a matching glass. He offered the brimming glass out to Brennan, who grasped it between his red-raw fingers, raised it to his lips and drank down a long gulp. 'That's better,' he gasped. 'I never used to touch the stuff, but now it's a comfort to me, you know.'

'The journals?' Ben said.

'There on the desk behind you,' Brennan said. Ben looked, and saw a neatly stacked pile of small books bound in wrinkled, aged grey leather.

'Only these four surviving volumes were found in the ruins of Glenfell House,' Brennan said. 'Not a diary in the modern sense, more of a serial letter to herself, which she kept going for several years as a way of recording her private thoughts and observations. The earliest dates back to 1841, when the newly married Lady Stamford first went to live on her husband's estate. From there, they cover the period of her life in Ireland until her departure in '49. There are two missing from the middle years, but I think you'll find most of the meat is still on the bone, so to speak. Go ahead, take a look. But treat them kindly, I beg you.'

'I don't suppose you'll let me take these away from here,' Ben said, picking up the top book from the pile.

'You're right about that. You'll have time to read through them, however. I hope you find what you're looking for.'

Ben flicked through the pages, scanning quickly left and right.

'Well? See anything?' Brennan said with a smile.

'I can see she had beautiful writing,' Ben said.

'She was a great beauty herself, going by the one portrait that was ever done of her. Anything else of interest?' Brennan had a twinkle in his eye, as though enjoying setting Ben a little test.

Ben was damned if he knew what he was looking for, and he didn't have much patience for games. He laid the book down, sifted through the pile and snatched up another. 'I don't know,' he said after a few moments of browsing. 'I'm going to need your help to figure out what could be so important about these diaries.'

'At first glance, not a great deal, that's for sure,' Brennan said, still smiling with that mysterious twinkle in his eye. 'Despite her remarkable achievements later in her short life, Elizabeth Stamford remains an obscure and minor figure historically. As for her husband Lord Edgar Stamford, aside from having been a bully and a brute who ultimately went insane and burned his own mansion to the ground with himself in it, his only real contribution to history, and what he's chiefly remembered for, was his scientific work.'

'He was a botanist, wasn't he?' Ben said, remembering what Kristen had told him.

'Something of a whizz-kid in his day. Distinguished himself in his studies at Cambridge, which he completed a year sooner than his contemporaries despite being a wild and intemperate young man. He was already a lord by then. His father, Colonel Montague Stamford, had been killed in action in the British campaign against the Xhosa on the Eastern Frontier, and his mother Amélie – half French – died of typhoid in 1838. Young Edgar was still in his teens when he travelled to Paris, where he studied for a time under the famous scientist Camille Montagne.'

'Montagne,' Ben repeated. 'French for mountain.'

'Stamford had come across him from reading his scholarly articles in the *Archives de Botanique* and *Annales des Sciences Naturelles*. It seems the two of them hit it off, because Edgar visited him twice more after he was married and living in Ireland, once in 1843 and again in 1845. Montagne's specialised area of interest, which Stamford shared, was the study of cryptogams.'

Ben looked at him, momentarily confused. 'Secret symbols?'

Brennan shook his head. 'Not crypto*grams*. In botany, cryptogams are things like mosses, algae, lichens and fungi.'

'I see,' Ben said, not seeing at all and beginning to wonder what the hell he was doing here. *This was a mistake*, a voice was screaming at him inside his head.

'Stamford was also great cronies with another botanist, his old Cambridge pal Heneage Fitzwilliam. But while Fitzwilliam went on to become a professor at Magdalen College, Oxford, Stamford's career was no great shakes as far as his contribution to modern science goes. He tinkered about in his lab and published the odd paper throughout the 1840s. Very few people today would remember his work. But . . .' Brennan seemed about to add more, then went quiet.

'But what?'

Brennan smiled slyly. 'As I said, at first glance there seems to be little of interest in the journals, except to nerdish historians seeking insights into the daily lives of the Victorian gentry. But when you look deeper, you'll come across . . . shall we say, some most unexpected surprises.'

'Like what?' Ben said impatiently. 'What's the big secret I'm supposed to find?'

'I've given you a clue already. Surprised you haven't picked up on it.'

Ben looked hard at Brennan, thinking that if the man hadn't been so ill and frail-looking, he might have been tempted to haul him out of his armchair and shake the answers out of him.

'Think about it, Mr Hope,' Brennan said. 'What was happening in Ireland in the latter half of the 1840s? What was the primary event taking place all around the author of these journals during that time?'

'The famine?'

Brennan nodded. 'Correct. Though I personally wouldn't use the term "famine". If you read, you'll see she didn't use it either. As she knew, and I know, it's hardly the appropriate word to describe the black events that overtook Ireland in the harvest of 1846 and created the veritable horror story of 1847 and beyond.'

'That's what people call it, isn't it?' Ben said. 'The potato famine?'

'Only those who don't know any better. The truth is quite different.'

'Different from the accounts in a thousand history books?'

Brennan looked grimly pleased at Ben's ignorance. 'Now now, I'm surprised that a man of your obvious intelligence, not to mention your background and skills, isn't more of a realist than to go believing in the tall tales of the majority of my fellow historians. To their shame, they love nothing better than to spout the usual pack of lies that passes for the official version of the story.'

'Then you'd better tell me the real one,' Ben said.

Chapter Twenty-One

'You are familiar with the potato, I presume?' Brennan asked.

Ben heaved an inward sigh. His idea of travelling all the way out here to the island of Madeira hadn't been to listen to a discourse on the topic of root vegetables. But he bit back his impatience. 'As much as the next man,' he replied.

Brennan leaned back in his chair, settling into lecture mode. 'The Irish rural population of the 1840 – that is to say some six million out of the country's overall population of eight million at the time – were very familiar with it indeed. It's a highly versatile vegetable. It grows prodigiously, keeps well and is easy to cook. Eaten in sufficient quantities it's a remarkable source of calories, protein and minerals, capable of maintaining health, preventing nutritional deficiencies like scurvy and supplying the energy needed for a hard day's work in the fields.

'There had always been plenty to go around in rural Ireland. Children would walk to school with their pockets filled with cold potatoes to eat at lunchtime. Labourers digging the fields would be allowed to roast as many of them as they could eat over an open fire. Fishermen's wives would weave stocking bags in which their husbands could carry mashed potato to eat at sea. A traveller and observer named Arthur Young described what he found to be a typical scene in the rural Ireland of the time: "*Mark the Irishman's potato bowl placed on the floor, the whole family upon their hams around it, devouring a quantity incredible, the pig taking his share as easily as the wife, the cocks, hens, turkeys, geese, the cur, the cat, and perhaps the cow – all partaking of the same dish. No man can often have been a witness of it without being convinced of the plenty, and I will add the cheerfulness, that attends it.*" He estimated that a barrel of around two hundred and fifty to three hundred potatoes could last a family of five, as well as the menagerie of livestock they often shared the same basic dwelling with, for a week. The father of the family would have taken the lion's share, consuming something in the region of twelve to fourteen pounds a day in order to get the necessary nutrients for the very difficult work that was his livelihood. Not the most varied diet, to be sure, but Young was surprised how very well they appeared to do on it. He described them as "*athletic in their form, as robust and as capable of enduring labour as any upon earth*", adding that "*When I see people of a country, in spite of political oppression, with well-formed vigorous bodies, and their cottages swarming with children; when I see their men athletic and their women beautiful, I know not how to believe them subsisting on an unwholesome food.*"'

'Just one problem with that,' Ben said. 'Dependence on a single food source made them vulnerable, if anything happened to go wrong with it.'

'Indeed it did,' Brennan said, nodding. 'An obvious risk, when you place all your eggs in one basket, so to speak. The potato harvest of 1846 was to have been the biggest ever. All of two million acres of land had been seeded across Ireland, and after the close shave they'd had the previous year with the blight that had narrowly missed devastating the crop, there was widespread optimism that this would be a year of plenty for all. And to begin with, it seemed as if all hopes would be fulfilled. Every planted field was teeming with the dark green leaves and purple blossoms of the thriving young plants.

'Then in early June, the first signs of the disease began to appear in a few localised spots. Within just a few weeks, it was suddenly everywhere, spreading like gangrene. It was said that farmers who had gone to bed dreaming of their lush potato crop awoke the next morning to the stench of the rotting plants. From one end of the country to the other, a desperate race began to stem the disease by salvaging whatever might remain of the crop. Many believed that by ripping up the stalks, they might be able to prevent the "infection" from reaching the precious vegetables below ground, where the earth would protect them. But when they dug into the ground to check, all they found was the same putrid, liquefying mush of black rot. They had failed to understand that the disease wasn't spreading downwards from the stalks. It was in the ground itself. A fortunate few who realised this fact in time were able to dig up a few surviving potatoes before the contagion hit them, saving a handful of their crop. But the vegetables that survived were small and soft, virtually inedible. All it did was to delay the inevitable.'

Brennan shook his head sadly and went on.

'What began to unfold over the following weeks and months was a crisis completely unprecedented in the history of the western world. The sole food supply of millions of people turned to slime before their eyes. Soon the hungry were streaming through the countryside in their hundreds and thousands, searching for anything they could use to feed their children and themselves. To begin with, those with a little food generously shared it out, even to strangers, as is the Irish way. If they were lucky enough to catch a fish or shoot a rabbit, they would gladly divide it out between ten or even twenty people. But even the most warm-hearted of them couldn't see their own families starve to death, and it wasn't long before they started closing their doors to outsiders.'

Ben listened quietly. He was able to picture the scene all too clearly in his mind.

'The weakest began to die. Some desperately tried to turn the black rot of their potatoes into something edible by drying it out into cakes. Others scoured the beaches, devouring seabirds' eggs, shellfish and seaweed, often poisoning themselves in the process. Bodies littered the coastlines, the fields, the roadsides, many of them with their mouths stained green from the nettles and grasses they'd been forced to eat in their desire to stay alive. The first so-called "death carts" were seen on the country lanes, gathering up mounds of bodies to be taken and heaped in unmarked mass graves. Meanwhile, the towns were suddenly filled with gaunt beggars, wretched figures looking more like skeletons than human beings. No longer able to work or pay their rents, tens of thousands were turfed out of their homes by forced eviction, beaten to a pulp if they tried to resist. And it gets worse. Believe me, it gets a lot worse.'

'Why didn't they eat the chickens, or the pigs?' Ben said.

'Oh, they did, of course, especially now that there was nothing left to feed them. The situation was as much of a death sentence for the animals as it was for so many of the people. But for most, it was a cruel decision to slaughter such an important source of revenue. You have to remember that these people had no money to speak of. Livestock was often all they had in the way of currency, for barter, or to sell to pay the rent. By eating them, you were devouring your only savings. And they were a one-off source of food, not sustainable. Some people resorted to other ways. One son of a County Mayo farmer gave away his father's last pig in return for an ounce of gunpowder, so that he could poach a few wild ducks. An ounce of powder wouldn't have lasted long, either. In many cases the family pig was sold for oats, barley, or meal. When that quickly ran out, the Irish resorted to selling their furniture, their farming tools, their fishing rods, even their ragged old clothing if anyone would have it.'

Ben listened, his jaw set, as Brennan went on with the gruesome scenario.

'Things became increasingly desperate. The starving would steal the swill from deserted pigsties. They'd seek out whatever was remotely edible in the offal bins of the fish markets. Those driven to crime often risked their lives to rustle sheep belonging to more affluent farmers, who protected them with rifles and often slept out on the hillsides to keep watch over their herds. Sometimes the poachers' families devoured the mutton flesh raw so that the smell of roasting meat wouldn't give away their crime. If they were caught, they were sometimes shot, sometimes beaten to death by the farmers' men. Fearing that hordes of the starving would sweep across their land and bring ruin on them, some landowners dug out pits ten feet deep, concealed with grass and weeds, with spikes at the bottom to impale any hungry thief who might come in search of something to eat. Man turning against man. The fabric of the nation gone. The music, the dance, the poetry, all of it silenced, destroyed.' Brennan gazed down at his lap, obviously deeply affected by the story he was telling.

'It was a tragedy,' Ben said. 'Anyone can see that. If they hadn't become so reliant on that single food source, things would have gone differently.'

Brennan looked sharply up at him. 'I'm afraid you still don't understand, do you? Have you ever considered the reason *why* the Irish diet was so limited to the potato? Do you think it was out of choice?'

'I suppose I haven't thought about it much,' Ben admitted.

'You and most other people,' Brennan said. 'Well, the fact is that the Irish peasant community, all six million of them, weren't living just on potatoes for the pleasure of it. It was the *only* food allowed to them by the gentry.'

'But why would that be?'

'Pure economics. The potato was a uniquely efficient and cost-effective way of sustaining the three-quarters of the population who were of the least worth to the country's rulers. For every poor peasant who might have been fed on wheat, you could keep three people alive, plus a pig and a small flock of chickens, on a potato diet – meaning that it would have taken three times the acreage to feed the same number of people. Even the type of potato allowed to them had been chosen for its growing efficiency. With so little land allocated to their needs, the rural Irish were forced to subsist on the most fertile, but also the worst-tasting, species, called the lumper.'

Ben remembered the ugly specimens he'd seen preserved in the famine museum in Glenfell. 'Okay, I get it,' he said, wanting Brennan to get to the point.

'Do you? Then perhaps you begin to see why the slow, terrible deaths of as many as two million people didn't result from some act of God. It was a disaster. But a famine, Mr Hope, a famine it was *not*. To use the term "famine" is to imply that the pathetic mounds of Irish bodies heaped like detritus upon the death carts and stacked twenty high in unconsecrated graves, often with their last breath still in their mouths, met such an end simply due to their foolish dependence on the vagaries of Mother Nature and a chance failing of the potato crop that they'd thoughtlessly relied on for all their needs. Well now, isn't that a bit like saying that the half million Jews who starved to death in the Warsaw ghetto a century later somehow managed to do so spontaneously, or because they'd neglected to stock their larders? No, no. To refer to such events as a "famine" is to miss the point entirely, and to insult the memory of the millions of lives lost.'

'So what would you call them?' Ben said.

'In the Irish language it was *An Gorta Mór*, the Great Hunger,' Brennan replied. 'Personally, I'd tend to side with George Bernard Shaw, as he went one step further in his *Man and Superman*. You may have seen the play?'

'I never was much of a theatre goer,' Ben said.

'"Me father died in Ireland in the black forty-seven", says Malone,' Brennan replied, affecting a thicker accent. '"The famine?" asks Violet. "No," says Malone. "The *starvation*. When a country is full o' food, and exporting it, there can be no famine." And that's exactly what it was.'

'A starvation,' Ben repeated. 'Implying what? That it was done . . .?'

Brennan's lips curled into a distorted smile. 'Why of course, Mr Hope. That it was done on purpose. Their so-called "famine" was in fact wilful murder. One of the worst acts of genocide you never heard of.'

Chapter Twenty-Two

Ben was silent for a moment as he tried to understand.

'Shaw got his facts right,' Brennan said. 'Even as millions of its people lay starving in the ditches and in their beds, so helpless and weak that the rats would swarm over them to rip what little flesh was left from their bones, Ireland was a country full of food. It was *abounding* with food. How could that be, I hear you ask?'

'Go on,' Ben said.

'The doomed potato, as widespread as it was, was hardly the only crop grown on Irish soil. During 1846 and '47 alone, some half a million tons of grain were exported out of Ireland, enough to have saved the lives of thousands of people. Not to mention the vast quantities of other exports such as butter, eggs and meat, all of which were being transported in bulk from Irish ports, on ships bound for England, throughout the entire period of the so-called famine. And who was doing the exporting? The British government, who had supreme control over agriculture in Ireland. For years the country had been supplying England with more than eighty per cent of its beef, roughly the same proportion of its butter, and even more of its pork.'

Ben blinked at the figures. 'I didn't know.'

'I suppose that's because it's not to be found in your

average history book,' Brennan said caustically. 'Another thing that's been conveniently forgotten is the pains the British took to ensure that not a scrap of their precious exports ever found their way into Irish hands. The escorts of heavily armed British troops guarding the convoys of wagons loaded with food on their way to the ports made certain that nobody could get near them. Any attempt whatsoever to steal a single egg, a single cup of grain or rind of meat to bring home to one's starving children, would be met with lethal response, or arrest – in which case the lucky ones faced immediate deportation to the penal colonies of the British Empire. The not so lucky ones were simply hanged.

'And even at the height of the famine,' Brennan went on, 'when their armed food convoys were passing within sight of the mounds of bodies and the death carts everywhere on the roads, the English rulers staunchly refused to turn over a single scrap of produce to feed the starving. Relief efforts devised by Whitehall were a joke, mere whitewash. It was largely left to humanitarian organisations such as the Quakers to set up soup kitchens and the like, while the British government simply sat on their hands. In contrast, other nations were doing what they could to alleviate the shocking situation in Ireland. Aid came from various quarters, saving untold lives: from Rome, from America. Even Turkish sultans sent shiploads of grain to the same ports from which British ships were snatching it away under military guard.'

Brennan shook his head in disgust. 'And there were worse disgraces to come. As the food supply for the Irish peasants was being shut off, the British authorities passed laws to restrict their ability to feed themselves even further. It became illegal for ordinary Irish people to fish for salmon or trout, which only the wealthy landlords and their guests were now allowed to do. New legislation was introduced that forbade the keeping of hounds, so that starving families could no longer catch a rabbit or a hare for the pot. The shooting of game was strictly forbidden. Arms were confiscated, to prevent the poor from hunting even a squirrel – and, of course, to deter them from getting any ideas about rebelling against their gentrified masters who, while all this was going on, were having shooting parties on the big estates, bagging grouse, pheasant and hare in vast numbers and hanging their catch off poles from the carriages they went hunting in, right under the eyes of the barefoot starving masses. It was more than provocation. It was sadistic cruelty.'

'Why?' Ben asked. 'These people were their workforce. The agricultural industry relied on them. Why starve them out like that?'

'For the same reason that colonial powers and globalist business interests, past and present, have sought to eliminate whatever indigenous peoples whose existence impeded their ability to exploit resources for vast profit,' Brennan replied. 'The attempts to exterminate the Australian Aborigine people by mass sterilisation in order to mine their traditional territories. The tricks played on South American tribes by greedy cattle barons wanting to deprive them of their rain-forests, to raze into ranches for the supply of a billion greasy beef burgers to the junk food industry. The devastation of Borneo's natural habitats in the interests of the west's insatiable demand for palm oil. And on, and on, all through history.'

He shrugged. 'In short, the British government wanted the land. As far as they were concerned, these poor Irish peasants were a waste of space, taking up acreage that could be put to better use raising livestock and wheat for England.

Consider the words of the influential British cleric Thomas Malthus at the time: "*The land in Ireland is infinitely more peopled than in England; and to give full effect to the natural resources of the country, a great part of the population should be swept from the soil.*"'

Brennan let those words hang in the air for a moment. 'Swept from the soil,' he repeated. 'That's what the English wanted, and that's what they got. On top of the enormous numbers who died of starvation, at least another million people fled Ireland during that time, mostly destined for America. An editorial of the *London Times* proclaimed jubilantly in 1847 that "*they are going! They are going! The Irish are going with a vengeance! Soon a Celt will be as rare on the banks of the Liffey as a red man on the banks of the Hudson.*" And it was true. Thanks to the "famine", approximately half of the rural population considered undesirable by the English rulers was eliminated, or should I say, ethnically cleansed, freeing up the land to create yet more produce for England. That's not too far off the proportion of European Jews estimated to have been killed in the Nazi Final Solution. Little wonder that one of my more enlightened fellow historians, AJP Taylor, was moved to say of the Irish starvation that "all Ireland was a Belsen".'

'So the British government took advantage of this natural disaster to suit their own agenda,' Ben said.

Brennan smiled coldly. 'Very convenient, wouldn't you say?'

Ben was silent for a moment as he sat digesting Brennan's tale of injustice, greed and callous disregard for human life. It wasn't the first one he'd heard, and he knew it wouldn't be the last. It disgusted him to the core.

But nothing he'd heard so far did anything to explain Kristen's murder. 'All right, let's say Kristen had uncovered everything you just told me,' he said to Brennan. 'Dug out all the dirt on the British government's policies of non-action, or whatever it was, during the fam . . . during the starvation. It was more than a century and a half ago.'

'You're right,' Brennan said. 'Ancient history. Yesterday's news. Who cares any more, now that everyone involved has been dead for so long? Nobody stands to gain, or to lose. Unless, of course . . .'

'Unless what?'

'I told you there were explosive revelations in the Stamford journals, and there are.'

'There's more?' Ben said.

'Oh, there's more, all right,' Brennan replied. 'The deepest, darkest of secrets, ones that have lain dormant for over a hundred and fifty years. The question is, does the nature of those secrets constitute grounds for murder? Does it threaten anyone's modern-day interests to such an extent? Who can tell?'

'Enough games, professor. I came a long way to find out—'

Brennan shook his head. 'It's all in there,' he said, pointing at the journals. 'You came here to read them, didn't you? That's what I suggest you do.'

'Anyone ever tell you you're an awkward customer?' Ben said.

Brennan smiled. 'Privilege of a dying man. You won't regret it.'

Ben leaned forward in his chair, rested his elbows on his knees and rubbed his temples in frustration as his mind struggled to put together the pieces of the puzzle. But even without knowing what deep, dark secrets the Stamford journal had to reveal, he could see a gap in the logic. 'No copies were ever made of the journals, were they?'

'None. It's impossible. I was one of the very first people to see them after their rediscovery, and they haven't been out of my possession since.'

'Then these revelations couldn't be known to anyone else?' Ben asked. 'There's no way she could have come by the information some other way?'

'I doubt it very much,' Brennan said, after a moment's consideration. 'Quite a few letters and other artefacts relating to Elizabeth Stamford have surfaced over the years, scattered about in the hands of historians and collectors. But nothing of the importance of these journals, and what they contain. If this particular cat were out of the bag, it would have caused no little stir among historical circles. That's the reason I was a little reticent about letting any old writer gain access to the material.'

'Then it's unlikely that she could have even known of the existence of these secrets you're talking about.'

'More than unlikely. I'm certain she had no idea at all. She wanted to view the journals only by way of general research. They were just another resource to her, albeit a key one she was keen on getting her hands on.'

'None of this makes any sense,' Ben said. 'I need you to recap for me, from the beginning. Kristen contacted you a couple of weeks or so ago by phone. She'd found out that you were the current owner of the Stamford journals, and she was interested in viewing that material herself. She left you a message asking if you'd agree to that. You weren't well enough to respond to her until after she was already dead.'

'Which I truly regret,' Brennan said. 'And I'm equally sorry I didn't have the chance to respond to the email she sent me. She must have written it not long before her death, two or three days at most.'

Ben looked up in surprise. 'What email?'

148

'Didn't I mention that?' Brennan said. 'It was about the letter.'

'Letter?'

'Yes, the one to Henrietta Wainwright.'

Ben shook his head.

'Let me see if I can find the email.' Brennan got stiffly to his feet and went over to the desk to pick up a small laptop, which he brought back to his armchair and rested across his knees as he flipped up the lid and powered the machine up. A blue rectangle reflected in each lens of his spectacles.

'Here we are,' he said after a few moments. 'I'll read it to you: "*Dear Professor Brennan, you might remember I phoned you not long ago asking if it might be possible to view the journals of Lady Elizabeth Stamford. Since I contacted you, it's become even more crucial for me to verify certain details that have come up recently in my research. I have in my possession a copy of a letter from Elizabeth Stamford to Henrietta Wainwright, written in October 1849, shortly after Elizabeth's return to England, in which she pays thanks to all the people she's indebted to for helping her: Stephen Wainwright and his sisters Henrietta and Cecilia, as well as one Padraig McCrory, whom she credits for having aided her escape from Edgar Stamford's clutches.*"'

Brennan paused reading and looked up at Ben. 'The Wainwrights were Elizabeth's second cousins,' he explained. 'She often refers to them in her journals, as you'll see. Stephen Wainwright was a well-known naturalist of the day, something of a reformist humanitarian. He and his twin sisters lived in Bath but were frequent visitors to Ireland in the years Elizabeth lived on the Glenfell Estate. When the marriage finally fell apart, they helped her to return to England and get back on her feet. They really were a very important influence on . . .'

But by now Ben was only half listening to what Brennan was saying. A startling connection had suddenly been made in his mind as the name had leapt out at him. *McCrory*. It wasn't an uncommon surname. But the coincidence stuck in his mind like something hard to swallow.

Padraig McCrory. Was this the same man, born in 1809, that Kristen had mentioned in her notes and about whom she'd gone looking for information at St Malachy's church?

If it was, now Ben had the surname to attach to the first name: the missing piece that had tripped him up when he'd tried to follow in Kristen's footsteps searching the parish records in Glenfell.

But what did it mean? Ben quickly pieced the bits together in his mind. Kristen had become interested in Padraig McCrory because of the letter. Quite why that was remained a mystery, but it had mattered enough that she'd contacted Gray Brennan a second time to try to find out more. Meanwhile, she'd been busy digging up information on the man herself from parish records. At the same time, she'd been in touch with her go-to guy Chris Ingram to get hold of the cellphone number of *Finn* McCrory, mayor of Tulsa, Oklahoma. As a result of which, she'd spent thirteen minutes on the phone talking to the Irish-American.

Discussing what? Family trees?

Ben reached into his pocket and took out Kristen's notebook. He flipped to the page and read it again.

PADRAIG BORN 1809
→ 107!!!! HOW POSSIBLE?????

While the man's identity and birth date now held no secrets, the line below was still baffling. What was the number 107 about? And what was 'how possible'?

'Did she say anything more about this Padraig McCrory?' Ben asked, interrupting Brennan.

'Just this,' Brennan replied. 'Let me read you the rest of her email. "*I'm now particularly interested in knowing more about Padraig McCrory, and anything that Lady S might have revealed about him in her journals. Looking forward to hearing from you,*" etc., etc.' He looked up from the screen. 'That's it.'

'And that's the last you heard from her?'

Brennan nodded sadly. 'I can only presume she was still waiting for my reply when . . .' His voice trailed off.

'And *is* McCrory mentioned in the journals?' Ben asked, puzzled.

'Oh, yes, a few times. But I was surprised that Miss Hall had suddenly become so interested in him. He was an Irish servant of the Stamford household, who looked after Lady Elizabeth's horses.'

Ben couldn't understand why this man was so important.

Brennan closed his eyes for a moment, then shook his head. 'It's late, Mr Hope. You'll have to forgive me, but Lady Elizabeth herself can tell you all you need to know. As for me, I'm feeling very tired and I must get to bed. We can talk again in the morning.'

Ben stood, picked up the four volumes and tucked them delicately under his arm. 'I'll take care of them.'

'I know you will,' Brennan said, rising from his armchair and laying the laptop back on his desk. 'I don't imagine you have a hotel booked, do you? But don't worry. You can stay here the night. There's a guest annexe adjoining the house. Follow me.'

Brennan left lights off as he led the way back through the house; now Ben knew why he preferred to be in darkness. Outside, the stars were twinkling.

'Let me just feed Romulus and Remus their evening meal,'

Brennan said. He disappeared into a little outhouse near the kennels and reappeared a few moments later carrying two enormous dishes heaped with dog food, which he placed at the entrances to the kennels. The mastiffs came lumbering out and fell hungrily on the food, slobbering and gulping.

Brennan lovingly petted them as they ate. 'They wouldn't harm you,' he said lovingly. 'A couple of teddy bears, but burglars don't know that. Isn't that so, my boys?' he added, cuddling the slavering beasts with unfeigned devotion.

Ben could see how desperately lonely he was.

'Now let me show you to your quarters for the night,' Brennan said. 'You'll be hungry yourself, I suppose. Help yourself to whatever's in the kitchen. There are tinned provisions and some not too bad local wine, for the visitors I never receive.'

'Don't you have any family?' Ben asked as they walked along a dark portico that skirted the courtyard.

'I'm the last of us,' Brennan said. 'Nobody to leave this pad to when I pop my clogs, which won't be long, I hope. I've already made provisions for Romulus and Remus.'

Ben made no reply.

'You're probably wondering how an old fuddy duddy professor comes to be living in such a ridiculous big place,' Brennan said with a chuckle. 'My academic pension would barely cover the maintenance costs. No, you see, it came out the arse of a chicken.'

Ben looked at him, wondering if his illness had touched his head a little.

'I had an old uncle in Dungarvan who'd become obscenely rich selling eggs, of all things, bless him. He had no children – seems the Brennans aren't much given to procreation – and I was his only nephew, and so he left me the lot. That's when I left the rainy shores of Ireland forever and moved here, looking forward to a long and happy retirement.' Brennan smiled morbidly. 'Next thing, this happens to me. Oh, well. As they say, life's a bitch and then you rot away in pieces. Here we are.'

They'd reached the door of the annexe. Brennan unlocked it and gave Ben they key. 'Make yourself comfortable, Mr Hope. Don't stay up too late reading. Good night.'

He turned away, and Ben watched the thin, dark figure for a moment as the dying man walked back towards the empty house and what remained of his empty life.

Chapter Twenty-Three

The villa's guest annexe was on two floors, with a spiral staircase leading up to a narrow passage with the twin bedrooms off it. One of them had French windows that opened out onto a balcony. That was where Ben stood leaning on the stone balustrade and watching his cigarette smoke trail idly off into the warm night as he reflected over the things Brennan had told him. He wasn't hungry, and hadn't touched any of the provisions downstairs. Behind him inside the room, on the lush blue velvet cover of the antique four-poster bed, lay the volumes of Elizabeth Stamford's journal.

He could only hope that he hadn't come all this way on a fool's errand. But it was late, and he had nowhere else to go right now.

He crushed out the Gauloise on the balustrade, showering the darkness with a tiny cascade of glowing embers, then flicked the dead stub into the thick of the bushes down below. Time to find out what dark secrets the journals had to tell.

'Let's get to it,' he said out loud.

Sitting on the soft bed with the window drapes shut to keep out the mosquitoes and only a small bedside reading light shining over the pages, he spread the earliest volume of the journal open in front of him. The faded date of May 14th, 1841 on the opening entry confirmed what Brennan had said: that Lady Elizabeth Stamford had first begun to record her private thoughts and observations soon after marrying and moving to her new husband's Glenfell Estate.

Carefully turning the pages as he read, Ben admired the quality of both her handwriting and her style, which was elegant without being mannered and vivid enough to make him visualise the beautiful, lonely young woman of nineteen sitting there at some dainty little bureau in the confines of Glenfell House putting these private words to paper, with no idea of who would come to be prying into them a hundred and seventy or so years later. It seemed strange to imagine that this journal he was holding in his hands had been written inside the very manor whose gutted ruin he'd been walking around only yesterday.

But as he read on and the minutes passed, he could see nothing yet that was even remotely explosive or contentious in what the journal's author had to say. He was looking at the account of the day-to-day existence of a fairly typical aristocratic young woman of her time; and in 1841 it seemed that Lady Stamford had been leading a pretty uneventful life. In her measured prose she complained of being excluded from everything to do with her husband's activities and the general running of the house.

'I cannot bring myself to suppose I shall ever like that man Burrows,' she wrote. 'How Edgar came to choose such a vulgar, savage brute for his manservant is a mystery to me. But Peggy, my maid, is a sweet creature, and if it were not for the distraction of her company, and that of my dear, kind Padraig, I should certainly run melancholy mad.'

So there was Padraig, Ben thought. He'd have been thirty-two years of age when Lady Elizabeth joined the household.

There was no indication yet why Kristen might have been so interested in learning more about the man.

Ben read on. Over the next few pages, Elizabeth described her resolve not to become bored with her new cosseted role as lady of the manor, and to fill her time instead with playing the piano and the harp, reading her beloved Miss Austen, and roaming the grounds of Glenfell House and the surrounding countryside with her lurcher, Aloysius. Riding was a passion, too, but she refused to condone the fox hunts Edgar delighted in, and expressed how sickened she felt at the fate of the poor fox: *'Surely life is hard enough already for the wretched things, without being torn to pieces for the entertainment – for that is all it is, as I can very well see – of my dear spouse and his bloodthirsty friends.'*

It was a few minutes later, in an entry dated October 1841, that Ben came across the next mention of Padraig McCrory. Elizabeth talked about him with warm affection; from her account, Ben quickly pieced together a vision of a gentle giant of a man, kind-hearted and obviously devoted to her as he was to her horses. A few pages further on, Elizabeth ventured to confess that it was from Padraig that she was secretly learning Ireland's native Gaelic. Secretly, because the language was strongly discouraged under English rule, which even forbade the use of the prefix *O'* in Irish surnames. *'I am sure that Edgar's fury would be immeasurable if he heard me utter but a single word of "that vile tinkers' dialect" for which he threatens to have the Irish servants horse-whipped by his man Burrows should they dare ever to speak it in their lord and master's presence,'* Elizabeth wrote in one of her more impassioned outbursts. *'Well, he can d— well have me whipped along with them, for I find its music as enchanting as these hills and glens he regards merely as so much grazing land.'*

Other than her contact with Peggy and Padraig, her social life at the Glenfell Estate appeared to have been severely limited. She looked forward to the visits from her cousins from England, the twins Henrietta and Cecilia Wainwright who, Ben gleaned, were about ten years older than Elizabeth, and their elder brother Stephen, who was a physician as well as a noted naturalist. She often mentioned him in glowing language as being *'quite unlike the roaring brutes who make up the majority of Edgar's friends. Preferring to eschew their after-dinner company as they guffaw and clamour over port and cigars with their endless, wearisome talk of money and politics, this evening he again sat with us ladies and enraptured us with his accounts of his travels to lands so exotic they seem to our limited understanding to belong to another world.'*

Stephen had captured rare butterflies in Brazil; had climbed mountains in Spain; had once had the honour of meeting the great astronomer and composer William Herschel at the Royal Society. Elizabeth recounted his stories in detail and, reading between the lines, Ben got the impression that she harboured a certain liking for this Dr Wainwright that went deeper than simple friendship. But even in her private journal, such things couldn't be said openly.

It was all very compelling and Ben found himself instinctively liking Elizabeth – but this wasn't what he'd travelled to Madeira to read about. He was getting nowhere after more than an hour, and there was still a hell of a lot of reading to do. Thinking he should skip forwards in time and pick the account up at a later point, he set aside the book and opened one of the other volumes to find the first entry dated September, 1846, cutting forward five years.

Maybe here he'd be able to discover more about the importance of this Padraig McCrory's role in the story.

The stable hand was an enigma to Ben. What had happened to him after Elizabeth had left Ireland? Had he remained at the Glenfell Estate until its downfall in 1851?

Why did he matter?

Ben was two lines in when he heard the sudden eruption of barking outside. The dogs must have sensed something. Some nocturnal wild creature, Ben thought. Maybe an owl. He remembered the way those used to set off the guard German Shepherds at Le Val.

For a second, his focus on the journal was distracted by fond memories that inevitably led back to Brooke. It took some effort to mentally shut them out, along with the noise of barking, and go back to reading.

Seconds later, his concentration was broken again. This time, what he heard made him put the journal down with a start and turn to face the curtained balcony window.

He tensed, listened hard.

Silence outside. But he knew what he'd heard. The muffled crump of two silenced pistol reports, rapid-fire, one after the other. Each instantly followed by a brief high-pitched squeal. Then back to silence.

Someone had just shot the dogs.

Chapter Twenty-Four

Ben's abdominal muscles tightened with a jerk and he sprang off the bed. He quickly reached out and turned off the little reading lamp, then crossed the dark room to the balcony window without a sound. He peeled back the edge of one of the drapes and peered out. He could see nothing but a stretch of dimly moonlit lawn and the shadows of the bushes and shrubs that filled the villa's garden.

He eased silently through the gap in the curtains and stepped out onto the balcony, dropped into a crouch behind the balustrade and listened. The only sound he could hear was the steady, rhythmic chirping of the cicadas.

Then, as he peered through the balustrade, a movement down below caught his attention. It was followed by another. A less trained eye wouldn't even have picked up on them in the darkness: two flitting shapes crossing the edge of the lawn towards the villa.

They moved with long, fast strides, keeping low, hugging the shadows. The silhouettes of two men who knew how to move silently and unseen over unfamiliar terrain. It wasn't an easy thing to do. Ben had mastered the skill a long time ago, after long and persistent training and years of honing the art of war. He knew right away that the intruders were schooled in it too. Perhaps to the same degree he'd been, or

159

close. In two seconds they'd melted invisibly into the shadows surrounding the villa.

Ben rose to his feet and peered over the edge of the balustrade. Beneath the balcony, the wall of the villa was clad in trellis thickly covered in ivy. It was a twenty, twenty-five-foot drop to the flower borders below. Without hesitation he swung himself over the edge of the balcony and scrabbled downwards, fingers gripping smooth stone and his legs dangling free for an instant before he kicked them towards the wall and let go. He dropped six feet or so before his hands locked onto the trellis and he checked his fall, pulling himself tightly into the rustling ivy. The trellis was strong and held his weight. He quickly found a foothold and began climbing down. In moments, he was standing on the soft earth of the flower beds. Ahead was the open-sided portico that skirted the villa wall and led to the main part of the house. Which way had the intruders gone?

He glanced around him, all his senses sharply focused. He could hear nothing. On the far side of the lawn, close to the high wall that bordered the property, he could just make out two patches of blacker darkness against the deep shadow. They weren't moving. Even as he trotted silently towards them, he knew what they were.

He crouched next to one of the dead mastiffs and touched his fingers where the moonlight glistened on a shiny, wet patch. Blood, still warm, oozing from a gunshot wound.

He ran back across the grass and entered the portico, his footsteps soft and stealthy on the flagstone floor. He reached the front door of the villa and found it hanging open. They must have gone through the lock in seconds. Whoever they were, they were good. Ben slipped inside the open doorway. The mosaic-floored entrance hall was dark. Ahead of him was the broad corridor that had led him earlier that day to

Brennan's study. To his right, the brass banister rail of the curving staircase gleamed in a glow of light that was coming from above. Ben moved closer to the stairs and heard voices.

Climbing a wooden staircase without a creak in the still of the night was another art Ben had learned a long time ago, and practised many times in the course of his work. But these were marble, with a soft runner up their centre. He bounded silently up them two at a time and reached the first floor, where the banister rail curved elegantly into the wall and formed a landing overlooking the stairs and the hallway below. The voices were clearer up here. From their harsh tone, Ben had the impression that it wasn't Brennan's long-lost friends who'd come to visit.

From the landing led a wide passage, and a little way up the passage was a half-open door. The light was shining from the gap. Ben moved closer. The voices grew louder. He couldn't make out what they were saying. He stopped. In the glow from the half-open door he could see the gilded frames of paintings hanging on the opposite wall. And something else.

The centrepiece of the display of antique arms was a Celtic battle shield. Irish, Ben guessed, the circular kind called a targe. Probably four hundred years old, wood and leather banded with iron. Fanned out over the top of the shield was an array of ancient daggers. Framing it left and right, with their blade tips crossed in an X below it, hung a pair of basket-hilted broadswords sheathed in steel scabbards.

Ben reached up and unhooked the one nearest to him. It came away from its wall mounting without a sound. He slipped his hand inside the steel basket and gripped the handle. It felt rough, like sharkskin. He didn't draw the blade out, for the *zing* of steel on steel that would give his presence away. He crept closer to the door, the sword substantial and comforting in his grip.

And peered tentatively through the gap into the room beyond.

Chapter Twenty-Five

The two intruders were dressed in black, from their combat boots to their ski masks. Black cordura holsters strapped to their hips. Black Glock pistols, one holstered and the other pressed tightly into Professor Gray Brennan's right temple.

The bed was a tall antique four-poster that dominated the far end of the room. Its fleur-de-lys covers were thrown back as if the two men had dragged its occupant bodily out of it as he slept, giving him a rude awakening. Now they were holding him in a chair in the middle of the room with his wrists bound.

One man stood behind the chair with a gloved hand cupped under Brennan's chin and the pistol at his head. Ben noticed the peculiar magazine loaded into the weapon's butt: not the usual double-stack box magazine, but an ultra-high-capacity double-drum mag. As if its user had anticipated the need to let off a hundred rounds in a hell of a hurry. The other man was standing in front of the captive with his back to the doorway. He was saying, 'Okay, asshole, one more time. Where are the fuckin' books?'

Ben took in the accent right away. An American, from one of the southern states, somewhere like Alabama or Louisiana. A thin, greasy blonde ponytail stuck out from the back of his ski mask. He was wearing his Glock in a left-handed holster. That sounded a note of recognition in Ben's mind.

'You don't tell us, I'm gonna watch your brains spatter all over that wall,' the man with the southern accent said. 'Your choice, douchebag.'

There'd been a struggle, even though Brennan was hopelessly overmatched. The front of his silk pyjama top was ripped, showing a welt of diseased and broken skin underneath. A vase of flowers on a table near the bed had been upset, the brightly coloured flowers trampled into the rug by the intruders' boots. The scent of flowers filled the room. So did another smell. A sharp tang that was strangely familiar to Ben.

Mint.

It was the same faintly unpleasant odour of nicotine gum he'd caught on the breath of one of Kristen's killers, that day on the beach.

The ponytailed man with his back to Ben was the one doing the chewing. With a chill of anger, Ben noticed the Ka-Bar combat knife in its sheath on the man's belt.

No coincidence. There wasn't any doubt in his mind that he was looking at the knife that had been used to murder Kristen.

The situation inside the room was surreal. Most men dragged out of bed at two in the morning, bound and held in a chair with a gun to their head by masked attackers, would have been ready to wet themselves in terror. Ben had seen more than a few of those. But not Brennan. He was grinning up at his captors as if he'd just remembered a good joke. If Ben found it weird, the two masked men found it even weirder. It was hardly the reaction they'd expected, and that was pissing them off.

As shocked as he was to see these two men here, Ben

knew he had the element of surprise on his side. He knew he could rush into the room unsheathing the heavy broadsword and split the gum-chewing bastard diagonally from shoulder to hip before he even had time to turn around. But the element of surprise would only take him so far. It wouldn't prevent his companion with the drawn pistol from pumping half of that big drum magazine into Ben before the sword could touch him. And that didn't make a lot of sense tactically.

The ponytailed guy drew his Glock. He thrust it furiously in Brennan's face and then averted the muzzle ninety degrees to let off a silenced double-tap that punched a pair of holes in the bedroom wall. 'Last chance. Where are they?'

'I know exactly what books you're talking about, and I know exactly where they are,' Brennan replied crisply. 'But I won't tell, so you'll just have to shoot me. Right here between the eyes. Go on, get on with it.'

The masked men stared at him.

'I repeat, I have no intention whatsoever of co-operating,' Brennan informed them. 'I am a witness to this assault and you have no choice but to silence me. What're you waiting for?'

In the brief silence that followed, Ben realised that nothing he could do would save Brennan. And that was the way Brennan wanted it.

The two men glanced at one another. The one holding him in the chair shrugged. 'This guy's nuts.'

The other nodded. 'Do it.'

Then the pistol at Brennan's temple fired. The impact of the bullet at extreme close range sent the historian toppling sideways, spilling out of his chair as he dragged it down with him. By the time he flopped to the floor, he was already dead.

He hadn't suffered. Probably hadn't registered anything more than an infinitesimal white flash as the bullet passed through his brain and out the other side. His killers couldn't know it, but it was the kind of clean, merciful death their victim must have prayed for a thousand times since his illness had struck. A doctor in a Swiss euthanasia clinic couldn't have given him a quicker end.

But they weren't going to get a medal for it.

'Now what?' said the one with the smoking pistol. 'We're never gonna find them.'

'No worries,' said the other, cracking a grin through his mask. 'Sometimes Plan B is just plain more fun. Let's torch this place and get out of here.' He flicked his pistol on safe and thrust it back in its holster, turning towards the door as he did it.

He stepped out of the bedroom and into the corridor.

Ben was waiting for him there.

Chapter Twenty-Six

A broadsword against two Glocks. It wasn't an evenly matched fight, but Ben couldn't do a lot about that. He wasn't about to let these guys walk away. He still had surprise on his side – and doorways offered advantages for combat that helped even the odds in ways that an open space never could.

As the first black-clad figure stepped out of the room and into the dark passage, Ben closed in on him fast, smelling the mint on the guy's breath.

He didn't want to kill them both, not yet, not until he found out who they were working for and why. Mint-stinker would be kept alive for now. Gripping the sheathed blade with both hands, Ben smashed the steel basket and pommel of the broadsword into the back of his ponytailed head. The blow sounded like a hammer hitting a cabbage.

The man fell forwards into the passage with a cry of pain, twisting as he went down, his hand going to his weapon as quick as a striking cobra. Ben lashed out a first kick that sent the pistol clattering from his hand and a follow-up that caught him under the chin and bounced his head against the floor. The other man was still in the doorway, his eyes wide in the holes of his mask. That split-second of hesitation was all Ben needed to rip the sword blade out of its scabbard and lunge at him.

This one he could kill.

With fast footwork and a powerful thrust, the tip of a sword could accelerate towards its target as fast as a thrown javelin and with enough forward momentum for even the heaviest, broadest blade to penetrate right through an enemy's ribcage. And Ben was fast. But the man was faster, dangerously faster. He threw himself backwards into Brennan's bedroom, drawing himself out of range of the lethal stab. Ben propelled himself towards the doorway, lunging the sword at him again with even greater force. The man grabbed the edge of the door, slammed it and drove it shut with a powerful kick. Ben had put too much energy into his sword strike to pull the blow. The sharp point of the sword sheared into one of the wooden panels, eighteen inches of blade passing right through. Ben yanked on the hilt to pull it out for another strike, but the fibres of the wood gripped it tight. It wouldn't budge.

He'd just lost his primary weapon. But there was another behind him on the floor. Abandoning the trapped sword, he dived away from the doorway to scoop up the Glock he'd struck from Mint-stinker's hand.

He'd hit the guy pretty hard, though evidently not hard enough. He was struggling to heave himself up from the floor and roll across to grab the weapon at the same time Ben went for it. Ben drove a knee into his chest and punched him in the face, felt his knuckles connect solidly against bone. It was a disabling punch, but this guy seemed able to absorb them with uncanny ease. Ben hit him again, blood smearing his fist. This time Mint-stinker flopped back down, but he looked as if he might pop right up again. Ben was losing precious seconds.

Too many precious seconds. The bedroom door burst open, the hilt of the trapped sword crashing against the wall. The second man reappeared in the doorway, his Glock with the bulky-looking twin-drum magazine thrust out in a two-handed grip and the sights rapidly acquiring a bead on Ben.

Ben's reaching hand was still a metre away from the fallen gun.

The second man took a step forward. As if in slow motion, Ben saw the well-practised flick of his thumb against his weapon's fire selector switch. He smiled. As if to say, *Gotcha, asshole.*

And in that fleeting fraction of an instant, Ben knew he was in more serious trouble than he'd bargained for.

Because pistols didn't normally have fire selector switches.

With a shock, Ben understood what was about to be unleashed on him. Getting shot at with a handgun was never good news, but now Ben was realising why these particular weapons were loaded up with twin-drum magazines. It was because they were Glock 18s, outwardly almost identical to standard pistols but officially classed as submachine guns. At the flip of a lever, they could be switched from normal semi-auto mode to spew out a constant stream of bullets at a rate of twelve hundred a minute.

Ben scarcely had time to think *Uh-oh* before he had to duck back through the dark passage, abandoning all notion of grabbing the fallen Glock. He kept his head down, weaving desperately as a zigzagging line of bullet holes churned up into the wall and chased him like a swarm of attacking hornets. Masonry chippings flew. Paintings dropped from their hooks, glass exploding. He dived, rolled, felt bullets zing past and flying bits of plaster sting his face. Twelve hundred rounds cycled per minute. One every five hundredths of a second. The air was thick with copper-jacketed lead alloy.

Ben reached the top of the stairs but knew that he'd never make it down without getting shot to pieces. He flipped himself over the landing rail as rounds sparked and ricocheted off its bars, and dropped into space.

For a moment he felt himself falling; then his shoulder and ribs exploded with pain as he hit the stairs ten or fifteen below. There was no time to worry about damage, as long as it wasn't crippling. He rolled down a few steps, then found his feet and went bounding towards the bottom.

The shooter appeared at the top of the stairs behind him, ejecting his empty drum magazine and slamming in a fresh one. His colleague was right behind him, hobbling slightly and holding his pistol in one gloved hand, with the other clamped to the back of his head.

Ben launched himself from the eighth step and hit the mosaic floor of the entrance hall running, heading for the front door. Nothing seemed to be broken, and if it was, he'd worry about it on the other side of that door. He could be there in six racing strides which, as long as the shooter fumbled his reload, might just be possible.

But the shooter didn't. He knew exactly what he was doing.

'Let's torch this place,' the guy had said. And as gunfire erupted around him again, Ben realised they weren't thinking of using matches. The stairway filled with bursts of white light as the rounds from the fresh drum mag ignited into flame like miniature Greek fire.

Incendiary explosive ammunition. Used in warfare to burn out vehicles and buildings and dispatch any and all enemy personnel inside them with the extra edge of efficiency that modern small arms munitions technology allowed. Ben had fired off more than a few crates of blue-tipped stuff in his military days, seen it light up tactical targets faster than rocket grenades.

And now he knew he had about a chance in a thousand of not getting lit up by one himself before he got to the door.

He felt a bullet rake the left shoulder of his leather jacket, bursting into a flash that burned his ear. He dived flat on his front and slid painfully across the floor as another burst zipped past him like tracer and shredded one of the drapes hanging over the high windows, instantly setting it alight. The hallway was filling with smoke and flame. The shooter kept his finger on the trigger, spraying bullets wildly. Bullets thunked into the door, exploding on impact and sending burning chunks of wood spinning through the smoke.

Ben knew he'd never make it to the door. Scrambling for a grip on the polished floor, he leapt to his feet. Changed course and sprinted up the corridor in the direction of Brennan's study. The shooters reached the bottom of the stairs and trained their weapons on him, both firing now. One of the ornamental plant pots exploded into fiery fragments of ceramic. Ben reached the bend in the corridor. His sore shoulder cannoned off the opposite wall. He staggered, kept running. Behind him, the whole corridor was a tunnel of fire. The flames licked and danced up to the ceiling, spreading fast and blocking the way for his pursuers.

Ben's mind darted back and forth between two options as he ran. He needed to get out of here, and fast, because if a bullet didn't take him down, the rapidly spreading fire surely would. But the volumes of the Stamford journal were still lying where he'd left them, on the bed in the guest annexe. If there was even a chance that the diaries could solve the unanswered questions that filled his head, he owed it to Kristen to rescue them from the fire. He hesitated, but only for an instant. He'd come this far. There couldn't be any turning back.

Half blinded by smoke, he kept moving.

Chapter Twenty-Seven

'Hold your fire,' said the one whose name was Matt Ritter. He lowered his own weapon and put a hand on his colleague's shoulder. The corridor the running man had disappeared into was a wall of flames.

Billy Bob Moon turned to him with a look of disgust. 'Tell me that wasn't the same prick we ran into in fuckin' Ireland.'

'Can't tell you he wasn't,' Ritter replied.

Moon spat out a chewed-up ball of nicotine gum. It was red with blood. 'Sonofabitch damn near stove my brains in. I don't care what he's doing here. All I know is, I'm gonna kill him.'

'You MARSOC pussies are all the same,' Ritter said. 'Quit your whining and let's move.'

The front door was burning fiercely from the incendiary rounds that had punched into it. Ritter crunched through it with his combat boot. After five kicks there was a ragged hole big enough for a man to pass. He burst through the blazing wood and outside, followed by Moon. They turned back to face the villa and emptied another fifty rounds apiece into the doorway and windows, until fire and smoke were pouring out of them. Ritter holstered his weapon, grabbed an incendiary grenade from his belt and lobbed it through a shattered window. The two of them averted their faces from the hot explosion that shook the villa.

'I love it,' Moon said, unclipping one of his own grenades and tossing it in after the first. Another blinding flash and deafening boom. When they turned back to face the house, the whole front of it was a raging inferno.

Sometimes Plan B is just plain more fun. In this case their orders were to burn the place to the ground if Brennan didn't give up the books the boss wanted. Neither man was much concerned with what exactly they contained or why the boss had such ants in his pants about them. They were just some bunch of old books. Paper and card and leather. They were combustible, and they needed to be disposed of. And that was good enough for them.

Ritter turned away from the burning house and stepped over to shine a torch through the window of the VW Touareg parked in the courtyard nearby. He could see paperwork lying on the front passenger seat. It was a car rental agreement. He used the solid aluminium head of the torch to smash the window. Reached in and grabbed the rental agreement and ran his eye down to where the name of the customer was printed, then to the box underneath containing the guy's signature. Ben Hope. Who the hell was Ben Hope?

He flicked the sheet of paper back inside the broken car window and said to Moon, 'Let's finish this. You go that way. You see him, you take him down.'

'You bet your ass I will,' Moon said fiercely. He was still smarting from the punches to the face and the blow to the back of his head. They split up, skirting the sides of the burning house in opposite directions. As Moon ran, he could see no sign of anyone trying to get out of the place. He must still be inside. Suffering, Moon hoped.

Flame and smoke were belching from most of the downstairs windows by now. Moon detached an incendiary grenade from his belt and hurled it at one of the dark windows on the upper floor. His arm was strong, and his aim was true. The grenade sailed up through the darkness and hit the window with a tinkle of breaking glass, followed by a wall-shattering boom and the breathy *whumph* of a fireball spreading through the villa's upstairs. Grinning, he shielded his eyes at the dazzling flash and ran on, ready to gun down anything that dared try to escape the burning house. Still no sign of life.

Moon stopped as he came to what looked like the back of a kitchen with the vent for an extractor fan and a wooden housing for two large butane bottles. Excellent. He skipped back a few metres and then hosed a short burst from his Glock into them. The blazing incendiary bullets punched through the steel.

The explosion almost knocked him off his feet. Shrapnel shattered windows and tore up the wall. A gigantic sheet of flame from the erupting gas threatened to set him alight as it mushroomed up as tall as the house, lighting up the whole night sky. Moon staggered back, whooping, 'Whoa, motherfucker!' Now there were flames rolling and licking out of almost every window of the villa. He'd burned out enough buildings in his time to know the chances of anything emerging alive from an inferno like that.

Four years out of MARSOC, the US Marines Special Operations Command, former gunnery sergeant Billy Bob Moon had never enjoyed his work so much. Who said civilian life had to be a drag? He ran on again, lobbing two more grenades into the house as he went, just for good measure. He'd covered the entire perimeter of the burning building by the time he met up with Ritter on the other side.

Ritter didn't look amused. 'What the hell was that explosion?'

'Someone getting the job done,' Moon told him. 'They not teach you boys anything at Fort Campbell?'

'Fuckin' shrap came right over the house. You trying to get us killed?'

'Now who's the pussy?' Moon said with a grin. His last words were drowned out as a chunk of wreckage broke away from the house in a surge of flames and tumbled down with a crash onto the roof and windscreen of the parked VW Touareg. The flames quickly got a purchase on the vehicle and in seconds fire was licking all over the bodywork.

'Come on, man,' Moon said. 'Job's done. Let's get back to the truck.'

Ritter was looking intently at what was left of the villa. 'Who the hell was that guy?'

'Who gives a shit any more?' Moon said. 'Fucker's barbeque.'

Ritter hesitated, still looking at the burning house. Then he did a double take and pointed. 'I wouldn't be so sure about that, bro. There he is.'

Chapter Twenty-Eight

Ben ran on through the villa as fire spread rapidly everywhere around him. Smoke filled his eyes and nose. Tears and sweat streamed down his face. He felt the walls shake from an explosion; then again, and again. He knew what the blasts meant. The killers were intent on reducing the whole place to a smouldering ruin. And if he didn't get out soon, he'd be buried in the ashes.

The villa was a labyrinth of passageways and connecting rooms. He sprinted from doorway to doorway, driven back repeatedly by curtains of flame that surged up at him, threatening to engulf him. The heat was intolerable. Just as he thought he'd taken a fatal turning, he suddenly found what he was searching for: a back stairway leading upwards. Only the first few steps were on fire. He bounded up them, heat scorching his shins and calves. Another shattering explosion rocked the building, far more violent than the others, and he had to duck as plaster rained down from the ceiling.

'Jesus,' he muttered, but the deafening noise drowned out his voice. It felt as if the building had just taken a direct hit from a bomb. He cringed on the dark stairway for a second, half expecting the whole ceiling to come crashing down on his head.

Onwards, upwards: he reached the landing and came to

a door, pressed his hand against it to feel for the telltale heat of fire in the room behind it. It was cool to the touch. He burst through into the shadowy room, blinked sweat out of his eyes and made out that he was in a spare bedroom Brennan had used for storage. Beyond silhouetted stacks of boxes and piled books, he saw the single small window that overlooked the front courtyard, ringed with ivy that flickered orange from the glare of the fire. He ran over to it, threw it open and clambered out. Cool night air hit him and his parched lungs sucked in oxygen. He grabbed fistfuls of the prickling ivy and swung himself right out of the window, clinging to the wall like a spider. He twisted his head to the right and saw that his bearings had been accurate – the balcony of the annexe bedroom was just twenty feet away. As long as the ivy held his weight, he could make it and get inside. Flames were surging from windows below and to the left of him. He could only hope that the annexe wasn't on fire too.

Ben began inching his way along the wall, finding hand-holds and footholds wherever he could and praying he wouldn't fall. The balcony edged closer. Closer. Almost in reach now—

And then he heard the shout from below. He barely had time to glance down and see the two masked men standing below in the courtyard before they'd raised their weapons to aim at him and started firing.

Ben leapt the last few feet across to the balcony as bullets stitched the wall and snipped ivy leaves into confetti. He scrambled over the stone rail and fell into a crouch behind the balustrade. Bullets ricocheted off the stonework inches away as he kicked open the French windows and scrambled through. To his dismay, he was met by a wall of heat, the choking stench of smoke and the flicker of flames inside the bedroom. He struggled to his feet and battled through it. Spotting his leather jacket and bag lying on the floor, he snatched them up. The drapes of the four-poster were ablaze, flames licking dangerously close to the volumes of the journal that he'd left on the bed. The one he'd been reading was beginning to smoulder. He grabbed it and beat out the flames.

Coughing from the smoke, he quickly stuffed the books into his bag. Now he'd got what he'd come for, and it had better be worth it. It was time to get out of here.

Gunfire from the window told him there was no escape that way.

The en-suite bathroom. Ben crashed through the door. He was almost blind from the thickening smoke but managed to find the bath towel hanging from the rail. Ripping it free, he plunged it under the taps of the old-fashioned bathtub. With the wet towel pressed tightly over his nose and mouth, he ran back out into the bedroom into the scorching heat. The fire was spreading all across the bed, greedily devouring the carpet, approaching the door in a liquid tide that seemed to move as if it was alive. Ben got there first and dashed out into the corridor.

Both ends were on fire. He was trapped. There was no way to run, no way out.

Except straight up. Ben yanked hard on the cord dangling from the loft access hatch. The trapdoor dropped down and a telescoping ladder slid with a clatter from the hatch. The aluminium rungs were hot to the touch as he went clambering up it into the dark attic space. Reaching the top, he lay across the rough attic floor and hauled the ladder up, slamming the trapdoor shut behind him. He couldn't block the spread of the fire, but he could at least slow it down.

A little. It wouldn't be long before the first flames began

to get a purchase up here. Already he could see the telltale flickering glow shining up through the cracks in the floor-boards, and the smoke trickling up between them. In the dim light he could make out the attic junk carelessly dumped up here, old chairs, packing cases, bits of spare timber left over from some carpentry job.

He got to his feet, dizzy from smoke inhalation and well aware that he might faint any time soon if he didn't get some air into his lungs. The attic space was low enough for him to grope blindly at the underside of the roof. He needed to find a skylight, some way to get out onto the roof, or it would be all over for him. He could find nothing, just the rough wooden beams, battens and roofing felt above him. He was getting desperate now, his chest heaving involuntarily hard and fast and drawing in nothing but smoke. The pouring sweat was stinging his eyes. Just seconds of consciousness remained. He had to do something.

Chapter Twenty-Nine

He half stooped, half fell to the floor. His fumbling fingers closed on the sawn end of a length of four-by-four timber. He dragged it towards him. It felt as heavy as a lead pipe to his oxygen-starved muscles, and he cried out with the effort that it took to pick the piece of wood off the floor and drive its square end straight up like a battering ram at the roof. He almost collapsed from the effort. Nothing happened. He gritted his teeth and put everything he had into a second blow.

This time he felt something give. There was a crack. Splinters of broken tile fell in, grazing his head and shoulders. Suddenly, he could taste fresh air again, and the sensation gave him the strength he needed for one final upward heave. The wood drove up through the roof. Tiles cracked and tumbled down through the ragged hole that had appeared above him.

Gasping, Ben let the length of timber clatter to the attic floor. Reached his hands up out of the hole and dragged himself painfully through, gulping lungfuls of blessed air. Dragging his bag up after him, he staggered to his feet on the slope of the roof, rubbed his stinging eyes and looked round to see the extent of the fire that was consuming the whole villa. The night sky was livid with its blood-red glow.

Below him, the figures of the two masked shooters were disappearing into the shadows, making their way to the perimeter wall. They must have a vehicle hidden nearby, he thought, and from the screech of approaching sirens he could faintly hear through the roar of the fire he understood why they were making their escape. Someone must have seen the red glow and called the emergency services; the perpetrators had no intention of being around when they arrived.

Neither had Ben, if there was anything he could do about it. Now his energy was rekindled and he needed to find a way down to the ground before the damn roof fell in and he found himself right in the heart of the inferno. He ran along the roof, careful not to slip on the sloping tiles. It was a long way down.

Ben would later hazard a guess that what happened next must have been a gas pipe rupturing. He'd never know for sure. All he knew was that the strong blast somewhere below him sent up a fountain of flame and splintering tiles right under his feet as he ran, and sent him flying.

There was nothing he could do to prevent himself from tumbling down the steep pitch of the roof, over and over. The left sleeve of his jacket had caught fire. He let go of his bag as he grappled to arrest his fall by hanging on to the iron guttering, but it came away with his weight.

Then he was falling, flailing in mid-air, trying to control his fall the way he'd learned in parachute training.

He hit the canvas awning below, bounced, rolled and then was tumbling through empty space again. The ground seemed to rush up at him: a terrace or patio area, the concrete amber-lit by the glow of the blazing villa. Thoughts of broken legs, or worse, flashed through his mind.

The impact knocked the breath out of him. But instead

of his body being smashed against the hard ground, he sank deep into something soft and spongy that gave under him. Wetness and coldness suddenly enveloped him, a shock after the heat of the fire. In his confusion he realised that he'd missed the concrete and splashed down on the plastic cover of Brennan's unused swimming pool. The force of his landing had ripped part of the cover from its moorings around the edge, and now the thick, crinkly plastic was wrapping itself around him like a shroud as he sank into the water, trapping his movements. The sleeve of his jacket wasn't on fire any more – it wasn't burning that worried him now. He struggled violently to free himself from the plastic cocoon that was hugging his arms tight against his body and preventing him from kicking out with his legs. Water was filling his mouth and throat. He managed to rip an arm free. His fingers closed around something – one of the pool cover anchor cords that hadn't snapped. He pulled against it, praying that it wouldn't come free.

It didn't. He pulled again, felt the plastic shroud loosen its grip around him. Suddenly his other arm was free, then his legs; and he hauled himself gasping and streaming with water onto the tiled edge of the pool.

He looked up as the roof of the villa caved in with a final groan of buckling timbers and collapsed into the burning shell of the house. The flames leapt high into the night sky, sparks and embers flying up like distress signals. The canvas awning over the patio burst alight and began to crumple towards the ground. At the last second, Ben saw his fallen bag lying on the concrete below it, and had to leap to snatch it away before the fiery canopy swallowed it up. Ben carried the bag to safety, inside it the books of the Stamford journal that he'd risked his life to rescue.

Away from the powerful heat of the fire, he began to

shudder with cold inside his wet clothing. His whole body was aching from the exertion of his escape from the villa, but he forced himself to break into a run as he crossed the lawn towards the shadows of the trees. He pressed through the branches, reached the wall beyond and lobbed his bag over the top before grabbing a handhold on the craggy stonework and clambering over after it.

The sirens were getting louder and closer every second. Ben could see the swirling lights in the distance as he dropped down on the other side of the wall. By the time the shrieking fire engines appeared and came speeding down the road towards the gates of the villa, he'd already slipped away out of sight.

In a patch of forest a kilometre away, he stripped off his wet things, rubbed himself down with a dry T-shirt from his bag and then changed into fresh things. He zipped up his jacket, shivering in the night air but knowing he'd soon warm up as he walked. Nothing he could do about his shoes, which squelched uncomfortably as he made his way, cross-country, through the darkness.

He still didn't know whether the Stamford journals would tell him anything. But he'd nonetheless managed to learn a lot from his visit to Madeira. He thought about the masked men who'd shot Brennan, now long gone and no doubt heading for home. They were Americans. Professional killers, without a doubt highly trained former military operatives – perhaps even from a Special Forces background, judging by the unmistakable skills they'd demonstrated that night.

Ben had known those kinds of men turn bad before. The ugly signs were often evident even before they quit the military and went off to pursue private contracts and a career that allowed them to kill for cash, sometimes also for pleasure. He thought back to the Ka-Bar knife used in

Kristen's murder. For decades, it had been the edged weapon of choice for the US Marines. He wondered whether either of the men had served with the Corps.

Whoever these two were, they had access to serious hardware and the means to transport it undetected from one country to another. Which meant there was big money involved: it was no cheap undertaking to hire men like that to do one's dirty work, equip them accordingly and move them from place to place without getting caught.

So the individual payrolling them would be someone of considerable means. That same someone must have known about the Stamford journals from Kristen's computer, and the email it contained from her to Gray Brennan in which she'd mentioned them. Somehow, the killer perceived the journals as enough of a threat that they were ready to snuff out anyone who got close to them.

And for reasons Ben didn't yet understand, it all seemed to revolve around the name McCrory.

He walked faster through the trees, his steps silent, his mind full of cold, brooding rage. The first streaky red-gold tendrils of dawn were working their way into the sky. He'd be off this island in a matter of hours, and he could clearly visualise the mental signpost telling him where to head next.

It was pointing towards Tulsa, Oklahoma.

Chapter Thirty

The soft thrum of the airliner filled the business-class cabin. The guy in the pinstriped suit in the aisle seat next to Ben had been asleep for the last hour or so. Ben glanced for a moment out of the porthole to his right and watched wisps of cloud break and whip over the expanse of the wing. Somewhere far below was the open water of the Atlantic.

It had been a mad scramble to get to Lisbon in time for the Iberia flight to New York. They were due to land at JFK in another five hours; then more sitting around waiting before his connecting flight, which was scheduled to touch down in Tulsa mid-afternoon, local time. There wasn't much for him to do until then but read and think. He returned to the volume of the Stamford journal that lay open on the fold-down table, flipped several more pages and went on with it.

April 15th, 1847
God forgive me when I so selfishly complain, as I have done many times before in these pages, that one of the more odious of my social duties as Lady Stamford is the role I must play as hostess on those frequent occasions when Edgar entertains his friends here at Glenfell. I can only suppose that the shooting on the estate offers so much more than is

to be had in England, for it seems the house is seldom free of yet another contingent of guests, most of them of the same raucous boorish coarse vain blockheaded variety as any of Edgar's fellow Members I have yet had the pleasure to meet. Who would have thought there could be so many Lords and Sirs? I have been introduced to such a multitude, I can scarcely tell one from another. They might all have been cut from the same cloth.

As I sit here writing these words in my chamber, the gentlemen have retired to the drawing room for their port and cigars and their frequent outbursts of laughter can be heard drifting upwards through the floor. I am afraid I excused myself early from the dinner table, feigning a headache, as I confess I sometimes do – but the truth is that I could not bear to be in the presence of those men for another minute. There were twelve seated for dinner, and not a decent soul among them. Can they possibly be so blind to what is happening here in Ireland? Is there no human compassion in their hearts at all? No, none, and as I hurried away from the dining room I did not know whether to fall weeping to the floor – or else take up one of Edgar's fowling pieces from the gun room and allow my rage to carry me to commit a heinous act upon them.

The conversation had yet been following a tolerably pleasant course until Lord Carlisle, seated to my immediate left, began his discourse on what the future of this country must be and what a lucky stroke the famine is for England. Another of Edgar's friends, a strikingly toadlike little man with whiskers growing like moss upon his jowls and whose name escapes me in my anger, then spoke up: 'I see old Bentinck is making noises in the House again. He will not keep quiet, continually accusing the government of the most *shocking neglect. Now he demands to know what is to be done with the 400,000 quarters of corn in stock in the ports of London, Liverpool and Glasgow that could be sent to Ireland to feed the starving people there.'*

At this, Lord Carlisle gave a derisory grunt. 'Bentinck is an imbecile,' said he, wagging his fork for emphasis. 'There can be no interference with the natural course of trade. Labouchere, the Irish Secretary,' he added for the benefit of the necessarily ignorant parties at the table, that is to say, myself, 'rightly states that the government has pursued a wise policy in not interfering with the supply of food to Ireland in any way which could compete with the efforts of private traders.'

I could feel the colour rising up in my cheeks. As hard as I tried to control my impulse, I could not but speak out: 'Am I to understand from your words, sir, that the calamity that has befallen this country cannot be allowed to affect the shipping of its abundant crops of grain and herds of cattle to England; that the traders' and speculators' profits, the landlords' rents, the agents' commissions, override all considerations of such terrible human suffering as we in Ireland witness every day, and that political economy is best accomplished simply by carrying on business as usual, as though nobody had died, or were dying at this very minute, a slow and cruel death from starvation?'

There was a weighty silence up and down the length of the table and I was aware of faces turning my way, most of all that of Edgar, who regarded me with a glower of disapproval for daring to address Lord Carlisle in such a manner. Whether or not L.C. had it in mind to reply to me (one does not, after all, enter into political discussion with a mere simple woman) it was Sir Harry Billington, the

Honourable Member for Guildford, seated further up the table to my right, who then weighed in with his view.

'It appears to me,' said he, 'that Ireland's soil and climate offer the conditions best suited for pasture; hence it appears that cattle, above all things, seem to be the most appropriate stock for Ireland. Corn can be brought from one country to another from a great distance, at rather small freights. It is not so with cattle. The great hives of industry in England and Scotland can draw their shiploads of corn from more southern climates, but they must have a constant dependence on Ireland for an abundant supply of meat.'

This drew several nods from around the table, and grumbles of 'Hear him, hear him', and 'A glass of wine with you, sir'.

'Is this your political economy, sir?' I cried, quite unable to restrain myself. 'To fill up every available corner of every field of Ireland with livestock reared solely for the mouths of England? And what of the common Irish people who would be swept aside to make way for such a plan?'

'What of them, madam?' said Sir Harry, fixing me with a whimsical air. 'There may not be many left, afore long; and may I say good riddance to 'em.'

Lord Carlisle, who had been eyeing me all this while from under his thick, white brows, smiled with benevolent condescension and cut short the protest that was forming on my lips. 'My dear Lady Elizabeth, I applaud your spirited defence of the Celt. However, we cannot doubt that by the inscrutable but invariable laws of nature, they are as a race less energetic, less independent, less industrious than the Saxon. This is nothing more or less than the archaic condition of their birthright.'

I thought of the many small Irish farmers and cottiers I

have known, of the worthy servants who keep this estate of ours running year upon year, how enduringly they all toil to feed their families. I looked at the round, protuberant bellies of the dinner guests, the buttons of their waistcoats straining to contain them, at the double or even triple chins greasy with sauce; and I wondered how many of our illustrious company had ever truly done a day's hard labour in their lives.

'But they starve, sir,' I protested. 'They are dying. Can you not see what is happening all around?'

"Tis a pity, to be sure,' replied Sir Harry, raising another great forkful of roast pork to his mouth. 'But madam, you must consider. Why, only last week in the House I heard Sir Robert Peel say, and I quote the great man: "I wish it were possible to take advantage of this calamity for introducing among the people of Ireland the taste for a better and more certain provision for their support than that which they have hithertofore cultivated." There's the truth of it. If they starve, they starve only by their own folly, this primitive and inexplicable lust for their beloved praties, at the exclusion of all else, and of all common intelligence.'

Speechless for an instant, I looked to my husband, but he was at that moment heartily digging into his plate. I could no longer touch mine. 'Allow me to say with the deepest respect, Sir Harry, that you are as sadly misinformed as the gentleman of whom you speak with such admiration. The Irish have not subsisted solely on the potato for any reason other than it is we who have forced this choice upon them. Therefore it is we who should be helping them to—'

Sir Harry broke into a laugh before I could finish. 'Upon my word, Edgar, your wife is as irrepressible as she is beautiful. We must be careful, eh?' Turning back towards me, he

189

gave a bow. 'My dear madam, I stand most humbly corrected.'

'Gentlemen, I ask that you forgive my wife's enthusiasm in these matters,' Edgar said with a twisted smile upon his face for his guests' benefit, the flashing look of warning in his eyes intended for mine. 'She may play and sing like an angel, ride like the wind and have been able to strip old Harte of nearly ten pounds at cards . . .'

'Did she, by God?' exclaimed Lord Carlisle.

'. . . But she is yet to be instructed in the wisdom of commerce and politics,' my dearest husband finished (and Heaven help me, should he ever read these words).

'I am sorry if I spoke out of turn,' I replied. 'And beg the gentleman's forgiveness of my woman's ignorance. I realise now how foolishly naïve I must appear in these subjects, and shall resolve henceforth to listen, and learn, and remain silent.'

This elicited smiles of amusement from all present, except from Edgar (whose wrath I expect to face later tonight). I looked into their eyes and could see no shred of humanity, no sparkle other than that which comes from too much wine.

How I wished, and still wish, that Stephen were here. Is it very wicked of me to reflect that I sometimes feel as starved of warmth and kindness as the poor Irish are of physical sustenance?

Ben's reading was interrupted by the clinking of the drinks trolley coming down the aisle and a smiling hostess asking whether he'd like a drink. His eye wandered over the row of malt Scotch miniatures on the trolley. 'Just some mineral water,' he said, with a pang in his heart. The trolley went clinking and jinking onwards down the aisle, and he returned to the journal.

He liked Elizabeth Stamford's spirit. His old friend Jeff Dekker would have described her as 'a lady with balls'. He was finding himself getting drawn deeper into her world, almost forgetting sometimes that he was meant to be searching for Brennan's explosive secret. He hadn't found it yet, after skimming nearly halfway through the four volumes of her elegant writing. He turned a few more pages.

May 3rd, 1847
How it appals me to witness the condition of those still living. Once hardy peasants now appear shrivelled and diminished in size and stature. Flesh and muscle has wasted away until the bones of their frames are barely covered, brittle and easily broken, their joints so weak that one might imagine their poor bodies falling to pieces before one's eyes. Their shoulders and necks are wasted so as to barely support the weight of their head. The skin of their limbs appears as dry and rough as old parchment and hangs in loose folds where once was strong muscle and healthy flesh. As their bodies feast upon their own fabric for sustenance, with each passing day their eye sockets grow larger and more cavernous, the eyes themselves sinking deeper into their skulls so that it becomes painful to look at them.

Many of the children, their growth brought to a halt, are in a condition still more deplorable. Arms stripped of flesh, like little skeletons, their inner structure as clearly visible as if bare bones had been covered in the thinnest muslin. Young faces as wizened and furrowed as those of the old. The hair falls in patches from their scalps, leaving their bald little skulls so pitiful and frail in appearance.

If but one child were so afflicted, even a stranger would come rushing to give aid. But there are thousands of them. They are everywhere, and all wearing the same look of utter desperation and hopelessness that rends my heart at the knowledge that I can do nothing whatever to save them. I am perfectly sure I will never eat a bite again without choking.'

The vividness of Elizabeth Stamford's account brought back painful memories to Ben as he remembered the victims of civil war, genocide and famine he'd seen in the Third World during his military days. Cadaverous children with distended bellies and hollow eyes, many near to the end and virtually unable to move as thick black swarms of blowflies clustered all over their dying little bodies. The worst thing had been their passive acceptance of their plight, young and old alike apparently quite peacefully resigned to death.

And death had been a certainty for most of them, with no chance of rescue. As a soldier, Ben's duty had been to walk on by, put it out of his mind and stay focused on the bigger picture of his mission. But he'd never really forgotten, and those awful reawoken visions now came flooding back so strongly into his mind that he could almost smell the stench of death and decay, hear the buzzing of the flies. Take out the heat and dust of Africa and the ever-looming presence of war, substitute the ruin of the devastated potato fields, the mud, the rats, the destitution and homelessness, the passing rumble of the death carts on the roads, and the distant laughter of rulers hundreds of miles away in London who couldn't care less, and the picture was just the same. The suffering of these people had been no less appalling. Perhaps even more so.

For what it was worth, Third World peoples of the modern

age had the solace of whatever the UN and other organisations could manage to do for them. They had famine relief, aid workers, food shipments. Usually too little, too late, and all too often hampered or hijacked by corrupt bureaucracy – but it was something, and it saved lives.

The Irish had had nothing. Only the faint, faraway hope of salvation in the promised land of America, for those few who could raise the price of the ocean crossing and survived the voyage. For those left behind, only the grim reality of death and disease, squalor and misery, with no end in sight.

Sickened, Ben had to close the journal and lay it aside for a while. The guy in the next seat was still sleeping, head thrown back and mouth open. Ben was glad he wouldn't have to get drawn into another conversation about the state of the energy market. He sipped his water and spent a few minutes gazing out of the plane window, thinking about the countless Irish refugees who had traced by sea the same eastward route he was travelling now towards America. It must have been bewildering for them to step ashore at the end of their long voyage, so far away from everything they'd ever known, strangers in a strange land with only each other for support.

Ben couldn't compete with someone like Gray Brennan for historical knowledge. But the Irish blood in his own veins had led him to read up on the subject in the past: he knew about how the Irish had been flocking to America for centuries, often to escape servitude and persecution such as they'd received at the hands of Oliver Cromwell, the so-called Lord Protector of England whose army had massacred thousands of Irish Catholic men, women and children in an unfettered campaign of bloody slaughter during the mid-seventeenth century. More than a century later, it had been said that half the Continental army fighting the British in the American War of Independence were Irishmen.

But at no time in history, before or since, had there been such an exodus of Irish to America as around the time of the Great Hunger. Some two million of them: a quarter of the entire population of Ireland. It was hard to imagine how the eastern ports and cities must have teemed with the masses coming off the ships. The poorest of all immigrant groups arriving in the New World, often living and working in the most squalid conditions imaginable, the Irish had clung fiercely together, creating tightly knit communities that grew and grew into strong enclaves in cities all across the country as the Irish-American population gradually spread west, deeply influencing the culture of their new homeland. They'd built its railroads and its canals, fought their own countrymen on both sides of its Civil War, toiled in its factories, educated its young, manned its police forces and its baseball teams, spawned many of its presidents. By 1910, there had been more Irish in New York than there were in Dublin. In modern times, some twelve per cent of Americans – over thirty-six million people, six times the population of Ireland itself – could claim Irish ancestry.

And they were proud of it. They even had their own flag, and nowhere else was St Patrick's Day celebrated with more passionate enthusiasm than in the streets of American cities: from Boston to New York to Philadelphia to Los Angeles; from Detroit to Chicago to St Louis, Missouri . . . to Tulsa, Oklahoma.

Ben took out the notebook on which he'd jotted down all that he'd been able to find online concerning Tulsa's incumbent mayor, Finn McCrory. As he'd quickly discovered, here was a man not just intensely proud of his third-generation Irish ancestry but seemingly hell-bent on milking every last drop of possible benefit from it. By all accounts he was a capable and effective politician, much loved by the many supporters who'd elected him for two consecutive terms of office.

From what Ben had managed to piece together, McCrory was something of a late starter in politics, having spent thirty years as a successful litigator in Tulsa before aspiring to the mayorship of the city. He'd been born in 1958, into considerable wealth, the source of which had been the oil boom of the first quarter of the twentieth century that had virtually overnight transformed Tulsa from just another dusty cowtown to the oil capital of the world. Arrowhead Oil had been one of the larger companies raking in vast fortunes, founded way back in 1935 by Finn's father, a notoriously outspoken and hard-drinking character whose physical size and tough ways inside and outside the boardroom had earned him the nickname 'Big Joe McCrory'.

By all accounts, Big Joe was as famous for settling deals with his fists as he was for being listed among the ten richest men in Oklahoma. Arrowhead Oil had been sold off to a conglomerate in 1990 for some mind-boggling sum, whereupon the elder McCrory had retired to his ranch near Sand Springs, Tulsa. The picture of him Ben found online showed a hulking broad-shouldered man with strong features, a mane of pure white hair and the penetrating eyes of someone who absolutely never took no for an answer, and never would. Still apparently going strong at the age of ninety-eight, Big Joe was credited with having been a major influence on his only child. Finn McCrory had described in an interview how his father had steered him with iron discipline from his earliest youth. Even as a fledgling lawyer, he'd been expected to shoulder big responsibilities within the family business.

'My daddy made me the man I am today,' he had declared to his interviewer.

Ben didn't yet know exactly what kind of man Finn McCrory was. But with every passing minute that the airliner neared its destination, he was becoming more and more determined to find out.

Chapter Thirty-One

Tulsa, Oklahoma

'How's my hair look?' Finn McCrory asked his assistant, Janet, in the small office the factory manager had let them use as a makeshift dressing room. Four other staff members from the mayor's office were crammed in with them. Bert Lessels was looking at his watch and Wendy Brandt was doing a last-minute check through the notes for the address the mayor was about to make.

Janet Reiss was a small, birdlike woman of sixty-two who'd been Mayor McCrory's personal secretary and general organiser during both of his terms of office. She reached up and flicked a couple of locks of his greying hair into place. 'Needs trimming at the back.' Janet was attentive to details that way.

'Yeah, but I don't look terrible, do I?' Finn asked. He was nervous about the speech. Public speaking was something he could do in his sleep, but today was special. He'd even bought a new pair of his trademark fancy tooled leather cowboy boots for the occasion. The tie was, of course, emerald green, neatly held with a gold shamrock tiepin.

'You look fine,' Janet reassured him in a motherly manner. For eight years she'd been fussing over his appearance, picking out his wardrobe, doing everything but wipe his nose for him.

'You look like shit. Now leave your goddamn hair alone and get out there.' The low growl came from the doorway, which was almost completely filled by the hulking, white-haired shape of Big Joe McCrory. At six foot three and with shoulders as broad as a power-lifter's, he dwarfed his son by a good four inches.

Finn darted a nervous glance at his father. He hated the old man being here and speaking to him that way in front of the staff. But you didn't talk back to Big Joe. That lesson had been learned the hard way, a long time ago. The old bastard could still break a man's jaw with a single punch.

'I'm ready,' Finn said to Janet. 'Let's do it.'

Today, the mayor was addressing over twelve hundred workers at Larson Engineering, one of Tulsa's largest aero-space plants, situated within the Cox Business Center, and producing wings and fuselages for Gulfstream G650 jets. The stage had been set up at one end of a factory floor. Partially assembled fuselages on gantries towered overhead.

It was stiflingly hot inside the building, but Mayor McCrory maintained perfect composure as he stepped up to the podium amid noisy applause. He was popular here, which was why he'd chosen this venue for today's speech. The blue-collar crowd were entirely male, virtually all white, and exclusively Republican. Just the kind of audience he liked. He'd slackened off the emerald green tie, and was jacketless, with his shirtsleeves rolled up in order to appeal to the working men.

Finn beamed and waved until the applause died down. 'How y'all doing?' he began, adding a few brief lines about what a valued mainstay of the local economy the plant was and how delighted he was to be back here. He sensed right away that the crowd were with him.

'You know, back during my courtroom days I was always known to be a man of few words. Juries loved me. Everybody got to go home early. So what I have to say to you today won't take long. I mean, hell, I *could* stand here all day and go on about all that's been achieved during my two terms as mayor of this great city of ours. I *could* talk about how we've reduced crime, cleaned up our town and boosted our economy. How we've reinforced Tulsa's already rich history with the energy and aerospace sectors while at the same time instituting new environmental programmes to protect our valuable natural heritage. I *could* talk about how fast we responded when ninety thousand Tulsans were left without power after last year's tornadoes, and about the huge success of the rebuilding programmes we put into place after that disaster.'

He paused, scanning the crowd and seeing nothing but attentive faces.

'But I didn't come here to yak and throw a bunch of facts and numbers in your face,' he continued emphatically. 'We all know that the last eight years have made Tulsa a better place to live, for you, for me, for the next generation. You only have to look around you to see that it's so. And I'm prouder than I can say to have been a part of it, thanks to the trust and support of the people of Tulsa who elected me for two terms running. Thanks to you.'

The crowd loved this, and the roar of cheers took a while to die down.

'In fact I'm so darn proud of this city and its citizens,' Finn went on, 'that after two terms as mayor, my service to you is far from done. I care deeply about Oklahoma. I know you do, too. That's why I'm here today, and that's

199

why I'm taking this opportunity to announce my candidacy for the governorship of this great state. I know I can count on your vote come November.'

There it was. The big one. More roaring applause.

The announcement hadn't been totally unexpected. Rumours had been flying for weeks, but this was the first official confirmation that Mayor McCrory was in the race.

He waited, smiling, for the din to subside. 'Now, I'm not one of your fancy-pants preppie types born with a big ol' silver spoon in his mouth,' he said, causing a round of laughter. This was an obvious dig at his chief rival in the coming November gubernatorial election, Maynard Leighton Jnr, who had been to Princeton. Liberal, pro-gay, anti-gun, Leighton was a sitting-duck target with this audience. 'I'm a straight-talking guy from good old Irish stock, just like a lot of you,' Finn went on, jutting out his chin. 'I understand what it's like for the working man. Those strong values have been in my family for generations, ever since my grand-daddy, Paddy McCrory, arrived in this great country over a hundred and sixty years ago from a little village on the west coast of Ireland called Glenfell. He came here as a refugee without a cent in his pocket and nothing but the strength in his two hands and the fire in his belly to sustain him.'

It was the same old account that Finn had enthusiastically repeated in speeches and interviews a hundred times over. The voters loved it and it worked every time.

'He knew what poverty was, and hunger,' Finn went on in a dramatic tone that had the audience hooked. 'You bet he did. He threw off the shackles of oppression to come to the land of the free. There *was* no Oklahoma when he got here. People like my granddaddy, and my daddy after him, built this whole country from the ground up and made our state the best place to live in America. And I mean to see it stays that way.'

Over the applause, Finn turned from the mike and said, 'Daddy, why don't you come over here and say a few words.'

To universal cheering and clapping, Big Joe McCrory stepped up to the podium. There was not a trace of stiffness in the old man's stride, and he didn't need to suck in his belly the way his son did. He bent down close to the mike, glowered severely at the crowd from under bristling white brows and said in a throaty bass rumble that filled the hall, 'Y'all vote for my boy. Hear me now.'

With that, amid whoops from the audience, Big Joe turned and calmly walked away.

Finn was beaming with filial pride. 'That's my old daddy, folks,' he said, returning to the mike. 'Ninety-eight years of age, and look at him. We McCrorys are famous for our longevity. That means I gotta lot of years left in me, and I intend to use every one of them for the benefit of my fellow Okies. That's all I have to say.'

Cue even louder and wilder applause.

The announcement speech had been a tremendous success. Finn was still wearing a mile-wide grin as he swept out of the building with his entourage trotting behind him to keep up. Big Joe had gone off on his own.

'Call Theo,' Finn instructed Janet as they strode out into the hot sun. Theodore F. Walsh was the campaign manager he'd hired three weeks earlier in anticipation of today's announcement, who had in turn hired a small army of strategists and media experts, all waiting in the wings for McCrory's candidacy to come out into the open.

'Now we can get this show rolling. We're gonna get our message out there, let rip and win this thing. Leighton hasn't a chance in hell. Come November, we're gonna roll right over him like a goddamn juggernaut.' Finn was on a high, walking fast and talking faster, already visualising himself moving into the governor's mansion at 820 NE 23rd Street, Oklahoma City.

'No going back now,' Janet sighed. 'I just hope we can afford these kinds of campaign expenses.'

'Money?' Finn scoffed. They were walking past the stationary Gulfstream jet that took pride of place in front of the main Larson Engineering building. Finn knew the type of aircraft very well, as it was the same full-spec model he owned himself. 'Don't you worry about money. That's the easy part. We got ten times more cash than Leighton can even dream of. That little faggot won't know what hit him.'

'Oh, that's great,' Janet said, rolling her eyes. 'You be sure to say that on NBC, now.'

Out in the sun-baked parking lot, their three vehicles were clustered side by side: the black mayoral Cadillac SUV, Finn's own Mercedes SL-class convertible – emerald green, naturally – and the massive red Dodge Ram crew-cab truck that Big Joe insisted on driving himself around in. With jacked-up suspension and massive chromed bull bars, the 4.7-litre monster reflected a lot about the old man's personality.

Big Joe was leaning against the door with his arms folded and his thick mane of snowy hair ruffling in the hot breeze. Finn caught the menacing look his father was shooting his way, and felt his euphoric confidence waver a tad. That was when his phone buzzed in his pocket, and he took it out to see he had a new text message. He read it, frowning, then slipped the phone back into his pocket and turned to Janet. 'See you back at the office later, okay?'

'Later?' she queried.

'Something I need to take care of first,' he replied non-committally, and Janet shrugged and headed off to climb into the SUV with the rest of the staff.

'Don't you ever call me your "old daddy" again, boy,' Big Joe growled at Finn. 'I'll beat the living crap outta you.'

Finn knew his father meant it. 'I'm sorry. It just slipped out.'

Big Joe snorted in disgust. 'Governor. Governor my ass. Can't even drive American.' He pointed at the Mercedes.

'Two hundred thousand bucks,' Finn said defensively.

The old man was not impressed. 'Two hundred thousand bucks' worth'a imported tin-can trash,' he spat, then reached for the door of his Dodge. 'I'm going home to the ranch. Be heading up to Topeka tomorrow for a couple days, week mebbe. Horse business.'

'Oh. Nice,' Finn said weakly.

With a parting hostile glare, his father clambered into his truck and fired it up.

Finn watched as the Dodge roared away in a cloud of dust. Very softly, as if the old man might be endowed with preternatural hearing, which he very possibly was, Finn muttered under his breath, 'When are you going to die?'

The answer was probably never. Finn sighed and walked with slumped shoulders to the two-hundred-thousand-dollar imported piece of tin-can trash.

Chapter Thirty-Two

As Mayor Finn McCrory knew very well, not all of his granddaddy's story could be divulged to the public.

On his arrival in New York City on a cold and windy October's day in 1851 after a long, harsh sea voyage, the immigrant Padraig McCrory, or Paddy as he'd later become known, stepped off the ship to discover a New World where a strong and growing core of Irish patriots were fiercely supportive of their own. Thanks to that support and the connections that it fostered, he'd quickly found his feet. He was a determined and single-minded man, not afraid to work. He knew horses, and America was the land of horses. By 1858, still playing heavily on his trademark Irish identity, Paddy McCrory had risen up to become a successful dealer in equine flesh, with livery yards all across New York State. When the Civil War broke out three years later, he secured supply contracts with the huge mobilising Union army that multiplied his wealth twenty-fold. By the end of that war, at the age of forty-three, he'd married Mary O'Kelly, an immigrant beauty from Mitchelstown twenty-five years his junior. Nothing would have pleased him more than to have a son and heir, but to Mary's heartbreak and Paddy's infinite disappointment, the couple found themselves unable to have children.

After fifteen years of building his business in the east, Paddy McCrory set his sights on new pastures, and in 1868 took Mary west to Kansas to realise a new dream out there in the Promised Land. It was a place of limitless opportunities for a man of wealth and ambition. From horses, Paddy diversified to that other staple of life on the frontier – guns. Percussion muskets to scatterguns to Colt's patent revolvers to the new Henry repeating rifles that had been the scourge of the Confederate army in the closing stages of the war; he couldn't sell enough of them and quickly developed a complete lack of scruple about who his customers were. He sold to lawmen and bandits alike. He sold to the European settlers who sought to protect themselves against Indian raids, then sold to the Indians so that they could better attack the settlers. Within a couple of years, Paddy McCrory had become richer than ever as one of the biggest traders of arms in the emergent Midwest.

Two decades later, Paddy 'Boss' McCrory was still strong and healthy and more ambitious than ever when the Oklahoma land rush of 1889 began. After that year's Indian Appropriations Bill essentially had opened up two million acres of Indian Territory to anyone with the means and manpower to grab it on a first-come, first-served basis, he jumped at the chance to join in the frenzy. He became one of what were known as the 'Sooners', the name given to those opportunists who moved to the new territory ahead of the legal date of 22 April 1889 so that they could pounce on the choicest bits of land before anyone else got a look in. 'Boss' laid claim to a vast acreage of prime ranch and pasture land that straddled miles of the Arkansas River, and in the inevitable land wars that followed he defended it with a small army of hired guns, professional killers who plied their trade with ruthless efficiency.

The area was booming. The newly founded Oklahoma City was established in half a day, bursting from a population of near zero to ten thousand within literally hours. Paddy McCrory was already the wealthiest man in the new state, and set to become even more so.

Soon after his seventieth birthday, Mary took ill with fever and died. Paddy mourned her, but more than anything he mourned the fact that he would never have an heir to inherit his fortune. He found solace in seeking out new territories to buy and sell, and in conducting campaigns against the scattered groups of Indians who were still bold enough to contest the white man's supremacy. How many Cherokee and others were slaughtered at the hands of his riders, nobody ever knew.

Old Paddy McCrory himself just kept on going and going. Portraits showed a large, tough and grizzled man of formidable bearing and stern manner, with piercing wild eyes and thick white hair, which he wore long. Time had seemed barely to touch him – he believed that old age was a state of mind, nothing more. When at the age of eighty-four he fell into a dispute with a cattle baron who tried to swindle him over a land deal, Paddy McCrory had ridden alone to the man's ranch and beaten him almost to death with his bare fists.

Finally, at the age of ninety, love re-entered his life in the comely form of Charlotte Polk, the daughter of a Tennessee planter. Truthfully, it had been something of a marriage of convenience: he was rich, she was young, he wanted a son, she was willing to provide in return for the lifestyle he could offer his new bride. It took some doing due to Paddy's advancing years, but finally by the age of ninety-four, he'd been given the heir he'd always wanted. The proud parents named the baby boy Joseph. It was 1916.

Paddy McCrory died shortly before the boy's fifth birthday, after a brief and painful illness. In his final years he was tormented by guilt over the wicked things he'd done during the course of his long and eventful life; on his deathbed he confessed to terrible sins and wept as he begged the Lord's forgiveness.

After his death, his widow Charlotte raised their son by herself and was a proud and loving mother. The family business took a bad hit in the Crash of '29, and for some years the spectre of poverty loomed over them. Then, in 1935, when Joe was nineteen, the McCrorys' ailing fortunes were spectacularly rescued: the chance discovery of black gold on their land turned out to portend the biggest oil strike the state would see for another decade.

With the boom of the burgeoning new auto industry, Big Joe McCrory was soon to ascend to the throne of an empire and become the youngest millionaire in Oklahoma.

The rest, as they say, was history.

From the Cox Business Center, Finn drove east on Route 66 with the top down and Foster and Allen's *Fields of Athenry* blasting on the car stereo. He then cut southwards, passing East Tulsa Bible Chapel and the Church of God of the Apostolic before arriving at Harvey Young Airport on 135th East Avenue. This was the smallest of the city's three airports and the base for some sixty aircraft, one of which was Finn's personal Gulfstream. Lately, he'd been making a lot of trips in it down south over Texas to Nuevo Laredo just south of the Mexican border. Nobody in Tulsa asked questions. He could fly in and out whenever he wanted, skirting the city's air traffic control area, and had his own private hangar.

The place was convenient in other ways, too. It was one of the only secret rendezvous points that were safe, from

Finn's point of view. His recognisability as mayor made it tricky to conduct illicit meetings with the employees of his real and main business, the covert and rapidly growing enterprise that the likes of Janet Reiss and the rest of his City Hall staff knew nothing about, and which – out of necessity – he'd become highly skilled at keeping totally separate from his political life.

People just assumed that his wealth came from his father. A lot of it did. But Finn's own money was pouring in faster and faster these days. And if he succeeded in becoming governor, the power he'd have would allow him to open the floodgates and shoot up the Oklahoma rich list.

Maybe he'd get even richer than Big Joe. Finn secretly dreamed of being able to tell the old bastard that on his deathbed, just to spoil it for him at the very end.

The dusty white GMC van was parked beside Finn's hangar with its windows down. As the Mercedes rolled to a halt, the van's doors opened and Ritter and Moon emerged. Ritter wore military-issue sunglasses and was all in black. Moon was in a blood-spatter T-shirt that said 'ZOMBIE HUNTER – KILL OR BE EATEN'. Classy, that Moon.

Finn got out of the car, glancing furtively about to ensure nobody was spying on them.

'Hey, nice boots, boss,' Moon said. Moon resented his employer's fancy clothes, just like he resented the two-hundred-thousand-dollar Merc. The McCrorys ate out at the upscale Palace Café two or three nights a week. Moon was more of a Dirty's Tavern kind of guy.

'What you been doing, chasing parked cars?' Finn asked, pointing at Moon's split lip and the purple bruising on his face.

'Ain't nuthin',' Moon replied sullenly, and popped another stick of nicotine gum.

'You boys sure took your time getting back here. Let's step inside the office.' Finn motioned towards the hangar's entrance. He led them into the shade of the building, where the Gulfstream sat cooling after its return flight from Madeira. The two men followed him up the gangway into the plush privacy of the aircraft, which Finn had had specially upholstered in emerald green with little golden shamrock motifs. He threw himself into his favourite seat and looked expectantly at them. 'Well? You got something for me?'

'There was a hitch,' Ritter said.

Finn stared at him. 'What the hell does that mean, a hitch? All you had to do was fetch me a buncha old books.'

'No sweat, boss,' Moon said, chewing. 'We dealt with the situation.'

'I'll decide when there's no sweat, okay? I want to know what happened.'

'Relax, Mr Mayor,' Ritter said. 'Your journals are all gone up in smoke.'

'Just like Brennan and the other asshole,' Moon said.

Ritter shot him a look. Moon talked too much.

'What other asshole?' Finn asked.

'The guy from the beach,' Ritter explained. 'Some guy called Hope. He was the hitch.'

'From what beach?' Finn asked in astonishment. 'You mean in Galway?'

'Yup. We, uh, we ran into him again.'

'That who banged Moon up? This Hope guy?'

Ritter nodded. Moon looked down at his feet and muttered, 'Looks worse'n it is.'

'What the hell was he doing there?' Finn demanded.

'We didn't exactly engage in small talk,' Ritter said. 'He turned up, got in the way, got taken out. End of story, end of problem.'

Finn shook his head, deeply perplexed. 'He made you, didn't he? Followed your incompetent asses all the way to Madeira. What is he, a cop? Some kind of goddamn private investigator?'

'Nobody made us,' Ritter replied in a flat tone.

'If he knew something, someone else might,' Finn said. 'I want to know more about this sonofabitch.' Taking out his mini-iPad, he quickly dialled up a news network and returned to the recent story of the unsolved fatal stabbing on the west coast of Ireland. Within seconds, he was scanning quickly through the article. 'Here he is. The hero who tried to stop the killers. Ben Hope.'

'That's the guy,' Ritter said.

'Hero my ass,' Moon muttered.

'What do we know about this guy?' Finn demanded.

'That he's toast,' Moon said.

Finn jumped out of the news item and quickly Googled the name. The search results popped up. A mountain in Scotland. A type of blackberry. A real estate salesman in Kansas. A teenage kid in Montreal. Some artist in London, and another Brit doing time for murder. Finn scrolled impatiently down the list.

Then stopped. Peered closely at the screen. 'Got it. You two, come and look. This is him, right?'

'That's him,' Ritter said, taking off his shades to look at the website image his boss had found.

'Guy's a goddamn ex-British soldier.'

'Fuckin' lobsterback,' Moon grunted.

'Director of some kind of training centre,' Finn said, reading more. 'Le Val. Normandy, France.'

Moon shrugged. 'So? Big deal.'

Ignoring him, Finn went on scouring this Ben Hope's résumé on the website. Words like 'tactical' and 'specialist' made him feel distinctly uncomfortable. 'Crisis response consultant,' he muttered, frowning.

'Sounds like bullshit, you ask me,' Moon said.

'I didn't ask for your opinion, Moon. I asked you who the hell this guy is.'

'Was,' Ritter corrected him. 'Some hotshot who thought he'd got the chops. Seen a million of 'em. Don't worry about it.' He was still pissed off at Moon for opening his big mouth.

'Says here he was a major,' Finn said.

'Major pain in the butt,' Moon chuckled. 'I never did like officers. Who cares why the fucker was there? Maybe he knew Brennan.'

'Yeah?' Finn said. 'And maybe you're a cretin, Moon.'

'Can't be, on account of I ain't never been to Crete,' Moon protested.

'It doesn't matter any more,' Ritter said. 'We handled it. That's what we do, right?'

'A man like this isn't someone I need on my case,' Finn said, pointing at the iPad screen. 'You're definitely sure he's dead?'

'As disco,' Moon said.

'Forget him,' Ritter said quietly. 'He's history.'

'He'd damn well better be,' Finn replied. 'Because we have some other business to deal with, and I don't need some meathead getting in the way this time.' He slipped a blank card from his pocket. On the back of it was written a name and an address in Crosbie Heights. He handed the card to Ritter. 'This needs to be done quickly and quietly. She can be knocked about a little, but I need her able to talk. Got it?'

'Who is the bitch?' Ritter asked, peering at the card.

'It's sensitive. She works for my wife.'

Ritter frowned. 'So?'

'So, Angela had her staying at the goddamn cabin that night. She was there.'

'When we . . .?'

'Uh-huh. When we took care of Blaylock. Damn woman videoed us and managed to sneak right out from under your noses. How'd you suppose that happened, huh? It's just luck that the evidence is in safe hands. But we have to make sure there are no copies. That's why I need her alive. Got that?'

Ritter didn't need to ask whose safe hands the video evidence was in. He showed the card to Moon, whose eyes glittered. Right up his street.

Finn shook his head, reading Moon's expression. 'Not you. She knows your faces. I can't afford for anything to go wrong.'

'Nothing will go wrong,' Ritter said.

'That so? She already got away once.'

'Don't make me beg, boss,' Moon whined.

'You heard me,' Finn said, casting a warning look at each of them in turn. 'Get one of your guys to take care of it. The sooner the better.'

Ritter currently had upwards of twenty men working under him virtually full-time to run McCrory's enterprise. He often thought about taking on more, as it was growing so fast. He rasped a hand over the stubble on his head as he reflected for a moment on who to give this job to. 'Joey Spicer,' he said.

'Spicer. He good enough?' Finn asked warily.

Ritter nodded. 'Oh yeah.'

'Then call him right away. Tell him it's worth three thousand bucks bonus.'

'Spicer'll want five for something like this,' Ritter said. 'Burglary gone sour, that's easy. Kidnapping, that's something else. He's gonna want to take a partner along.'

Finn waved his hand impatiently. He'd have doubled it to ten in an instant. 'Hell, make it seven-fifty. I don't care if it's two guys or twenty. I want her in front of me and talking by tonight.'

'What happens to her afterwards?'

Finn shrugged. 'Hell do I care? Feed her to the dogs. Give her to Moon. Do whatever you like with her. As long as she disappears. Understood?'

Chapter Thirty-Three

Erin had been home for a couple of days, with nothing to do but anxiously wait for something to happen. She didn't even know what that *something* was.

Officially, she was off work for a week, laid up with some kind of summertime virus. As the story went, she must have caught it before the weekend, forcing her to return early from the lake cabin. Angela had been sympathetic, wishing her a speedy recovery. 'I don't know how long I can manage without you, though. Things are crazier than ever around here.'

Erin couldn't stop fretting over the dilemma. She didn't want to lose her job any more than she wanted to let Angela down – but how could she go back to work there, after what had happened? She didn't know if she could look Angela in the eye. Worse, what if the mayor put in an appearance at the Desert Rose Trust offices, as he sometimes did? What would Erin's own reaction be if she found herself face-to-face with him in the same room? Would she give herself away? Would he twig? And if he did, then what?

And on it went. The torment of waiting and wondering. Long hours dragging by. Day merging with painful slowness into night and back into day. Still no news – and Erin's fear and frustration were preying on her more and more as she wondered what the hell the cops were doing.

She couldn't sleep. The thoughts that kept her staring at the ceiling into the small hours were still with her in the morning. She kept replaying the interview with Chief O'Rourke and Detective Morrell in her mind. Surely this thing couldn't just blow over as if it had never happened? Surely something had to be done about it? The situation couldn't go on the way it was.

It felt like being under house arrest. She couldn't focus enough to catch up on any work at home, couldn't go out for her daily run along the Newblock Park Trail that flanked the Arkansas River. The only time she'd ventured any distance from her house was when she'd taken a cab to go and collect her Honda from the repair shop. On her way home, she'd stopped at a Kmart for some groceries and a cheap cellphone to replace the one she'd given O'Rourke.

Now, with nothing else to distract her agitated mind, she'd finally been reduced to watching this crass afternoon talk show. Some peroxide four-hundred-pounder was crammed into a studio chair dithering on about her lawsuit against the food manufacturer who'd victimised her by maliciously tempting her to stuff her face with too many of their products: *'Look what they did to me!'*

Erin sat staring at the talking heads until she couldn't bear the inane babble any longer and launched herself off the couch. Camomile tea, she thought. Better that than Valium for soothing raw nerves.

Her kitchen was tiny, but neatly organised with everything within reach exactly how she needed it to be. All her utensils and cutlery were stored in the column of drawers under the small worktop. A row of shiny steel saucepans dangled from hooks on a little rail above. She turned on the kettle, which had exactly enough water in it for one person. While waiting for it to boil, she fetched down a stoneware mug from the cupboard in front of her and set it on the worktop. Picked up the little pot in which she kept the camomile tea bags. Dropped one into the empty mug. The kettle was coming to the boil by now. Its chunky plastic rocker switch automatically clicked itself off as it reached temperature. She lifted it off its base and poured the steaming water into the mug. As the homely aroma of camomile filled the kitchen, she reached towards the drawer to get a teaspoon to stir it with.

She didn't register the man's presence behind her until his black-gloved hand had clamped over her mouth, stifling her scream.

He drew her back against him, clasping her against his chest. She smelled the thin, rancid leather pressed under her nose. She struggled and tried to twist her head so she could bite his fingers through the glove, but his grip was like spring steel. He pressed her hard against the kitchen unit, trapping her tightly between his body and the column of drawers so that she couldn't move, couldn't turn or lash out backwards with her feet or elbows.

Then a muffled cry of fear broke from her lips as she saw the syringe he was grasping in his other gloved hand. It was a standard medical syringe with a protective plastic sheath over the needle and increments in millilitres marked along the length of its transparent barrel. The plunger was drawn back about a quarter of its travel and there was a pale, straw-coloured fluid inside. With his thumb he flicked the protective sheath away to expose the long, thin needle.

Erin struggled wildly but couldn't break the man's grip. He was taking his time. Enjoying the moment, knowing he was far stronger than she was. He pressed the syringe plunger, just far enough for a tiny squirt of the yellowish fluid to squirt from the needle's tip.

She watched, powerless, as he brought the needle closer.

It was pointing at her neck. She could see a minute drip of the fluid quivering on the end of the needle. In another moment or two, he was going to inject the whole contents of the syringe into her.

She knew then that the man hadn't come to kill her. If he'd wanted to do that, he could have snapped her neck already, or stuck a knife in her back before she'd even known he was there. He was going to drug her. Knock her out. Take her away and . . .

McCrory was behind this. He and his men were going to kill her. But not before they'd tortured and raped her. And when she was dead they were going to dismember her and dispose of her remains just like they'd done to the man in the cabin.

Her mind swam with horror. She felt faint and sick and her legs were shaking so badly that she might have collapsed if the man hadn't been pinning her against the worktop.

The needle moved closer.

'Hold still, darlin',' the man's grating voice chuckled in her ear. 'I just might poke out one of those pretty li'l eyes of yours by mistake.'

It was his mocking, jokey tone that made Erin focus. The icy grip of terror melted into white-hot fury that anyone could do this to her. She wasn't going to be anyone's victim. Not here, not in her own home, not today or any day.

With a shout of rage and effort she managed to rip an arm free. Grasping his gloved fist, she tried to push the syringe away from her. She was terrified the needle would puncture her wrist or forearm.

'Feisty, aintcha?' he rasped in her ear. 'Won't do ya any good.'

He was right. The syringe kept coming, inch by inch. Erin wasn't strong enough to resist him. This was going to happen and there wasn't a thing she could do to stop it.

Then she realised. One chance.

Her untouched hot drink stood on the surface in front of her. A wisp of steam was rising from the mouth of the mug.

She let go of the man's hand and reached out and grabbed it and dashed its contents back over her right shoulder. The boiling water had been cooling for less than a minute. She felt its scalding sting on her neck and ear.

But the yell of pain behind her told her that most of it had splashed right into his face.

'Fuck! Fuck! Oh, you *bitch!*'

He staggered back a step, his grip on her slackening momentarily, the syringe suddenly wavering in his other hand. Erin twisted and wriggled and managed to rip herself away from him, knowing he'd quickly recover from the shock.

She could see him properly now. He was a large man, solid and stocky. White, forties, ugly features made uglier by the twisted grimace of pain and fury and the livid scald like a birthmark across his right cheek and forehead. The burned eye was already beginning to swell shut. He stood between her and the door. Escape wasn't an option. Not yet.

Darting an arm across the worktop, she unhooked a saucepan from the wall-mounted rail. She gripped the handle with both hands and swung it at his head with all her might. There was a hollow clang. She felt the impact shiver the handle.

But the blow only enraged him even more. He lunged at her with the syringe and the needle scraped on the steel of the pan as she managed to shield herself with it. Jab, block; jab, block. She was reacting on pure animal instinct. No time to think or even breathe. It was simple survival.

'You ain't got a chance, bitch,' he sneered. 'I'm gonna stick you with this. You'll stay conscious maybe twenty seconds. Long enough for me to stick you with something else, and you're gonna feel me do it.'

He lunged again. Erin was quick, and the syringe stabbed into the worktop where she'd been standing a fraction of a second earlier.

'See what you made me do?' he said, staring at the bent needle. He hurled it away, reached under his jacket and whipped out a knife. 'Reckon we'll just have to do this the hard way, now won't we?'

He came at her. She dodged him again. Suddenly, she had a line of escape past him. She flung the saucepan at him, and it bounced off his chest and crashed to the floor. In the time that he flinched from the impact, she raced for the door, slamming it shut in his face as he came after her.

In such a small house, it wasn't a long run across the hall to the stairs. She went sprinting up them three at a time, heading for her bedroom door. He came bursting out of the kitchen like a mad bull and started up the stairs in pursuit, clutching the knife.

Erin crashed into her bedroom. The Springfield nine-millimetre was in its holster on the nightstand.

The man's thundering footsteps had reached the top of the stairs as she unsnapped the retaining strap on the holster and ripped the pistol clear of the leather and tossed the holster aside. At the same instant, she was swivelling on the balls of her feet to face the doorway and bringing the weapon up to bear in a solid two-handed grip.

He was already inside the room when he saw the gun in her hands. It was too late to stop. He charged at her, betting on getting to her before she could fire.

Erin squeezed the trigger.

The gun went *click*.

The gun went click, because in her panic she'd forgotten to jack a round into the chamber.

But now there was no time. Two hundred pounds of savage intent came rushing at her faster than she could get the weapon in battery.

Erin threw herself across the bed, rolling over the top of her quilted cover. Her feet hit the rug on the other side at the instant she managed to yank back the slide on the gun, released it and felt the distinct smooth metallic *snick* as the action scooped the top round off the magazine follower and drove it up and forwards into the chamber.

The man had been about to launch himself across the bed at her. He saw the purposeful look in her eye and hesitated just a split-second too long.

'Always shoot to kill,' her father had taught her. 'Half these sumbitches are on drugs. You gotta put 'em down hard.' Erin didn't want to kill anybody, not even someone about to kill her, not unless she had to. She aimed low and squeezed the trigger a second time.

The gun's ear-bursting report drowned out the man's cry as the bullet punched into his leg a couple of inches above the knee. The shot instantly disabled him. His leg buckled and he went straight down, hitting the floor with a heavy thump. The knife flew out of his hand as he went to grab his leg with both hands, writhing in pain, blood pouring out over his fingers.

She leapt over him, raced out of the bedroom and went pounding back down the stairs. At the bottom, she remembered to decock the pistol before thrusting it into her pocket. With trembling hands she grabbed what she needed from the hallway: jacket, car keys, purse.

She was halfway to the front door when she thought about the syringe. *Evidence.* She burst into the empty kitchen. The saucepan she'd flung at her attacker was lying on the floor, next to the shards of broken mug and the puddle of spilled camomile tea. A couple of feet away lay the syringe with its bent needle. Most of the straw-coloured fluid was still inside it. She quickly wrapped it inside a sheet of kitchen roll and dropped it in her purse. She could hear the man thumping about upstairs, and his cries of agony.

Erin burst out of the house and sprinted towards her little yellow Honda Fit parked in the dusty driveway. She glanced around her as she ran, and saw another car parked fifty yards up the street. A blue Ford Taurus she'd never seen parked there before. There was a man in dark glasses sitting at the wheel. He was reclined right back in his seat with his face turned upwards, as if he was dozing.

Erin didn't give him a second look. She dived into her Honda, stabbed the key into the ignition and went wheel-spinning backwards out of her driveway. The little car lurched to a halt, then she threw it into forward drive and hit the gas. She narrowly avoided colliding with an oncoming saloon that she hardly even registered as she sped off up the street.

She didn't care where she was headed, as long as it was far away from here. She drove like a maniac, overtaking everything in front of her, ignoring the horns that blasted at her. Several miles and several more near-misses had gone by before the dizzying, palpitating adrenaline rush took over completely, hitting her so hard that she couldn't hold the wheel any longer in her shaking hands. She swerved to the side of the road. After several gasping heaves, the tears came flooding.

And with them the realisation. She couldn't ever go home again.

Chapter Thirty-Four

On its approach to Tulsa International, Ben's plane swooped down over a vast landscape of vivid green hills, forests and sun-scorched swathes of flat prairie. From his window he got his first glimpse of the city from above: home to near half a million inhabitants, a gleaming modern metropolis of towering skyscrapers and criss-crossed highways, parklands and housing developments and industrial zones that spread far and wide along the banks of the broad, stunningly blue waters of the Arkansas River.

Within thirty minutes he was through arrivals and getting his bearings. He changed some euros for dollars, then picked up a Starbucks and sipped it while studying a map that told him he was just five miles northeast of downtown. From there, he made his way to Alamo Rental and selected a grey Jeep Patriot. It was a practical and sturdy vehicle, not too ostentatious or distinctive. Roomy enough to sleep in if he had to. But mainly, he chose it for its dark-tinted windows. Those would fit in with the plan he'd already worked out in his mind. He rented it for a week, which might turn out to be more than he needed, or might not.

The day was going to come when his name would be blacklisted by every car hire company on the planet, but seemingly it hadn't come yet. He'd just have to try extra hard not to destroy the Patriot.

His stomach was still on European time, and he filled it at a nearby steakhouse called Libby's that served bison burgers and homebaked chicken pies as big as a hubcap. It was hot, but the humidity was bearable and a fresh southerly breeze kept his shirt from sticking to his back as he left Libby's and walked back to the car.

He picked up the main highway, heading south. After Europe, everything seemed on a giant scale, wide and flat and spread out. He passed lumber yards and industrial plants and warehouses and used car lots before he spotted the general store he was looking for and pulled over.

Inside, the place was crammed with every kind of goods imaginable. He picked up two light denim shirts, two pairs of black jeans, compact binoculars, sunglasses, a baseball cap that said 'Tulsa Drillers', five plastic litre bottles of water and an issue of *Oklahoma Sports and Fitness*. The old guy behind the counter wore dungarees and had thin white hair and a face like crinkled tan leather.

'What's the nearest hotel around here?' Ben asked him as he paid for his stuff.

'English, huh?' the old guy asked, peering at him.

'Half Irish,' Ben said.

'Good for you. My people came over from Mayo, before the war. That's the *Civil* War I'm talkin' about. Name's Gallagher. Frank Gallagher.'

'Pleasure to meet you, Frank,' Ben said, wondering if he'd have got such a friendly welcome if he'd said he was English. 'I'm Ben.'

'First time in Tulsa, Ben?'

'First time.'

'Vacation?'

'Not exactly,' Ben said.

'Didn't figure you for a tourist. Stayin' long?'

'Long as it takes.'

'I reckon that's about right,' Frank replied with a wrinkled grin. 'Anyhow, you got the old Perryman Inn just down the road. Rooms're comfortable enough, I guess, nuthin' fancy.'

'Sounds like my kind of place,' Ben said.

'Maybe I'll see you around. Store's open day or night. I live right upstairs, so you just give me a yell any time. Got most everything you'll ever need.'

'You're not kidding,' Ben said, glancing around him at the sagging shelves.

Nuthin' fancy was the perfect description of the Perryman Inn, which turned out to be a motel only a couple of small notches above the rank of a fleapit. The proprietor was a guy with a beard and a paunch the size of a beach ball who was only too happy to take cash without asking for any ID. Ben was only too happy to do business that way, and he had no problem with the room either. It was cool and shady with the blinds down, and nobody in the world knew he was here. Ben locked the door, showered, changed into his new jeans and a new shirt. Then he put on the sunglasses and cap, grabbed his bag and went out to the Patriot.

As he drove into the heart of the city, the signs of the impact the oil boom had made were hard to miss. They were visible all around, in everything from the spectacular art deco architecture the Tulsans had built up with their newfound fortunes to the huge parks with manicured expanses of green, fountains and artificial lakes and waterfalls, all dominated by the looming presence of the Bank of Oklahoma tower, the tallest building in the state, a proud monument to big fat beautiful dollars. The place was an oasis of money in the middle of the prairie.

Ben used his map to locate City Hall on East 2nd Street in the heart of downtown. He parked the Patriot across from the modern glass-fronted building and the right distance away so that he could sit and watch the entrance and stay discreet. It was four forty and the sun was still bright and high and hot in the blue sky. He took out his phone and keyed in the same Tulsa landline number he'd called from Ireland. The same receptionist replied, in the same nice southern twang as before, 'Mayor's office.'

'Hi, this is Ronnie Galloway from Marshall Kite Enterprises.'

'You called a couple of days ago, right?' the receptionist replied coldly. 'From England?'

'That's right, London,' he said, scanning the building's scores of windows and wondering which one she was behind, not a hundred yards from where he sat. 'Is Mr McCrory available?'

'He's in his office,' she informed him. 'But he's not taking calls right now.'

'I'll try again another time,' Ben said, and switched off the phone. He'd no intention of speaking to McCrory, had only wanted to find out if he was in the building. He'd no intention of marching in and confronting him, either, because that was an obvious blind alley. Much better to sit tight, wait for McCrory to appear and then quietly follow him to see where the trail might lead. It might be days of cat-and-mouse games before it would lead anywhere interesting. Ben didn't care. Stake-out surveillance was nothing new to him.

He kept the windows rolled down, sipping water to keep cool and keeping one eye on City Hall while looking totally immersed in *Oklahoma Sports and Fitness*. He studied the layout of the building. There might be another entrance round the far side that he couldn't keep tabs on, but there appeared to be only one main car park. There was a good chance that anyone leaving the place would come into his field of view.

Five o'clock came and went. Soon afterwards, the first trickle of office workers began leaving the building. Some walked to their cars, others departed on foot. Ben wound up the Jeep's tinted windows. They made little difference to what he could see from inside, but passers-by wouldn't be able to see him. The inside of the car began to heat up quickly. That couldn't be helped. He reached into his bag and took out the compact binoculars he'd bought from Frank Gallagher's general store. They might not have suited Bernard Goudier for watching birdlife on the beach in Galway, but they fitted Ben's purposes just fine. He turned them up to maximum zoom and watched the office staff leaving City Hall.

Most were women, leaving in pairs and small groups, chatting and smiling and laughing now that their working day was over. He ignored them and focused on the men. Some were older, some were younger. Some wore suits and ties, some didn't. None of them was Finn McCrory.

Ben went on waiting, patient and watchful. Another half hour passed. The traffic of workers leaving the building peaked and then began to thin out. By quarter to six, there were just the occasional ones and twos filing out of the entrance. By six, the trickle had pretty much stopped altogether.

Unless he'd managed to slip out unseen, the mayor must be working late. Which wasn't unexpected, and wasn't a problem. Ben had nowhere else to go.

At half past the hour and still no sign of McCrory, Ben had had enough of *Oklahoma Sports and Fitness*, even if he was only half-focused on it. He tossed it aside and returned to his reading of Elizabeth Stamford's journals.

Chapter Thirty-Five

When Erin had been a little girl, her outings to the zoo with her father had been some of the happiest times of her childhood. Maybe that was partly why she'd driven straight there today, craving some kind of comforting nostalgia to soothe her after the shock of what had just happened. But it was also a deliberate strategy. The Tulsa Zoo and Living Museum was one of the most public places she could think of. At this time of year, it was milling with crowds all through the day. Nobody would dare attack her here.

Which gave her about forty-five minutes' space to think before closing time. The late afternoon was still sunny and warm. She stood at the rail of the elephants' enclosure. She liked elephants, always had. They looked wise and kindly and infinitely patient, like benevolent old uncles shuffling unhurriedly about in baggy grey boiler suits. She felt sorry that they were in captivity, but it was a lot safer for them here than in their own country. Nobody would butcher them and rip out their ivory and leave their ravaged bodies to rot in the sun. They'd escaped all that. They were protected.

Suddenly, she envied them.

She felt a lot less protected right now than the elephants were. Where would *she* be safe from the predators out to get her?

There was absolutely no doubt in her mind that the thug she'd shot in her house earlier that day had been sent by Finn McCrory. But how could she ever hope to prove that? Should she have tried to get him to talk? Leaned a knee into his injured leg and stuck her pistol in his face to torture and scare the truth out of him? Or maybe she should have stayed put and dialled 911? All she'd been able to think of was getting away. Maybe that had been a mistake.

But then Erin thought about the man sitting outside the house in the unfamiliar blue Taurus. Maybe getting away hadn't been such a bad idea after all.

The question now was what the hell to do next.

Erin took her new phone from her purse, along with the card with Chief O'Rourke's number on it. She stabbed the number out quickly.

'Chief O'Rourke?' she said when his gravelly voice came on the line. 'It's Erin Hayes. You said to call if I had to. Well, I had to. Something happened.' He listened as she breathlessly explained the incident at her house. She told him about the syringe. About the gunshot. Even about the man outside in the blue Ford. 'I don't think he saw me. I don't know if he was involved too. I just know they're after me and—'

'Try to stay calm, Miss Hayes,' O'Rourke said. 'Where are you right now?'

'City zoo. But I can't stay here long. It closes in a few minutes.'

'I know. Don't worry, you're perfectly safe where you are. A patrol car will be right there, okay? Meet the officers at the main gate, by the parking lot. They'll escort you here.'

'Please tell them to hurry.' She thanked him and ended the call.

Erin had started making her way through the crowds towards the main gate when she got that uneasy sixth-sense feeling that someone was watching her. It was an animal instinct. Almost a physical sensation, making her skin crawl and go cold.

She turned in the direction the feeling seemed to be emanating from. There were only crowds. Some kids were laughing. A little girl had ice cream on her face. A seal was honking and splashing about in the background.

Erin walked on. The announcement came over the outdoor public address system to say the zoo would be closing in fifteen minutes. She looked at her watch and walked faster, praying that the patrol car would be at the main gate waiting for her.

But when she got there, there was no sign of the cops. What was keeping them?

There was that feeling again. Erin spun around, and as she did she thought she saw a figure of a man slipping quickly into the crowd. There'd been something furtive about his movement, as if he was ducking out of her line of sight. She was certain he was following her. How long had he been there, furtive, watching? Since she'd got here? Maybe even before that? Who was he? He'd been too quick for her to get a glimpse of his face, but she'd got a look at what he was wearing: a check shirt loose over a red T-shirt.

Another uncomfortable chill came over her, despite the heat. She looked at her watch again. Peered anxiously through the main gate, up and down the road. No police car. *Come on. Come on.*

She walked through the gate towards the parking lot. The visitors were beginning to leave. In a few more minutes the zoo would be empty. And if the cops didn't show up in time, she'd be left alone with whoever was following her. She wasn't imagining things. There really was someone trailing her. Maybe the man in the blue Ford had followed her here.

Maybe he'd called in another accomplice. The moment she was alone, they'd strike. It would be as if she'd never escaped at all. It would be all for nothing. They'd take her.

Another long minute passed while all those thoughts were spinning around like pinballs inside her head. Erin stood at the mouth of the entrance, not knowing what to do as people filtered by her, heading for their vehicles. Engines were starting, cars pulling out of parking spaces and filing out the road. Still no sign of the police.

She glanced behind her. Thirty yards back, the man in the loose check shirt ducked out of sight around the corner of a wall. She only caught a fleeting glimpse, but there was no mistaking his intention.

Think, Erin. She was shaking. What was she supposed to do, pull out her pistol and start shooting and cause a mass panic and hope she wasn't getting it all wrong? Or wait for him to make his move? What if he got the better of her? She'd been lucky first time round, and couldn't take that chance again. Couldn't rely on the cops, either. They could still be miles away. There was only one thing for it. Staying here wasn't an option. She'd have to drive to the police headquarters herself.

Her mind made up, Erin joined the flow of the crowd and walked quickly towards her parked Honda. Glanced back twice, three times and couldn't see the man but could still feel his eyes on her like a touch. She reached the car. Breathing hard, she locked herself inside, started it up and backed out of her parking space, then turned round and filtered into the procession of traffic leaving the zoo.

She drove past the airport, heading south along the broad highway into the city. After five minutes she checked in her mirror, saw the silver Lincoln behind her and swallowed. She was certain it had followed her from the zoo. She couldn't take her eyes off the road long enough to get a good look in the mirror, but there seemed to be just a single occupant inside, a man. She could just about make out the red of his T-shirt through the sun's reflection on his windscreen. Her heart began to thump harder. She turned off at the next junction and took a right towards the Cherokee Expressway, testing to see if he'd stay with her. He did. She took a sudden left turn without signalling, heading due south again down Harvard Avenue. The silver Lincoln was still there in the mirror. If there'd been a shred of doubt in her mind, it was gone now.

She could feel the reassuring hard steel angles of the Springfield in her pocket, pressing into her hip as she drove. *Don't panic,* she thought. *You have a gun. You've made it this far. You're not defenceless.*

So why didn't she feel so sure?

Chapter Thirty-Six

With one eye on the entrance of the City Hall building across the street and the other on the volume of Elizabeth Stamford's journal resting on the Patriot's steering wheel, Ben lit a cigarette, slouched back in his seat and read through a series of entries from the summer of 1847.

He was frustrated and worried about losing sight of what he was even looking for in these journals. He was annoyed that Brennan couldn't just have told him what was so revealing about them. There'd been no more mention of the mysterious Padraig McCrory. No clues offered as to what Kristen had been hunting for.

And yet, as he kept reading, he couldn't help but become drawn into the story that had unfolded all those years earlier.

. . . Having learned from that villain Burrows that a number of the starving tenants on the estate were attempting to feed themselves by shooting one or two rabbit and grouse, my dear husband has forbidden the use or ownership of private arms. I did what I could to impress upon him that by such action he effectively condemns yet more Irish people to the same lingering death that now afflicts every morbid corner of this land. To no avail; his word is final. 'I will not allow these peasants to roam at will over the countryside with

loaded weapons,' said he. 'Today it is a rabbit they will shoot. Tomorrow a gentleman, for the pennies in his purse or the meat on his table. We shall not permit anarchy, and there's an end to it. Nor shall I allow you to meddle in the affairs of the estate.'

Yet meddle I shall, for I cannot simply stand by and do nothing.

. . . This morning I rode across the blighted fields to the cottages of our three nearest peasant neighbours, the Callaghans, McCormicks and Driscolls. To the Callaghans I gave a share of what little money I have been able to collect and keep hidden, ever fearing that Edgar might find it and discover that I have been secretly selling pieces of the jewellery he gave me. I then crossed the hill to the cottage of the McCormick family, to give them their share of the same in the hope that they might make use of it to provide for themselves. When I entered the cottage, stretched in one corner, scarcely visible from the smoke and the rags that covered them, were the three children huddled together, pale and shrivelled. They turned their sunken eyes upon me as I entered, but were too weak from hunger to rise. In another corner, prostrated on a bed of sodden straw, sat a poor creature, barely human in her squalor and evidently close to death. In a piteous croak, the old woman implored me to give her something to eat, but all I could give was the small sum of money I could spare.

Unable to bear the sight any longer, I hurried onwards towards the Driscolls' thatched hut beyond the wood, to find there a spectacle even more ghastly: the hut in ruins, reduced to burnt wreckage on the blackened ground. This I knew was the work of the house tumblers, unspeakable rogues employed by my own husband to force eviction upon their very countrymen. The family were gone, dead perhaps, buried in the pits now that the carpenters have no more wood for coffins, or else sent to the workhouse. I reined my horse around and wept for bitter shame as I returned to Glenfell House. I am weeping still.

. . . Yesterday I was attending to my stable when I came upon little Moira O'Brien, one of the servant girls, sobbing forlornly in the hay barn. 'What sorrows you, my dear?' I asked her, giving her a handkerchief. 'Pray dry your tears and confide in me.' Barely able to speak at first for her grief, she then related a tale so extremely distressing that I have not been able to shake it from my mind. I did not sleep for a single minute last night and my hand trembles as I force myself to write these words:

It is dreadful. Two of Moira's cousins, Sean and Liam McGrath, and seven other young men of the county are sentenced to death for the crime of armed robbery after gathering up arms and attempting to raid a convoy of food and livestock bound for Wicklow Port. What manner of desperation could have prompted such a foolhardy course? Everyone has seen the long columns of redcoats marching side by side with the wagons, muskets aloft and gleaming in the sun. Yet in their unthinking folly, Sean and Liam and their friends attacked from the wooded high ground as the convoy passed along a narrow road outside Loughrea. It is said the clamour of gunfire and the great clouds of powder smoke could be discerned for miles. How could nine inexperienced farmers have expected to succeed against English soldiers, to say nothing of escaping alive with enough food to feed their hungry families?

Three of their band were killed outright in the battle, if a battle it can be called. Michael Murphy received a musket ball in his right arm, shattering the bone so horribly that it was caused to be removed at the shoulder. The rest were *quickly rounded up and are now in the gaol awaiting execution. Their poor heartbroken families have petitioned for clemency, begging for the sentence to be commuted. Even deportation to the penal colonies of New South Wales must be better than hanging.*

'I shall do no such thing,' Edgar remonstrated with me when I pleaded, <u>pleaded</u> with him this morning to use his influence in the matter. 'These men deserve no less than the full punishment of the law; they shall have it next Thursday at dawn. I will be there in person to watch them drop, and to the Devil with them.'

Nice guy, Ben thought. He broke away from his reading for a moment to gaze across at the entrance of Tulsa City Hall. There had been no movement in or out of the place for the last several minutes. Mayor Finn McCrory was definitely working late today. This might be a long wait. That was okay with him.

Ben turned his attention back to the journal and scanned through the pages of angry indignation Elizabeth had poured out over the hanging of the Irish raiding party's six surviving members, including Michael, the amputee, who'd been dying of his infected wound anyway when they'd dragged him from the prison hospital to the gallows. Ben understood Elizabeth's sense of outrage, and he understood Sean and Liam, too. If he'd been around at the time, he'd probably have joined the raiders himself. They might not have fared any better, but at least they'd have taken a few redcoats with them.

The hanging had come and gone. There had been no surprises, no reprieves. It was sad. It was one of those tragic and unjust things nobody could have prevented.

Ben flipped more pages and went on reading. Then he

stopped. Blinked. Looked again. 'What the . . .?' he muttered aloud.

Explosive revelations, Brennan had said. *The deepest, darkest of secrets, ones that have lain dormant for over a hundred and fifty years.*

And suddenly Ben was thinking he'd found one of them.

He read the journal entry through to the end, staring at Elizabeth Stamford's faded handwriting so hard he could feel the blood rushing in his ears. Then, just to make sure he hadn't dreamed it, he went back and read the same passage again:

August 19th, 1847

I have made a discovery that shakes me to the core. I am at a complete loss as to what to think, or what to do with such knowledge. Oh, Stephen, where are you when I am in such need of a friend to confide in? I am alone and can do nothing but record upon these pages the turmoil of my mind.

I have often wondered what goes on behind the locked door of my husband's laboratory in the east wing. He will let no servant enter, nor have I ever been permitted to see inside. He habitually spends many hours shut in that room, refusing to speak afterwards of his work, on the grounds that his botanical and chemical researches lie so far beyond the limits of his wife's mental powers that to discuss them would be futile.

Inquisitiveness has not seldom driven me to venture to the laboratory door when he is inside, keeping silent as a mouse lest he detect my footstep and wondering at the peculiar odours that emanate from behind it. I have sometimes tried to peek through the keyhole, but could see only the opposite bare wall.

The only human being Edgar will allow into the laboratory

is his Royal Society colleague Heneage Fitzwilliam, whose visits to Glenfell have long been a frequent . . . I shall not say 'pleasure', for although the respectable gentleman's scientific eminence is without question, I have always found his manner somewhat odd. For days on end, many times repeated, have they closeted themselves inside the room, speaking in low tones as if conferring on matters of a highly secretive nature.

Now I come to my discovery. I shall not dwell on how the key fell into my hands today, or how I discovered where my husband keeps it hidden inside the cigar box on his desk. Seizing the opportunity while he is away on some business (whose nature he did not choose to reveal to me), I retrieved the key and ran to the laboratory, all sense of guilt quite overcome by curiosity.

The laboratory is a smaller room than I had expected it to be, yet containing such an amazing variety of instruments and other scientific objects whose names and purposes I cannot guess at, except to say they are connected with Edgar's botanical investigations. On a long table, covered with papers and books, I came across a heavy ledger filled with entries and notes in my husband's careful hand. I could make little sense of them, but they appeared to comprise an extensive record of experimental results, dating from the year forty-five to the present. In another book I came upon many drawings of plants similarly dated. Upon a wooden rack sit rows of jars filled with preserved plant specimens, which have been labelled in order and range from those apparently plucked in a state of perfect health, to others bearing signs of disease. The more recent the date, the more withered and ill-looking the plant, as though marking a progression.

Little do I know of botany — but to have lived here in Ireland for any length of time is to know and recognise these specimens as coming from the common potato plant that we see – used to see – growing everywhere around. What can Edgar and his colleague have been doing with them? I asked myself over and over, and could come to no answer until I discovered the box.

It is a plain wooden item, the size of a lady's sewing box, with a lid that hinges open to reveal the red velvet of its lining. Protected inside, I found a row of small glass tubes – I imagine one could call them phials – each stoppered with a tiny bung and containing some manner of thick brown fluid that resembles . . . well, I will not say what it resembles. I tentatively uncorked one of them and held its opening to my nose, only to recoil in disgust at its odour before quickly replacing the bung. The phial, like the rest, bears a label in Edgar's hand with the name 'Phytophthora infestans'.

Following my discovery, my mind awhirl as to what it could all signify, I replaced the items as I had found them and fled the laboratory, locking the door. Hastening directly to Edgar's study I returned the key to its hiding place, then perused his bookcase and brought down a Dictionary of Ancient Greek. My knowledge of such things being severely limited by the meagre education reserved for my sex, I spent some time looking up the words I had seen on the labelled phials of noxious fluid. From this investigation I quickly learned that the stem 'phyto' refers generally to the plant kingdom, and that 'phthora' is the old Greek term meaning destruction, corruption and ruin. 'Infestans' I did not need to be told must describe an infestation, an infection or blight.

A blight, intended to destroy plants? Is this what my husband and his scientific colleague have been working on all this time? The foul substance; the potato plant samples in their varying states of corruption; the profuse notes of all

239

their experiments; the conclusions are too unthinkable to contemplate.

Unthinkable, and yet inescapable. I am not a person of any great scientific understanding but it is clear to me that the goal of Edgar's researches has been the deliberate creation of as severe a withering and devastation of the potato crop as modern science could contrive. God help us. It is more than I can bear. Can my husband truly be responsible for the starvation that afflicts Ireland?

Completely stunned, Ben closed the journal. The enormity of what he'd just read was so overwhelming that he struggled to take it in.

After the initial shock, things that Gray Brennan had said back in Madeira began to fly into his mind. He remembered the historian telling him about the French scientist Edgar Stamford had studied with after leaving Cambridge, and then gone back to visit twice during the mid-1840s. What had been his name? Ben racked his memory for a few moments before he recalled it. *Montagne. French for mountain.*

He took out his phone and went online to look the guy up. Montagne had served as a surgeon in the French army before turning to botany. He'd later become one of the first scientists to study and describe the highly infectious plant disease known as *Phytophthora infestans.*

And Stamford had left the comforts of his estate to travel all the way to Paris, not once but twice, just to study with this guy. Working on what? The causes of a lethal blight that could wipe out a whole crop and plunge an entire country into starvation? If these nineteenth-century scientists could figure out how the disease worked, then was it possible they could invert the formula and figure out how to cause it, too?

Gray Brennan's voice echoed again in Ben's mind. *It wasn't a famine. It was a starvation.*

But it was one thing to talk about simply taking advantage of a chance natural disaster. One thing to bemoan the cruel neglect the English rulers had inflicted on the starving Irish, taking the food from under their noses as they died in the ditches.

This was different. It went further than Ben could have imagined.

One of the worst acts of genocide you never heard of.

Now Ben understood.

This was it.

This was the journal's secret.

He put the phone away and stared into space, still reeling from what he'd just read. Forget explosive. It was a hundred-megaton warhead.

That was when a movement across the street caught his eye, jerking him from his thoughts. He sat up straight behind the wheel of the Jeep and watched out of the window as a scuffed white GMC van pulled into City Hall's parking lot. The van's driver looked to be in a hurry. It squealed sharply to a halt in front of the building, and two men piled out and began walking fast towards the main doors.

Ben snatched up his binoculars to get a look at them before they disappeared inside. He felt his guts tighten with anger when he saw them magnified up close. Because these two guys were becoming familiar faces. Just like old friends he kept meeting up with. The combat kit from Madeira had been exchanged for a more casual look. The slightly taller one was in black, with a few more days' stubble on his shaved head than he'd had back in Ireland. The skinny one with the ponytail had 'PUT THE WHITE BACK IN THE WHITE HOUSE' emblazoned across his chest. Subtle. He reached into his jeans pocket as he walked, took out a wrapper and popped something in his mouth. Gum. Ben didn't have to smell it to know it.

'Hello, fellas,' he said.

Chapter Thirty-Seven

Portraits of the current Pope, JFK and Robert Kennedy smiled down upon Finn McCrory as he sat at his desk in the air-conditioned cool of the mayor's office. Some of Finn's Republican peers had been known to frown at the presence of such iconic Democrats hanging on his wall, but despite his party affiliation Finn remained staunchly loyal to the Kennedy name for what it meant to Irish-Americans.

Finn was reclining in his huge green chair with his boots up on the desk and the door locked. It was only at this time of the afternoon, when Janet and the rest of the staff had gone for the day, that he could make certain phone calls to certain people without having to hide in the bathroom or go out to sit in his car. Right now he was speaking with Xavier, one of his business contacts in Nuevo Laredo. Xavier sounded like he was standing out in the desert or somewhere, because the wind was crackling his phone's mike. Xavier had a thing about being listened in on, too – which, given the nature of their business, wasn't surprising.

No names were ever mentioned in their conversations. Specifics were referred to in the most oblique and vague way possible, so that even if anyone had been listening in, they wouldn't have understood what the hell the men were talking about. The call had been going on for over twenty minutes, because they had a lot to discuss about the shipment due to head south next week. It was a big one and both ends wanted it to go perfectly. Which Finn was confident it would, now that Blaylock had been taken out of the picture.

'Just a slight glitch in the system,' he told Xavier.

'Let's hope it's cleaned up now, huh?' Xavier said.

'Cleaner than clean. I don't think we'll have any more problems this end,' Finn said, smiling. 'Everything's looking good.'

Three rapid knocks at his office door interrupted what he was about to say next. He looked up from his call to see the door handle turning. Who the hell was that? One of the cleaners trying to get in, probably.

'So I'll be at the station as planned,' Xavier was saying. 'I expect the train will be on schedule.'

'It's always been a reliable service,' Finn replied.

'Tickets are getting kind of expensive lately.'

'But the passengers arrive right on time and everybody's happy, huh?'

Thump, thump.

Finn looked irritably over at the door. The handle was turning again. Hadn't that damned fool of a cleaner figured out it was locked for a reason?

'Later,' he said to Xavier, and ended the call. The knocking was getting louder and more insistent. Finn strode to the door, unlocked it and wrenched it open, ready to yell at the stupid cleaner.

But it wasn't the cleaner.

'What in the name of—?' he demanded, staring at Ritter and Moon, who were standing in the doorway. In a panic, he peered past them in case anyone might have seen them. Luckily, the place was deserted. 'Get in here,' he grated, lowering his voice. 'I thought I told you never, *ever* to show

244

your damn faces here.' He ushered them quickly into the office, shut the door after them and locked it again.

'You've been on the line the last half hour solid, boss,' Ritter said. 'We needed to talk to you. Something's up.'

'What in hell could be so important that you had to come to my office? Have you lost your minds?'

'Spicer's been shot.'

'He's *what?*'

'The Hayes bitch shot him,' Moon filled in, smacking gum and breathing mint.

Finn was stupefied. 'Is he dead?'

'He won't be trippin' the light fantastic any more, that's for sure,' Moon said.

Finn shook his head. 'Damn it, Ritter, you told me he was reliable.'

'Yeah, well, a nine-mil Springfield auto's pretty reliable too,' Ritter said. 'He took one in the leg. Blew a hole the size of Kansas above the knee, near enough took it off. She must've been using hollowpoints. Black Talons or something, I guess.'

'Jesus Christ,' Finn exploded. 'It was a simple job. How can you screw that up?'

'Take it easy, boss,' Moon said. 'It's under control. No cops involved.'

'It's not the cops I'm worried about, you imbecile,' Finn ranted at him. 'How'd you figure I knew about the video in the first place?' He turned back to Ritter. 'She's one woman. She's not the US fuckin' Marines. I thought you said Spicer took a partner along.'

'Jesse Zimbert,' Ritter said, nodding.

'So what happened to him, she shoot him as well?' Finn demanded.

'He was outside in the car,' Ritter admitted, looking down at his feet. 'Plan was to stay hidden until Spicer came out, then

245

move the car up close to the door and get her in the trunk. Instead, Zimbert's waiting in the car when he sees the Hayes woman run out of the house and take off.'

'His buddy gets half his leg blown off just a few yards away and he doesn't even hear the shot? Is the guy stone deaf or what?'

'Says he was listening to music,' Ritter replied, shamefaced.

'*Music!?*'

Ritter flushed deeper red. 'He's into Hideously Mutilated. That's a band. Goes around with earphones on. I guess he must have been wearing them when Spicer was inside the house.'

'You ever see him wearing them again, you put a bullet in his brain,' Finn raged. 'That's an order. No, in fact you put a bullet in his brain anyway. Now you're going to tell me he lost the bitch and we've no way of knowing where she is?'

Ritter could give a more positive answer this time. 'He went in the house, found Spicer halfway down the stairs, bleeding all over the place with his damn leg hanging off. Spicer told him what happened. Then Zimbert got back in his car and took off after her. Caught up with her Honda on the expressway. Meanwhile, he called in some more guys to take care of Spicer.'

'Spicer can live or die,' Finn said. 'It's her I'm interested in. Where'd she go?'

'Said she was heading for the zoo. That's the last I spoke to him. We tried calling you. Your line was busy. We came here.'

'The zoo,' Finn snorted. 'We sure about that?'

'That's what he said.'

'What's she gonna do, hang out with the monkeys?'

246

Moon tittered. Finn was going to tell him to shut up when his phone rang. It was O'Rourke.

'Guess who just called me,' the police chief said. 'Sounded all shook up. Says someone tried to pull a number on her. Was it your boys?'

'I don't know anything about that,' Finn replied, which meant yes. 'We have a present location?'

'City zoo,' O'Rourke said. 'I have people on their way. Awaiting further instructions. What you want me to do?'

'No damage,' Finn said. 'I don't want her harmed, not yet. Bring her to me. Usual place.' He slipped the phone back into his pocket, smiling. Things were under control again. The noose was retightening. Their little friend Erin Hayes was giving them the runaround but there was no way she was getting out of it this time.

Suddenly it was Ritter's phone ringing. 'Zimbert,' he said, fishing it out and looking at the caller ID. He put it to his ear, listened without expression, said nothing for thirty seconds. 'Okay. Keep me informed.' He ended the call and turned to Finn.

'Okay, she just left the zoo,' he told his boss.

'With the cops?' Finn asked.

Ritter shook his head. 'Alone.'

'Shit,' Finn muttered. They must have just missed her. 'So we're depending on this idiot Zimbert not to lose her?'

'We won't lose her. While she was inside, he found her car in the parking lot and put a GPS tracker under the wheel arch. She's heading south. He's on her tail. Just picked up a couple more guys for backup. Still want me to put one in his head?'

'I want you to get the hell after her, is what I want,' Finn yelled, pointing at the door. 'Bring the bitch back to me alive and talking. Got it? Now move your asses. And don't ever come back here.'

Ritter and Moon hurried out of the building. As they ran to the van, Ritter called Zimbert back. 'On our way. Keep your distance and no moves until we get there. Read me?'

'I can't wait to get my hands on this bitch,' Moon said, leaping in behind the wheel. 'Sweet, sweet. Come to Daddy.' He fired up the GMC's engine and hit the gas hard. The van pulled a tight U-turn in front of the building and squealed out into the traffic.

As they sped up the street, both Ritter and Moon were too intently focused on catching up with their target to notice the grey Jeep Patriot that pulled away from the kerb a little distance up the street, slotted into the steady flow and fell quietly in line behind them, three cars back.

Chapter Thirty-Eight

Erin was approaching the heart of downtown and still the silver Lincoln was close behind, following every way she went. Traffic was slow. She was still several minutes' drive from police headquarters.

Her thoughts raced. Why not just head straight to her destination? Maybe when her pursuer saw where she was going, he'd get scared and back off. Or maybe he wouldn't. He might just hang around and wait for her to come out. She had no idea what O'Rourke was going to do when she got there. For all she knew, she'd be turned loose again with nowhere to go except another motel to lie low in. Except it wouldn't be lying low if this guy followed her there. She quelled the panic that bubbled up inside her. She suddenly knew what to do.

She hung a left turn, then another, then a right. She blasted through a green light about to turn and smiled to herself as the Lincoln was forced to a halt at the red light. Sixty yards down the street was a shopping mall with an underground car park. Her tyres squealed as she turned in sharp left and went down the steep ramp. He'd have seen her, but it didn't matter. The red light had bought her some time, maybe two minutes, long enough to tuck the Honda away where it would be hard to find and make her way on foot up to the mall above. She could easily lose him there.

Then she'd emerge back out onto the street and hope to hail a cab. Tulsa wasn't New York; taxis didn't exactly come by every five seconds. But she might get lucky, and if not she could jump on the first bus she saw.

But Erin was too slow. Either her pursuer had jumped the red light, or she'd misjudged the time advantage it would give her. She'd left the Honda parked in the shadows between a thick concrete pillar and a dusty red Toyota pickup and was running in the direction of the lifts when the silver Lincoln came speeding down the ramp. It swerved towards her, engine echoing in the underground cavern of the car park. It squealed to a halt between her and the way to the lifts, cutting her off. The driver's door swung open and the man in the loose check shirt over the red T-shirt got out. An overhead neon was faulty, flickering on and off and throwing his face into shadow.

Erin instantly turned and started running back towards her Honda.

'Erin, stop,' he called out.

She knew that voice. She stopped and turned. He was standing by his car.

Erin narrowed her eyes and peered at him.

'Detective Morrell?' She stared. This didn't make sense. Why had Topher Morrell been following her? *Before* she called the cops?

'You're surprised to see me. I understand that,' Morrell said, stepping closer and holding up his palms as if to say, 'Trust me, I won't hurt you'.

'What are you doing here?'

'I can explain.' He took another step towards her.

Confused thoughts raced through her mind. She backed away from him. 'Then do it from right where you're standing. Don't come any closer.'

'I'm one of the good guys,' he said. His look was sincere, almost pleading.

'A man attacked me in my home and tried to stick me with a fucking needle. Now you're tailing me around the place. I don't know who the good guys are any more.'

'Erin,' he said. 'Can I call you Erin?' He approached another step.

'I mean what I say.' She took out the Springfield and pointed it at him in the same steady two-handed grip she'd used when she shot her attacker.

Morrell stopped. He looked at the gun. 'You don't need that.'

'Can't point a gun at a cop, right? That's a federal crime. Sorry. Right now I'd rather take my chances.'

'I'm not just a cop,' he said. 'I'm working with the FBI. That's what I need to talk to you about. Please, put the gun away. At least quit pointing it at me. Let me explain.'

'FBI?' she said, confused.

'Trust me.'

She shook her head firmly. 'Not a chance. Not until I see some ID.'

'All I have is my police badge. I said I was working with the Feds. I didn't say I was one of them. It's off the books.'

'Off the books?'

'Please. You need to trust me. You're in danger.'

'You don't say.' She sighed, then lowered the gun and let it dangle at her side with her finger off the trigger. 'Okay. Then talk. But don't come any closer.'

'The FBI are investigating Finn McCrory. It's a covert operation. I'm part of it. I've been part of it for months. That's why I was so amazed when you walked into my office with your story. I couldn't believe my luck. You're the key to this whole operation, Erin.'

251

'That's not how it looked to me. First you looked bored out of your mind with what I had to tell you. Then you sided with O'Rourke when he said my evidence was useless.'

He looked at her intently, as if he was earnestly willing her to believe him. 'If you let me speak, you'll understand why I had to act that way. I told you, this is a secret operation. We have to be real careful. One slip and the whole investigation into McCrory's activities falls apart. What he's into is worse than you could imagine.'

'I saw him shoot a man in cold blood,' she said, tight-lipped. 'What other activities could be worse than that?'

'How about the murder of thousands of innocent people? Drugs, organised kidnap and rape, torture, prostitution. Spreading misery and death. And getting obscenely rich off the back of it.'

Erin was too stunned to reply.

'McCrory deals in arms,' Morrell told her. 'And he does it in a big way, using a bunch of corrupt ex-military connections to supply millions of dollars' worth of weaponry to the criminal underworld. He's real selective who he sells to. His main customers are a gang called Los Locos. The fastest-growing and most bloodthirsty drugs cartel in eastern Mexico, used to be part of the La Familia organisation until it got ambitious and went its own way. The ATF and DEA come down heavier on them each year and now the Mexicans are tooling up for a major war to protect their billion-dollar industry. There's gonna be a lot more blood on McCrory's hands if he isn't stopped.'

Erin could hardly speak. 'The man they killed at the cabin—'

'He was one of their gang,' Morrell said. 'Name of Kirk Blaylock. He secretly approached the FBI some months ago, looking to make a deal. In return for full immunity, he was willing to blow the whistle on their whole operation.

McCrory's people must've sniffed him out somehow before he ever got the chance. Most likely it was Ritter. He's the smartest of all of them.'

'Ritter?'

Morrell nodded. 'Matt Ritter. Former soldier. About as good as they come, once upon a time. Served with 5th Special Forces Group. Gulf, Afghanistan, you name it, he was there. Then he turned rotten. Spent some years working globally as a private military contractor, doing things you don't want to know about. Gunrunning is nothing new to this guy. Now he's back in Oklahoma and he's got himself a nice cushy number as McCrory's chief of staff. You've met him.'

'He was one of the two men there that night?'

'Along with his crony, Billy Bob Moon. Ex-MARSOC. That's the US Marine Corps Special Operations Command. He's about as highly trained as Ritter is, and possibly even more dangerous. He's a psycho who loves to kill for the hell of it, whereas Ritter's the one with the business brains and the arms connections. The operation buys in hardware by the ton. McCrory flies down to meet his contact just over the Mexican border in Nuevo Laredo every few months. Xavier, but that's not his real name. Our intel suggests that the guy's a middleman for Los Locos.'

'Sounds like you know everything,' Erin said.

'Not nearly enough,' Morrell said. 'And without Blaylock's testimony, we couldn't prove any of it. We had zilch. McCrory's been way too smart to leave a trail that could lead back to him.' He smiled. 'Until now. Now we have a new star witness. That's you. Your video recording is the first real evidence that links McCrory to any criminal activity. Even without the Blaylock connection, we have him and his guys for first-degree murder.'

'Then why not use it?' Erin asked. 'The proof is right

there. McCrory could have been arrested the moment I handed it to you people.'

'It's a little more complicated than that,' Morrell said. 'Because it goes deeper than just McCrory. They're connected into everything. Corrupt quartermasters leaking military ordnance out of US arms depots. Police departments from here to Mexico taking bribes to look the other way. The Feds aren't about to make their move until the time is right to swoop in and take down the whole rotten bunch.'

Erin stared at him. 'Even the cops are in on this?'

'Yes, and it makes me sick. That's why I'm involved, see? Liam O'Rourke. The chief of police. He's one of them.'

'Jesus.'

'The FBI approached me last fall. After grilling me for hours, they finally revealed their suspicions to me about O'Rourke and asked me to be their inside man in Tulsa PD. I could hardly believe it was true at the time. Since then I've been spying on O'Rourke and reporting back to them.'

'That's why you were so quick to bring O'Rourke in after I showed up at your office,' Erin said.

Morrell nodded. 'I had to see his response. The way he reacted to the video footage, that was the final proof. I knew then for certain that he was covering McCrory's ass.'

'And you had to pretend to go along with it.'

'You understand now, right? But I almost bit my damn tongue off trying to cover up my excitement. This was the break I've been waiting for. The chance to nail both of those sonsofbitches. Ever seen the chief's house? Money like that doesn't come from a police salary.'

'This is incredible. You're telling me that both our mayor and our police chief are dealing arms to Mexican drug lords.'

'We don't think O'Rourke is directly involved in the trans-actions. He gets paid to turn a blind eye to McCrory's little

254

trips and the occasional bit of business he has to conduct in the state, such as the Blaylock killing. He also does his bit to protect the secret location of the warehouse.'

'The warehouse?'

'McCrory's arsenal. All we know is, it's somewhere in Tulsa County. Ritter and Moon have crews of drivers trucking the stuff out of the state. They cut south across Texas and over the Tex-Mex border to RV with the cartel. Different route every time, different rendezvous points. Impossible to pin down. That's another part of O'Rourke's job, to make sure the convoys never get stopped en route. Which means there has to be a lot more money passing hands among the local cops. He's not the only one. McCrory's been running a whole network, expanding it year on year. The Feds estimate that he's got at least thirty people directly working for him, maybe more. Now he's running for governor, there's no telling how big his operation could . . . What's the matter?'

Erin had turned pale and was looking distressed by something she'd suddenly remembered. 'O'Rourke,' she said. 'I called him. Told him I was at the zoo. He said he'd send someone. I was waiting there for the cops to arrive when . . . I thought you were one of *them*. That's why I ran.'

'You did the right thing. He won't find us here.'

'How did you know where I was?'

'Followed you from your house.'

'You've been watching me?'

He nodded. 'Whenever possible. It's not been easy, juggling a covert operation alongside all the regular duties O'Rourke expects from me, and I can't let him get suspicious. That's why I wasn't there when you were attacked. I wouldn't have let that happen, Erin, I promise. But O'Rourke called me away on another job and I couldn't get out of it. When I got back to your place, I saw you driving away like crazy. I figured something must have happened. I could either stick around and find out what, or follow you. Turns out I made the right choice. But you shouldn't have been allowed to be put in danger. I'm sorry.'

'Well, you're here now,' she said.

'The man who attacked you. Describe him to me.'

'Forties. White. About the same height as you, but much heavier. Real ugly.'

'Could have been any of them. Maybe Joey Spicer.'

'You'll know soon enough. I shot him in the leg. Self-defence.'

'If you'd shot him in the head, nobody would've missed him. Spicer's lowlife scum. We'll find him and lean on him. He's tough, but we're pretty tough too. If we can get him to snitch, it'll take us a long way to nailing McCrory.'

'What about me?' she asked. 'What happens next?'

'You're not safe. I'm going to call my FBI contact, Special Agent Dobbs. We'll arrange a rendezvous. I won't let you out of my sight until the handover.'

'Handover for what?'

'The FBI will arrange witness security for you.'

'You mean, a new identity? Relocation?'

'The full works. Should have been done days ago. Trust me, you'll be where McCrory can't possibly touch you. You're in safe hands now.'

She nodded.

That was when they heard the echoing roar of vehicles speeding down the ramp into the underground car park. At least two of them. Moving fast, rapidly approaching.

'That them already?' Erin asked, wide-eyed.

'No,' Morrell said, looking as alarmed and surprised as she was. 'That can't be them.'

Chapter Thirty-Nine

Ben followed the white van away from City Hall. He was good at tailing people, and had been doing it for a long time. The trick was to hang back by a decent number of car-lengths, using the vehicles between you and the target to block you out. Three was ideal. It worked best in heavy traffic, where you could maintain constant visual contact with little chance of being spotted.

But there were risks, too. Allowing a distance between you and the target made it possible to get separated. Traffic lights were a constant menace. Burn through a red to keep up, and bad things could happen – you might get into an accident, you might alert the target to your presence, and if you were really unlucky you might draw unwanted police attention into the bargain. That was why the best way to track a moving target was with a coordinated team in multiple vehicles, staying in contact by radio or mobile phone. A combination of cars, trucks and motorcycles was useful. Air support was even better. If one team member thought they were getting too conspicuous or had lost visual contact, they could call in another who immediately picked up the trail. When it was smoothly done, the target didn't have a clue they were being tailed.

Ben didn't have the luxury of a whole team of guys. He

was on his own, and for that reason he had to play it extra safe as he chased the white van through the streets of downtown Tulsa. Instead of three vehicles, he hung back four, his gaze fixed on the dirty panels of the GMC's back doors so as not to let it get swallowed up out of sight in the traffic. Even that didn't keep him completely hidden, because the van was moving fast, constantly stepping out of lane and slaloming left and right as it overtook just about everything in front of it, and Ben was forced to do the same. The two men were definitely in a hurry to get somewhere. He swore as the van sped past a station wagon, and wished they'd slow down. This reckless nonsense was going to get them all noticed.

The van turned this way and that, screeching through intersections, cutting a jagged path northwards through the city. After a few minutes, Ben realised that it had caught up with another fast-moving vehicle up ahead, a blue Ford. The two of them were keeping pace with each other. From this distance it was hard to tell how many occupants were inside the car – maybe three or four.

The blue Ford and the van were forced to slow a little as they came into a long right-hand sweeper choked up with traffic in both directions. From his three-quarter angle further back round the bend, Ben could see that the front passenger windows of both vehicles were wound down. The front seat passenger of the Ford was a heavy-looking ape with dark glasses. He was talking on a phone. So was the guy in the van. Ben would have bet money they were talking to each other. They were travelling in convoy. And taking it very seriously. Wherever they were heading in such a hurry, they meant business and it was a job for a crew of several men. Based on the Madeira experience, that almost certainly meant that these guys were heavily tooled up. Whilst Ben was totally unarmed.

Maybe this was going to get interesting after all.

Then, suddenly, it all started going wrong. A gap appeared in the slow-moving traffic and the driver of the blue Ford went for it, speeding along the solid line of cars on the right. The van followed. Ben muttered a curse and did the same. The Jeep accelerated to forty, then fifty. As he picked up speed, he could see the blue Ford coming to an intersection, chasing down the green light with the van right behind. Ben could see what was about to happen. They'd make it through the lights and he wouldn't. He'd have to choose between losing them or going right on through.

He was wrong. The green light turned to red before the Ford got there. But the Ford didn't slow down. As Ben watched, it went storming brazenly across the intersection with the van close behind, cutting across the path of an oncoming Nissan and causing it to swerve violently to avoid a collision. The Nissan's driver hit the brakes too hard, lost control and spun a full three-sixty and slammed hard into a Lexus that had been coming up behind it. The Lexus spun into a Subaru, which went careering straight into the path of a bus. Horns sounded in panic. Tyres screeched. Metal crunched and plastic splintered. The blue Ford sailed through the middle of the chaos without taking a scratch, but the dented Lexus rolled backwards into the way of the van. The GMC was bigger and heavier and smashed it out of the way in an explosion of flying wreckage as it followed the Ford away from the intersection and up the street.

Ben hit the brakes and sawed the Jeep's wheel this way and that, swerving wildly through the pile-up until he saw that the way ahead was almost completely blocked by crumpled vehicles. He pulled to a halt and scrambled out of the Jeep. Saw the blue Ford and the van disappearing away into the distance. He'd lost them. He clenched his fist and pounded it against the Jeep's bonnet.

People were getting out of their cars, staggering about looking dazed. Someone's horn was jammed on. The back door dropped off the badly buckled rear of the Lexus where the wing of the van had ploughed into it. The Subaru's front end had been mangled by the bus and a plume of steam was hissing from its radiator. The bus driver, a heavyset black guy in a uniform and cap, was scratching his head and staring around him at the damage. Some of his passengers were getting out, shaken and pale. A child was crying.

'Did you see?' an old woman said, pointing. 'That guy was a maniac!'

'Is anybody hurt?' Ben asked. All he got in reply were numb looks and a few head shakes. He couldn't see any blood on anyone. The only real injuries were to metal and plastic and insurance premiums. The only fatality of the situation was his chase. The Ford and the GMC were long gone.

At that moment, something caught his eye and he walked over to take a closer look, his shoes crunching on scattered bits of headlamp glass. Where the van had collided with the rolling Lexus, there was a big dark stain on the road. It had been quite a thump. There was a lot of smashed plastic everywhere. Most of the van's right headlamp unit had been torn out, like an eye ripped out of its socket. It looked as if the radiator had taken a bad knock, too.

Ben crouched down and touched a fingertip to the dark stain on the road. It was wet and warm. Water, not oil. It hadn't come from the Lexus. He could tell that from two things. First, there was little damage to the front end of the car. Second, there was a whole trail of black splotches leading away from the accident scene and in the direction the van had gone.

He got back into the Jeep.

'You can't leave, man,' the bus driver hollered. 'Cops will be here in a minute.' Ben ignored the guy, put the Jeep in gear and gently nudged a way between the two damaged cars blocking his way. If he returned the Jeep to the rental company with nothing worse than one or two scratches, nobody would die over it. Once he was clear of the wreckage zone, he hit the gas hard. His chase was back on, but how far would the trail lead him?

Chapter Forty

Both Erin and Detective Morrell stood frozen in the shadows of the car park, gawking in the direction of the fast-approaching roar of engines. Then, as they watched, a blue Ford Taurus burst into sight. Through the dazzle of its headlights Erin instantly recognised it as the one parked near her house earlier that day. Its front wheels hit the bottom of the slope, compressing hard against the suspension and making a squeal that echoed around the concrete walls and pillars of the underground space. The Taurus was closely followed by a white GMC van. Erin vaguely registered that the van was missing a headlamp and half its radiator grille.

But that was the least of her concerns as the two vehicles swerved across the car park and accelerated right towards where she and Morrell were standing.

'Look out!' the detective yelled, reaching out to grab her hand and haul her to safety. But Erin was already moving. She retreated quickly through the gap between her Honda and the Toyota pickup next to it, ducked down behind them and crouched low. Morrell quickly joined her.

The blue Ford screeched to a halt next to Morrell's Lincoln, rocking on its tired springs. The van pulled up at an angle to it. Doors flew open. Three men piled decisively out of the Ford, all wearing grim expressions. Erin only caught a glimpse of them, but she recognised one as the man who'd been sitting waiting for his buddy to dope her with tranquillisers so they could stuff her in the trunk and take her away. The other two she'd never seen before.

But the pair jumping down from the cab of the battered white GMC van: she got a clear look at them and she knew their faces very well. They were faces that had haunted her nightmares ever since that night at the cabin on Oologah Lake, and seeing them again hit her with a chill that made her gasp. McCrory's henchmen, his killers for hire. Moon and Ritter, Morrell had called them.

She recognised the van, too. It had been there that night. They'd used it to dispose of the dead Kirk Blaylock.

She looked at Morrell. His face was etched with tension. He reached under his loose shirt, and she saw the conceal-ment holster tucked into the hem of his jeans. He drew out a pistol. It was a Colt 1911 government model, big old-fashioned heavy iron. 'Stay down,' Morrell hissed at her.

The attackers were striding towards them, their steps echoing. Five against two. Erin heard a muttered command. She wanted to close her eyes and shrink into a tiny ball. Beside her, Morrell jacked a round into his Colt's chamber. 'Police!' he yelled. 'Back off or I'll shoot!'

The response was a deafening thunder of gunfire that filled the car park. Erin flinched, covered her ears, didn't know what to do. Bullets ripped into her little yellow car and howled off the concrete, tore chunks out of the wall behind. Morrell let off a wild shot and crawled around the back of the Honda. Now he and Erin were separated by about eight feet of open space. More shots sounded. The Honda's windows shattered as if a grenade had gone off inside it, throwing out hailstones of glass that bounced all around the concrete floor.

Cringing behind the Toyota pickup, Erin suddenly realised

that they were only firing at Morrell. The detective threw himself into a sideways prone position so he could aim his gun out from behind cover, firing back between the cars. Erin saw the white muzzle flash erupt three times, four times, from his Colt. The big .45 was extremely loud at close quarters. A spent shell case tinkled across the gap between the Honda and the Toyota and lodged under her arm, burning her skin. She hardly felt it.

Two of the men from the car dived for cover from Morrell's gunfire. The Taurus's back side window shattered. Morrell let off two more booming rounds, but he was in a bad position to shoot from and his shots went off target, punching fat round holes in the car's blue bodywork.

Erin shrank deeper underneath the back of the Toyota. It had jacked suspension and oversized tyres that lifted its chassis high enough off the ground for her to get tucked right under. Peering out from her hiding place she could see a pair of feet. Lightweight combat boots, belonging to one of the attackers sheltering behind the white van. Her mind was beginning to focus now after the initial panic. She could feel the Springfield inside her pocket. There was just space under the car for her to get it out, but not enough to aim it properly. She had to hold it flatways and had no idea whether her sights would still line up. She fired anyway, letting off three shots as quickly as she could control the snappy recoil of the nine-millimetre, screwing up her face at the lancing pain in her eardrums. Her hearing was now just one big singing whine of tinnitus. She saw the combat boots dance quickly away and realised that her shots had all gone wide, punching into Morrell's Lincoln.

The detective let off another round from his .45 and then its seven-shot magazine was empty. Exactly the reason why most people favoured high-capacity nines these days. Erin twisted around under the Toyota and saw him drop the empty mag from the butt of his gun, saw him reach to his left hip for the spare in his belt pouch. In the brief pause, the driver of the Ford broke cover from behind his car. He kept low as he sneaked up between the Honda and the pillar next to it, clearly intending to work his way around Morrell's flank. The detective hadn't noticed because he was focused on reloading his gun. Erin spotted the movement through what was left of the Honda's shattered windows. This was the jerkoff who'd come to kidnap her earlier.

'Morrell!' she shouted, and opened fire from underneath the Toyota. She couldn't shoot to kill. She lined the sights up on his shoulder. The Springfield snapped in her hand, twice, the bullets passing right through her car's interior. The man fell back out of sight with his face contorting in pain and his hand slapping to his shoulder where he'd been hit. There was blood on the concrete pillar behind him.

Morrell flashed her a thumbs-up sign and an earnest look of gratitude. Despite her terror, Erin's heart soared. *We can win this*, she thought.

But in the next few moments, she saw that she was wrong. A chattering blast of automatic gunfire riddled the side of the Honda and hammered the concrete between it and the Toyota, driving her back as far as she could scramble underneath for cover. She caught a fleeting glimpse of the two men from the van, steadily advancing towards Morrell's position. They were holding black assault weapons of a kind she'd never seen before, weird and futuristic. Whatever the hell they were, they weren't the sort of thing that was available to ordinary citizens, not even to ordinary criminals. They were full-blown military hardware and the two men seemed terrifyingly adept at using them. They were rapidly turning the Honda into Swiss cheese.

Morrell scampered for cover around the back of the car like a jackrabbit flushed out by hounds. The firestorm coming at him was so intense that he couldn't return a single shot from his pistol. The Honda was literally coming apart. One corner settled as its tyre was shredded, then another. Its thin yellow body panels were more silver-edged bullet holes than intact metal. The two shooters kept coming. The ponytailed one did a lightning-fast reload while the other covered him, then they switched over. Empty cases streamed from their weapons. Their muzzles were lit up with strobing white light. It was a continual outpouring of bullets, the noise so bad that Erin wanted to scream. She couldn't move, couldn't shoot for fear that they'd direct the fire at her.

Morrell didn't have a chance. He was so tucked in under the back end of the devastated Honda that all that was visible now was one leg sticking out, bent at the knee, bracing him tightly in behind his rapidly diminishing cover. Erin couldn't see the rest of him. But she saw the blood that spattered up the wall behind the parked cars as the bullets ripped into him. Still they didn't stop firing. The leg Erin could see started jerking and spasming, as if Morrell was having a fit. It was the impact of the bullets hitting him and the convulsions of his body as he died.

Now it was just her. She rolled over twice and wriggled out from under the dirty bottom sill of the Toyota. Leapt to her feet, squeezed off three shots behind her without looking back, and took off as fast as she could sprint between the wall and the line of parked cars. The way through towards the shopping mall was less than twenty yards away, but it might as well have been a thousand. She knew there was little chance of making it, and even if she did, they'd come after her. But she was going to try anyway. She'd rather die than let herself be taken captive.

She was nearly halfway to the exit when they shot her.

Chapter Forty-One

Erin sprawled face down to the hard concrete, dropping her gun, all her senses disintegrating into a wild tumult of pain and confusion. Something had pierced her shoulder, but it wasn't a bullet. A bullet would have blown right through her, spraying a mist of blood outwards and across her cheek. She'd have felt the wound channel open up inside her, sinew and bone and soft tissue turning to jelly with the shock of the impact. This was something else.

A terrible current of agony was rippling through her whole body. She couldn't control her movements. Her arms and legs were thrashing, her spine arching backwards so tightly that it felt like it would snap, if her muscles didn't first. She was only dimly aware of the curly wires connecting the dart in her shoulder to the device that the ponytailed man had clenched in his fist as he strolled casually up to her with his automatic weapon slung behind his shoulder.

'Hey there, darlin',' he said. 'How's about you take a little ride with your uncle Billy Bob?' He smiled as he peered down at her. There was a wad of white gum rolling around between his teeth; she caught a sharp minty smell off his breath that took her confused senses straight back to the nightmare memory of the cabin.

He did something with the object he was holding and the

awful electric convulsions stopped as suddenly as they'd begun, but Erin was too stunned to resist or even stand up. She was aware of figures of men circling her. Strong hands reached down and yanked her roughly to her feet. There was a jolt of pain as the thing stuck in her shoulder was plucked out. 'Get your fucking hands off of me,' she said. Her cheek was throbbing badly from the fall, and her voice sounded faraway and slurry. It was beginning to dawn on her that she'd been tasered. She kicked and struggled and lashed out with her fists. One of her punches made contact, but only weakly.

'She shot me!' It was the one she'd fired at through the Honda's windows. Blood was soaking through his shirt and he was unsteady on his feet, pointing at her with a look of amazement. 'She fucking shot me!'

'Try and run, bitch,' the one called Billy Bob said, taking out a pistol and shoving its muzzle under her chin. The steel was cool and hard. 'Go on. Be a sport,' he said. 'That's all I want, so I can blow your brains out.'

'Get the gun out of her face,' said the other man she recognised from the cabin, slapping the weapon away. 'Boss wants her back alive, remember?'

'Your boss. The mayor, right? Another one who's got it coming.'

'That's right, bitch. You got yourself an appointment with the mayor. Should be honoured. He's an important guy.'

'I know who you are,' she said. 'You're Moon. And you're Ritter. Call yourselves soldiers? You ought to be ashamed of yourselves.'

'How 'bout I wrap your head round and round with duct tape?' Moon said. 'Keep that smart mouth of yours shut.' He thrust the pistol in his belt and grabbed her roughly by the arm.

'Let's get the hell out of here,' Ritter said, walking towards the driver's side of the van. 'Put the bitch in the back. I'll drive. Moon, in with me.' He pointed at the wounded man. 'Jesse, you best let Skeeter drive the Taurus. Quincy, you ride in the back of the van with her. She tries anything, do what you have to do. But no rough stuff.'

'That part comes later,' Moon said, baring his teeth.

'You won't be grinning when they're dragging your scrawny ass into the deathhouse,' Erin seethed at him.

Moon's face turned sour. He spat out his wad of gum. 'I'm gettin' tired of your talk, lady.' With an iron grip on her arms, he began hauling her towards the van. She tried to kick him again, lost her footing and fell. He hauled her painfully along the ground.

Skeeter helped the injured Jesse into the back of the Taurus, leaving a blood trail. The one called Quincy walked round the rear of the van, opened up the doors. As he stood waiting for Moon to shove their captive inside, he heard something from the direction of the ramp and twisted his head around to see. 'I think we got company, boys.'

'That's their fuckin' problem,' Skeeter said, closing Jesse inside the car.

The sound of an approaching vehicle grew louder, a growing echoing rumble in the underground cavern. Ritter and Moon turned to look as the grey Jeep Patriot appeared around the bend and came down the ramp. It was moving fast. Much too fast. Its headlights blazed at them.

Ritter's eyes narrowed to slits. 'What the—?' Moon began. He let go of one of Erin's arms and his hand moved to unsling his assault weapon.

The Jeep hit the bottom of the ramp without slowing down. Its suspension bottomed out and sparks flew as its chassis scraped the concrete.

With a roar, it came right at them.

It wasn't going to stop.

'Jesus!' Quincy yelled as he realised the Jeep was speeding towards the back of the van.

Moon released Erin's other arm, letting her fall to the ground. Pulled the weapon from his shoulder and took aim at the Jeep. Ritter had his gun raised as well. A blast of automatic fire sounded over the roar of the Jeep's engine. Its windscreen fractured into a spider's web of cracks and its front end instantly became a colander of holes. But nothing short of a rocket launcher could have slowed its momentum as it sped towards the back of the van. The Jeep's driver's door flew open and a figure tumbled out, hitting the ground and rolling. The Jeep was an unmanned missile, three thousand pounds of metal hurtling towards them. Quincy let out a yell and grabbed the mini-Uzi subgun he had stuffed down the front of his trousers. A smart guy would have been leaping out of the way already. But Quincy wasn't very smart. He hesitated just a fraction too long.

The Jeep impacted against the van with an explosion like a Howitzer going off inside the car park. Quincy was caught between the crumpling back doors of the van and the radiator grille of the Jeep and cut almost completely in half, his right arm severed at the shoulder and sailing through the air in an arc that carried it across the Jeep's roof.

The impact lifted both vehicles clear off the ground. The front of the van was driven ten feet forwards and slammed into a concrete pillar.

As if in slow motion, wreckage and broken glass spun in all directions. The Jeep bounced back down on its suspension, rocked twice and was still.

Chapter Forty-Two

Ben hit the concrete and rolled twice as if he'd parachuted out of an aircraft, clutching his bag containing the precious journals. He sprang to his feet at the instant the Jeep smashed into the back of the white GMC.

He hadn't known exactly what he was going to find at the end of the drip trail he'd been following all the way from the intersection pile-up. He'd reckoned on finding trouble, but not the battle zone he saw as he sped down the ramp. In those short seconds, he'd taken in the whole situation. The van, the blue Ford and a silver Lincoln sedan all clustered together. Four men on their feet, two of them his old friends from Ireland and Madeira. The heavy-looking ape who'd been riding in the Ford was now slumped in its back seat, clutching a bloody shoulder. Another man he'd never seen before was lying dead in a pool of blood underneath what was left of a bullet-riddled Honda.

He'd spotted the woman there, too. Wondered who she was and what she was doing here. But there wasn't time to dwell on that right this minute. Two concrete pillars stood between him and the carnage of vehicles, spaced about twenty feet apart. He ducked behind the nearest.

Ben knew his dramatic entrance wouldn't faze these guys for long. Even before the echo of the crash had died away, gunshots began cannoning off the concrete pillar he was hiding behind. The problem with impromptu plans was that you didn't always get time to figure out the details in advance. Such as how to deal with a gunfight when you hadn't brought a gun. He also knew the two men well enough by now to know that if he didn't return fire, they'd quickly suss out that he was unarmed. All they had to do then was walk over and put him down.

That was when he noticed the arm. It was lying on the concrete midway between his pillar and the next one along, still twitching after being detached from its former owner. At one end was a bloody mush of flesh and trailing sinew and muscle. At the other end, the dead fingers were still wrapped around the butt of what Ben instantly recognised as a mini-Uzi submachine pistol.

There was a lull in the firing. Ben peeked round the corner of the pillar and saw Ponytail and his friend both changing magazines. Now or never. He leapt out from behind cover. One of the other men let off a shot that whined past his ear. Another punched through his bag. He ran straight for the fallen Uzi and bent down and snatched it from the disembodied hand and made it to the other pillar before the enemy could get him in their sights. Pressed tight against the pillar, he quickly examined his new weapon. Apart from the dead man's blood all over it, it was shiny and new and clean, with an extended mag, maybe fifty rounds. Not bad, but not enough. He was badly outgunned by these guys. It was getting to be an unpleasant habit.

Ben darted the Uzi's stubby barrel around the edge of the pillar. One touch of the trigger released a burst of fire that sounded like thick cardboard ripping, only massively amplified. A yellow stream of spent brass spewed from the ejector port. He saw the enemy fall back for cover behind their vehicles.

A tongue of flame suddenly leapt out from the clouds of black smoke that had begun to pour out of the crashed Jeep; then another. In a few more seconds, the whole thing might catch light. Another movement caught his eye as the back door of the blue Ford swung open and the injured ape staggered out, clutching a pistol. Ben scraped the Uzi along the bullet-chewed edge of the pillar and let off another burst. Before the guy could get a shot off, he'd been thrown half back into the car with his arms outflung and head lolling sideways.

Ben whirled back behind his pillar and checked the Uzi's magazine. About half his rounds were gone already. Submachine guns had a troublesome way of chomping through their ammo too quickly. Even more troublesome, when he didn't have a spare magazine. His opponents, by contrast, didn't seem to be short of them.

The smoke from the Jeep was thickening, drifting like a black fog over the vehicles and obscuring Ben's vision of his opponents. Then one of them came lurching out from behind the silver Lincoln sedan. At first Ben thought he was mounting an attack, then realised he'd been driven from cover by the choking smoke. He was bent double with coughing, his gun hanging limp in his hand. Ben wasn't interested in playing fair, not against these odds. He trained the Uzi on the guy and hosed out about half his remaining rounds. The man recoiled backwards and sprawled over the back of the Lincoln. The lightweight Uzi was hard to control and some of the bullets sprayed into the car's silver bodywork, shattering its tail lights. The smell of gasoline quickly began to pierce through the tang of cordite. Ben realised he'd punctured the tank.

A slick of spilled fuel rapidly spread across the concrete, under the dead man and under the wheels of the Jeep nearby.

Two seconds later, another dart of flame jumped from the smashed car and ignited the pool on the ground. A curtain of fire instantly leapt up. Both the Jeep and the Lincoln were engulfed in the fierce blaze.

'We need to get the fuck out of here,' Ritter said to Moon as the fire drove them back towards the van. They were three men down, and what should have been a neat, low-key job was quickly degenerating into an ugly mess. He looked around for the woman.

She was nowhere in sight. There wasn't time to start searching the whole place for her. He swore. The boss would be furious that they'd lost her. But there was nothing for it: this was downtown Tulsa, and not even McCrory's connections within the police department could hold the cops off an incident this major. He decided to cut his losses.

'Let's go,' he said to Moon. Moon looked disgusted, but he was thinking the same thing. They ran to the van, flung their weapons into it and jumped in after them. The flames from the burning Jeep were licking all around the badly bucked rear of the GMC. Its front end was almost as badly crumpled. But it was a tough old crate and it cranked into life, good for a few last miles before they'd have to abandon it.

Ritter slammed into reverse and stamped on the gas, shunting the blazing wreck of the Jeep backwards out of the way and crushing what was left of Quincy under his wheels. Then he swung the van violently around through the pall of smoke and headed for the ramp with a squeal of tortured rubber.

Ben emptied his last few rounds at it as it sped away, trailing plumes of smoke and debris. He watched it hit the ramp and roar up the slope and disappear around the spiralling bend towards street level.

Any minute now, there'd be more traffic as police and fire trucks began to arrive on the scene. Ben stepped quickly out from behind the pillar, tossed away the empty submachine gun and peered through the smoke. The two men he'd shot weren't coming back to life, and the mangled body of the one who'd been crushed and run over was just about as dead as anyone he'd ever seen.

So was the Jeep. A new speed record for destroying rental cars.

The woman Ben had noticed before suddenly reappeared and stepped tentatively out from between two undamaged parked cars a few metres away. Her face was sooty from the smoke. Her eyes were streaming with tears and she had a hand over her mouth. She ran past the blaze to the shattered wreck of the Honda and crouched briefly beside the dead man there, gazing sadly down at him. 'I'm sorry. I didn't know him well, but he seemed like a good man.'

'Who was he?' Ben asked.

She stood up and frowned at Ben. 'What do you mean? I thought you were working with him.'

Ben shook his head.

'Then . . . you're not Special Agent Dobbs?'

'I'm not agent anybody,' he said. 'My name's Ben.'

'You're a Brit.'

'I'm not from around here, that's for sure. But if we're going to have a conversation, we might want to do it elsewhere. We won't be alone here for long.'

She stared at him mutely for a second or two, as if trying to decide whether to trust him, then nodded. 'Wait,' she said, and ran back a few yards to retrieve a pistol that was lying on the concrete.

'You could take your pick,' Ben said, looking at all the weaponry scattered about.

'Sentimental value,' she said. She aimed the gun at him. 'You're telling me the truth, aren't you? You're not gonna try anything? Only I've just about had my fill lately.'

'Cross my heart and hope to die,' Ben said.

'All right,' she said after a moment. 'Just remember I have this. I've shot two men already today.'

'Understood,' Ben said.

She stuffed the gun in her jeans pocket. 'My car's seen better times,' she said, gazing wistfully at the Honda. 'And that was Morrell's Lincoln before someone set fire to it.'

'I think that was me,' Ben said. 'Sorry.'

She pointed. 'There are escalators leading up to street level. That's where I was headed before all this happened.'

Ben could hear the familiar wail of sirens fast approaching. 'Nothing like local knowledge,' he said to her. 'Lead the way.'

Chapter Forty-Three

By the time they'd ridden the lift up from the subterranean car park to the mall above and reached the exit, the whole place had been invaded by a swarm of police who were trying to contain the crowds of terrified shoppers driven from the mall in a mass panic by the sound of gunfire and explosions from down below. A pall of black smoke was pouring from the mouth of the car park entrance and climbing into the late afternoon sky as a fleet of emergency vehicles screeched onto the scene. A chopper was hovering overhead, its thud mingling with the chaotic noise of sirens and hysteria. Pitched gun battles evidently didn't happen every day in downtown Tulsa.

Gazing up and down the packed street, Ben could see no sign of the white van. It must have managed to get away unnoticed just in time. 'I didn't catch your name,' he said.

'Erin Hayes,' she replied, frowning at him. 'Aren't you going to tell me who you are?'

'Let's get some coffee,' he said.

The coffee shop they found quarter of a mile away was already alive with the breaking news of the incident. 'I heard an eye witness said it was a buncha Muslims,' one guy said. 'Goddamn a-hole terrorists,' someone else kept insisting loudly, over and over, until someone shushed him as a report came on the little TV above the counter and they all gathered around to stare. Ben bought two coffees and took them over to a booth by the window, far enough away from the focus of attention for him and Erin to talk privately. They could hear the helicopters and sirens even from this distance. Now and then a patrol car went screaming down the street outside, drawing stares from anxious passers-by.

'So, Ben,' she said after a long gulp of coffee. 'It is Ben, right?'

'Ben Hope. Nice to meet you, Erin.'

'I suppose I should be thanking you for saving my life.'

'That makes a difference from pointing a gun at me. My pleasure.'

'Except I still don't know who the hell you are, or where the hell you popped up from all of a sudden.'

'Long story. What did they want with you?'

Her eyes moistened suddenly and her coffee cup began to shake in her hand. Now that she was safe, delayed shock was beginning to set in. 'They were trying to kidnap me. They've been after me for days. My life . . . everything . . . just fell apart. They're going to kill me. I know it.'

'That's not going to happen, Erin,' Ben told her. 'Why are they after you?'

'Because of something I witnessed,' she said, working hard to compose herself. 'Something they did. Them and their boss.'

'You mean McCrory?'

She looked at him. 'So you know what this is about. You didn't just appear out of nowhere.'

'I have an interest in McCrory,' he said. 'Him, and his men. They kill people.'

She nodded. 'That pretty much sums it up.'

'What's your connection with him? Do you work for the mayor's office?'

'His wife runs a charity here in Tulsa. I work for her. She and I are kind of friends. That's why I was there at the McCrorys' cabin that night when they . . .' She paused, looking at him through narrowed eyes as a thought came to her. 'This isn't about Kirk Blaylock, is it? Some kind of revenge thing?'

'I've never heard of Kirk Blaylock,' he replied, with a look of sincerity that convinced her he was telling the truth. 'Who is he?'

'Was. The man I saw them shoot to pieces that night. He was about to betray McCrory to the Feds.'

'I'm not here because of him. I'm here because of someone called Kristen, Kristen Hall. She was murdered.'

She scrutinised him carefully. 'Then are you a cop? A detective?'

'I'm just a concerned individual,' he said. 'I was there when they killed her. I'm responsible for putting things right. She suffered. McCrory has to be answerable for that.'

'Was she—?'

Ben shook his head before she finished. 'No relation. Just a friend.'

'I'm so sorry.'

'Me too.'

'Why did they kill her?'

'All I know for the moment is that she was a threat to them. I'd like to know more, and I get the feeling you have more information than I do. I think we can help each other. Who was the man you were with? The one they shot?'

Erin hesitated before replying. 'He was a police detective. His name was Topher Morrell. He was helping the FBI. They're investigating McCrory because they believe . . .'

She paused again, and glanced anxiously across the coffee shop.

'Nobody's listening,' Ben said. 'The FBI believe what?'

Erin leaned forward and said in a low voice, 'Morrell said that McCrory deals arms to a Mexican drugs cartel called Los Locos. It means "the Crazy Ones".'

'I know what it means,' Ben said. He wasn't even that surprised at what he was hearing.

'McCrory supplies them with all kinds of military hardware. It's a big-time operation. If he becomes governor, it's going to get even bigger.'

After all, Ben thought, the higher you rose in US politics, the more illegal arms you could trade into Mexico. The efforts of a small privateer could never compete with the government's own Fast and Furious programme, which had deliberately and secretly introduced tens of thousands of firearms into the Mexican criminal underworld in order to create instability and justification for US paramilitary expansionism.

'McCrory was a lawyer. He's never been remotely connected to the military. Where's he getting the stuff?'

'The Feds think it comes through Ritter and Moon. They're his henchmen, or lieutenants, or whatever the hell is the right word.'

Ben's eyes narrowed. 'Ritter and Moon?'

'Billy Bob Moon, he's the one with the ponytail. Chews gum all the time. Matt Ritter is the other one. Morrell said they were both ex-Special Forces.'

Ben was silent for a few moments as he pictured the two men in his mind. 'It's what I thought,' he said quietly.

'About the arms dealing?'

'No, but I might have guessed about that too. Every time I meet up with those two, there are fireworks.'

'You've met them before?'

'The first time it was just sticks and blades. But the second time they were using automatic rifles and an awful lot of fancy munitions. Today they were using KRISS Vectors. Pretty newfangled hardware, and full military spec too. Not easy to get hold of.'

'Morrell said that Ritter's the one with the connections,' Erin said. 'They have a whole warehouse full of weapons, somewhere in Tulsa County. And crews of drivers trucking it down through Texas, over the border. This one cartel, Los Locos? They're getting ready to fight a whole war against federal firearms and drugs agencies who've been trying to clamp down on them. Scum like McCrory are only too happy to supply all the military hardware they can get. Like those things – what did you call them?'

'KRISS Vectors. Forty-five calibre submachine gun. Like a radical update on a Tommy gun. All polymer. Very advanced delayed recoil system, cyclic rate of over a thousand rounds a minute. I'd never even seen one before. I can imagine drug gangs would pay a pretty penny for a few crates of those.'

'How come you know all this stuff?' she asked, looking at him hard.

'Because I was a soldier too,' he said.

'Well, it doesn't matter who you were. You can't go against these people. It's not just Moon and Ritter. McCrory has about thirty men working for him. A small army.'

'That should even the odds a little in their favour,' Ben said with a grim smile.

'They'll kill anyone who stands in their way,' she insisted. 'Like Kirk Blaylock. He was ready to tip all the information over to the authorities. Your friend, Kristen, she must have known something too. That's why they got to her.'

Ben was silent for a moment as he considered what he'd only just that afternoon discovered in Elizabeth Stamford's journal. He thought about Kristen obtaining McCrory's personal number from Chris Ingram. Remembered her telling him with excitement that if her plan worked, she could give up work forever. 'I think Kristen was shaking McCrory down for money,' he said. 'A lot of money.'

'There, see?'

He shook his head. 'She didn't know anything about this. It's something else.'

'There's more you need to know,' Erin said. 'The police chief, O'Rourke – McCrory owns him.'

'Naturally.' No great surprises there either.

'Morrell was spying on him for the Feds. So we can forget about going to the cops.'

'That was never my intention,' Ben said.

'But we have to do something.'

'We?'

'I have evidence,' she said. 'Evidence that could put McCrory away forever. The murder at the cabin – I videoed the whole thing on my cellphone.'

'Where's the phone now?'

'I gave it to O'Rourke, along with a copy I burned on disc. That was before I knew he was one of them, and it's what made me a target the moment I told him what I knew. But there's another disc they don't know about. A second copy.'

'Got it with you?'

'You're kidding. It's hidden. Somewhere nobody would think to search for it.'

'And what are you planning on doing with it?' Ben asked her.

'I figure there's only one thing I *can* do, now I know what I know,' she said. 'Go to the Feds.'

'Then what?' he asked.

She frowned at him. 'They won't do nothing.'

'Maybe not. Maybe they'll come galloping into town on their white horses, arrest McCrory, put an end to his political career forever and then sling him in jail. Or else maybe they'll just keep doing what they've been doing so far, sitting it out until they have enough to nail the whole operation. Why else didn't they pounce the moment you handed Morrell the evidence?'

'I need a new life,' she said. 'I can't go back to the old one. I'm a single woman with no kids, no ties, no family worth hanging onto. I've already walked away from my job and my home. The FBI can easily make me disappear. Gone, forever, where I'll be safe and I can start over.'

'I've heard of people disappearing even more permanently when the witness protection programme didn't quite live up to the hype. It's a little too much faith to place in government agents. The authorities haven't exactly done a great job of protecting you so far. You've put your neck on the block for them, and they allow you to remain at risk. Does that sound as if they really care about what happens to you?'

'McCrory will be in jail. You said so yourself. He can't get to me from there.'

Ben shook his head. 'Think again, Erin. Think really hard. A man with McCrory's wealth can get to you from anywhere. How many Mafia hits have been sanctioned from inside, over lobster and champagne dinners with the prison governor?'

'Isn't that a little bit cynical?'

'Cynical, as in, not hopelessly naïve?'

'So what are you saying?'

'That you can run. You can run halfway around the world if you want to.'

'But I can't hide?'

'Not forever. Even if it all goes the way you hope and the FBI are true to their word and whisk you away under a whole new identity, and McCrory and his henchmen get slammed up in jail until they're very, very old men. Doesn't matter. They'll get you eventually, because nobody ever disappears. Not completely. It can't be done.'

'You sound pretty darn sure of that.'

'I am, because I'm the guy folks used to call upon to find those disappeared people. It's what I did for a living.'

'And now you're going to tell me you always found them.'

'If a person's still breathing, they can be found. Take it from me. What happens to them then depends on who found them. If it's someone like me, it can be a happy ending. If it's someone like McCrory's people, it won't be.'

'That's just wonderful,' she said sourly. 'So let me get this straight. Even if the Feds give a shit what happens to me – which they probably don't – and even if I can trust them to put me in the protection program – which I probably can't – I'm dead anyway?'

He nodded. 'More or less.'

'Thank you so much for the reassurance. You just made a fantastic day even better.'

'I don't want to have to think that the worst could happen to you,' he told her. 'Just like I don't want to have to think that McCrory is living it up in a nice warm minimum-security jail somewhere, with more privileges than most people on the outside and more power than it's safe for a man like that to have at his disposal. And he won't serve out the full term, either. No chance.'

'So what's the alternative?' she asked helplessly. 'What the hell am I supposed to do?'

'Drink your coffee.'

'It's cold.'

So was his, but he drained it anyway. 'Then let's go.'

'Go where?'

'The nearest used car place, for a start. There's not much we can do without transport. After that, I have an errand to run. Then we'll hole up and get some rest while we think about our next move.'

'Hole up?'

'My place.'

'Uh-huh. Your place.'

'You'll love it. Very snazzy. All mod cons.'

She raised an eyebrow.

'Don't you trust me yet?' he asked.

She looked at him. 'Do I have a choice?'

'Not if you want to live.'

'Okay,' she said after a beat. 'But we don't need to buy a car. I have another one we can use.'

Chapter Forty-Four

Evening was falling as they reached the row of lock-up storage units. 'This one,' Erin said, pointing at the third steel rolldown shutter door on the right. The graffiti on it was old and faded, matching the neglected-looking state of the rest of the place. She produced a pair of keys from her purse, knelt down at the foot of the shutter and undid the heavy padlocks that fastened it securely at each side. 'Help me out, will you? Mechanism's kind of rusty.'

'I hope the car inside isn't rusty, too.'

'Wise-ass. You'll see.'

Ben grasped the bottom of the shutter, tugged hard and it rose up with a grinding scrape. Erin ducked her head as she walked inside the dark space. He followed her, seeing nothing but shadows. The inside had the garage smell of car wax, old oil, cold metal.

'There's a light,' she said. 'But roll down the door first.'

Another grinding creak, and for a moment they were in total darkness before Erin found the switch and flipped it on. Overhead neons blinked and flashed brightly to life. Ben looked around him. The garage was bigger than it looked on the outside. Apart from a few old boxes of junk stacked up along one wall and a wooden workbench with an array of tools, all it contained was the long, wide, low shape of a car covered by a canvas tarpaulin. She walked over to it, picked up one edge of the tarp and began pulling it away.

Ben wasn't much of a car enthusiast. He appreciated automotive virtues like ruggedness, reliability and speed where needed, but beyond that he'd never regarded cars as anything more than tools. A vintage Land Rover was no more or less exciting to him than a Lamborghini, depending on whether he had to navigate a desert or race across Europe in a day. But even he had to give a low whistle as the tarp slipped to the floor. The lights gleamed on the sleek curves, deep black paintwork and chromed wheels of the classic American muscle car.

'1971 Plymouth Barracuda,' Erin said, gazing at the car with a wistful look in her eye. 'My daddy's pride and joy. He built most of it himself.'

'He lets you drive this old beast?'

'Daddy passed away some years back. He left it to me. This car was pretty much all he had to leave to anyone, security guards' pensions being what they are.' Erin opened her purse again and took out a set of car keys. 'It's not been used a whole lot since he died. I've only driven it a couple of times, but I keep it maintained.' Seeing Ben's look of surprise, she added with a smile, 'Daddy taught me a lot of things most little girls don't get to learn. How to strip down a Hemi V8, how to handle guns. I can skin and dress a whitetail, too, from when he used to take me deer hunting.'

She drew the Springfield nine-millimetre from her pocket. This time she didn't aim it at Ben. 'This pistol was the last thing he gave me before he died.'

'Now I understand why you didn't want to leave it behind,' Ben said.

'Said the world was going to hell in a hand basket. He wanted his little girl to stay safe after he was gone.'

'You will be,' Ben said.

'Maybe. Or maybe I'll end up like Topher Morrell. Poor Topher.' Erin walked around the back of the Plymouth, unlocked the trunk and opened the lid. Reaching inside, she took out a large brown envelope. Inside was a polythene bag that Ben saw contained a compact disc. 'Another reason I brought us here,' she said. 'This is where I've been keeping it.'

'The copy of the video?'

'You got a DVD player at your place?'

'I don't need to watch it,' Ben said. 'I don't need convincing. I've already seen what McCrory does to people who get in his way.'

'What are you going to do?'

'You already asked me that,' he said.

'And you never gave me an answer. What's your plan? Walk right in there and kill him, is that the idea?'

'Let's just say that you won't end up like Morrell. Not if I have anything to do with it.'

'What about Ritter and Moon? You want to get to McCrory, you're still going to have to deal with them sooner or later.'

Ben made no reply. He turned away from the Plymouth and ran his eye along the old wooden workbench. Its surface was rough and pitted. It had an old-fashioned steel vice G-clamped to its top. Ben sifted through the assortment of tools and picked up a heavy-duty hacksaw and a steel file. 'Mind if I borrow these? And the vice, too.'

'Be my guest,' Erin said with a shrug, too bemused to ask what he wanted them for.

'Will you drive, or will I?' he asked.

'I'll drive, you navigate. Your place, right?'

He shook his head. 'Shopping first.'

*

Frank Gallagher's general store was closed and in darkness, but when Ben walked around the side of the wooden building he saw there was a light on in one of the upper floor windows. Around the rear was a rundown porch with a back door. Ben tinkled a bell that hung from a bracket on the wall.

'This guy a friend of yours, or something?' Erin asked, frowning in the dark.

'We're like this,' Ben said. He tinkled the bell again. A dog started barking resonantly inside. A few moments later, he heard footsteps from the other side of the door, along with the scrabble of canine claws on bare floorboards. A light came on in the porch and a voice said, 'Quiet, Elvis.' The dog stopped its noise. An eye appeared in a small hole drilled through the door. It blinked and peered at Ben. Then there was the sound of locks rattling and the door creaked open.

'Back so soon?' the old shopkeeper asked with a wrinkly grin. He was barefoot and appeared to be wearing nothing but an ancient pair of dungarees. The smell of sour mash whiskey wafted from the dusty hallway. A large German Shepherd stood by its master's side, eyeing the visitors with a lolling tongue.

'Couple of things I left off my shopping list,' Ben said. 'You said I could give you a yell any time.'

'Like I said, store never closes,' Frank said. 'Come on in. How's the Perryman place workin' out for you?'

'A real home from home,' Ben said, leading Erin inside. 'Thanks for the recommendation.'

'Evening, miss.'

'Erin, meet Frank.'

'And this is Elvis,' the old man said.

'Ain't nothin' but a hound dog, right?' Erin said, patting the German Shepherd, which lathered her hand with its enormously long tongue.

'He keeps away the customers I don't want comin' round after regular hours,' Frank said as he locked the door shut behind them. He ushered them down the dusty hall. Another door led through to the back of the store. Elvis trotted along after them, having taken an instant shine to Erin.

'So what can I do for you, Ben? I never forget a name,' Frank said with a smile. 'You need some provisions? Beers? Some more clothes, mebbe?'

'I was thinking more along the lines of a Browning A5, Mossberg 500, something like that,' Ben said.

'Goin' hunting, huh?' the old man said without missing a beat.

'You might say that. And some boxes of shells, too. Double-aught buck and Brenneke slugs.'

'Little on the heavy side for a turkey shoot?'

'Christmas is a long way off,' Ben said. 'The turkeys are safe for now.'

'Then I reckon you're goin' after more dangerous game?'

'The most.'

'Whatever you say. Stay right there.' The old man vanished into a side room and came out a few moments later with a long box under his arm, which he laid on the counter and opened up. 'Ithaca 37 Featherlight,' Frank said, lifting out the shotgun from the box. 'Just like we had in 'Nam. Five-shot pump, slam-fire trigger, cylinder-bore choke. A regular Howitzer. How many shells you want?'

'As many as I can get in the trunk of a '71 'Cuda,' Ben said.

The old man grinned from ear to ear. 'Oh, boy. Didn't I say old Frank Gallagher's got everythin' you need?' He disappeared again into the back room, then re-emerged staggering under the weight of a teetering armful of cartridge boxes. 'Hornady and Federal mostly, some Winchester mixed in

290

there,' he panted, dumping them on the counter next to the gun before returning for more.

Ben ran his eye across the mountain of boxes. Each slug load propelled over an ounce of solid lead at twelve hundred feet per second – enough knock-down power to kill an elephant, if killing elephants had been his thing. The 00-buck cartridges blasted out eight round balls of .33 inches in diameter, roughly equivalent in firepower to three short bursts from a submachine gun, only delivered all at once in a lethal swarm that could blow a door off its hinges. He counted seventeen boxes of buckshot and thirteen of solid slug. Twenty rounds per box. The shotgun took four in the magazine and one in the chamber. He had enough to reload it one hundred and twenty times over.

'That should do it,' he said. 'I'll need a bag for this lot.'

'I'll throw the bag in for free,' Frank said, going over to a stand and picking up a black canvas holdall that looked strong enough to carry a full load of gold bars inside.

'One more thing. I need a knife, too.'

'Can't go huntin' without a knife, right?' Frank said. He reached below the counter and nonchalantly produced a monstrous survival knife, as if customers asked for them all the time. Ben popped the retaining stud on the sheath and inspected it. Cheap stainless steel and a short tang, mass-produced in some Far-Eastern factory and just waiting to snap in half at the first bit of punishment.

'No good?' Frank said, seeing his expression. 'Okay, hold on. I got somethin' back here that's a little more special. Didn't have no mind to sell it, but . . .' He disappeared once more and Ben could hear him rooting about in the Aladdin's cave he had back there. 'Here it is,' said the muffled voice, then Frank came back out holding something wrapped in a rag. He laid it on the counter and pulled back the folds of oily cloth.

'Hundred fifty bucks,' he said proudly. 'Because it's you.'

Ben picked it up. The knife was old, but almost immaculate. Its blade was long and double-edged. The steel hilt was shaped like a spiked knuckleduster, with four separate holes for the fingers to slip through. It had a skull-crushing pommel cap and stamped letters on the metal handle that said 'US. 1918'. This wasn't a hunting knife. It wasn't a survival knife. It existed for one purpose only, to kill. It had been designed a long time ago by a military mind that knew exactly what that involved and how to make an efficient job of it. And Ben could tell it had been used in the past for just that purpose. The faint dark stains on the blade were corrosion from the blood of someone who'd died many years ago with it inside him.

'Mark 1 US army trench knife,' Frank said.

'That'll work,' Ben said.

'If it don't, it means you got a serious problem on your hands. Which I'm guessin' maybe you do anyway. Am I right?'

Erin shot Ben an anxious look. Ben said nothing.

'I mind my own business,' Frank said. 'Just tell me one thing. You're not goin' to do anything crazy with all this hardware, now, are you, son?'

'I wouldn't dream of it in a thousand years,' Ben said.

'Good enough for me. You paying cash? That's even better.'

'It's been a pleasure doing business with you, Frank.'

'You enjoy the rest of your stay in Tulsa, Ben. You too, Miss. I'm sure glad you folks stopped by tonight.'

'Oh, sure,' Erin said, raising an eyebrow at Ben. Elvis padded across and slobbered over her hand, his way of saying goodbye.

Ben carried the Ithaca and the heavy holdall out to the Plymouth and got Erin to unlock the trunk. 'I can't believe I'm doing this,' she said, watching as Ben laid their cargo inside, next to the tools he'd brought from the lock-up garage and the brown envelope that contained the DVD. 'You drive,' she said, tossing him the car keys. 'I mean, you're not insured, but what the hell. We're past the point where it really matters any more.'

'Let's go and get something to eat,' he said.

'I'm not sure I have much of an appetite.'

'Then I'll get something to eat,' he said.

Chapter Forty-Five

They stopped off to grab a takeout from an all-night grill joint called Busby's, a few blocks from the Perryman. Erin's appetite seemed to make a rapid comeback when she smelled the quarter-pound burger patties sizzling on the open chargrill. Ben ordered two double cheeses, mayo on hers, chilli on his, large fries with both. Busby's sold beer by the bottle, and he bought three cold ones for Erin, along with some Cokes for himself. Booze was still strictly not allowed.

Returning to the motel, Ben backed the Plymouth right up close to his door so that he could transfer the holdall and the shotgun into the room discreetly and without frightening the neighbours. You had to think about these things, even in a high-class establishment like the Perryman Inn.

'Classy joint,' Erin said drily as she surveyed inside. 'You weren't kidding.'

There was an awkward silence as they both glanced at the double bed, which had seen a lot of use and was sagging in the middle. Ben offered to sleep on the bathroom floor that night. It seemed the least he could do. With that moment past, they unpacked the food and pulled up the room's only two chairs to eat at a little table.

'I didn't realise how hungry I was,' she said between bites.

'Getting shot at tends to have that effect on people,' Ben said.

'As long as they don't get killed in the process.'

'That helps.'

'You want a beer?' she asked, offering him a bottle.

He shook his head and cracked open a Coke. 'I'll stick with this.'

She shrugged. 'Suit yourself, if it's what you prefer.'

He sipped some of it and pulled a face at how sickly sweet it tasted to him. 'No, I hate the stuff. And I'd love a beer. That's why I won't have one.'

'Why, are you an alcoholic?' she asked.

He looked at her, taken aback by the directness of the question. In this light her eyes were vivid green, like a cat's. 'Let's just say I've been known to overstep the limits,' he said.

'My mom's an alcoholic,' Erin said matter-of-factly. 'It's what I grew up with, so I know all there is to know about it. Tequila and bourbon. Her favourite things in life.'

'Malt Scotch,' he said, jabbing a thumb at his chest.

'How long have you been on the wagon?'

'I'm still a newbie,' he confessed.

'Will it drive you totally crazy if I drink beer in front of you? It's just that I badly need it, after today.'

He smiled. 'I won't break your arm to get at it, if that's what you mean. You drink, and I'll smoke. Deal?'

'Deal.'

They ate a while in silence, then Ben said, 'So your mother's an alcoholic and your father's dead. Any other family?'

She shook her head. 'I was married a while. Had to walk away from it.'

'Why was that?'

'He used to hit me,' she replied.

295

'I'm sorry to hear it.'

'I never told my daddy. He'd have killed him.'

'Sounds like a sensible man.'

'What about you? Family? Kids?'

'I have a grown-up son,' Ben said.

'What's his name?'

'Jude.'

'That's a nice name. Does he take after you?'

'A little too much,' Ben said.

After they'd finished eating and the table was cleared, Ben lit up a cigarette, then went back out to the car and brought in the tools he'd brought from the lock-up. He clamped the vice to the table, then took off his belt.

'I'm not even gonna ask what you're doing now,' Erin said, sitting on the bed and sipping her second beer.

Ben picked up the shotgun and in a few quick moves removed the barrel, just a steel tube a little over two feet long with a fastening lug welded halfway along its underside. Setting the rest of the dismantled gun aside, he wrapped the belt around the breech end of the barrel to protect it from the jaws of the vice, then tightened everything up so that the muzzle end protruded immobile from the edge of the table. The next stage would get noisy, so he turned on the radio. 'Do they only play country music?' he said after the third station he tried.

'Boy, you're really not from around here, are you?'

Ben sat down at the table with the clamped barrel in front of him and the hacksaw in his hand, and began the process of turning a sporting weapon into a riot gun. It would become hopelessly inaccurate at longer ranges, but he cared as much about that as about the legality of it.

'You've done this before,' she said, watching him as the saw cut deeper into the steel with a grinding sound that set their teeth on edge.

'Once or twice,' he admitted.

'What a day this turned out to be. I've shot two people, I've been chased, tasered and almost kidnapped and now I'm sitting watch a strange Brit who doesn't like country music saw the barrel off of a shotgun.'

'Half Irish,' he corrected her.

'That's still a Brit, isn't it?'

He paused sawing, and looked at her. 'Careful.'

Fifteen minutes of metallic grinding and shrieking later, a length of discarded steel tube fell to the floor and Ben finally laid down the saw. Next he picked up the file and got to work smoothing off the end of the lopped barrel. He cleared up the mess of powdery metal that covered the table, and threw it in the waste basket before reassembling the now much-shortened Ithaca.

Meanwhile, Erin had finished her second beer and had kicked off her shoes as she began the third. Sitting back on the bed, she'd been idly sifting through the contents of her bag when she suddenly remembered the syringe. She took it out and held it in her hands, frowning at it. 'What do you suppose this crap is they were trying to stick me with?' she asked, peering at the pale-coloured fluid inside. Ben laid down the gun, walked over and took the syringe from her hand. He unscrewed the bent needle and dripped a couple of drops of the fluid onto the table. He moistened a fingertip and gave it a quick sniff. 'I'm pretty sure it's Zotepine,' he said. 'I've come across it before.'

'What does it do?' she asked anxiously.

'It's your typical chemical cosh,' he replied. 'Kidnappers use it. Powerful antipsychotic, antimanic, fast-acting in high doses. Before it was taken off the market for safety reasons, they used to pump the stuff into severely mentally ill people in hospital when they became aggressive, to make them nice and calm and compliant. Makes a handy date-rape drug, too, in low doses. A whole range of side effects you don't want to know about. If you keep taking it, you turn into a shuffling brain-dead zombie.'

Erin's brow was creased with anger. 'I took it away thinking it might be more evidence, or something. Now I just want to flush it down the toilet.'

Ben thought for a moment. 'There might be other uses for it.'

'Just keep it the hell away from me.'

'You've already come as close to it as you'll ever get. I promise.' Ben replaced the needle on the end of the syringe and laid it aside. He was quiet for a few moments, thinking. Then he walked back over to the bed and perched himself on the end of it. She moved her bare feet a little to make room for him.

'How do you feel now?' he asked gently.

'A little steadier.' She held up the beer bottle. 'This helps. Kinda sleepy.'

'Tell me about your boss.'

'Angela?'

Ben nodded.

'She and I get along great. She's a good boss, cares about the people who work for her, and is dedicated to her cause. I think she's a little sad and lonely. What else can I say?'

'How much does her husband trust her?'

'Believe me, she has no idea about what he's into. None, I swear.'

'You're sure about that?'

Erin nodded. 'Very sure.'

'That's fine.'

'What if I wasn't?' she asked.

'Then I'd have said perhaps she could help us fill in a few

298

blanks about hubby's little operation. Such as where they keep the merchandise.'

Erin shook her head. 'Leave her out of it, okay? It's going to be hard enough for her if all this comes out. I mean, it isn't much of a marriage, but something like this will destroy her.'

'So we can provisionally draw a line through her name. What about the father?'

'Big Joe?'

'Ever met him?'

Erin yawned. The luminous green eyes were getting harder to keep open now that the beer was taking effect. Her long day was catching up with her. 'Uh-huh. He was with Finn one time, when he came by the office. That old guy scares the crap out of everybody who meets him.'

'I've seen his picture,' Ben said.

'Angela's terrified of him. It's why she won't go near Arrowhead Ranch. That, and she's allergic to horses.' Erin stretched out a little on the bed, relaxing more with every passing second. 'Not like me. I love horses.'

'Let me guess. Your daddy taught you to ride.'

'Mm-hmm.' Her lips curled in a sleepy smile. One of her bare feet touched Ben's leg. He felt its warm pressure there, pressing against him. Maybe it was because she was getting drowsy that she didn't take it away.

'Arrowhead,' he said. 'Same name as the oil company the old man founded back in 1935.'

'The oilfields were all Indian Territory once. The whole state was. Native American names are part of the culture. It's pretty terrible, I guess. What the settlers did to them.'

'Have you been there, to the ranch?'

She shook her head. 'Know where it is, though. Who doesn't? Big spread out west of the city.'

Ben had a feeling that for an Oklahoman, big really meant big. 'Does old Joe McCrory live there alone?' he asked, wondering about all the hidden arms caches you could squeeze into several hundred, maybe even a thousand, acres of ranch land.

'I think so. His wife died a long time back.' She yawned again.

Ben stopped firing questions at her and soon afterwards her eyes began to drift shut. She'd had a long day. He took the empty beer bottle from her hand, laid it on the table. She murmured something and curled up on the bed with her head on the pillow, and he reached over her and pulled the covers across her body. Within a minute, she was asleep, leaving Ben alone with his thoughts.

Chapter Forty-Six

He was glad the beer was finished, because it hadn't been as easy for him to refrain as he'd made it look to Erin. 'Lead me not into temptation, Lord,' he muttered. 'I can find my own way there easily enough.'

He turned the lights off and paced quietly about the room for a while, clearing his mind of all the things that had happened that day and working back through what he'd learned from Elizabeth Stamford's journal earlier. Her revelation that her husband and his scientific crony Heneage Fitzwilliam had apparently been cooking up some kind of plant blight pathogen in their laboratory was still making his head spin. The implications were almost too much to take on board.

Almost.

Ben walked through to the bathroom, closed the door quietly so as not to wake Erin, and clicked on the string-pull light. Taking out his phone, he sat on the edge of the scuzzy old bathtub and went online to run a search on this Fitzwilliam character. With a name like that, there couldn't be many others.

The web had a few disparate pieces of information to offer. The man had been a reasonably well-known botanist of his day, a professor at Oxford, the author of a few books and some scientific papers which he'd presented to various scholarly institutes during the 1830s and '40s. All stuff that Gray Brennan had already talked about. So far, Heneage wasn't exactly setting Ben on fire. Not until a new piece of information popped up from the web search. Something Brennan *hadn't* mentioned.

Professor Fitzwilliam had died suddenly while sitting at his desk in his rooms at Magdalen College, Oxford, on September 9th, 1851, aged forty-seven. Not of a heart attack or a stroke, but of a single pistol shot to the back of the head. That, combined with the fact that no weapon had been found at the scene, had led the magistrates to conclude that his demise had been no suicide. Clever, those magistrates. Naturally, it hadn't been any more usual then than it was now for quiet-living Oxford dons to have their brains blown out in college by some sneak assassin.

September, 1851. A bell began to ring in Ben's mind. He searched for 'Lord Edgar Stamford death' and came up with September 20th of the same year, which was the date Kristen had said. Just eleven days after the murder of his friend and colleague, Stamford had burned himself to death.

Eleven days was probably about the length of time it would have taken in those days for the news to travel between Oxford and the rural west of Ireland. Had the aristocrat killed himself on hearing of Fitzwilliam's death? That didn't ring quite true to Ben – but then, maybe it hadn't been a deliberate act. Maybe he'd got badly drunk and knocked over a candlestick or something, inadvertently setting the fire that had blitzed Glenfell House. That was possible. But maybe there were other possibilities, too.

Ben went back to see what more he could dig up about Heneage Fitzwilliam, and after a few minutes he came across the first photograph he'd seen of the man. It was a typical period photo, very formally posed and taken at some science event in London in 1845. Fitzwilliam was a diminutive individual with half-moon spectacles, bald on top and sporting a ridiculous growth of side whiskers that could probably have been seen from behind on a clear day. A group of his peers stood stiffly clustered around him, all in dark suits and waistcoats. Beside Fitzwilliam, and looming over him by a good fourteen inches, was a large and imposing figure of a man who seemed to sneer disdainfully at the camera. When Ben looked at the list of names in the caption below the picture and counted left to right, he realised the man was Edgar Stamford. It was the first time Ben had seen him, too, and he looked every bit the arrogant tyrannical bastard that his long-suffering wife had made him out to be. He'd been as big as he was proud-looking, probably at least six-four, maybe six-five. When experts said people of the Victorian era were smaller than folks today, they obviously hadn't been looking at Edgar Stamford.

But it wasn't just the size of the guy. There was something else. Something that set Ben's mind churning and his blood quickening.

He keyed 'Lord Edgar Stamford Ireland' into the search engine and hit 'images'. The phone thought about it for a moment or two, then spat out the goods. Just one picture came up, but one was enough.

Ben stared at it for a long time.

The grainy, sepia-tinged photograph showed an assembled group posing in front of Glenfell House in 1844, in that particular self-conscious and solemn, almost funereal way people had acted around cameras at the dawn of the photographic era. Front and centre was Lady Stamford herself. Ben almost felt he knew her by now. Gray Brennan had said she was beautiful, and she was. Less beautiful by far, wearing the same unpleasant sneer and holding his wife's arm like the piece of property she was, was her tall, broad lord and master Edgar.

In the background were assembled various household members. There were a number of maids in uniform, some of them looking extremely young and nervous. To one side stood a brute-faced bloke in a tweed suit whom Ben could easily imagine to be Lord Stamford's villainous manservant, Burrows. Perhaps at Lady Stamford's request, even the horses had been brought out to have their picture taken with the group: a pair of handsome hunters, held still by a big guy clutching a halter in each large hand and staring with unnatural rigidity at the camera, as if he'd never seen one before. He probably hadn't.

Ben peered closely at the man's grainy image, thinking that this must be Padraig, Elizabeth's slow-witted but intensely loyal stableboy. If you could still be called a stableboy in your mid-thirties. He looked as strong as an ox, towering over everyone in the photo apart from Lord Stamford himself.

Ben's eyes narrowed to slits as his mind worked. So this was the famous Padraig McCrory Kristen had been so interested in, whose name Ben had followed in her wake trying to find in the parish records in Glenfell. There was little doubt that Kristen had seen the same photo Ben was looking at now. Somehow, this was the key to the whole thing.

Ben looked from the hulking stableboy to the lord. From the lord back to the stableboy. And in that moment, something flashed inside his mind and he knew.

He knew everything Kristen had known, and more. He knew why Finn McCrory wanted the journals so badly. Why Kristen had had to die for them.

The knowledge felt like a living thing inside him, pulsing, throbbing, stirring him up with excitement and anger. It was incredible, unbelievable . . . and yet it made perfect sense. He put away his phone. Stood up and clicked off the light and walked back into the other room.

Erin stirred on the bed, lifted her head from the pillow and looked at him. Her eyes were half-shut and her hair was tousled.

'What's up?' she asked, staring at him standing there.

'Tell me about the cabin,' he said.

Chapter Forty-Seven

Ben had done a lot more thinking by the time he stepped outside into the starry night, leaving Erin softly asleep inside the room. The night was humid, making his shirt stick to his back. It was after one in the morning and most of the other motel windows were dark. He could hear canned laughter from some TV show playing quietly somewhere. A couple of cats were hissing and growling at each other in the shadows behind a row of dumpsters.

Ben was running out of cigarettes. He put one between his lips, lit it up in the flickering halo glow of his Zippo and sucked in the smoke as he watched the lights of an eighteen-wheeler truck streak by on the distant highway, like a night train headed who-knew-where. He felt a little that way himself, every time Brooke entered his thoughts. She entered them often.

He took out his phone and dialled Finn McCrory's mobile number. It rang until the answer service cut in. Ben ended the call without leaving a message, then dialled the same number again. Same result. He tried once more, and this time he got a reply.

'Who the hell's this?' McCrory's voice was a raspy whisper. He sounded exactly like a belligerent, impatient VIP who didn't take kindly to being woken up in the middle of the night by an unexpected phone call.

'Careful how you talk to me,' Ben said. 'I might get offended and hang up. Then I might decide to call your wife's office in the morning and speak to her instead. She'll be interested in what I have to tell her about her husband's activities on the side.'

An opening line like that couldn't have failed to get McCrory's attention. There was a heavy silence over the phone. Ben could hear him breathing, waiting for more.

'Now I'm sure you'd prefer not to wake Mrs McCrory and have to face all those questions,' Ben said. 'So what you need to do is get out of bed, nice and quietly. Go downstairs and find a comfortable chair to sit in. You and I are going to have a little chat. Just us, in private. Do it now, McCrory. I'm waiting.'

He heard a grunt and a series of rustling noises as McCrory heaved himself out of bed, followed by a pause of almost a whole minute before the voice came back on the line. It must be a big house, Ben thought. Whichever part of it McCrory had hurried off to in order to talk, the sleeping Angela was well out of earshot, because her husband wasn't whispering any more.

'I know who you are, shitbird. I know all about you.'

'Of course you do,' Ben said. 'I'm the stone in your shoe. The guy who keeps getting in the way. Did your pal O'Rourke give you a hard time over the little incident at the shopping mall today? You might have to increase his retainer.'

'What do you want, Hope?' McCrory demanded.

'It's more a question of what *you* want, Mr Mayor. More precisely, what you're willing to give in return.'

'Oh, you called me up at one in the morning to talk business, asshole?'

'I've heard you're a pretty sharp operator when it comes to making deals,' Ben said. 'I think this is one you'll be eager to make.'

'Go on,' McCrory said warily.

'I have in my possession some items of interest to you. A set of books. Private journals of historical importance. Need I elaborate?'

'I know what books you mean.'

'That's what I thought. Now, what do I want with a pile of dusty old diaries? They're of no use to me.'

'I see. So you're looking to sell them, is that right?'

'To the highest bidder. The guide price is five million dollars.'

McCrory gave a snort. 'You've got this all figured out, huh, smartass?'

'Think about the alternative, Mr Mayor. It won't be pretty. A lot of people will get hurt. I'm sure we've all had enough of violence. Except maybe your psycho buddy Moon.'

'All right, fuckhead, let's say we do business. But five million for a bunch of old books? A little more than their auction value, isn't it?'

Ben took another drag on his cigarette. 'It's a seller's market. You know how that goes.'

'All the same, you tell me why I'd consider paying even half that much.'

'Because you stand to lose so much more if they should fall into the wrong hands,' Ben said. 'You know what I'm talking about, and you know this is a bargain price I'm offering here. I'm betting Kristen Hall was trying to shake you down for a lot more. Am I right?'

McCrory said nothing.

'And just to show you how generous I am, I'll even throw in something extra to sweeten the deal. Five million, and you can have Erin Hayes too. She's of no use to me either. Nor is the remaining copy of the little home video she made of you, Matt Ritter and Billy Bob Moon murdering one soon-to-be snitch by the name of Kirk Blaylock.'

McCrory remained very silent on the other end. Ben smiled. 'Hello? Are you there?'

'I'm here,' McCrory said in a tight voice.

'Now, I want the money in cash, and I want it tonight. We make the exchange, then you'll never hear from me again.'

'You're crazy. I don't have that kind of cash just laying around, you know. It'll take me at least two days.'

'Don't give me that. Your kind of clients pay by cheque, do they? It's cash, or else wave bye-bye to the journals.'

McCrory thought for a few moments. 'All right, all right. You have your money. But you mess with me, you're just another dead scumbag.'

'You know a good deal when you see one,' Ben said. 'Now here are my instructions. Meet me at the lake cabin at three thirty sharp. You come alone, with the money packed in two large holdalls. I'll be there with the goods. And the woman, too.'

'How'm I supposed to handle her, if I'm alone? Think I'm going to drive around with some screaming bitch in the back of my nice green Mercedes?'

'That's not going to be a problem,' Ben said. 'She'll be heavily sedated. I'll even help you stick her in the trunk, okay? Then she's all yours to do what you want with. Let the boys play with her a while first. Then grind her up into dog meat, for all I care. Makes no difference to me.'

'Real piece of work, ain't you, Hope?'

'Takes one to know one.'

'Maybe you should come work for me.'

'Why would I want to do that, with your five million in my pocket?' Ben looked at his watch. 'Best get moving, Mr Mayor. You have just a little over two hours. See you at the cabin.'

Chapter Forty-Eight

It was hot and sultry down by the lakeside, only the slightest of breezes from the north whispering over the water. An owl hooted from somewhere in the dark fringe of trees that hugged the shore. Clouds of moths danced in the glow of the cabin's veranda lanterns and the warm light that pooled out from its curtained windows. The front door was slightly ajar, as if to welcome the expected visitors. Music was playing softly inside the cabin: Mozart's Piano Concerto No. 21, Andante, the only thing Ben had liked from the McCrorys' CD collection. It was good music for waiting to.

At three fifteen, quarter of an hour ahead of schedule, headlights appeared on the single track that led towards the cabin. They weren't those of Finn McCrory's Mercedes, but of a van. The lights bobbed and jerked as it came lurching down the track. Another white GMC commercial panel van, just like the other. It drove up close to the cabin and pulled up next to the car that was parked there, with the engine running and the headlamps flooding the entrance on full beam.

As expected, McCrory hadn't come alone.

He hadn't come at all.

At the same moment that Matt Ritter and Billy Bob Moon jumped down from the cab, ready for war, the van's side and rear doors opened and another six of their accomplices clambered out. They all knew the plan. There was no talking, just the clacking of automatic weapons being cocked. They'd come extremely prepared. Every team member was equipped with a brand-new KRISS Vector, and between them these good ol' boys were carrying enough ammunition to spark off a rematch of the Civil War, one the Union would have lost for sure this time.

The men positioned themselves in a line facing the cabin, casting tall, bent shadows under the glare of the lights. There was a crackle of nervousness in the air. Despite Ritter and Moon's best efforts to stifle it, a certain amount of talk had been circulating among them about this badass mofo they were going after tonight. How he'd taken three of the gang down like skittles at the mall parking lot shoot-out and blown the crap out of a dozen cars, maybe even more; how he'd *cut off Quincy's arm* to take his gun. How sick and twisted was that? The man had even managed to evade Ritter and Moon not twice, but three times: a feat that nobody had ever, ever pulled off before. But if this Hope guy was swiftly becoming a legend, it would be a short-lived one after what was in store tonight.

Still, they were nervous.

Ritter walked a few steps towards the veranda, holding a megaphone that he'd brought from the van. His amplified voice cut through the stillness.

'All right, Hope. You know what we've come for. Toss out the goods. Then come out with the woman. Nice and easy. Hands on your heads where we can see 'em. No tricks. We get what we want, then nobody else gets hurt.' Nobody else, apart from Erin Hayes. That had been the deal.

There was silence from the cabin. The half-open front door creaked slightly in the breeze. The piano concerto tinkled faintly from inside.

'Hear me, Hope?' Ritter said into the megaphone. 'No messing around. You got five seconds.'

There was still no response from the cabin.

'What the hell's he doin' in there?' muttered Kurzweil on the far right of the line, nursing his gun.

Another of them, Meagher, laughed uneasily. 'Guess we caught'm screwin' the merchandise.'

'That is one hardcore dude,' said someone else.

Ritter silenced the chatter with a hard look, then exchanged glances with Moon. 'I don't think the sumbitch's comin' out,' Moon whispered.

Ritter gave a shrug. 'Fine. Wouldn't've done him any good anyway.' He tossed down the megaphone. He didn't show it, but he was a little disappointed in the boss's orders. He'd really wanted to kill this guy face-to-face. Moon was thinking along the same lines, but about the woman. Shame. But you had to do what you had to do. This was the second time they'd been sent to wipe out all trace of Hope and the evidence. Ritter was determined that there wouldn't be a third.

'All right, boys,' Ritter said to the lined-up team, unslinging his KRISS Vector. 'Let's rock and roll.'

Safeties were set to FIRE. Weapons were shouldered, fingers twitched on triggers. Then the tranquil night air erupted into a wall of noise, sending a panicked explosion of night birds flapping from the trees. The concentrated mass of firepower hammered into the front of the cabin, the pretty varnished oak planking shredded into splinters as more than a hundred and thirty rounds a second punched and tore through the wood. The porch railing blew apart. Windows shattered and fell in. The traditional-style lanterns Angela McCrory had gone all the way to Houston to buy for the entrance were blasted into a thousand pieces.

The shooters reloaded their guns and kept up a continual

fire as they spread out around the cabin, peppering it from a wider angle. Now the outer walls were beginning to disintegrate as over sixty kilos of copper-jacketed lead per minute poured into the building, destroying anything in its path. The music stopped abruptly as a bullet found the CD player. Bits of planking reduced to shredded tatters fell away from the structure. One by one, the interior lights went dark, until the cabin was illuminated only by the headlamps of the van. Nothing inside could possibly survive. Wherever Hope and the woman were desperately trying to take cover right now, they simply stood no chance against such a relentless unleashing of brute force.

Ritter ceased fire and held up his hand for the rest of the men to do the same. In the sudden heavy silence, something was fizzling from inside the shattered wreck in front of them. A bullet-riddled length of guttering swung loose and then dropped down onto the veranda, in the very spot where Kirk Blaylock had died crawling on his knees for mercy. After tonight, there'd be no more killing here. Because there was virtually nothing left of the place to kill anyone in.

Soon, there'd be nothing left at all. It was time to finish the job and go home.

Ritter turned and walked quickly back to the van, where a steel-lined box four feet long by two wide lay in the back. He flipped open the lid and took out one of his latest acquisitions, another toy that came courtesy of his special connections in the military. It was the new lightweight version of the M-32 forty-millimetre rotary grenade launcher, exclusively designed for the US Army Special Ops Command and capable of firing anything from non-lethal riot control rounds to chemical warfare munitions to high-explosive stuff, pumping out six shots in under four seconds. This would be a good opportunity to test it out before the first batch was sold on to their eager clients south of the border.

Ritter worked the trigger as fast as it would go. All six grenades slammed into the ruins of the cabin and detonated together in a fiery blast that lit up the sky and made the ground tremble. The force of the explosion lifted off the roof. Remnants of wooden walls and fragments of furniture and household fittings and wiring and pipes were blown upwards and outwards, raining down in a flaming circle that made several of the men step back; then the disintegrated roof collapsed into the furious blaze.

Ritter didn't need to reload. The destruction was total, the cabin's remains almost completely razed to the ground. Building demolition was getting to be a habit.

'Yeah!' Moon crowed, punching a gleeful fist in the air and forgetting all about his previous designs on Erin Hayes, now reduced to a smouldering corpse somewhere under all that wreckage, along with a certain Ben Hope who truly wasn't going to be a problem any more.

'That oughta do it,' Ritter said in satisfaction, his straight-faced composure slipping for just a moment. 'You know what, those trigger-happy beaners are sure as shit gonna love this baby.' Just the thing for taking out entire convoys of DEA agents. Oh, to be properly at war again. His grin vanished as quickly as it had appeared. 'All right, boys, party's over. Let's get out of here.'

A few looks and nods of relief were exchanged as the men gathered by the van, clutching their warm weapons, faces lit by the glow of the fire. Mission accomplished, and not a shot fired at them in return.

'That was something, huh?' Meagher said.

'Hey, where's Kurzweil?' someone asked suddenly.

Ritter turned to look around. Kurzweil had been on the

end of the firing line and Ritter had last seen him moving around the right-hand flank as they'd all spread out. He scanned the group, counting five excluding himself and Moon. Eight men had got out of the van. Now it was only seven. No Kurzweil.

'Anyone see him?'

Shaking of heads.

'He was standing right by me, coupla moments ago,' said Torres.

'Well, where'd he go?'

'Beats me.'

'Probably takin' a piss,' Moon said, peering towards the trees. 'Yo! Kurzweil!' he hollered, cupping a hand around his mouth. 'Get your retarded ass back over here now, you hear?'

Ritter looked hard into the shadows, but all he could see was the flickering outline of branches and leaves in the glow of the flames. 'Kurzweil!' he shouted. 'You wanna be left behind?'

But Kurzweil wasn't there. He was already several hundred yards away, totally unconscious and being carried off through the darkness of the forest.

Chapter Forty-Nine

Back in the olden days, the military brass had occasionally thought it worthwhile to pit small SAS units against superior numbers of regular British troops in tactical exercises, to test the training of both sides and practise covert operations and resistance-to-interrogation skills in realistic conditions. Ben and his team had used those exercises to become highly proficient at sneaking up on regular units in total darkness and in ghostlike silence and magicking one of them away, bound, hooded and utterly bewildered, to some secret location before his comrades had even noticed him gone. After a little roughing up, the thoroughly humiliated and slightly bruised squaddie would be stuffed in a Land Rover and dumped back on his unit, the butt of jokes for the rest of his life. It had all been a bit of innocent fun.

Fun wasn't what Lars Kurzweil was having as dawn broke over Tulsa. One moment he'd been carrying out his job along with the guys, the next, something had come up behind him out of the shadows and hit him so hard and fast he was down before he could make a sound. He'd felt a hand clamp over his mouth and then a sharp pain as a bent needle stabbed deep into the side of his neck. He'd lost consciousness too quickly to see his attacker's face or even to feel himself being dragged away into the trees.

As the drug's effects began to wear off, his eyelids fluttered open and he lifted his chin off his chest. His vision was watery and blurred, but he could tell he was in a darkened room. Something about it made him think it wasn't a normal room, but he was too fuzzy to figure out what, and so he tried to concentrate on his immediate situation. He was sitting upright on what felt like a wooden chair, unable to move his arms or legs. Slowly, he realised that he wasn't paralysed, but that he was tightly trussed to the chair with his hands tied behind its back and his ankles bound to its wooden legs. He struggled weakly, tried to speak but couldn't for the gag around his mouth. His head was pounding and awful nausea was washing over him in waves. He blinked to clear the wetness from his eyes.

The first thing Lars Kurzweil saw when his vision focused was the large black O of the sawn-off shotgun muzzle that was resting very still over the backrest of another chair in front of him, just a couple of feet from his face. His drugged brain was still lagging behind the rest of his senses, so it took a few seconds before he registered it for what it was and his eyes shot wide open.

Pant-wetting fear was a very appropriate reaction for someone awakening to the sight of a twelve-gauge in their face. A moan burst from his gagged mouth and he rocked in the chair, trying to recoil from the business end of the gun. The man pointing it was sitting backwards astride the chair opposite him.

'Welcome back to the world of the living,' Ben said. Three hours had passed since he'd carried his inert prisoner through the woods to where he'd hidden the Barracuda, far enough away for the rest of the men not to hear the throaty burble of the V8 Hemi as he made his escape. He could easily have put Kurzweil to sleep simply by compressing his carotid artery, cutting off the oxygen to his brain to knock him out almost instantly – but he'd needed the man to remain unconscious for longer, so he'd pumped about two-thirds of the syringe into him. That had allowed plenty of time to drive back to the Perryman Inn, pick up Erin and bring her and their captive here. The lock-up was proving useful in more ways than one.

The wide-eyed prisoner mumbled something through the gag that might have been, 'Where the fuck am I?'

'Where you are is up shit creek, without a paddle. I'm Ben. This is Erin. I think you already knew our names. I heard your buddies calling for you, so I know yours, too, Kurzweil. I know a lot of things, about Ritter and Moon, and your boss McCrory. When I take this gag off, you're going to be an obliging fellow and fill me in on the rest.' Gripping the shotgun butt in his right hand, Ben reached forwards with his left and yanked the dirty rag from the man's face. Kurzweil spat bits of fluff mixed with blood where the gag had chafed the corners of his mouth.

'Now let's get down to business,' Ben said. 'I don't need to tell a bad boy gangster like you that nothing says "instant brain death" like a twelve-gauge Brenneke slug at point-blank range. That's only if you act stupid and don't tell me what I want to know. Quick, concise answers. The whole truth and nothing but the truth. Or I will carve out a river valley through the middle of your skull. Are we clear?'

'Fuck you,' Kurzweil said, even though he looked no less terrified than before.

Ben leaned closer. 'I didn't quite catch that, Kurzweil. Do you want to start again and have another go? This time, think about what I just said.'

'Fuck you to hell,' Kurzweil quavered. 'Go right ahead an' shoot me if that's what you gotta do.'

Ben gave him a long, hard look. 'Do you have a death wish?'

'I talk to you, Ritter and Moon will kill me anyway. I ain't dyin' slow and ugly for you, not for nobody.'

Ben sighed. He laid down the shotgun. He'd had no intention of using it anyway. He needed information, and headless men weren't known for their loquacity. 'Looks like you have me over a barrel, Kurzweil. Which makes me very unhappy. It brings out my darker side.'

The prisoner was silent. His eyes were liquid and bulging.

Without looking back at her over his shoulder, Ben said, 'Erin, would you please mind stepping outside? Close the shutter behind you.'

'I want to stay.'

'No, you don't,' Ben said in a steady tone, not taking his eyes off the prisoner. 'Trust me.'

Erin hesitated anxiously for a moment, then nodded to herself and walked to the steel shutter. She knelt down, grasped its lower rim and raised it three feet, letting in the rays of the dawn light. The wheels of the Plymouth parked outside were visible through the gap, the wide tyres and arches still speckled with forest dirt. Erin clambered out and used her foot to press the rim of the shutter back down to the concrete, closing Ben and the prisoner inside alone. Ben heard the car door open and shut as she got inside to wait.

There was a silence in the lock-up. Kurzweil just went on staring at Ben, moisture glistening on his forehead.

'Everybody has a dark side,' Ben said after a few moments. 'But mine is so dark, it scares even me.' He paused. Stood up and walked over to the workbench where all the tools lay. 'It should scare you too. Because the things I'm capable of doing to you, right here, right now, on this beautiful summer's morning, are far more inhuman than what Ritter

319

or even Moon will do to you. You want to know where you are, my friend? You're in my torture chamber. Whether you leave it in one piece or in several, that's up to you.'

'I don't know anything!' Kurzweil blurted out, finally talking again. 'I was just doing what I was told!'

Ben turned and grinned at him. 'I've heard that one before. You'll change your tune. They always do, even tough guys like you. You'll be crying like a little girl, and that's before I even get started for real.'

He picked up a ball-peen hammer. It was a tool often used by bad guys to shatter kneecaps, break hands, tap out teeth and depress skulls. He inspected it thoughtfully, then laid it back down to pick up something else. 'Have you any idea how easily a pair of bolt croppers will shear through human flesh and bone? Let me show you.'

Kurzweil wriggled and cried out as Ben walked around the back of the chair with the bolt croppers. He levered its jaws wide with the long handles. The prisoner had a very clear idea of what was coming, and clenched his fingers into trembling fists. 'Oh God,' he moaned.

Ben grabbed the little finger of the man's left hand, winkled it out straight and fastened the jaws of the bolt croppers around it. 'After this one comes off, we go to work on the other nine,' he said.

Erin heard the piercing scream from outside in the car, and closed her eyes.

Chapter Fifty

Things were not going well at the McCrory residence that morning. After his late-night phone call, Finn had been so distracted that he'd managed to wake Angela by turning on the main bedroom light on his way back upstairs. Angela being Angela, that had led to a thousand questions about who he'd been talking to at one in the morning. His attempt to brush them off had only made it worse, prompting all her usual accusations of secretiveness and lying, and then a whole row that had ended up with him slinking off to spend the rest of the night alone in one of the other bedrooms. That wasn't unusual, either.

Finn had tossed and turned until six twenty, when a splitting headache had forced him to stagger downstairs in his emerald green pyjamas. He was greeted on the landing as usual by the life-sized colour statue of the Virgin, who stood with her back to a high Irish-themed stained glass window. Angela called her a 'gaudy monstrosity' but Finn loved to show her off to visitors, along with his Irish Room that sported, among other items, a giant tricolour flag, a beautiful cláirseach harp and Oklahoma's most comprehensive collection of Waterford crystal.

But Finn took no notice of the Virgin that morning as he stomped down to the kitchen to gulp down a handful of aspirin, which he was strongly tempted to wash down with a medicinal shot or two of Midleton Very Rare whiskey. Just as he'd been nursing his aching skull and thinking it couldn't get any worse, his mobile had buzzed to prompt him that he had a voicemail message.

Ritter: 'Call me.'

And so Finn had called him, and received news that had left him winded like a kick in the gonads. The mayor listened, sinking deeper into misery, as Ritter told him of last night's disastrous failure and Kurzweil's disappearance.

'The cabin?' Finn barely dared to ask.

'Cabin's not there any more. Sorry. Was your idea.'

Finn swallowed. The Midleton beckoned yet more enticingly. How was he ever going to tell Angela? She loved that cabin.

'Meet me,' Finn said. 'One hour.' Still reeling, he called Janet Reiss and woke her up to instruct her to cancel his appointments that morning.

'But you have the thing with the rail union delegates that we've already put off twice.'

'I don't care. Tell 'm I got run over by a train.'

'That's not funny, Finn.'

'Just say I'm feeling sick, okay?' Which was near enough the truth. By now, he could hear Angela was up early as usual, bustling about upstairs and banging doors in that way that told him he still wasn't forgiven for last night. Great. The other news he had for her would go down a storm. What the hell was he supposed to say to her? *Don't be mad, honey. I'll buy you another one.*

Desperate to avoid her, he scurried upstairs while she was in the bathroom, pulled on his clothes in a frenzied rush and managed to get out of the house without a confrontation. Seconds later, he was racing down the long drive of his imposing residence and beating the early-morning traffic on his way to the meeting with Ritter.

Which had been when his phone had rung again.

'How's it going, man?' This time, Xavier sounded as if he was calling from a raucous party or a nightclub, with wild heavy-metal music pounding in the background. It wasn't yet seven in the morning. The rock'n'roll lifestyle of the Mexicano drug dealer scene.

'Great! Just great,' Finn said, his face twisting.

'Listen, man, we need to move that shipment forward.'

Finn's jaw sagged and he almost ploughed the Mercedes into a line of parked cars. 'Okay,' he said, catching his breath.

'Yeah. They won't wait for next week, you know?'

Finn knew that Los Locos weren't people whose patience you wanted to try. 'So when they want it?'

'Two days, max. We cool for that?' As if loading millions of dollars' worth of illegal weaponry and munitions onto a convoy of trucks and transporting it more than six hundred miles across two states and over a heavily patrolled border without getting stopped was something to be cool about.

'Two days! Jesus Christ, you're killing me.' Finn's mind was in turmoil. Two days meant that the delivery would have to hit the road by early tomorrow, at the latest. Which inevitably meant that the job of loading the trucks would have to be done today. He'd barely have enough time, even if he rounded up every available man and got them started right away. And all of it, with Ben Hope still out there breathing down his neck and the Hayes woman running loose.

'No, man,' Xavier said, then added jokingly, 'but they might, if they don't get the goods.'

Finn knew that wasn't really a joke.

'I'll see you soon,' Xavier said, and was gone.

When Finn screeched the Mercedes to a halt outside his private hangar, the replacement GMC was there waiting for him and he saw to his intense irritation that Ritter was there, too, along with Moon, who was chewing his damn gum and wearing a T-shirt with the logo '100% BANDIT'. If Ritter felt bad about last night's objective going south, he wasn't showing it. Finn summoned them inside the Gulfstream 650, told them about the rescheduling of the arms delivery, and then launched straight in with the questions. What had gone wrong up there at the cabin? Why couldn't they eradicate Hope? Where was the damn woman? Where were the journals?

Ritter frankly didn't have a lot to say in response. By this time, the mayor was pacing furiously up and down the aircraft's aisle, his face a glowing shade of puce and his hair all in disarray.

'He's a goddamn pussy,' Moon insisted. 'Can't fight a straight fight because he's too chicken to face us out. He's gonna try and kill us off one at a time instead.' He snorted. 'Fuckin' Kurzweil. I mean, who *couldn't* kill that sorry piece of shit? My goddamn grandmother could—'

'Get your head out your ass,' Ritter said quietly. 'He didn't take Kurzweil away to kill him. He took him away to press him to rat us out. *Then* maybe he'll kill him.'

'Kurzweil knows jack.'

'He knows enough,' Ritter said. 'Hope will get it out of him, for sure.'

'Yeah?'

'Yeah. Because I would.'

'Okay, so what'f he does?'

'Jesus Christ, enough yakking!' Finn screamed at them. 'I'm trying to think.' He went on pacing, sweat stains beginning to show through his shirt despite the plane's cool interior. 'Damn it, maybe I should've just paid him the money.'

Ritter shook his head. 'Forget about the money, boss. The whole thing was just a set-up. He knew you wouldn't show. He had our moves figured out from the off. It was all about capturing one of our guys.'

'He's smart, all right,' Finn seethed. 'He's very, very smart. But money's money. For the right price, maybe we can make him go away.'

'I don't think he's interested in your money, boss,' Ritter said. 'It's you he wants. Because of what happened to the girl.'

That made Finn stop dead in his tracks and turned him cold. 'Then you'll just have to bury the sonofabitch, won't you? Maybe you'll get lucky next time. Or maybe I should just replace your asses. The fucking Mexicans could do a better job.'

'You don't mean that, boss,' Moon said.

Finn looked at him sharply. 'Don't I?'

Ritter took off his dark glasses and gave Finn a long look. His face was placid, but there was a cold fire in his eyes that almost made Finn take a step back.

'No more misses,' Ritter said. 'This time, Hope dies. That's a promise. I'll personally cut his heart out and bring it to you in a basket while it's still beating.'

'I don't care how you do it,' Finn said. 'I don't care what it takes or how much it costs. Just do it. He can't stand in my way again.'

'Hate to piss on your French fries, but there's just one problem,' said. Moon 'We got squat on this guy. We don't know where he's hangin' out, we don't know what he's drivin', we have no idea where the fucker might show up next.'

'Sure we do,' Ritter said. 'If he finds out what I know he'll find out from Kurzweil, he'll show up at Big Bear.'

'He wouldn't have the balls,' Moon said.

Ritter cocked his head doubtfully. 'I wouldn't be too sure. You ask me, that's where we'll see him next. I think we should let him walk right in there. I'll be waiting for him.'

Finn had pursed his lips and was thinking hard. 'No, no. You're wrong, Ritter. The woman – *she's* the key. Hope knew her name, he knew about the video recording, he knew about Blaylock. He's hooked up with her somehow. Maybe he was hooked up with her all along. Okay, so maybe we have squat on Hope. We have plenty on her.'

'I guess we could watch the house,' Moon suggested, ever hopeful that he'd finally get his hands on the woman in private.

'Tried that, remember?' Ritter answered.

'Yeah, well, maybe if y'all had let me take care of it instead of that dickweed Spicer, she wouldn't've gotten away so easily,' Moon countered.

'She's bound to go back there,' Finn insisted. 'So that's what the two of you are gonna do, get over there and stake the place out. She can't stay under the radar forever. Meanwhile, I'll have O'Rourke's guys scour the whole of Tulsa for the bitch.'

Ritter didn't like it one bit. Stake-out duty was for the lower orders, not for someone of his experience and seniority. There were more urgent matters to take care of. 'These trucks ain't gonna load themselves. I need to be there.'

But Finn was adamant. He shook his head. 'Meagher and the boys can handle it without you. Make the calls, tell 'em to haul ass right now, this morning. Then shift yourselves to Crosbie Heights and *get me that woman*. We get her, we get Hope.'

Chapter Fifty-One

Erin sat waiting in the car for eight long minutes, then ten, with nothing to do but stare into her lap and try not to imagine what Ben Hope was doing to the man inside the lock-up. The scream she'd heard earlier had been cut abruptly short and she'd heard nothing since. The silence from behind the steel shutter was even worse.

Waiting made all kinds of dark thoughts pass through her mind. Who was this guy Ben? How the hell had things gotten so desperate that she'd resorted to hooking up with some crazy ex-military type tooled up with guns and ammo and dragging her into a personal revenge quest of his own? Could she trust him? Should she just take off? The key was in the ignition.

But she didn't touch it. *He isn't like that*, she kept telling herself. *He's one of the good guys.*

When a whole quarter of an hour had gone by and she couldn't stand it any longer, she was about to shove open the door when the shutter suddenly screeched up and Ben walked out and stepped towards the car. He had the .40 calibre auto taken from Kurzweil tucked into the waistband of his jeans.

She stared at him. He wasn't spattered from head to foot with blood, or grinning maniacally clutching gory implements of mutilation. He didn't look like someone who'd just tortured a man to death. But then, what did she know about torture?

'Well?' she said. She peered into the lock-up, but it was too dark to see. There was no sound from inside.

'Well what?'

She frowned. 'What happened in there?'

'We talked,' Ben said.

'I heard a scream.'

'And you thought what?' Ben asked, looking at her with the faintest of smiles.

Erin suddenly felt embarrassed.

'It's what I wanted you to think,' Ben told her. 'Him too. I wanted him to believe I'd sent you away so you wouldn't have to witness something horrible. Then when I told him I was going to cut off his fingers one at a time, he didn't take a lot of convincing.'

'You haven't—?'

'The scream was just me giving him a little pinch. Didn't even break the skin. After that, he was ready to tell me anything.'

Erin stepped inside the lock-up. Kurzweil remained tied up in the chair. There was no blood. He still had all his fingers attached, both his ears, and appeared undamaged apart from the fact that he was stone-cold unconscious again.

'There was enough in that syringe to knock out a rhino,' Ben said. 'I've just put the last few ccs into him. He'll be out of action for a bit.'

'What happens to him next?'

'Dump him. I don't need him any more. I know every-thing he knows.'

Erin looked at him quizzically, but he made no reply. That was when she spotted the torn-out notebook page lying on the workbench. Peering at it, she saw that some notes had been written on it. All she was able to make out were the words 'BIG BEAR' before Ben followed her eye and snatched the paper up before she could read more.

'What's big bear?' she asked.

'It's not important,' he replied, folding the paper into his pocket. He turned away and walked back outside towards the Barracuda, got in, fired up the engine and reversed the car through the open shutter and half into the lock-up.

'Looked like something to me,' Erin said as he got out of the car.

'Help me get him in,' Ben said, and Erin sensed that he was deliberately holding back from her. Together, they tipped Kurzweil over backwards and heaved him, chair and all, into the trunk. It was large enough to take a chair on its side with a large man strapped to it. Ben slammed the lid, then got back behind the wheel, put the Plymouth in drive and nudged the gas, edging forward far enough to clear the shutter. Leaving the engine idling, he climbed back out and grasped the shutter sill.

'Aren't you going to tell me anything?'

'We're leaving now.'

She stepped outside into the morning light, and watched him as he pulled the shutter all the way down on its rusty fittings and replaced the padlocks to secure it in place. He shrugged on his jacket to cover the pistol in his belt, waved for her to get into the passenger seat, then got back behind the wheel. He revved the gas and the powerful V8 propelled the car away from the lock-ups and back out into the street. He was beginning to get the hang of Tulsa's geography.

'That's the real reason you sent me out,' Erin said tightly after a few minutes' silence as he gunned the big car through the city streets. 'I get it now. You didn't want me to hear what he told you. You found out where McCrory's arsenal is, didn't you?' She could see from the look in his eyes that she was right. 'Looked like a set of directions you'd written on that notepaper.'

'Forget about it.'

'Big Bear,' she said. 'Is that a town? I never heard of it before.'

'Erin, enough of the questions. I won't answer them.'

'Why won't you tell me? I'm just as involved in this as you are.'

'Because what you don't know can't hurt you,' Ben replied.

'If you're going, then so am I.'

He shook his head emphatically. 'No way. I'm doing this alone.'

'Don't do this to me. I've come this far. You can't leave me hanging.'

'You've been lucky. Now you need to quit while you're ahead. Too many innocent people have been hurt already. I can't take you where I need to go. I can't be responsible for you.'

'So, what, I just sit tight in that Perryman roach-hole?'

'We're not going back there. I'm taking you to a better place, downtown. You'll be safe there for now, as long as you keep a low profile.'

Erin just looked at him and made no reply, but he could tell she didn't like it. Ben pointed backwards with his thumb. 'Then I'm going to offload Sleeping Beauty there. He'll wake up in an hour or two, counting his fingers and feeling the joy of living like never before. Then if he's got any sense he'll start running and not stop until he's in Barrow, Alaska.'

'I'm glad you didn't hurt him. You're a good man, Ben.'

'You don't know me that well.'

'I'm worried about you going after McCrory alone. Let me come with you. Please? There's got to be something I can do to help. I could . . . I don't know. Keep watch, or something.'

'I work best alone. Always have.'

'Even if it means getting killed? It's insanity. People don't do this kind of thing. Not in the normal world.'

'There is no normal world, Erin. Just this one.'

'You'll be dead. I won't ever see you again.'

He glanced across at her. It almost sounded as if she cared.

'No,' he said. 'I'll come back for you when it's over. Then you're going home.'

Erin was checked into room 421 at the Hyatt Regency on East 2nd Street, under the name Rosie Lang. The plush decor and amenities were a welcome change from the Perryman. Ben thought she'd earned it. He stayed with her until she was safely in her room, which was spacious and comfortable with floor-to-ceiling glass that looked out over neighbouring scenic gardens. He told her to lie low and wait for his call, promised he'd see her soon and then left quickly, saying no more than he had to.

Back out on the street, he got in the Plymouth and sped away, heading southeast across Tulsa. Mid-morning, the sun was hot and he kept the windows rolled down to blast the inside of the car with cool air as the Muskogee Turnpike took him through the adjoining city of Broken Arrow. A few miles beyond, he left the highway and followed a series of turnings onto progressively smaller and quieter roads, past dotted farms and holdings until an unsurfaced country lane took him to the quiet kind of spot he was looking for. He stopped the car in a cloud of drifting dust and climbed out into the heat. There was nothing around but patchy

331

scrubland and rocks. The grass was tall and burned, and the air was full of the buzz of insects.

Ben popped the lid and manhandled the chair out of the trunk, then dragged it a few yards from the roadside to a spot screened by bushes. Kurzweil was still semi-conscious, his head lolling sideways like a drunk's. Ben left him sitting there and walked back to the car to fetch his bag and the shotgun, then returned to join his slowly awakening prisoner.

Ben sat a few yards away on a rock, laid his bag down at his feet and the shotgun next to him. He removed his jacket and rolled up his sleeves. The chirping of the crickets was loud, a harsh pulsing rasp from all around. Ben closed his eyes. A stolen moment of reflective stillness. The quiet before the storm. It would be soon.

He thought about Ritter and Moon. They'd been through a level of training reserved for the cream of the world's dedicated warriors. They were younger than him. Faster. And they'd got the better of him twice already.

He lit up his last cigarette and took his time over it, knowing it might be a while before he had another. It might equally be never. But Ben didn't let that thought concern him. It never had in the past, and there was no need for it to now.

While he waited for Kurzweil to wake up, he checked the Stamford journals. They looked a little more beaten-up since he'd dived out of the moving Jeep with them, and one of them was scored along its cover from the bullet that had gone through the bag during the car park shoot-out.

He thought for a while about what to do with the journals. He'd no further use for them himself. They'd served their purpose, as far as he was concerned. The rest was just paper and leather. He wasn't much of a bibliophile. But he couldn't bring himself to dump them, and there was no denying their historical value. After a few moments' reflection he remembered the little museum in Glenfell. It was decided, then. If he came through this okay, he'd send the books there for posterity.

And if he didn't come through it okay, then maybe one day they'd be found again by someone who gave a damn. Or maybe not. It would be out of his hands then.

He sat and smoked and soaked up the sun's heat and watched Kurzweil until the last Gauloise was just a stub. He flicked it away and ground it into the dirt with his heel. By then, the prisoner's eyes were open and gazing resentfully at him from the chair. The eyes followed him, widening, as Ben reached once more into his bag and drew out the US army trench knife.

Ben stood up and walked over to Kurzweil, slipping his fingers through the knuckleduster hilt and unsheathing the blade. Kurzweil began to struggle again before he realised that Ben was cutting him loose. The ropes fell slack and Ben stepped away. Kurzweil eased himself stiffly from the chair, grimacing with discomfort and rubbing his chafed wrists.

'I told her I'd let you go,' Ben said. 'Because that's what a good and decent person would do. Because it would have upset her if I'd said that things don't work that way. You understand?'

Kurzweil nodded. Acceptance.

Ben drew the forty-calibre from his belt. It was cocked and locked, a round in the chamber and the safety on. He tossed it to Kurzweil, and Kurzweil caught it.

'First move's yours,' Ben said.

A sharklike grin spread over Kurzweil's face. He hefted the gun. 'You're a crazy man. You coulda killed me.'

'I'm not an executioner,' Ben said. 'I was once. I can't do it any more.'

They locked eyes. For two long seconds, they stood completely still. Then Kurzweil went to shoot. In the time it took for him to punch the pistol up and out at arm's length and disengage the safety and square his sights on Ben, the shotgun was up off the rock and a blasting roar of flame ripped from the sawn-off muzzle. The Brenneke slug hit Kurzweil in the sternum and cut him in half.

Ben picked up the pistol and wiped the blood off it, then collected his things and walked back towards the car, leaving what was left of Kurzweil spread out over the ground. The buzzards would find him soon enough.

The Plymouth rumbled into life and moved off in the dust haze.

The killing had started.

Chapter Fifty-Two

Eleven miles further southeast, after crossing the county line at a steady ninety-five miles an hour with the wind blast roaring around his ears, Ben reached the town whose name was on his sheet of directions. Adonis, Muskogee County. Population: zero. It wasn't the most vibrant of places. As Ben sped through the single main street, which seemed to be pretty much all Adonis had ever consisted of, just a cursory glance at the empty, tumbledown clapboard houses, the fallen-in roofs and glassless windows and the sprawl of weeds everywhere was enough to tell that the town had been abandoned for at least seventy years, perhaps longer. Even the local vandals looked to have stopped bothering with it.

Following the directions, Ben turned left, then left again, leaving the ghost town behind and heading into open, flat country. Barbed wire sagged from fence posts left to rot along the lonely roadside. The occasional dead tree and clump of tangled bushes dotted the landscape, and the rest was desiccated grass and dust and rock. The road was unmetalled, just two compacted-earth wheel-tracks worn into the dirt.

But for a place long since abandoned, it seemed nonetheless to get more than its due share of traffic. That certainly tallied with what Kurzweil had told him. As he drove, Ben's eye picked out many overlaid tyre tracks. Wide, heavy vehicles had been making frequent journeys along here. Stopping to examine the tyre marks in the dirt, he found that the freshest of the tracks were recent. Very recent, unevaporated moisture pressed from the ground, telling him that the road had been used within the last couple of hours.

He felt a stirring in his heart and stomach. They were here.

Left again at a stand of bushes, like the directions said; the car bumped up a short incline and onto a narrower track. The trucks had been this way before him, and not long ago. Three hundred yards further on, Ben came to a tall locked metal gate in a high fence that stretched as far as he could see in both directions.

He drew up to the gate and got out. The fresh truck tracks passed under the fence and carried on up the dirt road that sloped gently upwards to the collection of old farm buildings whose tops he could see just over the brow of the hill some four hundred yards away. The fence that barred Ben's approach wasn't new, but it wasn't old. Eight feet high, strong weld-mesh wire, and it seemed to go on for miles. Who would splash out the money for security fencing out here in the place that time forgot? He already knew who. The same illegal operator who'd ensured that the gate was secured with three stout padlocks, keeping unwanted visitors firmly out.

The remains of the original gate were still visible inside the perimeter, along with the ancient weathered hand-painted sign that depicted a snarling bear's head. Big Bear Farm, as it had once been.

Ben got back in the Plymouth and backed it up all the way down to the turn-off, where he tucked it out of sight behind the cluster of prickly, thirsty-looking bushes. He grabbed the binoculars, tucked Kurzweil's pistol and the trench knife into his belt and put on the leather jacket, despite the oppressive heat. He popped the four solid-slug rounds out of the shotgun's magazine and replaced them with heavy buckshot. In close, hectic combat against multiple moving targets, you needed a street-sweeper with spread-out killing power, not something you had to stop to aim like an improvised rifle. He jacked a round into the chamber, topped the magazine up to make five, then dropped extra cartridges into his jacket pockets where he could get to them quickly. He slung the loaded gun over his shoulder and checked the time. Almost noon.

He didn't pause to think about what he was walking into. This was the job he'd come to America to do, and now he was ready to do it. It was as simple as that. He locked the car and walked back to the gate, scaled the wire mesh and jumped down to the other side, dusting his hands. To stay on the track was asking to be spotted by any lookouts posted on guard, so he kept to the long grass and whatever shrubbery he could use as cover as he cut a zigzag path towards the distant farm buildings. As he got closer, he moved with extreme caution. He was on his own out here with no backup against an enemy force who greatly outnumbered him and knew the terrain. There was no margin for tactical errors.

He'd been right about sentries keeping watch. The guy was standing in knee-high grass cradling a scoped bolt-action Ruger scout rifle and gazing absently down the track in the direction of the gates, which were obscured by the slope of the land. He looked bored and deep in his own thoughts, whatever those might have been.

Ben worked his way painstakingly around the guard's flank, keeping low as he slipped smoothly from bush to tree to clump of grass and pausing now and then to check that

337

the guy hadn't seen him and wasn't tracking him through the grass with the riflescope. He hadn't.

Ben crept closer, until he could almost smell the guy. Then closer still. Within a few feet of the guard's back, he slipped the trench knife from his belt. He counted mentally, *one – two – three – GO* and covered the remaining distance like a leopard that had stalked up within charging range of an antelope for that final, explosive attack. He took the guard down fast and silently and cut his throat in a sawing motion. The British army had taught Ben long ago to kill at close quarters without thinking twice. Thinking made you hesitate. Hesitation meant you were the one getting killed.

Ben rolled the corpse over in the bloody grass and checked for ID. He found a phone and a wallet and took both, then relieved the dead man of his rifle and his sidearm and moved on.

The final approach was painstaking and awkward, laden down with two long guns. Ben worked his way around the side of the old farm to a vantage point between two dead tree stumps that formed a V on slightly raised ground, from where he could scout the layout without being seen. He laid the scoped rifle in the crook of the stumps, where he could return to it later. Lying flat on his belly, he scanned the range of buildings through the binoculars. It looked exactly like what it was, a sad old place that had fallen into disuse a very long time ago and had all the hallmarks of dereliction to show for it. Old tyres and rusted-out oil drums and abandoned farm machinery lay scattered about between corroded sheet-metal buildings.

Ben had known many such places in his time. Some had been battle zones heaped with dead bodies. Some had been hideouts where kidnappers kept their victims in appalling conditions. Others had been a cover for sophisticated drug production facilities. Big Bear Farm had been put to a different purpose.

It was a hive of industry down there. In a broad dirt yard maybe fifty yards across between rundown buildings, three large trucks, several miscellaneous 4×4 vehicles and a whole team of men were gathered around what looked at first glance like a dug-out hole for an Olympic-sized swimming pool, only much deeper. The hole was lined with concrete and until very recently had been covered with an enormous iron sheet that was now attached by chains to the back end of a tractor and had been dragged aside, leaving scrape marks in the dirt. It was probably half-inch steel plate, weighing several tons.

Inside the hole, Ben could see stack upon stack of crates. Some were square, some oblong, some plain white wood and others painted military green with white stencilled lettering on their sides and lids. A crane lorry like the kind used in builders' yards to shift tons of sand and stone was parked up by the edge of the hole. A guy stood beside it working a remote control panel and guiding the big yellow steel arm downwards. Powerful claws clamped around another crate and the crane lifted it out, swivelled its dangling, swaying cargo across to the rear of one of the trucks and deposited it on a hydraulic lift where two men jacked it up onto a cart and wheeled it into the bowels of the truck's loading bay.

Meanwhile, more men were descending into the hole on ladders and hauling out some of the lighter crates to be passed along in a line for stacking inside the truck. They were working hard. Even at this range Ben could see the sweat and dust on their faces. They'd been at it for some time, because the first truck was already loaded and had been moved back from the arsenal store, where two guys were securing the straps holding the sides in place. With the second truck half loaded and the third waiting in line, they were halfway through their job.

Scanning back and forth, Ben counted eighteen men. All were carrying sidearms in belt or hip holsters. They'd propped their rifles untidily against the side of the nearest building, the way criminal rabble or the worst kind of crappy guerrilla soldiers would do. He couldn't see McCrory, which was no surprise or disappointment. Ben wasn't here for him – not yet.

No sign of Ritter or Moon, either, but they might have been supervising things from inside one of the buildings. Nearly all the focus was on the truck that was being loaded. Just one guard was standing by the one that was already full, nursing a Benelli twelve-gauge auto and looking quietly relieved that he'd been given such light duty.

Ben put away the binocs and slipped away from his vantage point. It took less than three minutes for him to thread his way down among the buildings and reach the truck unnoticed. He drew the knife again as he crept silently up behind the second guard. Same routine. Same horrible sensation of the cold steel blade puncturing flesh and slipping deep inside. Same muted cry of shock and surprise as Ben eased the wriggling body gently to the ground behind the wheel of the truck and kept his hand clamped over the guy's mouth until he was still.

Ben peered around the side of the vehicle. Nobody had seen him or noticed the guard's sudden disappearance. A quick glance through the truck's cab window told him that it was empty and the key was in the ignition. He moved back down the side of the truck and quickly undid two of the side straps before clambering up into the loading bay. There was little room to move among the stacks of crates.

He used the knife to slash the straps holding the cargo in transit, and then to prise open the lid of the first crate. He dug into the packing material to reveal a neat row of brand-new KRISS Vectors. Ten of them; at a quick count there were maybe forty more crates of the same type inside the truck. Between three trucks, some hundred and twenty crates. Over a thousand weapons, all destined for the trigger-happy little hands of the Los Locos cartel.

The next crate he checked was bigger. It was full of rotary grenade launchers, like the one he'd watched Ritter use to lay waste to the lakeside cabin. There were about twenty of the damn things, enough to take on an army division. A whole stack of crates nearby was marked HIGH EXPLOSIVE; Ben levered it open with the tip of the blade and pulled away the lid. He gave a low whistle. He was looking at more forty-millimetre grenades than he'd seen together in one place for a very long time. And that was just one crate out of over a dozen he could see at a glance.

How US army quartermasters could fail to sound the alarm over the disappearance of this much ordnance was beyond him. But there was no time to dwell on such questions. He could hear the crane and the voices of the men outside. He grabbed two of the rotary launchers from one crate. Loaded five grenades into each, snapped them shut and slipped out of the cargo bay with a launcher in each hand. Quickly, quietly, he moved towards the cab door and opened it. He tossed the launchers inside, then climbed in after them and swung himself up behind the wheel.

'Here we go,' he muttered.

And twisted the ignition key.

Chapter Fifty-Three

Erin paced her comfortable room in the Hyatt Regency until the restlessness building up inside her like steam pressure made her feel as if something was going to pop inside her mind if she didn't get out of this place and *do* something. Part of her resented that Ben had left her stranded here in this gilded cage while he went off on his own. Another part of her was deeply concerned about him and wanted to help. She shouldn't have let him go, damn it.

She stalked out of the room, took the lift down to the lobby and after asking at the desk was directed to a business centre with superfast broadband access for hotel guests. Settling in behind a free terminal, she ran the search phrase BIG BEAR TULSA through Google to see what came up. It was what Ben had written down after talking to Kurzweil. It had to mean something.

After some hunting around, the search led her to a website called www.Abandoned-Oklahoma.com, which gave listings of ghost towns and settlements classed as barren, neglected, abandoned and semi-abandoned. She'd never realised there were so many. From the site, she learned that the town of Adonis in neighbouring Muskogee County, de-established in 1949, had once been the nearest community to the old Big Bear farmstead, a wheat-growing concern that had gone bust some time in the fifties and fallen into rack and ruin.

'Bingo,' she murmured.

Google Maps helped her to quickly pinpoint the farm. The satellite image zoomed in close enough to get a blurry view of a scatter of agricultural buildings. She blinked. Was this where McCrory had kept his arsenal hidden from the FBI all this time?

'I'm going,' she said out loud, drawing a couple of looks from other computer users in the room. She had no idea what she was going to find when she got out there, or even how she could get to such a remote and distant place without a car. Public transport was minimal in these parts. She only knew she desperately wanted to be involved, and that every minute lost was time that Ben was on his own without a soul to help him.

Erin returned to her room to collect her things, then headed quickly out into the street. A cab was her best chance. If she had to, she'd get the driver to take her all the way to Adonis, and worry about paying the fare later.

The sun was beating down hard, and the paving was blinding white in the glare. Erin crossed East 2nd Street and hurried along in the shade of the tree-lined sidewalk in the direction of the towering Bank of Oklahoma high-rise. *Please God let there be a taxi*, she prayed. *Please God let a taxi appear right this moment.*

Her heart leapt as, moments later, precisely that happened. The yellow checker cab slowed as she hailed it, cut out of the traffic and pulled into the kerb twenty yards up the street near the entrance to the bank. Erin broke into a jog, amazed at her good fortune. But before she could get to the waiting car, an obese man in a drumskin-tight business suit carrying an attaché case came striding out of the bank, eyes front and talking on a phone, and barged in ahead of her.

'Too bad Conroy is upset, Artie,' he was saying in a piping voice, loud enough for the whole street to hear. 'I want the goddamn Radisson deal closed today. We're bleeding money on this.'

'Excuse me,' Erin said, catching up. 'But that cab's mine.'

He jerked around and stared at her in indignation. 'Hold on, Artie. *What?*'

'I said, this cab's mine,' she said levelly. 'I need it.'

He shrugged, and gave her an alligator smile. 'I just made it mine.'

'I saw it first,' she said.

'What are you, twelve years old? Shit happens. Get another.'

She moved between him and the taxi door, laid a hand on his arm and gave him what she hoped was her best pleading look. 'I have important business. Please. You don't realise how important—'

'Kiss my ass, lady.' He used his bulk to push past her, almost knocking her down, then opened the taxi door and started wedging himself inside as he resumed his phone call. 'Nah, just some stupid skank. Like I was saying, Artie. *Fuck* Conroy.'

Erin stared at this insolent sonofabitch stealing her taxi right out from under her nose. That was when the pressure finally went *pop* inside her mind.

She took her pistol out of her bag and aimed it in his face.

'Okay, you asked for it, cheesehog. Out of the damn cab. I said, get out of the taxi, *now!*'

A few bystanders scattered in alarm. Someone yelled, 'Whoa, holy shit!'

The fat guy dropped his phone and his case and put up his hands. 'Jesus Christ. Okay! Okay! Whatever you say, ma'am.' He plucked his bulk out of the taxi door and stepped away in a hurry, his chins wobbling. The cab driver craned his neck from behind the wheel and gaped at Erin, too stunned to move.

'POLICE! DROP YOUR WEAPON!'

Erin froze. She hadn't noticed the two beat cops approaching. They were just ten yards away, Glocks drawn and trained right on her.

She let her pistol clatter from her fingers and put her hands up. One cop covered his partner as he darted across to pick up her gun. 'Against the car!' Erin did what they said.

The arrest didn't take long. Within what seemed like just seconds, a police cruiser screeched up with lights flashing, and in front of the gathering crowd of onlookers Erin was bundled into the back and read her rights through a wire mesh.

She was too shocked to register where the patrol car was taking her. A hand pressed to the top of her head as she got out; she was walked inside a building, handed over, processed, fingerprinted and finally banged up inside a cell. She slumped on a fixed metal bench and put her head in her hands, feeling ready to throw up out of self-disgust and anger.

Minutes went by. Then the cell door rattled and she looked up to see a craggy face leering at her through the bars.

'Well, what have we here?' Chief O'Rourke growled. 'Look what the cat brought in.'

Chapter Fifty-Four

The commotion Ben had been expecting kicked off one startled beat after the truck engine roared into life. McCrory's men dropped what they were doing and began yelling and running towards the truck, grappling for their pistols, leaping to grab their rifles.

Ben crunched the gearstick into first, stamped on the gas and the truck lurched violently forwards, bouncing over the uneven ground. He could feel the sheer weight of the cargo of weaponry and munitions in the back. There was no way he could have tried to use it as a getaway vehicle and outrun the 4×4s belonging to the crew. That was fine by him, because theft wasn't his intention.

His purpose was simple: to inflict maximum damage. Hit McCrory where it hurt most, hit him hard and whittle down his forces with all the speed, aggression and surprise the SAS had taught Ben to deploy.

He drove the loaded truck straight towards the half-loaded one, revving the diesel to a scream and bracing himself for the impact that bounced his ribcage off the steering wheel amid a rending crash of heavy metal. Men hurled themselves out of the way as the half-loaded truck was rammed sideways into the crane lorry. The crane toppled over the edge like a falling tree, crushing its operator who hadn't been able to get out of the way in time. As if in slow motion it went smashing down into the concrete pit, crushing ladders and equipment and crates, followed by the truck which tumbled over on end, shedding its cargo everywhere.

By then, bullets were thwacking into the bodywork of Ben's truck, which had ploughed to a halt at a crazy angle at the edge of the pit. With the shotgun still slung around his shoulder, he grabbed the two grenade launchers, kicked open the driver's door and hurled himself out. He hadn't hit the ground before he squeezed off the first grenade. It sailed into the side of one of the 4×4s and the vehicle was lifted off the ground and flipped like a toy in a rolling ball of fire. Shrapnel cut down the three men who'd been too slow to escape the range of the explosion. Another managed to dive clear. He fired at Ben. Ben fired another grenade that caught the guy square in the chest, carried him off his feet and backwards into the pit before it went off, setting off a chain explosion of the spilled munitions down there that rocked the earth like a volcanic eruption and sent up a spout of flame bigger than the blazing oil-wells of Kuwait.

Ben felt the skin-peeling heatwave gush by him like dragon's breath as he ducked around the side of a building. One of the big barns was instantly engulfed in the conflagration, its flimsy wooden structure collapsing, buckled and blackened sheet metal raining down to bury several more of the 4×4s while McCrory's crew ran like ants.

Never let your enemy get up once he's down. Tacticians from Napoleon Bonaparte to General George Patton had said it, and with eight grenades to go, it was wisdom Ben intended to honour. He didn't stop squeezing off shots until both launchers were empty and both trucks and two more farm buildings were blazing skeletons. The fireworks shooting up from the arsenal pit were lighting up the sky with one massive mushrooming blast after another that melted into a rising skyscraper of black smoke they could probably see in Oklahoma City.

Ben threw down the launchers and unslung the shotgun. The first round was already in the chamber. He fired a round of buckshot at a guy who was aiming a pistol his way from behind an old trailer. The shotgun kicked against Ben's shoulder. The guy's head dropped out of sight. Ben racked the shotgun lightning-fast. *Ker-chunk*. Fired again, swept the man's legs out from under him with the second shot and racked it again and blew out his heart and lungs with the third as he went down.

A bullet skipped off the ground near Ben's feet and he danced away between the buildings, topping up the shotgun's magazine from the loose cartridges in his pockets. He kept moving, running back in the direction of the higher ground where he'd stashed the dead sentry's rifle. Hastily aimed gunfire followed him as he went. He whirled round and fired back from the hip, saw a bite-shaped chunk of masonry disappear from the corner of a building and the guy leaning out from behind it go down with a red flower spreading over his white T-shirt.

Ben kept running. He reached the tree stumps, threw himself down prone behind them in the tall yellow grass and switched weapons. The blunt instrument of a sawn-off shotgun was out of its depth at this distance, but the rifle was a scalpel. Scanning left to right with the ten-times magnification scope, with the gun mounted in the V of the tree stumps, he picked out running figures through the smoke. Still no sign of Ritter or Moon. He wondered where they were, and why not here. What was left of the loading crew was a disorganised rabble. Ben smoothly tracked the rifle after one of them, crucified him in the scope's fine cross hairs and squeezed the trigger. The .308 punched his shoulder

348

and his eardrums; Ben saw the red-pink mist of blood spray from his target and instantly moved on to acquire another in his sights. Fired again. Same result. Then the wind changed, and a sweeping pall of black smoke engulfed the battlefield that had been Big Bear Farm, obscuring everything from view.

Ben took his eye from the scope. Time to leave. Enough damage had been done.

For now.

Turning his back on the burning farm, he returned unnoticed to the place he'd hidden the car. As he walked down the track he checked through the wallet he'd taken from the sentry. Two hundred and eighty dollars cash, driver's licence and assorted cards. This guy was the kind of rent-a-thug who actually carried ID on a job. His name had been Dwayne S. Gulick. Next Ben did a quick inspection of Gulick's phone. There might be one or two contacts on there that could be useful to him.

On the way back through Adonis, he tried calling Erin. There was no reply, and her phone was turned off. He left a brief message asking her to call him. But something didn't feel right. He pulled over at the side of the road, got the Hyatt Regency front desk number from Google and called them to ask to be put through to Miss Lang in room 421. After a few moments, the receptionist informed him that Miss Lang had gone out.

A tingle of worry began to grow inside him, and he drove on more quickly.

Chapter Fifty-Five

Finn McCrory was alone at home, gnawing on a cold meat sandwich at the bar in the kitchen and still avoiding the office, even avoiding his campaign manager Theo Walsh, when he got the call that spoiled his lunch.

'I told you how it'd go down,' Ritter said. 'Hate to say it, but you shoulda listened to me.'

'You told me what?'

'You'd best sit, boss.'

'I am sitting. Spill it, goddamnit.'

'It's not good news, boss. I just got a call from Meagher up at Big Bear. Or what's left of it. Ain't much.'

Oh no. It couldn't be true. Finn plunged his head into his hand. His guts began to churn.

'Hope?' he said in a small voice.

'Who else? You got me and Moon sitting on our asses in fucking Crosbie Heights while he's doing exactly what I warned you he'd do.'

'Oh, Lord. When did this happen?'

'Just now. Minutes ago.'

'How bad is it?' First the cabin, now this. If Hope was involved, the answer was predictable enough.

'Couldn't be much worse. The trucks are blown to shit, along with everything in them and the entire stock. They're still draggin' bodies out of the wreckage. Twelve confirmed dead, three missing. It's only Meagher, Lukas and Strickman left, and Strickman's lost an ear.'

Strickman's missing ear was of small concern to Finn. His heart was rattling along like a train. 'Jesus Christ, how'd he get into the place? Who was on the gate?'

'Gulick had the watch. Looks like he never saw it coming. Hope slit'm from ear to ear. Took his wallet and his phone. Used his rifle to kill Hannigan and Stearns.'

A plug of hot bile rose up in Finn's throat, though not out of sympathy for Gulick or the others. He managed to swallow it back down again, only just.

'When you say there's *nothing* left—'

Any tiny glimmer of hopefulness was swiftly dashed by Ritter's reply. 'Sounds like what it is, boss. Meagher said the place looks like fuckin' Hiroshima.'

'Oh, Lord,' Finn repeated. His stomach didn't feel good at all. 'Where are you?'

'Still here clocking an empty house,' Ritter said pointedly. 'You want me and Moon to head down to Big Bear? Boss? Boss?'

Finn had hung up, in order to dash to the kitchen sink and let go of the rising tide that wouldn't be kept down any longer. He was violently sick twice, then gulped down a glass of water and a fistful of antacids and collapsed in a wicker chair. A cold sweat rippled down his body like witches 'fingers at the thought of his precious stock all gone, gone, blown to smithereens. But the cold sweat was nothing compared to the dread terror of what would happen when the Mexicans found out about this. Those guys were as paranoid as they were ruthless. They'd instantly suspect that the attack was the work of the DEA or the FBI – that a massive law enforcement operation was closing on a supplier it was now time

351

to cut their ties with. Cutting ties meant visits in the night. It meant carjacking, kidnapping and heaven knew what else. It meant slitting throats. Colombian neckties. Slow dismemberment. Blood-spattered shower curtains. Screaming horror and death.

Finn rose from his chair and made it to the kitchen sink before throwing up a third time. He splashed water in his face, screwed up his eyes and let out a miserable groan.

That was when the phone rang again. He wiped his chin and stared at it, thinking it must be Ritter calling with even worse news. Like the Mexicans were on their way already, armed with chainsaws and blowtorches. 'What the hell,' he croaked wretchedly, and picked up.

'Guess what I got for you,' said the gravelly voice of Liam O'Rourke, sounding uncharacteristically upbeat.

A small ray of sunshine beamed down over Finn McCrory as he listened to the news. O'Rourke's version of events naturally gave him all the credit for tracking down the Hayes woman and bringing her into custody.

'She's under arrest?'

'Sure, but I wouldn't worry about that. Paperwork can disappear, just like people can. The officer who booked her, he's my guy.'

Finn was beginning to smile as the black clouds overhead rapidly dissolved away to clear blue sky and he suddenly could see how he was going to get through this. It was a magnificent turnaround. The Hayes woman was no longer a threat, and soon neither would Ben Hope be. His secrets would be protected. He would survive. Even the Mexicans didn't seem like such a big deal. In his elation he quite believed that things would be smoothed out just fine. It was just a glitch. He'd come out on top, like always. He was Finn McCrory.

'What you want me to do with her?' O'Rourke asked.

The chief of police, at his beck and call, awaiting orders. Finn's smile widened. With the cabin and the farm gone, there was only one place he could keep his new hostage. Certainly not at the house, and the aircraft hangar was too public. Serendipity had provided a nice alternative.

'Bring the bitch up to the ranch,' he said.

O'Rourke hesitated. 'Arrowhead? Big Joe's place? Christ, Finn, you sure?'

Unbelievable. The old bastard managed to intimidate even Liam O'Rourke.

'He's out of the way for a couple days,' Finn said. 'Topeka. Seeing a man about a horse, I don't know what. Point is, we have the place to ourselves.'

O'Rourke seemed relieved to hear that Big Joe was two hundred miles away in Kansas. 'Okay. I'll take care of it personally.'

'Get rolling, chief. And bring as many of the boys as you can get hold of.'

'We expecting trouble?'

'Not that we can't handle,' McCrory said with a grin. 'Not any more.'

Chapter Fifty-Six

Ben tried again to call Erin's mobile as he crossed the line back into Tulsa County, then once more coming into the outskirts of Broken Arrow. Still no reply.

'Come on, answer the damn thing,' he said out loud.

Of all the things that worried him at the moment, it was Erin that worried him the most. The fact that she'd left the hotel when she'd been supposed to lie low there, and that she wasn't responding to her phone when she was meant to be waiting for his call. It wasn't like her.

The other two things on his mind were Ritter and Moon. Ben had little doubt that their not being present at Big Bear Farm that day had made his work there a lot easier. That was a plus. But now he'd lost his biggest tactical advantage – the element of surprise that had enabled him to strike hard and fast and get out again before the enemy had known what hit them. Now they knew he was coming, and they'd be waiting for him to make his next move, ready to respond with everything they had. That was a big negative.

Nor was Ben happy not knowing where Ritter and Moon were, especially now that Erin had strangely disappeared off his radar screen. Put all those concerns together, and they added up to a set of possibilities that he didn't like. He didn't like them one bit.

His jaw tightened and he pressed a little harder on the gas, shooting past slower cars and trucks to the throaty tune of the Barracuda's Hemi V8. The turnpike led straight into the heart of Tulsa. He'd be there in just a few minutes. Then he would see what he would see.

That was when the sudden shrill of the Dixie ringtone sounded in the car next to him. He glanced across to see that it was coming from the phone he'd taken from the sentry called Gulick, which was lying on the front passenger seat next to the dead man's wallet.

The phone kept ringing insistently. He hesitated, then reached over for it, thumbed the REPLY button and pressed it to his ear without saying anything.

'Hey there. How are you feeling on this fine sunny day?'

Ben's fist tightened on the steering wheel as he recognised McCrory's voice. He sounded bright and breezy, like a friend calling up for a catch-up chatter. His amicable tone gave Ben a chill.

'Congratulations, Mr Hope. You sure had some fun at my expense today, didn't you? I'll bet you had a ball. Yes, sir.'

Ben said nothing.

'Well, I just wanted to call and let you know that the fun ain't over,' said the cheery voice in his ear. 'In fact, it's just about to begin. We got ourselves some female company, me and the boys here. That lady friend of yours is quite something, isn't she?'

'Put her on,' Ben said. He felt numb. The road kept spooling towards him at ninety miles an hour.

McCrory laughed. 'Sorry, bud. She can't talk right now.'

'She'd better be all right.'

'Oh, we're taking good care of her. Don't you worry about that.'

'What do you want?'

'Why, just the pleasure of your acquaintance. I was thinking, how about you come and join us all here? We'll have ourselves a party. Talk things over. Kind of square things up, man to man.'

'Tell me where,' Ben said.

'Arrowhead Ranch. Out by Sand Springs. You'll know where to find it.'

'I'll see you there,' Ben said.

McCrory laughed again. 'Delighted to hear it. I'll be waiting. Put on a nice reception for you. Just like old pals.'

'Soon,' Ben said. He tossed the phone out of the car window and hit the gas harder.

Chapter Fifty-Seven

Finn McCrory smiled as the line went dead. He turned off his phone and tucked it into the pocket of the fancy hand-stitched jeans he was wearing, along with a cool white shirt and his favourite tooled cowboy boots. The jeans were tight around the middle, cinched with a silver-buckled alligator belt on which was riding his .44 Magnum Smith & Wesson revolver in a custom John Bianchi holster. The gun was a special order in mirror-finish nickel plate, with scroll engraving and cocobolo hardwood grips by Hogue, mono-grammed with his initials in mother-of-pearl. It felt pretty good there on his hip. Made him feel invulnerable.

It was a beautiful afternoon. Finn stood by his still-ticking Mercedes and gazed up at the sky, an unbroken azure dome above the green pastures of Arrowhead Ranch that stretched for miles in three directions, a world of peace and tranquillity as far from anything as a man could ever want to get. The thoroughbreds were grazing in their neatly fenced paddocks. The birds were singing in the old oak trees that pleasantly shaded the big whitewood century ranch house. Yes, a beautiful day – one that might not have started so well for him, but which was now turning out just fine.

Hadn't he said it? Hadn't it been his brainwave that the

woman was the key to getting Hope? Finn was pretty pleased with himself. And soon, very soon, the rest of the plan would fall into place as nice as pie.

An approaching dust cloud on the long private road that wound up to the ranch turned out to be the white GMC van. Finn walked out to greet it as it rolled up. Ritter and Moon sprang down from the cab while the side door slid open and Meagher, Lukas and Strickman got out. Strickman was wearing a thick makeshift bandage covering one ear and the side of his head, and looked like death. Moon's chest slogan for the day was 'I DON'T CALL 911'.

'This all you could get?' Finn asked them, surveying the crew through narrowed eyes. Never mind, it would be enough.

'This is all that's left,' Ritter said. 'She here?'

'Any time now,' Finn replied, and shielded his eyes with his hand to scan the horizon. Moments later, a second dust cloud appeared in the distance. They watched the two faraway cars turn off the road and grow steadily larger. Chief Liam O'Rourke's silver Mercury Grand Marquis led the way, followed by an unmarked Crown Victoria.

The cars crunched to a halt up next to the other vehicles. O'Rourke stepped out of the Mercury, jacketless in a shoulder holster rig and accompanied by fellow Irishman Mike Corcoran. Finn knew all three cops in the Crown Vic: Lou Wylie, Dixon Coyle and Cliff Duhame. All three were on his payroll.

Duhame got out of the back seat clutching their guest of honour by the arm. She was still protesting as violently as she'd been when they'd hauled her from her cell for an unauthorised ride out into the country.

'Spirited little thing, ain't she?' O'Rourke grunted.

Moon was almost salivating.

'Afternoon, Miss Hayes,' Finn said with a broad smile. 'Welcome to Arrowhead Ranch. Pleasure to have you with us.'

'Rot in hell!' Erin spat back at him.

'See what I mean?' O'Rourke said.

'She'll soon cool down.' Finn motioned to Ritter and Moon, who stepped forward and took Erin from Duhame, one arm each so that she was powerless to fight them. Finn led the way from the house to the stable block around the side. Most of them were unused nowadays, since the old man had laid off the ranch-hands and drastically scaled down his stock in latter years (hopefully a sign of age finally catching up). So was the brick-built tack-room at the end of the stable building. 'In there,' Finn said, and Ritter and Moon shoved Erin inside.

'See ya real soon, sugar tits,' Moon said to her, and then lolled his tongue obscenely.

The door banged shut and Finn double-bolted it, snapping the padlock shut and giving the key to Moon. 'You're the jailer.'

'My pleasure,' Moon said with a wolfish smile.

Back at the house, the mixed group of gangsters and bent cops were eyeing one another warily. 'Hope doesn't stand a chance,' Finn said, surveying his little defence force.

'So this Hope guy is the one who's been causing all the trouble, huh?' O'Rourke said.

Finn gave a dismissive wave. 'He's nothing.'

'He's a little more than that,' Ritter said. 'You called down the thunder. Storm's coming.'

'He won't be so tough when we start peeling his girl-friend's skin off,' Finn said.

'All the same, boss, I think you should find somewhere to take cover when he gets here.'

'You worry too much, Ritter.' Finn laughed, and the cops

laughed with him. But Finn stopped laughing before they did, and his hand found its way to rest on the butt of his revolver.

Ritter looked at his watch. 'He could be here any time. Dave, break out the gear.' Meagher nodded and opened up the back of the van. Coyle peered inside. 'Crap. You boys bring enough hardware?'

Moon tossed him an M4 battle rifle. 'Gonna need it. This guy ain't easy to kill.'

'Why, Billy Bob, I do believe you're afraid,' O'Rourke said. He and Moon had crossed paths on a few previous occasions.

'Up your ass,' Moon replied, giving him the finger. 'Sonofabitch I'd be afraid of ain't born yet, and his mother's dead.'

The next couple of minutes were taken up with the unloading of weapons from the van and the cars. Corcoran and Wylie had raided the police armoury for a couple of Remington twelve-gauge pumps. Everyone had brought their sidearms for backup, too. Conversation dropped to a minimum amid the pre-battle sound of magazines being loaded and inserted, bolts being clacked and general tooling up.

Moon smirked as all five cops put on their bulky Kevlar vests. 'Now who's pussy?'

'Let's go inside,' Finn said, ignoring him.

The interior of the ranch house was traditional Okie, the way the old man had designed it. He liked big rooms, big furniture, sumptuously varnished wood and acres of steer-hide leather. The walls were decorated with mounted animal heads, racks of antlers and pictures of Big Joe posing with all manner of stuff he'd killed on scores of hunting trips. An original Wells Fargo stagecoach wheel had been made into a chandelier. A section of the enormous living room was fashioned after a western saloon bar, complete with cow horns and a spittoon. Cherokee spears and tomahawks hung above doorways and antique six-guns and Winchesters were everywhere. Finn had grown up with all that Roy Rogers shit and didn't even look at it. He threw himself into a deep leather couch while the others stood around or sat in chairs or leaned against the walls, biding their time.

They waited. And waited. Finn got up and began pacing. Ritter sat completely immobile with a blank thousand-yard stare, nursing his rifle as if it were a part of his flesh. Moon smacked gum and thought about Erin Hayes.

'How 'bout a drink?' Coyle suggested, eyeing the spirits cabinet. It was hot sitting about in those damn bulletproof vests.

'I'd stay sharp if I was you,' Ritter said, without moving his eyes.

More time passed, and nothing happened. The sun sank in the west and the sky turned golden-red and then purple.

'Why ain't he here yet?' Mike Corcoran asked. Nobody replied.

Evening slowly merged into night, the stars came out. Still nothing. They drew the blinds so that Hope couldn't see inside the house. A coyote yipped and howled in the distance and Coyle and Duhame exchanged uneasy glances. The cops hadn't reckoned on this. They had anxious wives and hot dinners and TV and warm beds waiting for them at home. The silence and the waiting had them rattled.

'Maybe he ran,' Finn said, breaking another long, tense silence. 'Hell, maybe he won't come at all.'

'He'll come,' Ritter said.

Twenty more minutes had passed before they saw the approaching car lights shining brightly through the gaps in the blinds. Everyone moved nearer the window, tense, listening hard. Soon afterwards, they heard the growl of a big V8 getting closer.

'This is it, boys,' O'Rourke said, assuming command as befitted his rank. 'He's here.'

Chapter Fifty-Eight

'I don't believe it,' Wylie said, watching through the blinds as the lights drew steadily closer. 'He's just driving right up to the house. Fucker's as bold as brass.'

'Guy's got some balls, gotta give'm that,' O'Rourke muttered. He had beads of sweat breaking out on his brow. He puffed out his chest. 'All right. Let's take care of business.'

O'Rourke drew his Colt Python from the shoulder rig. Corcoran racked a round into the chamber of his Remington pump with that bright, crunchy *snick-snack* that had put the fear into a million hearts. Moon quietly pressed off the safety of his M4 and swapped glances with Ritter. Both thinking the same thing. *Fuckin' cops.* On another day, they wouldn't have hesitated to gun down the whole stinking bunch and do themselves and the world a favour. The people you had to work with.

'What the hell's he doing?' Finn murmured, watching from another window. But as the dazzling lights drew up close to the house and he recognised the vehicle, he deflated like a punctured ball.

The Dodge Ram.

It wasn't Hope. Big Joe was back.

'Oh, shit,' Finn said under his breath.

He watched, paralysed, as the pickup truck stopped

outside. The lights and engine died. The old man got out, showing no apparent stiffness after his long drive from Kansas. He was in his travelling clothes, jeans and denim jacket, and had a sling bag over his shoulder. He lingered for a moment to stare at the four vehicles parked outside his house, and Finn saw his face crease up into a deep, dark frown that Finn had seen before.

'Oh, shit,' he said again. He swallowed.

The sound of the front door opening; heavy, deliberate footsteps in the hall. Then Big Joe walked into the room, stopped and glared from under beetling white brows at his son and the armed men inside his house.

'I thought you were in Topeka,' was all Finn could think to say at first.

'What the hell's this?'

'Let's go in the other room, Daddy,' Finn said, stepping over and anxiously taking his elbow to steer him back through the doorway. Big Joe resisted, then emitted a long, low sound like a snarl and let Finn guide him across the hall to the room opposite, which Big Joe used as a TV lounge.

Big Joe looked grim. 'I come home early and there's a bunch of gorillas with guns in my house. You owe me an explanation. Let's have it.'

'It's none of your concern, Daddy. I got some business to take care of, that's all. You keep out of the way, now, before you go and get yourself hurt.'

'Don't you Daddy me. What business? You wouldn't know business if it crept up and chewed your butt off.'

'Now listen, Daddy—'

'I want these people out of my home right now.'

Finn flushed. 'No way.'

'What did you say?'

'I said no way. This is a meeting. These are my associates.'

'Associates,' Big Joe said, clenching his teeth. He gripped Finn's arm. 'Associates my ass. You think I never saw a bunch of cheap hoods before?'

'That's the police chief in there.'

'Exactly. You think I'm blind, boy? Think I can't see what this is?'

The hold the old man had on Finn's arm felt like a steel pincer. 'Let go.' Finn wrenched his arm free and backed away.

'What's the matter with you?' his father seethed at him. 'What the hell are you into? This what I brought you up to be? A goddamn criminal?'

Finn felt something break inside him and the anger gushed out. 'Oh, it was easy for you. You made something of yourself. What about me? How'm I supposed to make my way, with your reputation hanging over me? You ever stop to think about that?'

'I always knew you were a coward and a cheat. Now you're fixin' to kill a man right here in my own home. That's what this is, right? An ambush.'

'I—'

'This is what you call your business. This is what you do when my back is turned. Don't lie to me, boy!'

'He – he knows our secret, Daddy. I did everything I could, but he knows. I can't let it go any further.'

Big Joe's eyes bugged in fury. 'So that's it. You opened your big mouth. You let it out.'

'No! I—'

'Not a soul,' the old man rasped. 'Not a living soul ever knew. I've been keepin' it locked up like the holy of holies since twenty years before you were even born. Now you just up and spill it right out. You got horseshit for brains, son? Don't you know what's gonna happen to you if folks know the truth about our family?' His big fists were clenched as he advanced on Finn.

Finn unholstered the revolver from his belt. 'I've taken enough abuse from you. All my life you've been putting me down.'

Big Joe showed him yellow teeth as he kept on coming. 'I put you down, boy, you won't be getting back up again.'

'Don't you come any closer, you hear me? Back off!' Finn pointed the gun and thumbed the hammer.

But Big Joe just glanced disdainfully at the revolver. He seemed eight feet tall. A granite mountain looming over Finn, ready to fall on him like a million tons of rock. 'What the hell are you going to do with that? You gonna smoke me? You gonna ventilate the old man with your roscoe? Huh? Show us all what a big tough guy you are? Huh?' He kept prodding Finn in the chest, shoving him back harder each time.

'I'm warning you . . .'

Big Joe regarded him with pure disgust, as if he could spit blood at the very sight of him. 'You shame me, Finn McCrory. I shoulda strangled you the day they pulled you out of your momma, God rest her soul.'

Finn's back was against the wall. He could retreat no further—

Big Joe lunged to wrench the gun from Finn's hand—

The stunning BOOM of the magnum seemed to drive all the air out of the room. For a terrible moment, Big Joe stood rocking on his feet, staring in speechless apoplectic disbelieving rage at his son who'd just shot him. Then his eyes rolled down and he saw the blood. He staggered back a step. One knee buckled first, then the other, and Big Joe twirled and hit the polished floor face first with a crash almost as loud as the gunshot.

Finn stared down at him. Stared at the revolver in his hand.

The door burst open. Ritter ran into the room, stopped and looked down at the inert hulk of Big Joe.

'I didn't kill'm,' Finn said, talking loudly like a deaf person over the ringing whine in his ears. 'Hope did. We all saw it, right? Hope came here and murdered a defenceless old man. You're a witness, Ritter.'

Ritter said nothing.

The blast of a second gunshot made them turn. It had come from the other room.

Chapter Fifty-Nine

Ritter ran back across the hall, Finn behind him still clutching the handgun. Everyone in the other room was on their feet and staring either at the shattered window overlooking the front of the house, or at Mike Corcoran who was standing there with the pump-action levelled towards the broken glass, smoke oozing from its barrel.

'What happened?' Ritter said.

Corcoran wet his lips with his tongue, still pointing the shotgun at the window. 'I saw something. Outside. A movement.'

'You thought you did.'

Corcoran shook his head. 'No, man. I saw it. A shape. Just for a moment.'

'Could've been some animal,' O'Rourke muttered.

Ritter drew his pistol and stepped to the window, carefully drew aside the shredded blind and peered out through the jagged remains of the pane. He could see nothing out there except darkness. Maybe they were just jumping at shadows. Maybe not.

The silence outside was disconcerting. If Hope was here, he could be anywhere around the house.

'What was the shootin' in there?' O'Rourke asked, pointing towards the other room.

'Forget it,' Ritter told the chief with a sharp look. 'And keep your voice down.' O'Rourke was no longer in command, if he ever had been. Ritter took charge as effortlessly as breathing. 'Dave, hit the lights. You, you and you' – pointing at Corcoran, Wylie and Duhame – 'I want you at the front of the house. Spread out, keep to the shadows, shoot anything that moves. It starts to kick off, do not leave your position.' He turned to Meagher, Lukas and Strickman. 'You three cover the rear.'

'I'll stay here,' O'Rourke whispered, taking up position near the window. 'In case he tries to get inside.'

Meagher switched off the lights. The milky light filtered in through the blinds, the sudden darkness turning them all into dark silhouettes. Ritter liked the dark. It was his element. He turned and gestured to Moon, an unspoken command that was clearer than daylight between them. It meant 'go check on the woman', and it was music to Billy Bob.

Moon tapped Coyle on the shoulder. 'You come with me, copper.'

Corcoran, Wylie and Duhame picked up their weapons and headed outside to guard the front, while Moon led Coyle around to the rear.

Ritter led McCrory aside, speaking low. 'I can't stay with you, boss. Is there someplace you can close yourself in?'

'The old man's study.' Finn was shaking with nervous excitement, not even so much because of Hope, but because of the realisation sinking in of what he'd just done. The thought hit him that it was *his* study now.

'Show me the way,' Ritter told him.

Finn led Ritter up the hall to the broad wooden staircase, then up it and through the rambling house to the south-facing study at the far end. The moonlight from the window shone dimly on the old man's desk, the fireplace behind it and the six-point deer antlers that hung on the wall above.

'Lock yourself in,' Ritter told him. 'You hear shooting, stay put. Anyone comes through that door . . .'

'I have this.' Finn patted the holster on his belt. It was the same gun he'd shot Blaylock with. Ritter knew he wasn't afraid to pull a trigger.

'Keep the light off,' Ritter said, and left.

'Kill him good,' Finn called after him.

The ranch house was filled with a silence that could almost be touched. Like a chill, thick mist had descended on the place, shutting it off entirely from the outside world. Ritter was tingling with the thought of what was coming. The seconds counted down like chimes inside his head.

As he reached the bottom of the stairs, the silence finally ended. The triple gunshot came from outside. A pause, then two more blasts.

Front of the house.

Ritter moved fast up the hallway to the door. Outside, he found Wylie and Duhame standing under the shadows of the oak trees, guns waving left and right as if every pocket of darkness held a threat. Ritter saw the Remington 870 pump lying on the ground. Corcoran's.

'Mike's gone,' Wylie said, breathing hard. 'He was right there next to me, and then he was gone, just like that.'

'Didn't you see anything? You must've seen something.'

Wylie's eyes glistened in the darkness. He swallowed audibly. 'I didn't see or hear a goddamned thing. He was there and then he wasn't.'

'Like a fuckin' ghost took him,' Duhame muttered.

Ritter glanced around him into the deep darkness. The cop wouldn't be far away, dead in the bushes. Ritter didn't believe in ghosts. He knew what had taken Corcoran, and Hope was already somewhere else.

Ritter had hunted men all his life. Nobody could escape him.

His eyes narrowed. Was that a movement up along the side of the house? He stared hard, at the darkness. He was certain that part of the shadows had shifted. Black moving on black. Ritter didn't want to use a flashlight and betray his own position. The dark could work for you as much as against you. That was why he loved it.

Ritter turned back to Wylie, and whispered close in his ear, 'Behind me. Single file, three yards apart. Not a sound.'

They moved up the side of the house towards where Ritter thought he'd seen the movement. Ritter led the way, light and quiet as a panther, then Wylie, then Duhame. Ritter could almost hear Wylie's thudding heart a few steps behind.

He flinched as the crunch of a snapping twig came from the rear. All those times he'd led US Special Forces patrols through enemy territory in the total confidence that none of his men would leave the slightest sign of their passing; now he was in charge of a bunch of keystone cops who advertised their presence with a sound trail like a fuckin' rhino. He glared back in anger, and saw Wylie's pallid face behind him in the darkness. Ritter put his finger to his lips. Wylie shook his head, as if to say 'it wasn't me'.

Ritter's eyes narrowed. He peered past Wylie's shoulder, at where Duhame had been tagging along behind them just a moment ago.

Duhame was gone.

Ritter spun back, brushed by Wylie, then stopped after five yards and looked down.

Duhame was lying sprawled out with his face in the dirt. Ritter dropped into a crouch and rolled the cop over. His larynx had been crushed and his neck was broken.

Ritter felt himself go cold. That was a feeling he hadn't had in a long, long time. He looked into the shadows and felt them looking back at him.

I know you're there.

Wylie saw the body and drew in a sharp intake of breath. 'Jesus Christ. What the fuck—?'

'He's hunting us,' Ritter said.

Then the lights came on inside the house.

Ritter ran back to the door, not even caring if Wylie was with him or not. The front hallway was lit up, as was the room with the blown-out window where they'd all been waiting earlier.

O'Rourke had never left it. But it wasn't him who'd put the lights on. He was sitting in an armchair with a Cherokee tomahawk buried in his skull. The blood pool at his feet was still slowly spreading, catching the lights' reflection.

Ritter sensed Wylie enter the room behind him, heard the gasp of shock. Wylie just wasn't used to this kind of stuff. He was going to have to learn fast.

'Don't move,' Ritter told him, and left the cop standing there open-mouthed while he moved quickly back out of the room and up the hallway to the stairs, turning off the light as he went.

He reached the door of the study and rapped with his fist.

'Who's that?' came the nervous voice from inside.

'Just checkin', boss. Stay tight.'

Before McCrory could reply, Ritter's head whipped round at the percussive single *boom* of the gunshot downstairs. He sprinted back down the staircase, back down the hallway and into the room.

Wylie had moved, but only as far as the shotgun blast had blown him. He was sprawled backwards over the bar with half his head gone. Blood was drip-drip-dripping off the edge of the bar and into the spittoon on the floor.

Ritter whirled around at the sound of approaching footsteps in the hall, raised his rifle to point it at the door, then lowered it as Strickman, Lukas and Meagher came into the room.

'Yeugh,' Lukas said at the sight of the dead cops.

'Told you not to leave your positions,' Ritter said. 'Where's Moon?'

Chapter Sixty

The stable block was dark. Billy Bob Moon reached into his pocket for the key McCrory had given him, shone his torch on the tack-room door and popped open the padlock. He undid the top bolt, then the lower, opened the door a crack and shone his torch inside, peering in after it. 'Li'l pig, li'l pig, let me in,' he said softly.

Erin was sitting in the corner, her back against the white-washed wall, her knees drawn up and her arms wrapped around her shins. She looked up in fear and defiance, blinking at the light beam playing on her face, and Moon had a stab of pleasure when he saw she'd been crying.

'Told ya I'd be back, angel wings.' He pulled the torch back to hold it under his chin, flashed her a demonic smile, then withdrew his head from the crack in the door and turned to Coyle. 'I'll be a couple of minutes. Keep your eyes open and your fuckin' ears shut. Know what I mean?'

'Nobody said anything about this, bro,' Coyle said, getting the message.

'Ain't your bro, copper.' Moon grinned at him. 'S'matter, you worried you won't get a piece when I'm done?' He stepped inside the tack-room and shut the door.

'Together at last,' he said, shining the torch in her eyes.

Erin rose blinking to her feet, but before she could make

a sound or a move, he rushed her and stunned her with a blow to the neck, then punched her in the face. Her head flopped back and he caught her as she fell. Moon helped himself to a good, long feel as he lowered her to the floor. 'Oh, yes,' he breathed. 'You and me. Sweet baby.'

'Everything all right in there?' Coyle's voice said from outside.

'Shut it,' Moon snapped back.

He knelt beside her, unslung his M4 and laid it on the floor, then positioned the torch so that its beam shone across her body. Reaching behind his hip, he drew the black USMC Ka-Bar knife from its leather sheath.

Sitting holding a knife over the yielding body of a woman was such a good feeling. Moon pushed the point of the knife in between the buttons of her blouse and angled it so he could peer inside, giving himself a sneak preview of what was to come. Nice. Very nice.

The knife froze in his hand for an instant as multiple gunshots sounded, muffled by distance and the buildings.

'Something's happening,' Coyle said.

Moon heaved a sigh and twisted his head round to bark, 'Hear your voice one more time, dude, I swear.' He'd waited too long for this to be distracted. Ritter could handle things out there.

Moon slashed a strip of cloth from Erin's shirt with the razor-sharp blade and used it to tie a gag around her mouth. The knife was no longer needed, for now. As he was slipping it back in its sheath, he heard more distant gunfire; a single shot this time, the fat low boom of a twelve-gauge that sounded like it had come from the house. Moon paused, detecting the sound of Coyle moving about nervously behind the tack-room door. This time the cop had the good sense to keep his mouth shut.

'See, they got'm,' Moon muttered under his breath. 'Nothing to get all jacked up about.'

He had better things to do. Oh, so much better. He ran a hand up along the curve of the unconscious woman's thigh and hip, savouring the moment, taking his time. The hand continued upwards, slithering over her. It reached her shoulder then moved across her throat, lingered there for a second as he wondered what it would be like to strangle her when she was still unconscious, totally yielding and passive. That was something he'd never tried before. Then he could do her when she was dead: which was something he'd only done once before, and enjoyed; but it was hard to decide whether it would be more fun than doing her while she was awake and fighting back, and *then* strangling her. Or using the knife on her.

So many options. These were the kinds of fundamental questions that generally preoccupied much of his thinking. Whatever he chose, nobody would mind. Why hold on to the bait now that the fish were biting?

He decided to do her while she was still alive, then use the knife. There'd be others. His hand continued moving. Very slowly, he undid one button of her blouse. He ran his tongue over his lips. Undid another button, inserted a finger and drew the soft cotton back a little so he could see the lacy material of her bra. 'Ooh. Baby. Uncle Moon's gonna give you some lovin'.' He moved down to the next button.

'There's something—' Coyle began outside the door, but never finished.

Moon heard a thud. 'Damn it, I told you to keep quiet!' he yelled.

Something hammered the door, hard. Moon snapped his body up and away from the woman on the floor, snatched up his torch, stepped furiously to the door and wrenched it open to shine the light in Coyle's face and aim a punch through it, knocking the fucker's teeth out for disturbing him.

No Coyle.

Moon stepped out of the tack-room, shone the torch up the aisle that ran alongside the stalls. 'Hey cop, where'd you go?'

No reply. Coyle must have gone back to join the others.

'Fuck'm,' Moon said, only mildly disappointed that he wouldn't get to kill the guy after he'd done with the woman. He'd been toying with the idea for a couple of hours, for no other particular reason than he didn't like Coyle's face. And he was a cop. It had been a while since he'd iced a cop. Somehow it was more fun than killing real people. Killing a bent cop was even better. What could anyone do about it? Call the police? Moon thought that was hilarious.

He turned back inside the tack-room and something hit him a slamming blow to the face. His vision exploded white and he was suddenly on his back, trying to look up through the mist of stars. Blood filled his mouth and nose.

The man standing over him seemed to have appeared from nowhere, as if he'd risen out of the ground.

Chapter Sixty-One

Ben had checked Erin's pulse and removed the gag. She was unconscious. Her lip was cut from the blow that had knocked her cold. But she was alive. Less could be said for Billy Bob Moon, a few moments from now.

'Look at me, Moon,' Ben said. 'You know who I am, don't you?' He pointed the sawn-off shotgun in Moon's face.

Moon blinked, spat blood, and his teeth bared in a red grin. 'Sonofabitch.'

'I knew I'd find you here, Moon,' Ben said. 'I smelled you. Stand up.'

Moon was hurt, but not that hurt. He was on his feet quickly, knees slightly bent, every muscle tensed ready to fight. 'You gonna shoot me, better do it quick.'

Ben tossed the gun down and touched the hilt of the trench knife in his belt, without drawing it. He shook his head. 'You already know what it feels like to be on the handle end of one of these. Now you're going to find out what it feels like going in.'

Moon spat again. 'Think I've never been cut before?'

'This'll be the last time. That's a promise.'

'Takes more than some drunk to get the drop on ol' Billy Bob.' Moon grinned bloodily. 'Hey, stumble fuck. Where's your bottle? How about I slice your fuckin' arms and legs off and have you eat your girlfriend's liver? Wash it down with some nice corn whiskey.'

Ben just looked at him.

Moon began to laugh, then cut the laughter short to whip out the Ka-Bar and lunge forwards in a quick two-step round-house slash that would have caught most men off guard, even some well-trained soldiers. He was rattlesnake-fast, but Ben was so far ahead of the curve that he knew what Moon was going to do even before Moon did. He stepped out of the arc of the strike, took Moon's wrist and mashed the nerves in his hand that made his fingers let go of the knife. At the same time, Ben's elbow crashed into Moon's face. Moon staggered, but Ben still had his arm, so he could only stagger in a circle as Ben drew the trench knife from his belt.

Ben gripped the knuckleduster hilt tightly and popped Moon in the face with it. Moon was blinded by pain and didn't see the strike coming or try to block it with his free arm. The spiked steel handguard hit him full on with all the force Ben could put behind it. Moon's nose became a bloody bubbled pulp crushed up beneath his left eye. Ben hit him again, just as hard, and smashed his jaw and followed through and felt his teeth give. Then he hit him again, and again. *Crack.* Cheekbone. *Crack.* Eye socket.

Moon fell, hitting the floor on his back. Ben still had the arm. He pressed Moon's elbow against his knee and bent it the way it had never been meant to go, with a crackling and splintering that was drowned out by Moon's gurgling scream. Ben let go of his broken arm, caught the other and did the same to that one. Moon wasn't screaming any longer. He was squealing like a pig. Ben pressed the sole of his boot against Moon's throat, pinning him down hard and choking off the sound. He leaned down and looked into the man's ruined face.

'Kristen Hall,' he said.

Then he pushed the tip of the trench knife into the soft flesh under Moon's chin and rammed it through his broken jaw, through his tongue and palate and up through bone until it pierced deep inside his brain. Ben watched the eyes roll back and the light in them go out. He jerked and twisted the blade free, wiped it clean on Moon's 'I DON'T CALL 911' T-shirt and slipped it back into its scabbard. He felt nothing as he stepped away from the dead man, no anger, no satisfaction. What was done was done. Ben picked up Moon's rifle and hung it over his left shoulder from its two-point tactical sling, then grabbed his shotgun and slung it over the other.

Erin was still out cold, but her pulse felt normal and her breathing was regular. He couldn't leave her here. Ben scooped her gently up in his arms and carried her out of the stable block. He passed the stall where he'd dragged the body of the man who'd been with Moon, paused at the entrance, looked left and right. The enemy were six men down. By Ben's calculations he still had three more of McCrory's soldiers to deal with.

Not including Ritter. Ritter was the worry.

Ben felt exposed as he retraced his steps past the house, expecting a bullet in the back at any moment. He already knew where he was taking her, and had the keys in his pocket. It wasn't the perfect hiding place, but it was the best he could do for the moment. Reaching the Dodge Ram parked at the front of the house, he supported Erin's weight on one arm and shoulder, opened the back passenger door and eased her limp form inside. Even in bright daylight, she couldn't have been seen through the dark-tinted glass.

He was certain that she'd come to within the next few minutes and was sorry he couldn't be with her when she awoke, confused and disorientated, in a strange new place. He shut the door silently and clunked the central locking with the key fob. Another button allowed him to remotely disarm the alarm system. He was concerned that if she woke up and moved around inside the cab, or tried the door, she'd set off the siren.

'I'll be back for you,' he promised her, even if she couldn't hear him.

He slipped away.

Back inside the hallway of the ranch house, Ben looked in the door to his right. The tall grey-haired man was still sitting there with the Indian tomahawk buried in his brain. Not all household ornaments made such useful improvised weapons. The one with half his head missing was still slumped over the bar. Nobody else was around. Ben moved back into the hallway. To his left, a pool of blood was spreading out from underneath a closed door. He opened it a crack, smearing the blood along the floor like thick paint. A dead arm lay stretched out in the blood on the other side of the door. The man who owned it was big and old and looked a lot like Joe McCrory. That accounted for the shot Ben had heard coming from inside the house earlier. He didn't know why they'd killed the old man. But Joe might have been a problem for Ben, and if he was dead, that just made things easier for him.

Ben moved on. He needed to find McCrory Junior. He knew that Finn was here, because the green Mercedes SL-class was here. Ritter would want to protect his boss when the trouble kicked off, perhaps not out of love or loyalty but certainly to keep the gravy train rolling. Where would you hide such an important non-combatant in a big house like this? Not on the ground floor. Somewhere as far away from the action as possible.

Ben walked to the staircase at the end of the dark hallway and tested his weight on the first step. It creaked in the middle but not at the side, so he kept to the edge. From a landing, the stairs switched back 180 degrees for another flight. At the top, a broad passage led from the upper landing, with doors either side. More dead animal heads with glassy eyes adorned the walls. Ben didn't know if he could have lived in a house filled with the things he'd killed looking at him like that.

He made his way along the passage, checking doors left and right. He was checking the fourth door along, which opened onto a spare bedroom, when he heard something and stopped, head cocked, listening. It was the soft creak of at least three men stalking up the stairs after him.

McCrory's soldiers were back inside the house.

Chapter Sixty-Two

Ben ducked inside the bedroom. He stood close to the door and listened in the darkness to the footsteps reach the top of the stairs and come padding along the passage. He heard doors being opened and shut, each room being checked the way he'd been doing himself. As each door closed, the footsteps came closer and he could hear them more clearly. He reckoned on four men.

Now they reached the bedroom he was in. The steps paused outside. A ray of torchlight licked along the gap at the bottom of the door. Ben thought he heard the faintest whisper.

The handle began to turn.

Ben stepped back, pointed the shotgun from the hip at the middle of the door and slam-fired three rounds of buckshot into it as fast as he could work the slide while keeping the trigger held back. The muzzle flash lit up the huge ragged hole where the centre panel of the door had been.

Through the ringing in his ears, Ben heard running steps heading back towards the stairs. Just one man. He dropped a slug round straight into the Ithaca's breech, rammed the pump into battery and swivelled on his feet to chase the runner like a trap shooter chasing a moving clay. With a Brenneke slug, it didn't matter that there was a wall between him and the target. The gun boomed and kicked hard against his shoulder, and a crater exploded in the wall showering plaster back at him.

Something tumbled down the stairs. Ben rushed for the shattered door and wrenched it open. He jumped over the three splayed-out, piled-up bodies lying on the other side and raced towards the stairs, plucking more buckshot cartridges from his pocket as he went and thumbing them inside the shotgun's magazine tube. To his right was the huge hole in the wall where his slug had gone through. To his left on the opposite wall was a splat of dark blood. More blood on the stairs. Ben chased down them after his wounded target, reached the first landing and then had to pull back as gunfire sprayed up the stairwell, ripping shreds out of the heavy oak banister. Ben shoved the Ithaca between the stair rails and loosed four buckshot loads in the direction the shots had come from.

The firing went silent. Ben waited, perfectly still in the darkness. He was good at waiting. A minute passed. Then another. No sound from below.

When he was satisfied, he returned up the passage towards the three dead men. There was a lot of blood on the floor and the wall opposite the shattered door. Even in the gloom, he could see that flying splinters had done as much damage as the shotgun blasts. He stepped back over the bodies and walked on.

He checked from room to room until he found the locked door. He twisted the handle. Solid wood. Not the kind of door that could be broken down with a kick or two.

'Ritter?' said a voice inside. McCrory's voice.

When Ben didn't answer, McCrory opened fire from inside. Three splintered bullet holes opened up in the thick wood.

Ben reeled back from the door. Whatever McCrory was packing in there, he didn't want any. But his gun was bigger. He popped another Brenneke into the Ithaca's breech, then rammed the muzzle against the door lock and fired. It was the way military entry teams breached closed doors, and Ben hadn't seen a lock yet that didn't burst into pieces under that kind of punishment.

Finn McCrory ducked for cover as the door blew open with such force that it crashed against the wall. By the time he'd straightened up and pointed the .44 Magnum, Ben was already inside the room and right on him. He snatched the big, heavy revolver out of McCrory's hands and smacked him hard across the face with the butt end. McCrory cried out and staggered back against a desk.

The study was decked out in much the same style as the rest of the ranch house. A traditional brass and green glass banker's lamp threw out light from the desk. A leather captain's chair stood between it and a tall fireplace. Above that hung a big rack of antlers mounted on a shield. Resting across the antlers was an old Winchester lever-action hunting rifle that presumably had been responsible for the trophy.

Ben hardly noticed any of it. He saw the beach in Ireland. Kristen running from the men McCrory had sent to kill her. He pictured her in his mind the way Moon and Ritter had left her lying there on the rocks.

'No,' McCrory said. His eyes were big and round. He raised his hands as if he thought he could stop a twelve-gauge round from the gun Ben was pointing at his face.

I'm not an executioner, Ben had told Kurzweil.

But in McCrory's case, he was willing to make an exception.

He worked the pump on the shotgun, the way he'd done a thousand times before. *Clack*: the rearward movement for the extractor claw to get a grip on the rim of the fired case, draw it back out of the chamber and fling it away as waste material out of the ejector port. *Clack*: the forward movement to chamber the next round as it was pushed up out of the magazine tube.

But something felt wrong. The pump wouldn't go back forwards. The action wouldn't close, because something was stopping the round from chambering. The empty had failed to eject.

Classic pump-action stoppage. Every cop and soldier who'd ever received firearms training was schooled in how to fix the jam. It was something talked about in classrooms but which very seldom actually happened in the field. A one in a million chance. Just one of those things, like a flat tyre or a dead battery. Except it was very liable to get you killed.

Ben could either clear the jam by ramming the gun's butt vertically down against the floor, or he could toss the weapon and bring into play the rifle he'd taken from Moon, which was still slung behind his back. Neither option was something you could do in less than two or three seconds, and two or three seconds was all the time Finn McCrory needed to see that his opponent was in trouble. McCrory looked startled for an instant, then stumbled around the back of the desk, almost fell over the captain's chair and made a grab for the Winchester hunting rifle that rested on the deer antlers above the fireplace.

McCrory worked the lever. No malfunctions there. Just the unmistakable sound of a well-oiled rifle action chambering a long, high-powered cartridge. It looked as if Big Joe liked to keep his guns loaded.

McCrory grinned and levelled the gun at Ben's head.

Chapter Sixty-Three

Staring down the wrong end of the Winchester's octagonal barrel, Ben dropped the shotgun.

'Long gun too,' said Finn McCrory.

Ben unslung the M4 and let it fall.

'And the rest,' Finn said.

Ben drew the trench knife out of its scabbard and thought about throwing it at McCrory. But of all the knives in the world, none could have been less suited to throwing. The weight of the big steel knuckleduster would pull it completely out of balance as it flew. Whereas McCrory only had to flick a finger and Ben was as dead as the deer who'd donated his antlers for Big Joe's wall.

Ben dropped the knife.

Finn's eyes glittered. 'So you thought you'd come in here and shoot me, did you, dipshit?'

'You have it coming, McCrory.'

'You're talking about the girl, right? Kristen Hall?'

'Surprised you even remember her name,' Ben said.

'You think I wanted that to happen? Think I wanted her dead?'

'I'm sure she left you no choice,' Ben said.

'That's how I see it. Anyone in my position would've done the same thing.'

'Of course. You're just a normal guy.'

'You think I should've paid her off? You think she'd have gone away? Forget it. No chance. She'd've bled me dry.'

'She was the one who did all the bleeding,' Ben said.

'Everyone has secrets, Hope. Just happens I have more than most people, and your friend knew way too much about them.' Finn smiled at Ben over the rifle sights. 'But what am I saying? You do too, don't you?'

'It was Kristen who worked most of it out,' Ben said. 'All I did was fill in the gaps. I think she picked up on the name McCrory from her history research, and connected it with this up-and-coming US politician she must have read about, who was getting so much mileage out of his grandfather escaping Ireland and becoming a success in America. Good human-interest angle, McCrory. But you should've kept your big mouth shut. It was the dates that gave you away.'

Finn chuckled. 'Is that a fact?'

'Yes it is, because Kristen dug deeper and found out from the birth records in Glenfell that the real Padraig McCrory, a simple Irish stable hand who worked on the Glenfell Estate, was born in 1809. He'd have been a hundred and seven years old when your father was born. Biologically impossible. It didn't add up, and Kristen was the kind of journalist who likes to get their facts straight. When she contacted you initially, she just wanted to tidy up the details. She told you about the anomaly with the dates in the parish records. You could have brushed it off so easily. But instead you flipped, because that's the kind of stupid arsehole you are. That just raised her suspicions and made her dig deeper. By the time she contacted you again, she knew the truth and challenged you with it. By doing that, she made herself a target. Because you had so very much to lose if the truth came out, didn't you, McCrory?'

Finn's jaw tightened and his eyes narrowed. His finger twitched on the trigger of the Winchester.

'That's how she found out who your real grandfather was,' Ben said.

'Really. You know that, do you?'

'He was born in 1822. That still makes him a very old man when his only son was conceived, but then, your family are a long-lived bunch. His real name was Edgar Stamford.'

Finn cracked another smile and shook his head. 'I'm impressed, Hope. Truly, I am. You get the cigar. That's right. Who'd have thought that my granddaddy was a blue-blooded lord?'

'That's not all he was, is it?' Ben said. 'He was a bully and a coward who enjoyed having people beaten and hanged, who abused his servants and tormented his wife. Then he murdered the real Padraig McCrory and stole his identity, so that he could fake his own death and escape to America before the things he'd done would catch up with him. *That's* what you're descended from. Funny how your genetics will catch up with you.'

Finn's smile didn't waver. 'Got me all sussed out, don't you? That's what the family legend says, all right. My daddy didn't know it himself until 1937. My grandmother Charlotte waited sixteen years, 'til he was twenty-one, before she told him what ol' "Padraig" had told her on his deathbed. His final confession. Or did you know that as well, you limey smartass?'

'Does the family legend mention what your granddaddy Stamford had been cooking up in his lab with his crony Heneage Fitzwilliam?' Ben asked. 'The disease agent that Elizabeth Stamford discovered by accident and wrote about in her journal? *Phytophthora infestans*. They engineered it. Cultivated it. Contaminated the potato crop with it.'

Finn nodded slowly. 'Oh, sure. That *is* part of the family legend. I don't mind telling you, seeing as I'm gonna kill you pretty soon anyway. The old bastard spilled the whole story out when he was rat-ass drunk one day. Told me everything. I must've been twenty-six, twenty-seven.'

'It must have come as quite a shock to discover that your grandfather was a cold-blooded mass murderer responsible for implementing a deliberate plan of genocide against the Irish people and causing up to two million deaths,' Ben said. 'And that he was a British government spook.'

'There's no goddamn proof of that part,' Finn said, flushing.

'Wrong,' Ben said. 'Kristen hadn't figured that part out yet. But I did. After Elizabeth Stamford got back on her feet in England, in 1851 she went to consult a London lawyer called Abraham Barnstable. A real high-flyer. I think it was to tell him what her former husband had been involved in, and that she intended to spill the beans. That was her big mistake. She didn't know that Barnstable was connected with government intelligence. All the way to the top of the pyramid. The only people who could have known that Stamford and Fitzwilliam were secret agents on a mission to wipe out half of Ireland's population so the English could move in on their land.'

Finn's eyes had narrowed to slits. He clenched his jaw. 'You just keep talking, Hope. I'm not in a hurry to blow your goddamn head off.'

'When they knew what she knew, they didn't waste any time in orchestrating her murder, which got pinned on some innocent teacher. Three days after Elizabeth was killed, Heneage Fitzwilliam was shot dead in his room in Cambridge. He must've managed to warn Stamford before his death, maybe that someone had been following him and they were in danger. Knowing what was coming, Stamford set his plan. He needed a corpse, a big one that could double as his own.

The stable hand Padraig McCrory fitted the bill very nicely. Stamford murdered him, dressed him in his clothes and put a family ring on his finger that would identify him. Then he burned down the mansion with the dead man inside, and fled to America with all the money he could carry. He discovered that keeping up the Irish image was good for him in the New World. Or maybe he was just too scared to drop the pretence in case someone cottoned on to who he really was, and the British intelligence guys decided to come knocking on his door to cut the last connection between them and what had happened in Ireland in 1847. Whatever the reason, he kept up the lie until almost the very end of his twisted life.'

'Smart. Very smart. Finished now?'

'You were just continuing a family tradition, you and your father before you. After all, the McCrory reputation was built on your phoney Irish heritage. It was too good a thing to let go of, especially for a man of your political ambitions. You had too much to gain from the whole deception, and too much to lose if your future electors found out that their poster boy was not only about as Irish as the Queen of England, but that his ancestor was the guy the British government paid to lay waste to their country and murder millions of their people. Can't see that going down too well with the Irish-American voters. You said you had no choice but to murder Kristen Hall. You know what, McCrory? I believe you.'

The whole time Ben had been talking, he'd been moving towards McCrory, maintaining eye contact to distract the man with the gun from the barely perceptible shifting of his feet. The desk was between them. Ben was now almost close enough to make a grab for the rifle.

But Ben never had the chance.

Chapter Sixty-Four

If Ben had been keeping his ears open instead of focusing every shred of attention on the rifle that was pointing at him, he might have heard the laboured noises of a mortally injured man crawling up the stairs, inch by blood-smeared inch. The staggering footsteps making their way towards the study door—

There was a sudden crash. Big Joe McCrory filled the doorway. His face was streaked with pain and rage and blood and his teeth were bared like an animal's. His breathing was a tormented rasp as he lurched into the room with the last of his strength, eyes wide and fixed on the man who had taken his life. His own son.

'I'm going to kill you, boy,' came the croaking wheeze. Blood bubbled from the old man's lips as he spoke. He was dying on his feet, and yet the force of the willpower that had driven him all his life kept him moving.

Big Joe raised a bloody fist. In it was clenched one of the old six-guns he'd kept on the wall downstairs. The hammer was cocked. The trembling barrel pointed straight at his son.

Finn McCrory looked stricken, beyond horror. He turned the Winchester he'd been pointing at Ben towards his father.

The two gunshots filled the room in a single ragged crashing explosion. The express bullet from the Winchester caught the old man in the chest, blowing out his heart and killing him instantly. The .45-calibre soft lead slug from the old six-gun caught Finn right in the centre of his brow. It didn't have the energy to blast an exit wound through the back of his skull. It ricocheted and rattled around like an angry bee inside his head, carving wound channels in so many directions that his brain was churned to jelly before his knees even gave way under him and the rifle slipped from his lifeless hands.

Father and son hit the floor almost simultaneously, both stone dead.

Ben stood looking from one to the other. The chronicle of blood and deceit that was the Stamford line had ended forever, tonight, in front of his eyes.

He left the study and went back for Erin.

Outside, the night had grown sultrier, and the clouds that had gathered to blot out the stars were pregnant with rain. The Dodge Ram sat deep in shadow under the trees. Ben took the key from his pocket and was going to clunk the central locking when he realised that the back door was hanging open.

Erin was gone.

She might have opened the door from the inside. Might have gone to hide in the house, or wandered off among the ranch buildings to look for him. Or someone else might have popped the central locking from outside and taken her. There was no way to tell. Ben scanned the grounds, but saw nothing, no trace. He was berating himself for having disabled the alarm system. Either way had been taking a risk, but he understood now that this risk had been worse. It was too late now. He just had to find her.

'Erin!'

Nothing.

He felt the first fat plop of rain hit his face. Then another tapped his shoulder. Then the clouds let go, as if they couldn't hold the weight of the deluge any longer. The water soaked his hair and drummed on the roofs of the cars. Within seconds it was spouting from the gutter pipes of the ranch house and running in rivers across the ground.

'Erin!' he called again, louder.

'Right here,' said a voice that wasn't Erin's.

Ben turned.

Ritter limped out of the trees. He had Erin clutched to his chest, her body in front of his like a shield. One hand was clamped over her mouth and the other held a pistol against the side of her neck. Ritter's face was pale. Ben could see that the gun was shaking slightly and that Ritter was swaying on his feet.

It had been him on the stairs. He was badly wounded from at least two shotgun blasts, and must have lost a great deal of blood. He was frightened, and more dangerous than ever before.

They faced each other through a curtain of rain. Erin was struggling in Ritter's grip, but he had her tight and helpless. Her eyes were locked on Ben's and full of terror.

Ben laid down Moon's rifle.

'You don't give up,' he said.

'Neither do you.' Ritter's voice was unsteady and racked with pain.

'Let her go, Ritter. Everyone's dead.'

Ritter blinked rain from his eyes. 'Not everyone.'

'Let her go,' Ben repeated, 'and we're done. You can walk away from this.'

Ritter dug the gun harder into the side of Erin's neck and his eyes flashed.

'It's not her you want,' Ben said.

Ritter gritted his teeth and said, 'No.' He took the gun away from Erin and pointed it at Ben. 'On your knees. Fingers laced on top of your head.'

Slowly, Ben raised his hands in plain view. He spread his fingers and interlocked them against his wet hair. He kneeled on the ground, head bowed, peering up at the man with the gun. The rain streamed from his hair and down his face. He could feel the cold wetness soaking into his trousers where he knelt.

Ritter's face was hard and expressionless. The gun wavered in his hand. He blinked again. Then let go of Erin and shoved her hard. She stumbled and fell.

Then Ritter fired.

Ben keeled over backwards into the dirt.

Erin screamed.

Ritter stepped closer. Smiling now.

Ben rolled on the wet ground. The pain in his chest was blinding. He tried to focus.

Ritter aimed the gun down at Ben. Now he'd finish him. He was in no hurry. Then he'd kill the woman. *Then* they were done.

'Say goodbye, asshole.'

'Goodbye, asshole,' Ben said. He pulled McCrory's .44 Magnum from the back of his belt. It had two rounds left.

He fired them both into Ritter's head.

Ritter crashed backwards as if he'd been hit by a truck. The pistol cartwheeled out of his hand and he went straight down and landed spreadeagled on his back on the wet ground.

'Ben!' Erin picked herself up and ran to where he lay. 'Oh, God! Ben! No!'

The pain was blinding. Ben flung away the revolver. He propped himself up on one elbow as she reached him and fell to her knees beside him. With his other hand, he unzipped his jacket.

Erin stared at the vest that Ben had taken from O'Rourke. The bullet was a flattened lead disc circled by splayed-out petals of copper jacketing. It slid down the front of the Kevlar and disappeared in the wet grass.

'You're not shot,' she said, stunned.

'Might have cracked a rib.' He held out his hand and let her help him clamber to his feet.

'You took a bullet just to get him away from me,' she said. She brushed her dripping hair away from her face, looking up at him with big wondering eyes.

Ben shrugged. 'Seemed like a good idea at the time.' He looked down at Ritter. The rain was washing his blood into the dirt.

Ben took the dead man's phone from his pocket. There was one last call to make before this was over. First, he took out a set of car keys and tossed them to Erin.

'The Plymouth.' She'd never thought she'd see it in one piece again.

'Not a scratch on it,' he said. 'It isn't far away.'

She nodded. 'Where are we going?'

'You're going home.'

As they walked back to the car, Ben used Ritter's phone to call 911. He told them they'd find the mayor dead at the scene of a shooting at Arrowhead Ranch, along with several detectives from the Tulsa PD including the police chief. He told them to call FBI Special Agent Dobbs. They might also like to send some officers to Adonis and check out the remains of Big Bear Farm. That was going to keep them busy for a while. Ben said all he needed to say, then threw the phone into the bushes.

By the time the flashing lights lit up the sky and the fleet of police descended on the ranch, the Plymouth was already long gone.

'You won't be staying, will you?' she asked as they drove back towards the city. The wipers were beating fast, lashing away the rainwater.

He shook his head. 'The FBI won't waste time turning up at your door. I don't intend to be there when they do.'

'Aren't you even going to come back to my place tonight?'

He looked at her. 'You can drop me off on the edge of town.'

'You mean you're just going to disappear into the night.'

'Something like that.'

'Where will you go?

Ben kept his eyes on the road ahead and said nothing.

'I wish you didn't have to leave,' she said softly.

He reached across and clasped her hand. Squeezed it for a moment, and then let it go.

On the outskirts of Tulsa, he told her where to drop him off. He watched the car disappear into the night, then turned and walked off to make his own way.

Like he always would.

Read on for an exclusive extract from the new Ben
Hope adventure by Scott Mariani

The Martyr's Curse

Prologue

France
January 1346

The crowd looked on in awed silence as the pall of smoke drifted densely upwards to meet the falling sleet.

Four attempts to light the pyre had finally resulted in a dismal, crackling flame that slowly caught a hold on the pile of damp hay and twigs stacked up around the wooden stake at its centre. So thick was the smoke, the people of the mountain village who'd huddled round in the cold to witness the burning could barely even make out the figure of the man lashed to the stake. But they could clearly hear his frantic cries of protest as he writhed and fought against his bonds.

His struggles were of no use. Iron chains, not ropes, held him tightly to the thick wooden post. Rope would only burn away, and the authorities overseeing the execution wanted to make sure the job was properly carried out – that the corrupted soul of this evil man was well and truly purified in the cleansing flames.

He was a man of around forty, thin, gaunt and known locally as *Salvator l'Aveugle* – 'Blind Salvator' – because he had only a right eye, the left a black, empty socket. The robed and hooded traveller had first turned up in the village in late November. He'd declared himself to be a Franciscan priest on a lone pilgrimage to Jerusalem, where almost for the first time since its fall to the Muslim army of Salah al-Din in 1187, Christianity was re-establishing a lasting foothold. Salvator's mission was to join his fellow Frenchman and Franciscan, Roger Guérin of Aquitaine, who had managed to purchase from the current Mamluk rulers parts of the ancient city, including the hallowed Cenacle on Mount Zion, and was in the process of building a monastery there.

But Salvator's long journey hadn't started well. He'd scarcely covered eighty miles from his home in Burgundy before a gang of brigands had beset him on the road, taking his nag and the purse containing what little money he had. Bruised and battered, he'd plodded on his way on foot for a month or more, totally dependent on the goodwill of his fellow men for shelter and sustenance. Finally, fatigue and hunger combined with the growing winter cold and the unrelenting rain had brought on a fever that had nearly ended his pilgrimage before it had properly begun. Some children had come across him lying half dead by the side of the path that wound up through the mountain pass a mile or so from their village. Seeing from the dirty tatters of his humble robe that he was a holy man, they'd run to fetch help and Salvator had soon been rescued. Men from the village had carried him back on a wagon, he'd been fed and tended to, and fresh straw bedding had been laid down for him in an empty stable that he shared with some chickens.

During the weeks that followed, the priest's fever had passed and his strength had gradually returned. By then, though, winter was closing in, and he'd decided to delay resuming his journey until the spring. To begin with, most of the villagers hadn't objected to his remaining with them two or three more months. It was an extra mouth to feed, true; but then, an extra pair of hands was always useful at this hard time of year. During his stay, Salvator had helped clear snow, repair storm damage to the protective wall that circled the village, and tend to the pigs. In his free time, he'd also begun to draw a crowd with his impromptu public sermons, which had grown in frequency and soon become more and more impassioned.

Needless to say, there were those who were unhappy with his presence, and this became more noticeable as time went on. It was a somewhat closed community, somewhat insular, easily given to suspicion and especially where strangers were concerned – even when those strangers were men of God. And most especially when those strangers frightened some people with their odd ways.

The first rumours had begun to circulate about a month after Salvator's recovery. Just a few passing whispers to begin with, quickly growing to a widespread consensus that the presence of this itinerant priest was cause for deep concern. Increasingly, villagers complained that the content of his sermons was scandalous. He railed against core doctrines of the church, even attacked the views of the Pope, which he declared to be ignoble and ungodly. But that wasn't the worst of it. What really worried people were the seizures.

Once while feeding the pigs and again in the middle of delivering one of his sermons, Salvator had been seen to suddenly go rigid, then drop to the ground and begin to thrash about in a way that absolutely terrified those who witnessed it happening. During these inexplicable convulsions, his limbs would twitch violently and his face would contort in the most horrible way, foam drooling from the corners of his mouth and his one eye rolled up in its socket so that only the white showed. Most alarmingly of all, it was reported that he would babble and croak in a strange, guttural language that none of the villagers had ever heard before.

As the rumours inevitably picked up momentum, so did the growing belief that Salvator was possessed by demons. They'd all heard of such things, though never before seen it with their own eyes. What else could explain these frightful episodes?

It was after the third seizure happened that the village elders convened to discuss the urgent situation. The assembly of greybeards unanimously decided that such evil could not be allowed to remain in their midst. Despite the risks posed by the weather, they all agreed that their best horseman, a young carpenter named Guy, should be dispatched at once to the nearby town to notify the higher church authorities. In the meantime, Salvator should be locked up in a stone barn outside the village walls and guarded day and night, so that whatever sinister forces had taken hold of him could do no further harm.

When, after several worrying days, Guy returned from his trek, he was accompanied by an envoy of the bishop and a small party of officials and soldiers, who rapidly set up court in the village's tiny stone chapel and summoned the prisoner to be brought before them. Covered in chains, Salvator was forced to prostrate himself in front of the bishop's envoy, explain himself for preaching such scandalous and profane sermons and provide evidence to all present that he was not in league with powers of Satan.

The evidence Salvator gave them was all they needed. Right before their eyes, and to their equal horror and satisfaction, he succumbed to yet another bout of convulsions that proved beyond any doubt that some devilish entity had taken possession of this man's soul. There was no alternative but to purge it out, to banish the demon and cleanse the corrupted fleshly vessel that had been its host.

Death by burning was the only way.

Bit by bit, the sluggish flames gained on the pyre, helped by a chill wind from the mountain that picked up and cleared the smoke. Salvator screamed in agony as the fire began to dance around his feet, then up his legs. Part of his robe burned away, exposing blackened and blistered skin.

'I curse you!' he screamed through the heat mist at the church envoy on his high seat, and at the lesser authorities and the soldiers gathered nearby to watch.

'And you!' Salvator bellowed at the crowd. 'Damn your souls, for what you have done today to an innocent man!'

The people shrank away, terrified in their belief that it was the voice of the tormented demon inside him that they were hearing. Children buried their faces in their mothers' robes; hands were pressed over their ears to protect them from evil.

The flames leapt higher around Salvator, and still he wouldn't pass out but kept on roaring at them.

'God sees the shameful sin that has united you all. May His eternal curse be on you all, and your children, and your children's children after them! May a thousand years of pestilence rot this unholy place and everyone in it!'

One of the soldiers glanced nervously at the bishop's envoy, ready to raise his bow and fire an arrow into the heart of the flames in order to silence the voice that was rattling the nerves of even the most hardened man present.

But the envoy shook his head. For purification to be effective, no mercy could be allowed. The heretic must burn to death.

And burn to death Salvator did, but it took an unbearably

long time. To the villagers, it seemed as if the flaming human torch went on railing at them even as the sizzling flesh peeled from its bones. Then, finally, his cries diminished and he hung limply, no longer resisting, from the blackened chains that held him to the stake. The remnants of his robe burst alight. Then his tonsured hair. By now he could barely be seen for the flames. His one rolling eyeball seemed to peer balefully at them from the scorched ruin of his face.

Long after the carbonised skeleton had fallen into the cinders leaving the chains hanging empty, Salvator's voice went on ringing inside the heads of the horror-struck villagers. They would never forget the promise of everlasting pestilence that had been heaped on them and their line.

Within a year, Salvator's words would come true.

The martyr's curse had begun.

Chapter One

Udo Streicher knew it was over before his entry team had even penetrated the inner core of the building.

His information had been first-rate. The materials he'd been looking to acquire were exactly where his sources had said they would be, and he'd come within a hair's breadth of having them. Millions had been spent on intelligence and equipment. An entire year had been devoted to planning. Twelve hour days. Sometimes sixteen. Checking every possible detail. Obsessing over the layout of the hidden complex. Analysing the security systems. Evaluating the risk. Assessing their chances of making it out alive.

And for all that meticulous planning, now the raid had gone badly wrong. The mission was blown. The ten-strong group was down to nine. The equipment was lost. They'd ditched everything they'd brought with them, except their weapons.

Behind them in the white-walled, starkly neon-lit corridor, three dead bodies lay sprawled in pools of blood. Two of them belonged to the armed Korean security personnel who'd surprised the intruders just as they were about to make it through the final set of doors that separated them from their objective. The third belonged to an Austrian called Dieter Lenz, a follower of Streicher from the beginning. But Dieter wasn't important any more. What mattered was getting out of here. Streicher refused to consider the alternatives. He'd rather die by his own bullet than face a lifetime of incarceration in the roach-infested hellhole of a North Korean prison camp.

The nine remaining members of the team ran in tight formation, their clattering footsteps all but drowned out by the shriek and whoop of alarm sirens that were sounding off all through the facility. The platinum-haired Hannah Gissel had her pistol drawn and her teeth bared in a kind of animal ferocity. Torben Roth was clutching the Uzi he'd gunned the guards down with. Bringing up the rear were the Canadian, Steve Evers, and Sandro Guidinetti. Guidinetti looked like he was losing it under the pressure.

'Which way did we come?' Wolf Schilling yelled as they reached a fork in the corridor. Every door and wall in the lab complex looked the same.

'This way,' Streicher said, pointing left. He gripped Hannah's arm and they raced on. The sirens seemed even louder, a wall of sound that permeated everything. Another door. Another bend in the corridor.

A side entrance swung open, and suddenly the way ahead was blocked off. A four-man security patrol, dressed in the same khaki paramilitary uniform and wielding Chinese-made assault rifles. Screaming at them in Korean. Streicher only knew a little of the language but the message was clear: DROP YOUR WEAPONS! SURRENDER OR WE WILL SHOOT!

The stand-off lasted less than two seconds. Torben Roth was the first to open fire, shooting from the hip and hosing nine-millimetre rounds up the corridor. Hannah snapped off three, four, five shots from her Glock. The guards crumpled up and fell. Streicher shot the last one with his own Heckler & Koch. He did it without hesitation or compassion. It wasn't the first time he'd shot a man.

'Come on!' Hannah yelled. Her eyes were flashing with a mixture of aggression and terror and pure adrenalin. She leapt over the heap of dead men. The other eight followed. Streicher felt a strange surge of pride in his woman as he followed her. Weeks earlier, he'd already decided that in the event of the mission going bad, he would kill her before he took his own life. A wild, untamed spirit like hers didn't belong in captivity.

They ran faster. The alarms drowned out everything. Every door they passed, Streicher kept expecting to see fly open and hordes of guards swarming through. But there was nothing. Nothing like the level of resistance he'd feared. The North Korean economy was dismal to the point that even a hardcore military dictatorship could be forced to make serious defence cuts. That could be the reason. After all, nobody knew about this facility. Security could have been pared down to the bone, with nobody any the wiser. Maybe the remaining few guards were locked down elsewhere in the building, unwilling to face the armed intruders' superior numbers. Maybe there were no more guards at all.

All of which was making him begin to wonder if they'd been premature in beating a retreat.

Before he could decide what to do, they'd reached the main entrance. The jungle air enveloped them like a hot, wet cloak as they burst outside. The alarm sirens were even louder out here, their echo bouncing off the buildings, distortion crackling in the team's ears. The compound was grey concrete, as vast and forbidding as a high-security prison yard, and ringed with a wire fence supported on steel posts fifteen feet high and topped all the way around with coils of razor wire. The main building was far larger than the rest, white, squat, windowless, like a giant bunker. The smaller buildings clustered around it, mainly storage units and maintenance sheds, were painted in military drab green. The high galvanised steel and mesh main gate was directly opposite the white building, eighty yards away. From there, a concrete road spanned the patchy open ground surrounding the facility, where the jungle had been roughly cut back to clear room for it.

Officially, this place had never been built. The North Korean rulers firmly denied its existence. US Intelligence had long suspected otherwise, but their satellites had never been able to distinguish the facility from hundreds of others across the country that looked outwardly identical. The American spies were clever, thorough people.

But Udo Streicher was cleverer, and took thoroughness to a level that verged on the pathological. If anyone could find out what was really in there, he could. And he had, though it had cost him a fortune and a lot of hard work.

Needless to say, Streicher and his people hadn't used the main gate to get inside. The hole in the wire was a hundred yards along the length of the perimeter fence, on the east side of the compound where the bushes grew closer and the no-man's land was at its narrowest. Beyond, the verdant thicket of trees hid the small clearing where the team's two choppers were on standby. Waiting to whisk them and their precious spoils back over the border to the RV point on the coast, from where a motor launch would carry them eastwards to the safety of Japan. A chartered jet from Tokyo back home and dry to Europe, and the mission would have been accomplished.

A successful end would then have become the start of the next phase in the plan, one that Streicher had dreamed about for a long, long time.

'We're clear,' Roth said, glancing around them. He seemed to be right. The compound was deserted and empty apart from a parked row of Jeeps in Korean People's Army colours, used to ferry security and other facility personnel back and forth.

'We've taken them all out, that's why,' said Hannah. 'It was a mistake. There's hardly anyone guarding this place. Which means we need to turn around and go back inside and get the stuff. Right now. Before it's too late.'

Streicher said nothing. He stood still, his head cocked a little to one side as if he was smelling the air.

'She's right, Udo,' Schilling said. 'We have time. We can still do this.'

'It's what we came here for,' Hannah said. 'It's why we chose this place, remember? That's what you told us. Our best chance. Our only chance.'

Streicher said nothing.

'I'm up for it. Or else we came all this way for nothing,' Roth said.

'And Dieter died for nothing,' Schilling said.

Streicher said, 'There's no time. It will have to wait.'

'Wait how long? Months? Years?'

'As long as it takes.'

'No. I want to do this,' Hannah said.

So did Streicher. He wanted it more than anything in the world. But he shook his head. 'Listen.'

He'd heard it the moment they stepped outside. It had been barely audible over the sirens, but now the sound was growing. It was the growling rumble of vehicles approaching. Hard to tell how many. Enough to be a serious problem.

411

Enough to have made him absolutely right about getting out of here, right this minute.

'Oh, shit,' Hannah said, as she heard it too.

Then they saw where the sound was coming from, and suddenly things were very much worse.

The line of military vehicles emerged at speed from the jungle, roaring along the road right for the main gate. Six of them, ex-Russian GAZ Vodnik troop carriers in Korean People's Army colours, each carrying up to nine men. The column made no attempt to slow for the gate. The first vehicle crashed straight through, steel frame and galvanised wire mesh crumpling and folding underneath it as it stormed inside the compound followed by the rest of the convoy. The vehicles fanned out and skidded to a halt. Their hatches flew open and a mass of men spilled out. More than fifty fully armed troops. Against nine.

'Fuck them,' Torben Roth said. He snapped another magazine into his Uzi. Hannah raised her pistol. Gröning and Hinreiner looked at each other, then at Guidinetti.

The clatter of small arms fire filled the compound. Roth held his ground. A burst to the left; a burst to the right. Then he staggered and dropped his Uzi and blood flew and hit the wall behind him. Streicher ducked down low and ran to the fallen man and saw that his face had been ripped open by a rifle bullet. Streicher grasped him by the arms and began dragging him behind cover, helped by Gröning. Hannah kept on firing until her pistol was empty. Several of the soldiers were down, but now the Russian GAZ Vodniks were advancing and bringing their onboard heavy machine guns into play. The roar of the gun shattered the air. 14.5mm bullets ploughed through the parked Jeeps, gouged craters in the buildings, chewed up the concrete.

Streicher now knew beyond any doubt that he'd been right.

412

Things were bad enough already. If they'd stayed inside the building a minute longer, none of them would have made it this far alive. 'Help me,' he said as he dragged the bleeding, disfigured Roth. Between them, he and Wolf Schilling and Miki Donath managed to manhandle the injured man out of the field of fire and between the buildings while the others did what they could to hold back the soldiers.

The firepower was withering. Hannah fell back when her pistol was empty. Guidinetti was hit in the shoulder and Evers was supporting him as they made their retreat. How so many of them made it back to the hole in the wire without getting shot to pieces, Streicher would never know. Staggering through the bushes towards the trees with Roth's weight slippery and bloody in his arms, he was praying that the soldiers hadn't already intercepted the waiting helicopters.

Sixty seconds later and the choppers would have been gone anyway. The pilots had heard the gunfire and were quickly powering up their turbines in desperation to get the hell away from here. Their skids were dancing off the ground and the vegetation was being flattened by the down-draught as the surviving team members clambered on board. Streicher, Hannah, Donath and Schilling and the injured Roth on one; Evers and Guidinetti and Hinreiner and Gröning aboard the other. The soldiers were coming. Flitting shapes in the trees. Muzzle flashes lighting up the shadows of the thick green forest. Bullets cracked off the Perspex screen of Streicher's chopper.

'Take it up! Get us out of here!' Streicher yelled to the pilot.

As the choppers lifted off, the thicket suddenly crashed aside. Like a great scarred green armour-plated dinosaur hunting through the jungle, a Korean People's Army VTT-323 armoured personnel carrier lurched through the trees, trampling down bushes and saplings and anything else in its path. Its twin machine guns swivelled up towards the escaping aircraft. But those weren't what Streicher was gaping down at in horror from the cockpit of the rising helicopter. It was the turret-mounted multiple rocket launcher that was angling up at them, tracking its targets and ready to fire at any moment. 'Higher!' he bawled over the din of the rotors, thumping the pilot on the shoulder. 'Higher!'

Two rockets launched simultaneously in a twin jet of flame. They streaked through the trees and hit the second chopper and blew it apart in an expanding fireball.

'No!' Streicher howled as he saw it go down.

The burning wreck dropped from the air and crashed down on top of the armoured personnel carrier. A secondary explosion rocked the jungle, and then Streicher saw no more as his pilot spun up and away at full thrust, nose up, tail down.

They flew in numb silence over the forest. The green canopy zipped by below. Wolf and Miki were trying to hold down the bleeding, squirming Torben Roth and pump morphine into him from the first-aid kit. Hannah was lost in a world of her own, her face drawn and grim and spattered with someone else's blood. She made no attempt to wipe it away.

And Udo Streicher was just beginning to contemplate the scale of the disaster. It would be a long time before he was fully able to calculate his losses, both human and financial.

But he'd be back. This wasn't over. It would never be over. Not until he'd attained his goal. One way or another, the world would know his name before he was done.

It was, after all, his destiny.

Chapter Two

Hautes-Alpes, France
The present day

When they'd found the stranger, at first they hadn't known what to do with him.

It was young Frère Roby, the one they affectionately called simple, who'd first stumbled on the camp high up on the Alpine mountainside during one of his long contemplative rambles one morning in early October. The nineteen-year-old would later say that he'd been following a young chamois, hoping to befriend it, when he'd made his strange discovery.

The camp had been made in a natural hollow among the rocks, sheltered from the wind, out of sight and well away from the beaten track, only accessible along a narrow path with a sheer cliff face on one side and a dizzy drop on the other. It was like nothing Roby had ever seen. In the middle of the camp was a shallow fire pit, about two feet deep, over which had been built a short, tapered chimney made of stone and earth. The fire was cold, but the remains of a spit-roasted hare showed that it had been used sometime in the last couple of days. Nearby, almost invisibly camouflaged behind a carefully built screen of pine branches, was a small and robust tent.

That was where he'd found the stranger, lying on his side

415

in a sleeping bag, with his back turned to the entrance. To begin with, Roby had been frightened, thinking the man was dead. As he dared to creep closer to him, he'd realised he was breathing, though deeply unconscious. The chamois completely forgotten, Roby had dashed all the way back to the monastery to tell the others.

After some thought, the prior had given his consent, and Roby had led a small party of older men back to the spot. It was mid-afternoon when they reached the camp, to find the stranger still lying unconscious inside his tent.

The men soon realised the cause of the stranger's condition, from the empty spirits bottles that littered the camp. They'd never seen anybody so comatose from drink before, not even Frère Gaspard that notorious time when he'd broken into the store of beer the monks produced as part of their livelihood. They wondered who this man was and how long he'd been living here undetected, just three kilometres from the remote Carthusian monastery that was their home. He didn't look like a vagrant or a beggar. Perhaps, one of them suggested, he was a hunter who'd lost his way in the alpine wilderness.

But if he was a hunter, he should have a rifle. When they delicately searched his pockets and his green military canvas haversack in the hope of finding some identification, all they came across was a knife, a quantity of cash, some French cigarettes and an American lighter, a battered steel flask half-filled with the same spirit that had been in the bottles. They also found a creased photograph of a woman with auburn hair, whose identity was as much a mystery to them as the man's.

The monks were fascinated by the fire pit. The blackened mouth of the stone-and-earth chimney suggested that the stranger must have been living here for some time, perhaps weeks. The way it was constructed indicated considerable skill. They were themselves men who'd been used to a hard, simple existence close to nature all their lives, dependent through the harsh alpine winters on the firewood they'd gathered, chopped and seasoned themselves. They understood that the fire pit was the work of someone highly expert in the art of survival. That, as well as the green bag and the tent, made them wonder whether the stranger might at one time have been a soldier. A Wehrmacht infantryman had been found frozen to death not far from here in the winter of 1942, hiding in the mountains after apparently deserting from his unit. As far as the monks knew, there weren't any major wars happening at the moment, down there below in the world they'd left behind. The stranger was dressed in civilian clothes – jeans, leather jacket, stout boots – and his blonde hair was too long for him to have belonged to the military anytime recently.

Whatever clues they could derive about his past, it was his immediate future that concerned them. Despite their isolated, ascetic lifestyle, the monks were worldly enough to know about such things as alcohol poisoning, and they were afraid that the stranger might die if left. The monastic tradition of helping travellers was just one of the many ways in which they were sworn to serve God. The question was, what should they do?

There'd been some debate as to whether to bring him back to the monastery, where the prior would know best how to help him, or whether to call for outside help. It hadn't been a hard decision, as none of them possessed a phone to dial 15 for the SAMU emergency medical assistance service.

So they gathered up his things and carried him back along the winding, steep and sometimes dangerous mountain paths to their sanctuary, Chartreuse de la Sainte Vierge de Pelvoux, where the stranger had remained ever since.

That had been over seven months ago . . .